DARK & LIGHT

SHORT STORIES

Oliver Eade

www.olivereadebooks.org

Cover design copyright © Fiona Ruiz

UK spelling observed
Typeset in Georgia

ISBN: 978-1-912513-60-4

Silver Quill Publishing

Dedicated to Yvonne

my love

'A short story is a shard, a sliver, a vignette.
It's a biopsy on the human condition
but it doesn't have this capacity
to think autonomously for itself.'

Will Self, author of 'Umbrella'
short-listed for the Man Brooker Prize.

Acknowledgements:
I wish to thank fellow writers, including those
In the Borders Writers' Forum and the Society of
Medical Writers, for encouragement and
advice over the years. As always, I am indebted
to my unbelievably patient wife, Yvonne, for
coping with my annoying ups and downs. Lads, but not
least, I must thank everyone in Silver Quill Publishing
for helpful support and for proofreading suggestions.

Reviews of some of the author's other publications:

Moon Rabbit

'...Moon Rabbit will lead children's imaginations to fantastical realms. It is a magical mix enhanced by gentle and ethereal illustrations...'

Mairi Hedderwick, author of the Katie Morag books, 2009

'...Enchanting tale of two children who embark on a dangerous mission... Ideal introduction into Chinese culture... to be enjoyed by children of all ages...'

A Good Read, Sunday Express, 2009

"Magical Experience..."

PA News, 2010

Northwards

'...A witty and heart-warming novel packed with adventure...'

Sunday Express, 2010

A Single Petal

'...Carefully researched, well plotted and more full-blooded than you might expect, A Single Petal's spiritual dimension is solidly grounded in traditional narrative rules...'

Alastair Mabbott, The Herald, 2013

'...There's an abundance of beauty in this book...: it is a sensitive, poetic account of the faith, fears and irresistible forces within a community...'

Raymond Hume, The Writer, 2020

The Terminus

'...Once you pick up this chilling book, be prepared to climb onto an emotional roller-coaster...'

Wendy Leighton-Porter, award winning author of the 'Shadows of the Past series', 2013

The Parth Path
'...A momentous novel. The reader is drawn into a post-apocalyptic nightmare... In the face of overwhelming evil, good prevails...'
Iona Carroll, author of the 'Oisin Kelly' series, 2018
The Kelpie's Eyes
'...An extraordinarily good fantasy novel... so well- handled that it grips throughout...'
Frost Magazine, 2018
In the Blink of an Eye
'...Powerful stories following key developments in medicine... clearly written and hugely informative...'
Ray Cartwright, Emeritus Professor of Medicine, 2021

Contents:

All Because of a Girl called Hayley

She did not even turn around for a last look. Just stepped up onto the carriage and slammed the door shut. The train containing his wife curled out of Berwick station and once gone, it seemed as though he might as well stay forever on that platform staring at the timeless ruin of the old city wall whilst thinking about his personal ruin. His life.

She had been his life, and he had always assumed their love to be something permanent. Indestructible. Now it was little more than a scar cutting his existence in two. Permanent, but dead. Like that old wall.

God, what the hell did I do to make everything go so horribly wrong?

He had brought up her to the Scottish Borders *because* of its ruins and its history. Before they met, history had been her thing. She had a brilliant academic career ahead of her.

So why?

Had the childlessness of their seven-year-old marriage encouraged Hayley? Doubtless *she* blamed everything on him and his work, though never said as much. In fact, of late, she never said much to him at all. For which *he* blamed Hayley. He had often thought about ways of quietly killing the girl after realising the effect she had on his wife. Now he thought of only one thing. To dispose of her in the cruellest way possible. Death by burning, her final resting place being the council tip.

Everything had been so carefully planned. After the drive up from Suffolk, they would spend a night in Jedburgh, see the abbey, move on to Kelso, another abbey, followed by Dryburgh and Melrose, then the starkly austere Smailholm Tower, afterwards taking in the long-defunct mills of Selkirk and Galashiels plus the ruined church and old bridge at Stow. By using history, they could revisit their past, put things back on the right track and rebuild the crumbling ruin of their marriage. She might even be persuaded to use her writing skills to become a historical novelist. Even forget Hayley.

Perhaps?

Forget Hayley? If only! *Those piercing eyes, that pert, up-turned nose, sweet chin and ruby lips. How could I ever destroy her?*

Of course, things never do work out according to plan. The more ruins they visited, the more distant she became, as though reminding him, and in a small bookshop in Melrose, he saw Hayley. That did it!

On the final leg of their Borders tour he decided to pull out one last stop. He had seen the ruined Peel tower on a promontory near the River Tweed whilst heading towards Peebles. On the way back, with not one word having been spoken all morning, he drove the car up onto a verge near the ruin.

Not much of a building, but could this provide a turning point?

"Let's sit there a while," he said, looking across a field pock-marked with sheep at the old tower. "Enjoy those rolls I got in Peebles. Years since we last had a picnic together."

"That ancient pile of stones? Come off it!"

"Looks sort of romantic. Think of its past. Christ knows what might have happened within those old walls. *Real* history! Who knows, you might get inspiration for your first historical novel? The life of a Borders reiver must've been quite something. Intrigue, deceit, wall-to-wall fighting, thieving... and their women. Well... you know... they—" He fell silent.

"They what?"

He thought about those Borders women of the past, dutifully subservient to their menfolk. Would it have been different for the two of them back then, a life within that Peel tower? And might its past rub off onto them even now, if they were to sit together, their backs up against its ancient wall? Not that he wanted her to be subservient. Just... well, a just *little* responsive towards him. That was all he asked for.

"Dunno! Anyway, I'm hungry. And you could... you know..."

"I know what?"

"Plan your historical novel. Starting here in the Borders. Inside that Peel tower. As it used to be."

"Bloody couldn't! Hayley would have kittens!"

"For God's sake, can't you forget Hayley? For an hour or two?"

I promise I will kill Hayley if she refuses to speak to me about what's troubling her. Work it out to the last detail, including the burning and disposal of the ashes.

Soon, they found themselves seated, side-by-side, up against the tower wall and staring in silence at the river. His hunger had left him, and both rolls lay untouched on his bent-up knees.

"I've been thinking, Sara," he said at last. "We need to do something together for a change. Whilst you were involved with Hayley, in that bookshop in Melrose, I..."

He flicked away an ant that was wandering uncomfortably close to his foot. If only he could have done the same to Hayley.

3

"Well, if you were to write a novel about reivers and stuff, I could perhaps help with the research," he suggested. "Things should be less busy for me at the hospital now that I've a new colleague. Look, I know I have been rather—"

"It's over, John!" she interrupted, cutting into his sentence with surgical precision.

"No, Sara. Please hear me out."

"I'm expecting a baby. His!"

He looked at Sara, at the river, the sky, his feet, then at the ant searching for something. Something that might tell him this was only a bad dream, maybe? But reality stared back at him wherever he looked.

"*His*?"

"I... I was going to tell you sooner, John, honest but..."

"Wait a minute, Sara. I'm lost here. *His* baby? What... I mean, who on earth are you—?"

"Pat."

She turned to face him. She was crying but averted his gaze when their eyes met.

"Your agent? But she's a bloody woman!"

"Pat? He's a man all right! Very much a man. You never asked, never seemed the slightest bit interested in what I did. Oh God, John, I wanted to tell you at the time, three months ago, before I toured the States with Hayley, but—"

"Damn Hayley! How could I know Pat was a man? Jesus Christ!"

"You never asked and I felt so confused. So lonely. But when I found out I was expecting last week, I—"

"You love him?"

4

Sara paused before shrugging her shoulders.

"But how can you be so sure it's...?"

"We were together for two months during my tour. He was the only one who made love to me. Besides..."

"Yeah, yeah! No need to bloody rub it in! *Jesus!* A baby by another man? Sara, I—"

"Look... I think I should just take the train back. Sort stuff out at home—"

"*Whose* bloody home?"

"Get my things together and—"

"Move in with the bastard? Oh God, Sara!"

He, too, was crying.

"I don't know! Like I said, I've been confused. Go to Mum's, perhaps. Look, I really—"

"I'll kill him!"

"That wouldn't change things. John, I'm so sorry. It happened, and that's all I can say."

"Happened? Christ, only because you bloody let it. And all because of a girl called Hayley, the little bitch."

Not a word was exchanged until they reached Berwick Station where she repeated, 'I'm so, so sorry,' over and over without turning to look at him.

Nothing made sense. The ruins, Hayley, and now a baby by a man he had assumed to be a woman. His mind in a whirl, he drove back across the Borders, alone, towards the town of Melrose. He would buy every Hayley book they had in that little bookshop, take them to the ruined Peel tower and watch her suffer with all the hatred he could muster whilst she burned. No, more! would go to *every* bookshop in the Scottish Borders, buy up *all* their stocks of Hayley books, burn them, then set off around the country to rid the rest of the world of Hayley. Not even on

Amazon would the ruddy little girl be able to flaunt her silly little grinning face that had bought Sara world fame and ruined his life.

At Home with Hayley; Hayley on Holiday; Hayley at the Zoo; Hayley the (Fucking!) Girl Detective....

Hayley just went on and on and on, the little cow! Christ, he would make Hayley suffer for what she'd done. Was burning good enough? Should he soak every book in cat's piss and vinegar before setting it alight? But wet things don't burn and their cat was already dead. Like his marriage.

Hayley, Hayley, Hayley!

He could think of nothing else as he sped towards Melrose, his foot pressed fully down on the accelerator. Hayley and the life she had destroyed formed a dark cloud filling every corner of his mind. Hayley's big smiley eyes taunted him through the windscreen, blocking out the road, the fields of corn, rape, cows... and the trees.

*****

On seeing the police car waiting outside their home in Norfolk, Sara's first thought was for Pat. Had John carried out his threat and killed her lover? But the truth was a thousand times worse, in no way softened by the officer's words...

"He wouldn't have felt a thing when his car hit a tree."

It got worse. Returning to the Scottish Borders to identify the body was unbearable beyond endurance, but she stayed on there, in the Borders, close to the ruins and to him. She had finished with Pat, the randy bastard. That's what she was trying to say to him after she told him about the baby, but somehow only anger showed and it was turned against Pat for using Hayley to ruin her marriage; against herself for not saying, 'No!' to the bastard.

She had the child in the Scottish Borders. She bought a house there and she read about the reivers, their lives and the ruins they'd left behind. She wrote that novel about the Scottish Borders reivers and the suffering of their womenfolk. It became a best-seller...

And her daughter's name is Hayley.

A Hoovered Life

Humphrey Pilkingshaw was fastidious about cleanliness, both for himself and his house. 'Self' was easy. Three showers a day, spotlessly clean clothes after each shower and vigorously brushed teeth following every meal. Circular motion, as he read at the dentist's, not up and down. Oh, and the shoes. Polished daily to a high 'see-your-nose-in-them' sort of shine, and, of course, every piece of fluff and dust that appeared on those shoes and on his suede slippers would be dealt with immediately. With the hoover. Oh yes, the hoover. Never picked off with fingers lest unsightly prints should appear on the shiny leather or pockmark the suede.

Humphrey could not imagine an existence without his hoover. If he had been born before the invention of that most noble of civilisation's engineering achievements, he would most probably not have survived for long, for how else could he have kept his house truly clean? Cleanliness was essential for his continued existence. Since retiring from his position in a local government office, one might have been forgiven for believing that the job of keeping his home spotless would have become a whole lot easier. Not so! Hoovering had always taken up all of Humphrey's spare time. Now that all of his time was, so to speak, 'spare', all that time was spent in hoovering.

Every morning, after showering, brushing his teeth, de-fluffing and polishing his shoes, Humphrey would be off around the house with his hoover. *His* hoover, although he did have a wife. You would hardly have noticed her at 36 Beehive Close. Just a shadow somewhere in the background, sometimes moving about, mostly not for fear of getting in the way of Humphrey. Elspeth was her name. Ellie for short. By now, Ellie had turned into a grey-haired, little woman with sad Labrador eyes and pink slippers. Yes, she, too, had to have her slippers hoovered by Humphrey. Every day.

How Ellie hated that hoover. She hated the sound and she hated the smell but above all she hated the aggression with which the hoover, controlled by her husband, attacked every corner of every room in their late fifties property, including the hallway and the carpeted stairsteps. Particularly the stairsteps.

Unfortunately, 'aggressive' was the only operative mode available to Humphrey when in command of that awful appliance. He simply did not do 'gentle' whilst in charge of the hoover. Poor Ellie knew only too well that basic mathematical equation of 36 Beehive Close:

Humphrey+Hoover = Aggression.

Of course, this was not aggression for the sake of aggression alone. There was true purpose behind it, the quick zip along by the skirting boards, the frantic zigzag spider dance on the landing, the speed hound swish across the living room carpet, all executed with a single purpose in Humphrey's mind...

The Guinness Book of Records.

Every day, now, was a hoovering competition day for Humphrey, as day after day he competed with his own previous best hoovering-time record. Twenty minutes, eighteen minutes fifty-five seconds, eighteen minutes forty-three seconds, eighteen minutes thirty-seven seconds. Gradually, with the aid of a super-accurate stopwatch, which recorded the passage of time to the nearest hundredth of a second, Humphrey saw himself getting slowly closer to his target time as he observed seconds and tenths of seconds being shaved of his personal best. Plus, he had his own special, secret formula. One that adjusted for the surface area to be hoovered. All one thousand three hundred and forty-seven square feet of it. And a mathematical adjustment for spotlessness failure.

The latter was assessed after each episode of hoovering by Humphrey going around the house with ten strips of two-centimetre-wide Sellotape, each measured to precisely ten centimetres, and sticking them to the floor at ten different randomly chosen sites. The strips were then peeled off, and placed on a special light box, and all the adherent, hooverable bits of dirt counted and fed, in a negative way, into his formula to produce a final numerical result, the 'hoovering index' which was carefully recorded in Humphrey's hoovering logbook.

All this fully occupied Humphrey for whenever he wasn't actually showering, brushing his teeth, polishing his shoes, or, of course, hoovering. Sometimes he did manage to sit for short periods, proudly perusing his logbook, and observing, with great satisfaction, that his hoovering-index was getting close to three point seven. Nobody, apart from Humphrey, had any idea what three point seven represented, or meant, and Humphrey's ability to explain this figure was rather poor, but a hoovering-index of three point seven was the target that would, he felt, justify contacting the Guinness Book of Records. Details on how to do this were recorded in his hoovering logbook kept on his bedside cabinet.

So where did Ellie fit into the scheme of things at 36 Beehive Close? Well, apart from keeping out of the way when Humphrey was active with the hoover, she would prepare his food, at precise, pre-determined times, and see to all the essentials such as shopping, cooking, paying bills, contacting tradesmen and services, whenever necessary, as well as washing, drying and ironing all the clothes. Humphrey was far too busy trying to achieve three point seven to be concerned with any of these things. So, as you can imagine, Ellie had a miserable life.

Completely, totally and utterly miserable. But all this was to change quite suddenly, one nice, bright Sunday morning in May. Humphrey was all set to increase his hoovering index by a vital zero point two six that morning. This, he told himself, on rising, would be the day, for he had a feeling that something special was about to happen. He felt thoroughly excited by the thought of appearing in the G B of R for achieving the fastest hoovering time ever as judged by the Pilkingshaw Hoovering Index. He felt certain he could succeed this by revamping his hoovering circuit. He would alter his course at the landing at the top of the stairs. Instead of the usual zigzag, he would hoover half the landing on the way to the bedroom and half on the way back, to cut out any unnecessary reduplication of effort caused through retracing his steps with an active hoover. He was sure it would work. Ellie would, on his command, readjust the position of the electric cable, in his wake, to ensure it was not in the way on his return, then she could scuttle back into the kitchen and stay well out of his way. And all might have gone according to plan had Humphrey informed Ellie of the change in routine. As it happened, in his excitement about the changes, with the near certainty of getting into the G B of R, he forgot to tell his wife.

From the safety of the kitchen the noise was

terrifying. Ellie cowered in the corner like a frightened rabbit at the sound of it, and waited several seconds—or to be honest, several minutes—before emerging from the kitchen and venturing to the foot of the stairs. Understandably, she wished to wait until the twitching was over, for there was sure to be twitching. Just like after Humphrey drove into a pheasant. It had carried on twitching for a very long time.

When Ellie arrived at the scene, it was very much as one might expect to see after a man, intertwined with a hoover, had somersaulted several times down a steep flight of stairs. There had been surprisingly little vocalisation from Humphrey. Just an aborted yelp, followed by the tumbling crash of body and machine. They said his neck would have been broken instantly, and that he would not have suffered, although whether or not Ellie was pleased to hear this was difficult for the emergency crew to ascertain from her vacant expression. But she was, in truth, a gentle, if simple, soul, and certainly would not have wished him to suffer.

At first, Ellie noticed that the hoover had gone quiet, and this made her really happy, for she so hated the sound of that hoover. The cable had been pulled free from the wall socket, and Humphrey, focused on zero point two six, was dragged out of the bedroom by his hoover of which he refused to let go. Because of that zero point two six. Ellie, unaware of the route alteration, had moved the cable when he was in the bedroom just as she had done, under orders, for countless past hooverings over the years. And Humphrey did not know that she did not know, so the explanation for what happened was very simple. Man and hoover were launched, horizontally, into the air, at the top of the stairs where gravity took over. Humphrey landed on his head, his neck was snapped and a few downward twirls later man and machine lay in an untidy heap at the foot of the stairs.

"Oh dear, oh dear!" exclaimed Ellie as she extricated the well-used appliance and playfully patted her husband's ashen cheek. "Humphrey?"

Humphrey's dead eyes stared blankly at the ceiling.

'Accidental death' the Procurator Fiscal recorded at the inquest. 'Accidental death' Ellie told her family and her few acquaintances. 'And he died doing what he loved best,' she would proudly add. 'Hoovering!'

They tried to persuade Ellie to wear black at the funeral. 'It's the done thing,' they all said. So she wore yellow and pink, and had on a white, wide-brimmed hat with a flower in it. And later—very much later—a flagstone was erected in the local graveyard:

'In loving memory of Humphrey Pilkingshaw who departed from this life during an attempt to set the world hoovering speed record. Sadly missed by his loving wife, Elspeth.'

She did not want to put in the 'sadly missed' bit suggested by a friend, for Ellie was honest, if nothing else, but they finally persuaded her that Humphrey would have appreciated it.

Never again was the sound of the hoover heard at number 36 Beehive Close. Humphrey's beloved hoover appeared at the local council tip even before the funeral. By the time of the funeral, big changes were already happening at Humphrey's old residence. Dust and fluff settled in layers, fragments of crisps, previously banned, and bits of peanut shell decorated the carpet in the living-room, and red wine spills added a touch of colour. Ellie developed quite a taste for red wine and wondered why

Humphrey never touched alcohol himself. It also helped her to see herself in a different light. She would often stand, for long periods, in front of the mirror in her bedroom, wine glass in hand, trying on this newly bought top or that newly acquired dress after returning from the Oxfam shop with armfuls of clothes. As for her hair... it soon changed, at the hairdresser's, from mouse-grey to bright, vivid blue in a fashionable new style. She had always fancied the idea of blue hair. And, naturally, with that colour change, plus a manicure and a full facial, came the desire for passion. Something she had never before had the opportunity to experience. Within two weeks after the funeral, an advert appeared in the dating columns of the local paper:

'Attractive, widowed, blue-haired, forty-five, WLTM dashing, romantic, handsome gent of similar age with view to fun nights and long-term relationship.'

Ellie received one reply in response to her advert. The old fellow had clearly interpreted 'similar age' in the loosest possible way. The 'fifties plus' label he used failed to hide his immobility from advanced osteoarthritis, his age-bent posture and the obvious fact that his topping was a toupée, but the trendy jeans, the trainers and the sparkle in his eyes were enough to kindle Ellie's long-dormant romantic spirit. Particularly when she left off her glasses. A 'would-be artist' he called himself. He recited poetry too, and whenever he did this, Ellie would sit with her eyes closed, swooning like a lovesick schoolgirl. And in bed? Ellie never let on, but 'Fifties Plus' soon moved in to 36 Beehive Close where sixties pop music and much laughter was now to be heard in the once quietly spotless residence of the late Mr Humphrey Pilkingshaw.

Of course, Humphrey's name never did appear in the

14

Guinness Book of Records. Buried somewhere amongst the cobweb-connected heaps of paper and books that once belonged to Humphrey Pilkingshaw, and which now littered the floor of his one-time office, now a music room, junk room and spare bedroom rolled into one, was the hoovering logbook. Needless to say, the Pilkingshaw Hoovering Index, an explanation of the mathematics of which was contained within, never did become widely used as a measure of hoovering speed and efficiency.

Christmas at Great Aunt Daphne's

Christmas at Great Aunt Daphne's was always something special. You see, she had these dolls called Belinda, Flossie and Mildred. They were even older than Daphne. When she told us this, we reckoned that they must be the oldest dolls in the world. Despite this, she always let me and my cousin, Cathy, play with them when our two families met up, every Christmas, in that large and lonely Victorian house on the cliff top. We never stayed more than two nights because Dad complained it was too far from the pub and our pimply, elder brothers went into non-stop moan-mode because Great Aunt Daphne did not have a television. Cathy and I, on the other hand, would make use of every waking minute of those two days and, whenever we were about to leave on Boxing Day, we, too, would moan. Because of those three dolls. And because they spoke. Not through some factory-made gizmo hidden in their stuffing, or a fancy, battery-driven voice-box. They just spoke.

"Nonsense!" chuckled our great aunt when we first found out and told her.

No one else knew, and it remained our little secret. Cathy and I would spend hours with the dolls, in the attic, after opening our Christmas presents, and having left them strewn about the living-room, untouched, with half-sozzled grown-ups stretched out on the sofa and in armchairs, bleary-eyed, whilst our brothers squabbled like Siamese fighting fish over their presents. The fairy lights on the tree would wink prettily, out of sync with the Christmas carols squawking at us from the radio, as we tittering girls disappeared upstairs to play with Great

Aunt Daphne's dolls.

Or did the dolls play with us?

Together, we would act out family, school and shop scenes. Whatever took our fancy. And the dolls would join in. Of course, Flossie, the bossy one, *always* had to be teacher, shopkeeper, whatever. Even, on one occasion, a policeman who arrested us girls for 'creating a disturbance'. And she did not like it when we giggled for Flossie took our games *very* seriously. She hated being made fun of, but we could not help it. We thought it so hilarious to be arrested by a little doll in a pink crinoline dress. Cathy, who refused to be serious for more than two seconds, said 'sorry' to Flossie, then giggled again.

The following Christmas, having seen the movie, Cathy and I persuaded the dolls to join us in a fun version of the Wizard of Oz. I was to be Dorothy and Cathy offered to play the Wicked Witch. Whilst the dolls argued amongst themselves over the other characters, I sneaked downstairs to the kitchen. We girls were hungry, and I went to steal some of the lovely stollen cake Great Aunt Daphne made every year. I took it up to the attic, with a breadknife, where I cut a few slices whilst the dolls decided who should play whom. In the end, predictably, Flossie was to be the Wizard of Oz and the others were told to share the remaining parts between themselves.

"Why does Flossie *always* have to get her own way?" Cathy whispered to me through a mouthful of stollen. "Don't know how the other two put up with her!"

Flossie had very good hearing.

"*I* do!" she snapped.

And Cathy collapsed with laughter, unable to stop herself.

After we got going, Flossie sang a superb 'Over the Rainbow' for me since I could never sing in tune. Cathy made a convincing Wicked Witch of the West, Belinda and Mildred had fun doubling up as other characters, and everything seemed to be going so well. Until it happened.

"You're still alive!" Flossie-the-Wizard-of-Oz boomed out to Cathy in a strangely deep voice.

"Of course I'm still alive!" laughed Cathy as she got up from the floor after being 'destroyed'. "This is only a game, Flossie."

Flossie turned to face me. Oh, I forgot to tell you, the dolls could move about by themselves. And we girls never questioned how or why.

"She's still alive!" repeated Flossie. "The Wicked Witch should be dead!"

"Oh, lie down on the floor again," I suggested to my cousin for the sake of some peace. "Play dead for a while, then we can move on to the next game."

"Just because bossy-boots Flossie says so!" grumbled Cathy, before stretching herself out on the floor. "Hey, Sally, get me a drink. The stollen's made me really thirsty."

I crept down to the kitchen again, prepared a jug of orange juice and brought it up to the attic on a tray. As soon as I put my head through the open hatch at the top of the stepladder, I dropped the tray. It crashed to the landing floor, and the noise must have been drowned by my scream. The attic floor was red with blood. Cathy's head was only a few feet away, her eyes fixed and staring blankly ahead. Her body was at the other end of the attic where I had left her. The three dolls were lying motionless on the moth-eaten sofa, staring innocently up at the ceiling. On the floor, in the pool of blood, was the breadknife I had used to cut the Stollen, my fingerprints all over it. No one else's.

And no one believed me when I said Flossie did it. I told them what happened over and over and over. Then I repeated everything to the policeman. About Cathy upsetting Flossie and Flossie hating to be made fun of. The dolls, being just dolls, remained stock-still and silent. Their enigmatic, painted smiles gave nothing away. I cried and cried, and I told the children's officer, then more policemen, the truth, and I begged Mummy and Daddy to believe me, but no one would. Looking back on it, all these years later, from the locked ward of a long stay psychiatric unit for the criminally insane, I ask myself the same question that they must have all been asking themselves:

Why should they have believed me? A fit young girl, as Cathy indeed was, to have her head cut off by three inanimate Victorian dolls dressed in pretty crinoline dresses? No way! Particularly not after the SOCO only found one set of fingerprints on the murder weapon. Mine.

I have often wondered what happened to Flossie, Belinda and Mildred. Great Aunt Daphne died a week after the event. Probably from shock. After a while, my parents and my big brother stopped visiting me. They were too horrified by what I had done. Or, rather, what everyone thought I had done. And it must have been a thousand times worse for them when I got splashed all over the newspapers. 'The Child Fiend', I was labelled, and the awful thing is that no one else knew how much I truly loved Cathy. She was my best friend ever.

The dolls? Great Aunt Daphne's house was sold, the contents auctioned off. Perhaps the dolls are in someone else's attic now, or maybe gathering dust in an old antique shop that smells of the past, waiting for an unsuspecting child, like Cathy or me, to play with them again.

You do believe me, don't you? I'm dying. Cancer, they say. I would hate to leave this life without anyone else ever knowing the truth about Flossie, Belinda and Mildred. And about what really happened that Christmas in an old Victorian mansion house out there on a lonely clifftop.

Blind Dates

Arabella Nuthatch was not unattractive. Some would even have called her pretty. But she had never been with a man. Not because she didn't like the opposite sex. Quite the opposite. She thought a great deal about men. The trouble was her shyness. Now, at thirty-four, she began to think this had gone on for too long, the 'not having been with a man' thing. She had made timid attempts to flutter her eyelids at Dennis, the young postman, but stopped this when her friend from up the road, Claire, pointed out that Dennis was already married and to a most gorgeous blonde.

"What about a dating agency?" Claire suggested.

Arabella protested that she was far too shy, but soon eagerness to experience the things hinted at in her Mills and Boon books became too strong to resist. Claire helped her to compose the details about herself:

Attractive professional lady (as Claire insisted, supermarket checkout is a sort of profession) *into walking the hills* (it was uphill from the bus stop to the supermarket), *theatre* (sometimes watched East Enders), *sport* (and Wimbledon, on the telly) *dining out* (MacDonald's) *WLTM handsome gent* (it's much better if they're handsome, particularly for first timers, Claire told her) *40-50* (needed to be experienced since Arabella was a virgin), *view to friendship, fun nights and more.'*

The 'and more' was important, Claire told her. Means 'sex' and they would know, then, that they could forget about the walking, the theatre, the sport and the dining out.

When she got a reply from the dating agency, she felt both nervous and excited. He did, indeed, look handsome in the attached passport photo, and they were to meet in the station café at Kings Cross. He said he would wear a brown jacket with a red flower on the left lapel to be sure she could recognise him. *Should she bring anything with her?* she asked Claire. Claire, the ever-dutiful friend, gave her a couple of condoms.

"Will it hurt?" asked Arabella, staring suspiciously at the little packets.

"Not if he's experienced," reassured Claire. "Handsome, you say?"

Arabella smiled.

"Very," she replied. There was a distinct glint in her eyes as she hid the little packets at the bottom of her handbag.

Kings Cross station was teeming and the café packed. She hoped she would recognise Nigel, or that he might recognise her. The photo she had sent was thirteen years old. Still... a brown jacket with a red flower in the lapel? She felt certain there would be no problem in identifying her would-be lover as she queued for her coffee, and she soon spotted him. Seated, alone, in the far corner of the café, looking very contemplative.

Arabella patted her hair and smoothed down her miniskirt. 'Miniskirt a must,' Claire had said. 'You've great legs!' She paid for her coffee, and walked with caution, unused to wearing such high heels, between the crowded tables and towards the seated man. He hadn't yet seen her.

Doesn't look much like the photo, she thought as she approached him. *Must've been taken a while back, like mine. Bound to be experienced, though.*

22

The very idea of, at last, sharing her secret desires with a real man sent tingles of anticipatory excitement around her body.

"Nigel?" enquired Arabella, holding her cup of coffee.

The man glanced up. He looked awfully sad.

"Why, yes," he replied.

Funny, but he looks nervous too, thought Arabella as she put her coffee mug on the table and sat down.

"Annabelle?" he questioned. Arabella laughed.

"No, Arabella!"

His diffidence gave her confidence. 'Latent motherly instincts,' Claire said later when Arabella recounted the event to her friend.

"Oh, I'm so s-sorry," stuttered Nigel, clearly apologetic. He looked anxiously at her with his soulful Labrador eyes. Not at all as she had imagined. "I thought you would be a little older," he added, offering a weak smile.

Older? And the photograph she had posted was already thirteen years old. Her confidence soared like a skylark as she sat beside Nigel, her stocking tops visible when she crossed her shapely legs.

"I'm so very grateful to you for coming," continued Nigel. "You've no idea what it's been like for me. They say it's worse for men, you know."

Worse for men? His first time too? Golly, she thought, *I had no idea.*

She noticed Nigel's hand tremble as he lifted his coffee cup to his lips. She felt sorry for him and so wished to give him a big hug, there and then. She placed her hand over his after he put down his cup.

23

"It's all right, really. I was scared too, you know."

"Scared?"

Nigel seemed puzzled. Arabella noticed him looking at her legs. She felt pleased. Claire was right about the stockings.

"Yes," said Arabella, timidly. She looked down and bit her lower lip. "It's the first time for me, you see."

Claire had told her he would come on even more if he knew she was a virgin.

"Oh, I suppose there always has to be a first time."

Nigel smiled again. She liked his smile. It wasn't the least bit lecherous.

"Look," he said, "perhaps this isn't such a good place to talk, after all. A bit inhibiting. I might get emotional with all these people around. So... erm... would it be okay if we went back to my place? I know there are memories there, but perhaps that's a good thing."

So soon? Arabella felt really turned on. And memories? *Must* have tried it before, but maybe a long time ago. She knew could help him. She uncrossed her legs, revealing even more of her thighs.

"Your place? Why of course, Nigel."

They left the station café together. Moments later, Annabelle, a sternly dressed, middle-aged bereavement counsellor, entered Kings Cross station café. She looked around at the crowded tables, spotted an empty one and went over to it, placing her newspaper on the seat beside her. She seemed to be looking for someone as her keen eyes scanned the other tables. She went to get herself a coffee, then returned to her table, looking up as a man entered the café. Not exactly like the photograph they'd sent her. In fact he looked somewhat younger, but he had on a brown jacket with a red flower on his lapel. It had to be him, and she knew photographs could be so misleading. She stood and waved at him. He waved back. Right after all.

"Nigel?" she asked, offering her hand, expecting him to shake it.

"Indeed!" said Nigel, taking her hand and kissing it. Annabelle frowned and quickly pulled back her hand. Still, she knew how disturbed men in his situation could become. It was her job to help him through the bereavement process, and she had vast counselling experience.

"Such a pretty name, Arabella," Nigel said, grinning broadly.

Annabelle frowned again.

"It's Annabelle," she corrected. Nigel laughed.

"Prettier still!" he said. "Look, do sit down. Sorry I'm late, but you know how it is. Forgot a 'you know what' so had to pop into the gents. I'll get myself a coffee. Won't be a tick!"

Nigel wondered why Annabelle continued to frown as he looked across at her whilst buying his coffee. A lot older than her photo, but not bad looking despite this. Just no dress sense at all. Still, he was sure she'd be wanting what he was wanting. 'Fun nights, and more'? Why else would she have put that in? And boy, did he need it?! It had been so long since Freda left him.

Funny, thought Nigel, shrugging his shoulders as he sat next to Annabelle with his cup of coffee, *but I could have sworn her name was Arabella.*

"I know we'll get along together very well, Annabelle," he said, winking at her.

"Look," Annabelle began, sensing that the man was

25

blocking out the issue, "I realise this is going to be awfully painful for you, but…"

Nigel's eyebrows shot up a couple of centimetres. *Painful? Wow!* he thought, *she must be into S&M or something. Probably explains the drab clothes. Never done that, but game for anything, as long as it moves on from the old slap and tickle.*

Annabelle really could not make him out, this suave-looking man sitting opposite her. Probably so totally overcome with grief that he had difficulty showing it.

Denial, that'll be it, she reassured herself. *Perhaps not such a great idea to meet in the station café. Inhibiting for him. Terrified of breaking down. Could explain his strange behaviour? He said in his letter that the memories of his wife were just too strong back home, in his flat, for them to meet up there.*

She could understand that. How about her place?

"Look, Nigel," Annabelle continued, smiling for the first time, "this isn't going to be the best place for what we need to do. We do really need to talk, eh?"

Talk? About whips and shackles, no doubt. Somehow I can't imagine her wielding a whip or whatever they use in that S&M stuff.

He liked the shape of her bosom. And her hips and her legs. She had a friendly smile.. He did not like the idea of talking too much, but they could always cut that short.

"So," ventured Annabelle as Nigel sipped his coffee, "I'm afraid the agency gave me very few details. Confidential information, you see. Look, I do understand how difficult it must be for you. All that pain. But beyond that there is… well… relief from the pain, I suppose."

She smiled so pleasantly. Nigel was still unsure about the pain thing. Not his cup of tea, really, but she had

26

a such nice smile. He grinned back at her.

"Always straight, myself," Nigel said. "*Very* straight. Normal, like, you understand. Not really into pain, but game for anything, if you get my meaning."

Annabelle frowned again. *Why does she keep frowning like that?*

"Of course! Please be straight with me. Look, there are ways of coping with the pain, and really here is not the place (*Bloody right,* thought Nigel). You see, my flat is just around the corner (*Fast worker,* thought Nigel). Why don't we go there when you've finished your coffee? It'll be so much easier to address that pain (*Oh, here we go again!*), and reach beyond it when there aren't others around who might hear you (*Hear me scream, you mean? Christ, I'm really not sure about this!*)."

Despite Nigel's ambivalence, his male needs were too overpowering to ignore. When his coffee cup was empty, he followed Annabelle out of Kings Cross Station café.

*****

"I can't... I can't even talk about it just now," another Nigel said, his eyes moist. "It's... it's all too painful."

He seems so upset, the poor darling, thought Arabella, as she moved up closer to her first date on the pale-blue, floral-patterned settee. She had no idea men could get so emotional their first time, if this was truly his first time, or indeed that it might be painful for them as well. Odd, she reckoned, the floral settee and the obvious feminine touch about the décor. She did wonder whether he might be gay-trying-to-go-straight, though her instinct told her he was not. She put a comforting arm around Nigel's shoulders as he looked at her with his hang-dog eyes. His tears boosted her confidence.

"Look, Nigel," she said, quietly, "we don't have to talk just now. I've come prepared, you know." She tapped her bag in which were hidden the two condom packets. Nigel, of course, assumed she had a bag full of tissues. But he did find the warmth of the woman comforting, and it was impossible not to look at those wonderful legs. Nigel smiled. He was still smiling as Arabella slowly unbuttoned her blouse. Still smiling when she reached back and unfastened her bra. His smile broadened at the sight of Arabella's bared, soft white breasts. It had been so awfully long. He moved up close to his counsellor. Really close, and, his hand trembling, he reached up and touched...

*****

Annabelle ushered Nigel into her small Islington flat.

"Cup of tea?" she asked, smiling dourly. "It does help, you know. Please, make yourself at home. Know what I mean?"

Oh, he knew what she meant, all right. Wow, what a fast worker! Bet she can hardly wait. The purpose of the tea was a mystery to him, but he wasted no time. Soon, he stood in Annabelle's sitting room, bereft of all items of clothing, including his Y-fronts, aware of blood pulsing into his manhood. He caught a glimpse of himself reflected on the telly screen. *Still a fine physique,* he reckoned. *Can't think why that bitch, Freda, left me. Have everything a woman needs. At least this Annabelle woman will appreciate what I have to offer, and perhaps I could talk her out of that whips and shackles nonsense.* He watched his reflected penis slowly rise up like the proud mast of a sailing ship, but a loud crash disturbed his musings and caused the 'mast' to sag.

"Aaargh!" screamed Annabelle, dropping the tray with the tea mugs. Map-shaped spills of tea decorated the carpet around her as she stood staring in terror at the naked man in her sitting room.

"Oh, my God!" she cried out, backing towards the door "This has never happened before!"

"Yes," Nigel called out, chasing her into the kitchen. "Your God! Your very own Adonis!"

This is more like it, he told himself. He was so pleased she had changed her act. That S&M stuff would not have suited him.

*****

Nigel found his counselling session with Arabella truly comforting. He really did feel better afterwards, and honestly had no idea this was what counsellors offered. None at all. But it was wonderful. Funny she never once asked him about his recent loss, or how he felt after his wife died, but in a way he was glad he didn't have to talk. She even made him a cup of tea, afterwards, and he told her how he would call the agency and express his gratitude plus tell them how wonderful she was. He told her that he was very keen for further sessions and was simply delighted when they went on to have another one after he had finished his cup of tea.

*****

It was years since Annabelle last saw an erect male member. It pointed aggressively towards her as she stood in the kitchen with her back to the sink, wondering what to do. She was an experienced counsellor and yet had no idea bereaved clients could behave like this. There had been no mention of this sort of behaviour during her training.

"Come, sweet Venus," urged Nigel with a weird look on his face. "Come to your Adonis. Be not shy!"

Flipped, reckoned Annabelle. *Totally bloody flipped!*

"Look," she said, trying hard to regain her usual composure, "I know hard it is..."

"No you don't! Not yet, my beloved Venus. Come, hold it, feel it."

"Oh my God," muttered Annabelle, as Nigel came closer, his face horribly distorted by that daft look.

"Yes, yes, your God, your one and only Adonis," persisted Nigel. He was loving her little game of hard-to-get innocence.

Adonis stepped forward again. Too close. Venus reached back, fumbled for something beside the sink, grabbed it and struck out...

*****

Arabella apologised to Nigel for only bringing two of 'those rubber things' and promised to bring a bagful the next time. And Nigel was so pleased that there would be a next time. And a next and a next. He thought this bereavement counselling, suggested by his doctor, had been such a tremendous idea and decided to thank the man in writing.

Arabella left. Immediately she arrived home, she called Claire on her mobile.

"Claire, it was fabulous!" she said. "Disappointed at first because he looked a bit different from the photo. Not so handsome. And he seemed rather sad and very nervous, but wow, he made up for it all right. Used them both, we did. He was so pleased. And you know what? I'm seeing him again tomorrow!"

*****

30

"There was nothing else I could have done, doctor. Honestly! Oh dear, oh dear, what will the agency say?" Annabelle could hear the hysterical screams about Venus and Gods still issuing from the emergency room and wondered where she had gone wrong, and how else she might have handled such a disturbed client.

"He's going to be all right," the A & E doctor said, looking forlornly at the blood on his gloved hands. "It'll heal. But you're not his wife, then?" he added, glancing up at Annabelle.

"Indeed not! His bereavement counsellor!" she retorted. The doctor appeared puzzled.

When Annabelle got home from the hospital, she was still worrying about what the agency would say. Or do. So, the following morning it came as quite a surprise when she got a call from the agency to say how delight her client had been, and that he had no idea that they were able to offer such an amazing service.

Sumimasen[1]

When I started my walk, I felt the sort of elation that only nature can excite as I breathed in the dew-wet scent of the forest. A cool breeze caressed my face whilst spear-shafts of sunlight found their way through the dense growth, spotlighting a prickly bush here and a lichen-covered rock there. For me, there was something magical about the scene. Something that Zen poets of the past might have captured in the sparing words of a haiku poem.

How quickly all of this changed when the mountain that I had decided to climb became engulfed in a violent storm. Within the space of only two or three hours I was feeling utterly wretched as I struggled on up the steep, dwindling path that should have led me to the peak.

All I wanted was to reach the road that I knew cut through the forest, over the pass, and on to the small fishing town on the east coast of this remote peninsula in northern Hokkaido. Soon, strong gusts of wind replaced the gentle breeze, transforming the forest into a roaring beast. Worse than the wind was the rain. It began as a light refreshing drizzle, but slowly, as though an unseen hand was turning up a celestial shower tap, it became a drenching downpour. Cold water dripped from the hood of my anorak onto my numbed face, and the rucksack tugging at my shoulders seemed to get heavier by the minute as it soaked up the rain. It seemed pointless, if not dangerous, to make for the summit, and I just prayed that I would hit the road where I felt certain I would be able to get a lift. One thing that had impressed

---

[1] Japanese for 'sorry'

32

me in Japan was the kindness and the generosity of the Japanese. I was sure someone would pity a wet and bedraggled *gaijin*[2] begging for help, even if I did resemble a half-drowned rat.

It was as I urged myself on towards the only road crossing the mountain range that I first heard the voice. My heart leapt. *The road at last,* I thought. It was the voice of a young woman, that gentle disembodied feminine voice heard all over Japan. In lifts, shops, trains, buses... almost anywhere where there might be enough people around to listen to her. In these places, I would have absolutely no idea what the female owner of the voice might be saying, but its softness alone was always like music to my ears. On this occasion it was no different. The voice had the same, reassuring quality. It lifted me out of my deepening despair and reminded me of all those delicately beautiful Japanese women I tried so hard *not* to stare at on Tokyo Metro.

The voice, only just audible above the tearing gusts of wind, appeared to come from behind a dense clump of bushes ahead of me. I stopped and called out.

"Hello! Anyone there?"

The voice stopped. I tried out my meagre Japanese, of which I spoke only a few words:

"*Ohayo*[3]!" I cried out, loudly.

All that came back to me was the furious sound of the wind. Certain that I had not simply imagined it, I stumbled on up the path in the direction of the bushes whence the voice seemed to have emerged. I was convinced that I would find the road just beyond those

---

[2] foreigner
[3] Hello

bushes, but when I got there was no road and no person. The path ahead was empty.

A chill fear gripped the back of my neck as I continued on. Still wondering whether some quirk of nature had carried someone's voice, from the valley, high up into this Godforsaken forest, I froze when I heard the voice again. Louder and quite distinct, and it came from very close by. I peered ahead, my eyes half-closed in the driving rain. Again, the voice stopped. All I saw were the trees swaying wildly in the wind. The gentleness of that voice now did nothing to allay my mounting panic as I searched the gloom of that storm-swept forest for an explanation of what I heard. I summoned courage to call out again.

"Ohayo!" I yelled again.

It started up once more. Quite abruptly. On this occasion, it came from behind me. I almost overbalanced as I turned around, quickly, to confront the elusive owner of the voice, but to my horror all I could see was the empty, narrow trail along which I had just walked, winding its way back down the slope. Not a soul to be seen. Rooted to the spot, I whispered, slowly, in English.

"Where… are… you?"

Silence. I called out again. Almost shouted:

"Where are you?!"

The voice answered from right behind me:

"Sumimasen! English I speak no velly well. So solly."

I turned. Only the cold emptiness of the forest. Emptiness and the wind and the rain. I tried hard to control my fear.

"Who are you?" I enquired, speaking slowly and clearly. "Please show yourself."

The reply came straightaway...

"Ah! *Sumimasen!* I speak not well English."

There was a pause, after which the voice continued, softly.

"Next stop *Rausu-ko.*" This was followed by a girlish giggle. "Aw-light sir, I speak you English." Another giggle. As the voice giggled, I could see, in my mind, a young, charmingly pretty Japanese woman covering her smiling mouth, and looking shyly up at me as I stood alone in the cold driving rain. But there was no one there.

"Yes," I replied, still searching my brain for some rational explanation. "Yes," I repeated. "But you speak English very well."

"*Domo arigato*[4]," the voice said. "Oh! *Sumimasen!* So solly! I say, 'thank you,' sir."

Slowly, I started off, again, up the steep path, peering around, in vain, all the time, for a human presence for that voice. For a while, I heard only the wind and I focused my thoughts on reaching that road as quickly as possible. However, after a period, the voice spoke again. Annoyingly. "Next stop *Rausu-ko.* Ticket prease." There was another girlish giggle, but I just continued up the path. "Prease sir, pay ticket," followed by more laughter. I remained silent, clenching my teeth. I was afraid. *Very* afraid. This the voice that I had heard on every bus I had ever taken in Japan, a beautiful gentle voice, but disembodied in this unfriendly forest it seemed so very different. I simply wanted to escape from my fear of the voice and from the torture of the mountain. "Oh, prease sir, *sumimasen!*" Why are the Japanese forever apologising? '*Sumimasen*' was one of the few Japanese

---

[4] Thank you

words that I had learned. 'Excuse me', it seemed to mean. I sensed that the voice had noticed my increasing annoyance. "Where you flom?" the voice enquired, as though by becoming more personal she might win my sympathy. Starting off again, and just wishing the voice would stop, I replied, reluctantly, "Scotland. I'm from Scotland". "Ah so! Scotalandu!" said the voice. "Oh, *sumimasen!* I say not well, sir. Scot-a-land." "Yes, that's right," I said, with irritation. "Scotland!" There was a short pause, followed by: "Oh! Whisky!" and then another giggle. I hastened up along the trail accompanied by the voice... "Oh sir! No whisky. So solly." Apologies again. It, or she, seemed so aware of my feelings that I even began to wonder whether the voice was actually coming from inside my own head. Was I going mad? "You been 'rong' time in Japan?" asked the voice, now just to my right. *Rong? Wrong? Oh... 'long'!* I was getting used to the Japanese mixing up there 'l's and their 'r's. *I can't avoid this,* I thought, briefly. "Two months!" I replied. "Ah so!"

The voice sounded genuinely interested. I tugged on the straps of my rucksack, as though this might help to speed me up the slippery path. For many minutes, the only audible sounds were my laboured breathing and the rush of the wind through the trees. Then, for some strange reason, perhaps not really wanting to be abandoned altogether by that pleasantly musical female voice, I took up the odd conversation myself:

"Where... are... you... from?" I panted, slowly, as I scrambled over the slippery stones that lay across the path. Silence. I stopped and repeated my question, feeling distinctly silly talking to myself. Quite suddenly, she spoke again. From just in front of my face.

"Prease, no ask. So solly," the voice faltered. For the first time she seemed to show emotion. She was no longer just a matter-of-fact mechanical, albeit pretty, feminine voice.

"No ask," she repeated, clearly sobbing. "Prease, no ask." She went silent.

It was then, as I started up the hill again, that I glimpsed something large and blue showing through the trees to the right of me. There were traces of diesel fumes in the air. At first, I imagined this to be a hut beside the road and, with renewed energy I left the path and struggled on through the sodden undergrowth towards the blue shape. The smell of diesel grew stronger, and, as I approached the shape, I realised that I had been looking at the roof of an overturned bus. The rain drummed, angrily, on the contorted metal. I could not immediately see the road, but I knew the bus would not have been able to travel far through the forest. It soon dawned on me that this was not just an old wreck. The sickly smell of diesel fuel, now almost overpowering, was obviously due to leakage from the vehicle. *A very recent accident,* I reckoned. *There might even be survivors.*

Hurrying forwards, I slipped off my wet rucksack, enabling me to run faster. I could now see, quite clearly, where the blue bus had left the road above and where it had cut a broad swathe through the undergrowth before coming to rest on a craggy outcrop of rocks. It lay half on its side, its wheels pointing accusingly back towards the road. The windows were shattered, and the front of the bus was a mass of crumpled metal. Worst of all, I could see the lifeless, crushed face of the driver amongst the twisted wreckage.

37

Forgetting my voice companion, I clambered onto the sloping side of the battered hulk and peered through a jagged space that had once been a window. In the dim light, I saw the distorted bodies of passengers strewn haphazardly amongst the broken bus seats. The ghoulish sight caused me to retch, but I somehow managed to control my reflex reaction after realising I simply had to get on with checking for survivors.

I squeezed through the broken window, trying to avoid the jagged glass, although I noticed my hands were covered with blood as I pulled my way slowly over the wrecked seats, checking for signs of life in the partially dismembered bodies below me, and in the limbs dangling from above. The bus must have been almost full at the time of the accident and the carnage was awful.

I was still edging towards the back of the bus when, from a speaker at the caved-in front end, a soft female voice that I knew only too well, by then, called out clearly:

"*Tsugi wa Rausu-ko*[5]! *Arigato.*"

In my anger, I screamed back at the voice as I struggled on towards the rear of the bus.

"Shut up! For God's sake, shut up!"

I stopped briefly when the voice, now 'freed' from the speaker, spoke again, quietly, in my right ear.

"*Sumimasen*, sir. In English I say next stop *Rausu-ko.*"

I closed my eyes, tightly, hoping this might shut out the voice.

"Just go away!" I said, quietly, and continued with my gruesome task.

"Oh solly! So solly!" sobbed the voice.

---

[5] Next stop Rausu-ko

38

The voice cried on, softly, as I approached the rear of the bus. This section appeared, initially, to be empty, and I saw that it bore less damage. Then I caught sight of a young woman's bared leg, bent and sticking up into the aisle. Peering over the seat, I was overcome with horror and sadness as I found myself looking at a teenage girl lying on her back on an unbroken window. Even in death she was exquisitely pretty, her lifeless eyes gazing in disbelief at a world to which she no longer belonged. Although at first glance her young body appeared intact, I was sure she, too, must be dead. Nevertheless, I had to be certain. I climbed over the seat and, perching on the armrest, reached down to grab the girl's small hand. I began to search frantically for a pulse at her wrist. There was none. Her limp hand felt cold. Dead.

It is not easy for me now to describe exactly what happened next. I dropped the girl's hand when a powerful shock jerked my own hand that held hers. A sensation I can only describe as like a thousand hot needles shooting down my arm to the fingers. Immediately before this, I had experienced what felt like a blow on the back of my neck. Not a physical blow. More of a pulsing warmth, though not heat. At the same time, my whole being became overwhelmed by intense sadness and countless other indescribably powerful emotions that sprang from the back of my neck down to my fingertips in contact with the girl's wrist. That was when I dropped her hand. The whole experience lasted a mere fraction of a split second, but the impact on my memory of that infinitesimally brief moment in time will never leave me. It was as though all thoughts, fears, hopes and passions of a lifetime had been caught and distilled into a small vial, the contents of which were injected into me and then travelled, in that instant, around my entire body and my soul; as if an independent existence, entity, life, whatever, had just shot through my body.

"What the...?" I gasped but stopped short when I saw the dead girl's lips twitch. Her eyes looked different. They had lost that waxwork stare. Then her fingers moved. She appeared to be trying to grasp something.

She was alive. Of this, I had no doubt. I grabbed her arm again, tears welling in my eyes as I felt a faint, but distinct, pulse at her slender wrist. At the same time, her eyelids flickered and, slowly, she turned to face me. With tears streaming down my cold cheeks, I squeezed her hand.

"You'll be all right. Okay!" I said, just wishing that I could speak Japanese. The girl looked both bewildered and frightened as she stared up at the strange-looking *gaijin* addressing her.

"I'll get help for you. Quickly. Help. The road," I said, pointing in the direction of the bus's final journey after careering off the road. The girl just stared at me in disbelief. She was trembling, so I removed my anorak and covered her with it.

"Who are you? What's your name?" I asked in English, trying to put her at ease before going for help. The girl's eyes seemed to be searching for something before fixing on mine. She smiled. I knew then that she understood me. She spoke:

"*Wakaranai[6]!*" she said softly. A single tear trickling down her pale cheek, her voice continued... "I don't know. *Sumimasen!* English not good. Prease no ask."

I knew that voice only too well.

---

[6] I don't know

Helpline for Phobias

He stamped at the black spider as it ran over the silken white material, but missed. "Ouch!" screamed the bride, in pain. The spider scuttled away.

Unable to lift her stricken foot pinned down by the minister's own foot, the bride raised her other foot. Startled by the volume of her scream, the minister leapt off the dress, and, with both feet now in the air, the bride fell backwards. On top of the bridesmaid. All eighteen stones of her. Squashing the bridal bouquet and pinning the spreadeagled bridesmaid, a slip of a girl, to the floor.

The minister had frequently prayed to his heavenly boss about his arachnophobia, seeking divine assistance, but whenever he saw a spider, however small, the result was the same. Reflex reaction. Stamp, swat or run. He could not run whilst officiating at a wedding, so, for a ground-based arachnid it had to be 'stamp'. No time to think about where the bride's feet were.

The groom, too, was startled by the shrill scream of his about-to-be wife. Having just taken the ring from the best man, standing beside him, he dropped it. *His* reflex reaction was to dive forwards after it. Unfortunately, the minister did the same, and their heads collided with an audible bang. Both concussed, they landed on top of the bride. The bride's father caught sight of the ring, still rolling. Unable to run, due to his arthritis, he staggered after it... sadly, without his walking stick. His daughter had a phobia about walking sticks and he had promised her he would leave it behind for the wedding.

After catching his shoe on the hem of her dress, he had nothing to help him maintain an upright posture. He flip-flopped forwards, headfirst, into the wooden pulpit. Another bang. The impact of the bride's father's bald head with the edge of the pulpit sent the man into reverse and caused the pulpit to topple over with a resounding crash as he fell backwards. On top of the bride.

"Blood!" yelled the bride's mother who had been standing beside her husband before his noisy journey to and from the pulpit. Blood, gushing from a wound in the man's head, was everywhere. She hated blood. Had a phobia about it. The mere sight of blood *always* made her faint. So she fainted. On top of the bride.

By now, the slim bridesmaid's face, the only part of her still visible, had turned a dangerous shade of blue.

"Do something, Henry, for God's sake!" the groom's mother shouted at her husband. "Call an ambulance!"

Henry slapped his pockets.

"There's no phone in this funny suit I'm wearing."

"It's not funny! It's a morning suit. Do something. Quick! Alice is turning blue!"

The groom's mother tried, unsuccessfully, to push the heaped up, groaning figures off her daughter-in-law-to-be, beneath whom lay Alice the bridesmaid, whilst the best man chased the still rolling ring.

"Take *my* phone!" shouted the beadle, throwing his mobile phone to the groom's father. How was he to know that Henry had a thing about mobile phones? Hated them, though never dared tell his wife. Guess you could call it a phobia. He was quite relieved that the beadle's phone never reached him. This was because his wife got in the way of its trajectory. The downside was that it hit her on the temple, stunning her. She fell on top of the those already spreadeagled over the bride who still lay on top of the bridesmaid. As did the groom's father when he stumbled and fell whilst trying to catch her.

It was quite a long time before the beadle, the best man and other wedding guests, who *could* stand the sight of blood, managed to free the poor bridesmaid, still an unhealthy shade of blue. It was a very long time before the ambulance arrived. Because of yet another NHS workers' strike.

The following week they were all back in church. The bride, the groom, both sets of parents, the best man, the beadle, the minister and the bridesmaid... in her coffin. Quite a small coffin, being a mere slip of a girl.

At the end of the service, muted by the tragedy of events of the previous weekend, they filed past the collection plate. 'All donations to go to *Helpline for Phobias*' was written on a card propped up behind the collection plate. The plate overflowed with banknotes and generous cheques, and *Helpline for Phobias* made a lot of money out of one wedding and a funeral. They also received calls about fear of spiders, horror of blood, distaste for walking sticks and mobile phone phobia.

One month later, the minister was still praying to the highest authority about spiders. The groom's mother would faint at the mere thought of blood. The groom's father conveniently forgot his mobile phone whenever possible, and the bride's father was still forced to shuffle about in pain, without a stick, in his daughter's presence.

An Teallach

Approaching Braemore, she turned off the main road and drove on, slowly, towards Gruinard. The mist had closed in and she saw only the road, the heather colouring the edge of the moorland and wet rocks patterned with lichen, all of which disappeared into the haze beyond a radius of about a hundred yards. Soon, out of the mist, a road sign appeared. Dundonnell. Remembering the name, she pulled into a layby, looked again at the map, peered out through the car window at...

At nothing. It was certainly the right place. She would simply have to rely on the map. Determined to see this through, she felt reassured about what they had told her at the B&B. That the mist would lift. Showers with sunny intervals, they said.

She opened the car door, walked round to the back of the vehicle, took out her hiking boots then sat, sideways, on the car seat, with the door open, as she pulled them on.

So many times, Alan must have done this, she thought. She pictured his amusement at seeing her struggling with the laces. It was the first time that she had ever worn hiking boots, bought especially for the occasion.

A full year had passed since Alan died. She had wanted to do what she was now doing ever since his death, but, until then, had been unable to find enough courage. 'An Teallach' had stuck in her mind after recalling that last meal they had shared with old friends of Alan one week before *it* happened; the event that stopped Alan from 'living' and which lead to his death. When she listened, that evening, to Alan talking with his old pal, those mysterious Gaelic words remained stuck in her head. Later, after his death, they just seemed to grow and grow. They became, for her, a symbol of the strength of the soul inside the Alan she knew and that the system had destroyed. *That* was why she needed to come to see the place for herself. She would not be put off by the mist or rain.

Over dinner, that evening, Alan had asked his friend, Peter, now an anaesthetist in Huddersfield, whether he wanted to join him on a hike to An Teallach.

"A hike, and perhaps a short climb, although I'm not that fit now," Alan said. Peter was reluctant. He had given up climbing altogether, and his wife had even managed, over the years, to put him off Scotland. "Because of the rain," Peter said. "We always head for the sun now. Spain, Corsica, Italy. At least, when it rains in the Mediterranean, you know it's going to stop. Not so in the Scottish Highlands."

Alan had disagreed.

"Well," he replied, "I'm afraid I can think of nothing more enjoyable than standing in the rain, looking across Loch Toll an Lochain at the massive face of An Teallach, and then seeing the mist slowly clear from the dark grey summit of Sgurr Fiona. And if you're lucky the rain does stop, the sun hits the mountain, and, well... pure bloody magic!"

She recalled how Alan sometimes became lost for words when he tried to explain how the Scottish hills affected him, but now she understood.

Why had *they* refused to understand him? Alan the person. That evening, he was over the moon at the thought of travelling up to Scotland for a long weekend and hiking the An Teallach range It was his favourite spot.

45

He planned the trip during the two weeks after that meal with Peter and his wife. He wished to be on his own that time, but now she just felt so sad that she had not at least offered to join him on the trip. She had never been much of a walker herself and liked to do her own thing whenever Alan went walking. Shopping in Oxford Street, visiting friends. Alan respected her independence. He was like that. Kind and understanding where others were concerned. That's what made him such an outstanding doctor. But it also destroyed him. Now she could see how the sensitivity that had made Alan so compassionate towards his patients might have left him feeling so bad about himself.

It happened on Alan's Saturday on call, a week before he planned to go to An Teallach. It had been horrendously busy, but Alan would never allow this as an excuse for what happened. Late that night, he had a call from a woman whose family was well known to his practice. It was about her nine-year-old son who had been complaining of a headache. The woman had five young children from four different fathers. The boy had never known his real father, and his stepfather, at the time, was a brute of a bully. Unemployed, somehow the man found enough money to drink himself silly several times a week. The social work department had more than once become involved because of suspected physical abuse of the children by their stepfather.

The woman was fond of her children, but she could barely cope, forever in the surgery, asking for help with her own and with the children's problems. Particularly young Sean's. Sean had major behavioural problems, both at home and at school, and recently had been prescribed Ritalin. There were emergency callouts from Sean's

46

mother two or three times a week, mostly about Sean. 'Headaches' were his stock complaint. None of the children were ever *really* ill, and, more often than not, Sean would deny having a headache whenever the doctor arrived. He or she would often turn up only to find the young tearaway beating up one of his little sisters. That Saturday seemed no different to Alan. When he entered the living room, he found Sean, seated on the empty-beer-can-littered sofa, watching television. Sean grumpily said that he felt 'all right.' and refused to get up, remaining stubbornly glued to the television whilst Alan examined him as best he could in the dim light.

"There doesn't seem to be anything serious," Alan reassured Sean's mother. "We'll just give him some paracetamol. Call me back if you have any concerns about Sean." He was aware of the mother's drunken boyfriend lurking in the background.

Alan thought no more about this visit and had a peaceful night's sleep. The following day he was off call, and spent his free time poring over his maps, getting everything ready for the trip to An Teallach. She remembered his childlike excitement. But when Alan arrived home Tuesday evening he appeared to be in a state of shock. He sat down, put his head in his hands, and would not look at her. It took a long time to discover why he was like this, but finally it all came out...

Sean had become ill overnight. When his mother found him the next morning, he was drowsy and barely able to speak. He was rushed to hospital but died shortly after admission.

"Meningitis," said Alan. "There'll be a coroner's autopsy. And an inquest."

Alan found it hard to speak and appeared frozen

47

beyond tears. He kept on saying to her that he should have picked it up, that he hadn't examined the child as thoroughly as he might have, and that, anyway, he should have had the boy admitted to hospital. Nothing she said seemed to reassure Alan that he'd done nothing wrong. She found it impossible to reason with him. As far as *he* was concerned, to miss a case of fatal meningitis in a child was unforgivable.

Alan's colleagues were wonderful. Not for one moment did she blame them. They even came round to Alan's home to talk with him. Alan was a good listener, but he was not good at talking about his own feelings. They all said they would have done exactly the same themselves, and that there was no way that Alan should take the blame. Besides, they told him, he had told Sean's mother to inform him if she had any concerns. If she had been worried enough to call the doctor out, then why did she not check on him overnight? Alan replied that it was his duty to tell her to check on Sean every hour or two. For every reassuring comment made, he responded by putting himself down.

Alan cancelled his trip to An Teallach. That's when she knew how badly he had taken Sean's death, and even at that early stage Sean's stepfather was targeting Alan with his wrath. He arrived at the health centre, after Sean's funeral, drunk and raving about that 'bastard who calls himself a doctor.' The inquest loomed like a gathering storm cloud, and it seemed to Alan that it would herald the end of the world. His, at least. There was nothing she could say nor do to alleviate his inner misery over Sean's death. She merely hoped that some of the load might be taken off his shoulders after the inquest, and she prayed that they would not be too hard on him.

Meanwhile Alan's colleagues and many of his patients continually praised his ability as a doctor.

The inquest, she realised, later on, was only the beginning. The coroner recorded Sean's death as due to 'natural causes' but the boy's stepfather, who was becoming increasingly vitriolic in his verbal attacks against Alan, demanded a judicial review on the grounds of 'medical negligence.' It all hinged on what sort of examination Alan had made of Sean that Saturday evening. Alan maintained that he had checked for a skin rash and had tested for irritation of the meninges, an indication of meningitis, but Sean's family was adamant that all he did was to say there was nothing wrong with Sean, claiming that the child had not been properly examined. It did not help Alan that he clearly carried a huge burden of guilt about the case, for he had his own concern that his examination of Sean seated in a dim, poorly lit room, and being his usual uncooperative self, had been inadequate. What really let Alan down, however, was his very brief note in Sean's record. He had simply written 'no signs of meningitis.' Without documentary evidence as to what that actually meant in terms of completeness of examination, it became a question of his word against that of the family, and his waning self-confidence made 'his word' come across as very weak.

The judicial review left an element of doubt in many peoples' minds, although Sean's death was still attributed to natural causes. It was as though they were bending over backwards to make it easier for Sean's family to take action against Alan through the courts. Alan was so low and depressed about everything that he was no longer able to work. Sean's stepfather, however, seemed to thrive on the unfolding course of events, growing in strength all the time. He had the whole extended family behind him, and they had even managed to trace Sean's true father and got him wound up as well, although the man had never once come to see Sean during the boy's life. Sean's stepfather wanted to have Alan 'done for murder', as he repeatedly put it in writing to the practice, although correspondence from the man ceased after the lawyers became involved. Finally, Alan, whose medical defence lawyers failed to help him in any meaningful way, was to face a charge of unlawful killing through negligence, a charge which, if upheld by the court, would carry a prison sentence. His defence counsel repeatedly said that they had no case to make such a charge, but Alan barely heard what people were trying to tell him. He had withdrawn so much into himself that he was just existing from hour to hour, from meal to meal, and from fitful sleep to sleepless night.

She felt so powerless. She desperately tried to support Alan, to help him see that this would all blow over, and to persuade him that many a good doctor would have done exactly as he had done in the same circumstances, but Alan was beyond help. He refused admission for psychiatric assessment. In truth, no one seriously believed his problem was caused by psychiatric illness. Fate had dealt him a heavy blow, and because of the way he was made, something that had ensured he had always been a caring doctor, he was unable to pick himself up.

As she traced her way through the mist, on foot, with the aid of a compass and a map, she once again felt some of that guilt herself. Although she had done all she could have done to help Alan, after he killed himself she bore the blame. It was only recently that she felt able to turn her anger out towards those who had hounded Alan so mercilessly. Particularly Sean's stepfather who had shown no love for Sean when he was alive, and who had, himself, been accused of violence against the troubled boy. To add to her personal trauma, she was struggling financially. None of Alan's life policies could be cashed in since he had taken his own life.

She followed the burn for about two hours, climbing a little all the time, until, out of the mist, a small loch appeared up ahead. It was almost black in the dim light. She knew this was Toll an Lochain. A fine, cooling drizzle, that gently caressed her face for the first hour of her walk, had stopped, and, as she sat on a rock and pulled a sandwich box from out of her rucksack, gaps in the mist began to open up. These grew and grew, before merging, until she found herself looking across the loch at the towering wall of Sgurr Fiona, the highest peak in the range. The summit was still partially hidden by soft curtains of mist.

After sitting for a while, she became aware that her body was casting a long shadow. She glanced over her shoulder and saw the sun emerge between the clearing clouds. She looked back at the cathedral majesty of Sgurr Fiona. The mist had vanished and the summit of the mountain seemed almost alight with the warm glow of the sun.

She had always known how lucky she had been to have found someone like Alan. They had shared so much together, and now, at long last, she felt she could share, with her memory of him, the magic of Sgurr Fiona.

51

The Cat Who Snored

Doña Rosa Piñeda Galdós never needed to worry about money. The widow of a wealthy Andalucian industrialist and landowner, she lived alone in a fine house on the outskirts of the village of Monachil in the foothills of the Sierra Nevada. Alone, that is, except for Paño, a large, blue-grey, Persian cat. Paño—Spanish for 'cloth'—acquired his name after a friend of the widow commented on what appeared to be a grey cloth on the settee shortly after Doña Rosa had acquired the Persian kitten. The widow thought it was extremely funny that her aristocratic cat, with a distinguished pedigree, had been called a 'cloth' so she decided to rename him 'Paño'.

Paño was fond of sleeping on Doña Rosa's settee, and, since he spent most of his life asleep, the grey 'cloth' which grew to be quite large, was usually seen occupying this prime space in the sitting room of the widow's sumptuous residence. Something else about Paño… he snored. Loudly. And the extraordinary thing about Paño's snoring was that it sounded totally human. Doña Rosa always said that the sound of Paño's snores gave her comfort in her spacious, grandiose old house, for it reminded her so much of her dear, late husband, Don Pedro. He, like Paño, had been a champion snorer.

"Paño knows," the widow would tell the villagers. "He only snores because he knows it reminds me of Don Pedro." Then she would laugh, for Doña Rosa was always laughing and joking. The children of Monachil thought that Paño's snores were very funny and always joked about them. Should a lorry cause a rumbling noise by tipping its stony load onto a construction site, then they

52

would say, amongst themselves, '...Listen to Paño snoring!' Or a giggling group of teenage girls, caught in a storm, might attribute the distant roll of thunder to Paño snores.

When Paño was awake, and disappointingly for the children that was not very often, he was the friendliest animal imaginable. The children loved to hear him purr as they ran their small hands through his long, soft, grey fur. Paño was too large for the smaller children to carry, but the larger boys and girls took great delight in lifting him up for the little ones to tickle his tummy. The children would laugh when Paño let out his strange deep-throated 'miaow,' for it sounded like no other cat in the neighbourhood. Someone once likened the sound to the call of a lynx, although no one had ever heard a Spanish lynx. Indeed, some claimed that a lynx made no noise at all.

The children of Monachil loved to visit the grand house of Doña Rosa not only to see Paño but also because of the widow herself. She was a large woman, Doña Rosa, and for those who did not know her she could appear quite fierce. However, only a brief acquaintance with the good lady was required to realise that she not only had an extraordinary sense of humour, but also a heart of gold. The children adored her. Doña Rosa was an excellent cook and she loved to bake cakes and magdalenas for them should they happen to 'drop by'. And drop by they did. Any time when not at school. Often, at weekends, her garden was alive with the voices and shrieks of excited children, and the villagers were always happy if their little ones had gone off to play in the widow's garden.

Set on a slope, the garden had been levelled off where it descended the hillside. Consequently, it was surrounded by a four-metre high wall on the inside, although, from the road, the wall appeared to be only about two metres. There was no gate nor other outside access to the garden, which could only be accessed by going through the widow's house, so everyone knew that Doña Rosa's garden was a totally safe place in which their children could play. Also, they knew that the widow would keep a careful watch over their youngsters, and on their comings and goings. She reliably telephoned parents to let them know if their children were on their way back home.

There was one thing about Doña Rosa, however, that did worry the people of Monachil. Her total inability to worry. About anything. Of course, everyone knew that she was extremely wealthy, for her large house was simply full of valuable artefacts and items that Don Pedro had amassed during his lifetime. He had been a great collector. There were priceless paintings and decorative plates and vases, beautiful silverware, a few exceedingly valuable items of Visigoth gold plus antique furniture that really would have been more suitably placed in a museum...

And his collection of old books.

The books had been Don Pedro's most prized possessions. Amongst them were several wonderfully illustrated medieval manuscripts which Doña Rosa would often off show to the children. She loved to see their little eyes light up in amazement as she turned over pages full of painstaking calligraphy and delicately painted illustrations, explaining how these books had been created by humble monks hundreds of years before, working away in cold, dimly lit monasteries for no reward other than the knowledge that what they had made was something sacred to God, and very beautiful. On the widow's bookshelves were also a number of eighteenth-century volumes, including botanical treatises embellished with strange and neatly drawn plants bearing long Latin names, old books of long-forgotten Spanish and French verse, and a number of autographed first editions, including one signed by Garcia Lorca himself.

Naturally, the villagers became particularly concerned for the widow after hearing reports that a gang of Romanian thieves had descended on the area in and around Granada. These thugs began by preying on foreign tourists in the Albaicín, stealing bags, wallets and cameras. Soon, the increase in petty crime in a wider area was attributed to these Romanians. More worryingly for the people of Monachil, there had been break-ins as far out of the city as Cajar and Bella Vista. They knew it was only a matter of time before the thieves got to work in the quiet little village of Monachil. The men of the village helped each other as they set about tightening up the security of their homes. Many times, they offered to check on Doña Rosa's house. They told her that they would fit better locks and bolts to her doors and windows, and cement broken glass onto the top of her garden wall, but she would have none of it.

"Nobody has ever burgled my house," she argued, "and, besides, if they did break in then they would have Doña Rosa Piñeda Galdós to contend with!" At this, she would put on as fierce an expression as she could, drew herself up to her full height, which was pitifully short, then burst into laughter. They were completely unable to make her take the threat of burglary seriously. Admittedly, she could look very imposing indeed, if and when she was able to stop herself from laughing. Her posture and her appearance was then reminiscent of the huge, old portraits of distinguished Andalucian ladies from the past that adorned the walls of her living room and her reception rooms. These images of matriarchal power gazed sternly down at the widow's visitors, though the children were not the slightest bit intimidated by them.

"Who's that?" they would ask, "And what about her? Who's she? Her face looks funny! And that person over there, Doña Rosa, wearing a mantilla? Can you tell us who she is?"

Of course they *all* knew who the beautiful young lady in the mantilla was. It was a younger Doña Rosa, but they loved to hear it from the lady herself, again and again, and she loved to tell them, for this would invariably lead on to stories about her life as a girl in Sevilla, and her courtship with Don Pedro. She spared them the unpleasant bits from her life history. The oppression and the horrors of life under General Franco whom Don Pedro hated.

No, the villagers had little confidence in Doña Rosa's ability to look stern for longer than a few fleeting moments before a mischievous twinkle appeared in her eyes; something that usually meant the widow was about to erupt into fits of laughter.

Repeatedly, they begged her to allow them to make her fine old house secure against those Romanian thieves." It will be so easy for us," they insisted. "The locks, the broken glass on the wall, and we could fit grilles to your windows. Nothing at all. Half a day's work, that's all. Payment for looking after our children."

Of course Doña Rosa knew that 'half a day' in Spain could mean anything from a few hours to a few weeks, and she did not want any prolonged work on her house disturbing Paño's sleep. So she merely shook her head.

"But Doña Rosa, all those precious things of Don

Pedro's in your house! Just imagine if they were stolen."

"Nothing is more precious to me than to make your children happy," she insisted. "And to hear Paño snore like my late husband. Anyway, who would want to steal an old grey cloth that snores?" Then she collapsed with laughter, leaving the villagers to worry on her behalf.

*****

One chill night in March, when a cold wind blew off the snow-covered Sierra Nevada, and all the houses, save Doña Rosa's, were firmly bolted and shuttered, like small fortresses, against intruders, a solitary figure walked into Monachil. He was a short, swarthy man of indeterminate age. Somewhere between mid-twenties and late thirties. He had come to Spain hoping to find work. There had been nothing for him back home, where unemployment was widespread. The fact that three fingers were missing from his left hand, as a result of a childhood injury, had not helped his prospects of finding a job. He found nothing in Italy, France and Germany, and people in these countries had been unfriendly to him. "Try Spain," a fellow Romanian suggested, "for there you will be sure to find work and make friends."

The man had hitched his way down through Spain, finding neither work nor friends. Only a rough band of compatriots who ruined tourists' holidays by fleecing them of their money, credit cards, cameras, mobile phones and anything else of value that tourists might have on them. The man who came to Monachil, at two in the morning, was unlike these men. He was a loner. He hated the idea of stealing from tourists in the streets. Having seen their distraught faces, he would immediately feel sorry for them. Stealing from large shops and wealthy houses, however, was different.

The man was clever and had managed to teach himself enough Spanish to understand and make himself understood in the country in which he now found himself. Unfortunately, despite his intelligence, circumstances had always prevented him from being anything other than desperately poor. He was seeking something better for himself. And for his mother and his young unmarried sister back in his homeland.

That night, he had walked all the way to Monachil from the outskirts of Granada. He carried a shabby suitcase and all that this contained was an empty rolled-up potato sack. He had not come to Monachil at two in the morning looking for work. He had exhausted *all* possibilities of finding work in Spain, just as he had in those other countries; when people heard his accent and saw that three fingers were missing from his left hand, they simply said, 'no work here, *chico!'*

Perched on the wall, the man was somewhat surprised to see such a long drop into the garden of Doña Rosa's house, but he was desperate. He hadn't eaten for two days. He leapt soundlessly to the ground, certain that he would find another way out when his potato sack and his suitcase were full. He was both frightened and excited. Excited at the thought of acquiring something that would earn him money. Enough to keep both him and his family back home alive. He'd heard that there were wealthy houses in some of the outlying villages away from Granada. Houses which were less like fortresses than those in the city, and this house seemed to be just what he had hoped to find after his long walk up towards the foothills of the Sierra Nevada. The owner might just as well have left the back door into the kitchen open, he thought, as he cut a neat hole out of the windowpane, through which he reached his arm and released the catch on the other side of the door. He crept silently into the house and switched on his torch.

The first room he entered was a kitchen, large and old-fashioned. A pile of unwashed dishes and utensils littered a draining board beside a deep porcelain sink. On an old oak table, in the centre of the kitchen, was a dish covered by a cloth. The man raised the cloth and saw, to his delight, that it had been hiding a large number of magdalena buns. These had been made especially for the children of Monachil by Doña Rosa, it being the weekend. He popped one of them into his mouth. It was simply delicious. So he took another, then another. He had forgotten how anything could taste so good.

The man moved on through the house. He had work to do, a sack to fill. First, he passed a pantry with a fridge and a freezer, to the contents of which he decided he would help himself on the way out. Then, on through a utility area, with buckets, mops and brushes. A washing machine stood in the corner. If only he could have washed his few items of clothing in it, for he felt so ashamed to be wearing dirty, smelly clothes all the time.

Making no noise whatsoever, the man crept along a short corridor into a large dining room. Here he wowed at the grandest of furniture imaginable. A huge polished, walnut table shone back at him as his torch lit up the room. Around the table was a set of beautifully upholstered, carved, antique chairs. Against one wall stood a cabinet full of exquisite china, decanters, glasses, and goblets, and along the opposite wall another filled with valuable ornaments. However, what really caught his eye was the enormous silver candlestick right in the centre of the table. He took great care with this as he

59

slipped it into the potato sack. With the candlestick alone, he felt sure he would be able to buy food and new clothes and still have plenty left over to send back to his mother and his sister. He went on into the next room. The ornaments could wait until he knew what else was worth taking, for the candlestick took up a lot of space.

The sitting room was darker and gloomier than the dining room in the torchlight. In the dim light, the man could just make out a comfortable settee on which were several cushions, one of which was strangely fluffy and grey. There were two large armchairs, and at the far end of the room an old bureau next to a curvaceous, ornate chair. Beside this stood a large bookcase, and even in the poor light the man could see that the books in it were antique and probably worth a lot of money. He placed his sac carefully on the floor beside this and picked out several of the best-preserved books. It was as he lifted the now heavy spoil off the floor that something caused the hair at the back of his neck to stand on end. No mistake. It was the sound of someone snoring, so distinct that it could only have come from the room in which he now stood. He froze, for there was nobody else in the room. He tiptoed quietly around the settee to see whether anyone might have fallen asleep in a drunken stupor on the floor behind it. There was nobody, but to the man's absolute horror the snores seemed to come from the settee itself, near where he had been standing just a moment beforehand. Terrified, he remained rooted to the spot.

Having been brought up in a Romanian village, where stories of ghosts and vampires abound, he feared that he was about to awaken some ghastly ghoul of a creature that would suck out his blood and send him on a nightmare journey into the land of the undead. He had to

60

escape from whatever it was. Slowly, very slowly, he inched his way around the settee, took hold of his potato sack and turned to make for the door. Unfortunately, he had failed to notice a tall, slim, rosewood pedestal beside the bookcase, on which was balanced a huge black Qing dynasty Chinese vase, virtually invisible in the darkness. His sac caught the foot of the pedestal. The heavy vase hit the marble floor with the sound of a discharging cannon. Then, complete silence. The snoring stopped. The man caught only a brief glimpse of the apparition that had been responsible for the ghostly snores. On the settee. His torch picked out two large yellow eyes. They had materialised from nowhere and were turned towards him. He fled. Through the door and into the dining room, knocking into chairs as he made for the corridor leading to the kitchen, and out of the kitchen door into the garden. Relieved that whatever it was had not yet caught up with him, he used his torch to search for a door leading out onto the street. He scanned first one wall, shone his torch at the next wall, and the third wall, and then all the way back again. No door!

Despite the cold wind, he was sweating as he had never before sweated. Surely there had to be a door, he thought. Some other way out of the garden. He frantically swung his torch this way and that, but only illuminated an expanse of blank, white-washed wall. Somewhere to hide, he hoped. A tree or a bush? There were only three or four small citrus trees with trunks no thicker than broom handles, and a few leafless shrubs looking very sorry for themselves in the cold spring air.

It was whilst he was deciding where he should try to conceal himself when the whole garden suddenly lit up. He whispered a small prayer when an ominous, black figure appeared, silhouetted in the kitchen doorway. The creature seemed much larger than he had envisaged from his brief encounter with it in the living room of the house. Like a witch, it was wearing a tall dark hat, and brandishing what appeared to be a sword. Without a doubt, this had to be a magical sword, one thrust of which would caste him down into an underworld of demons and the most hideous of crawling things imaginable. The man stood there, shaking with fear, still clutching his potato sack.

Doña Rosa had grabbed the first thing she saw on her way down the stairs after being awakened by a terrific crash. It was a blunt, old ceremonial sword of Don Pedro's that hung on the wall at the foot of the stairs. It was so blunt that it would have been useless for cutting bread, let alone inflicting injury as a weapon of self-defence. The widow had also quickly picked up her black mantilla and fastened it on the top of her head to give her added height.

"Thief, thief!" she called out. "Stay still whilst I call the police."

The man was almost relieved that the creature appeared to talk like an ordinary human. It was female, and this somehow seemed less threatening despite the sword. However, what really reassured him that perhaps this was not, after all, a ghost or a vampire was the mention of the police. Why would a vampire need to call the police? There again, the thought of being handed over to the police was almost as terrifying as facing some supernatural monster. He knew only too well what the police were capable of doing from the days of Nicolae Ceaușescu.

But this had to be a human woman, and the man found his voice...

"Please," he called out in broken Spanish, "Please, no police. I do no harm. See... I give back!"

The man held out the potato sack for the woman to see.

"Borrow only! No steal nothing!"

"Borrow?" repeated the lady with a tall, black thing balanced on her head. "Borrow!" she bellowed again.

Suddenly, she dissolved into uncontrollable laughter. The man just stood there, in the garden, as the woman laughed and laughed and laughed. He began to wonder whether he might have broken into a madhouse. After all, this would have explained the strange thing on her head and the absence of any means of escape from the garden. Gradually, the woman's laughter subsided.

"Oh dear, oh dear, that *is* funny," she muttered. "Borrow indeed!" She began to giggle again.

"Give back," the man insisted. "No steal. No thief! Please, no police!"

Doña Rosa had not the slightest intention of calling the police. Ever since Franco's men had murdered her elder brother, she'd hated anything to do with the police or with any government authority. She only wanted the intruder to be put in his place and to know who was boss. The man edged forwards, hoping that he might be able to slink past the crazy woman, but he stopped as soon as Doña Rosa raised her sword and pointed it in his direction.

"Stay!" she commanded, blocking the doorway with her imposing frame, magnificently draped in a long Andalucian shawl. She squinted to get a better look at the man.

"Rather scruffy looking, aren't you?" she observed

"Obviously not a very good thief!" The widow laughed again. The man just could not make her out.

"Please," he said again, "no say 'thief'. No mean to be thief. Please, no police. My little sister, she soon wedding. Marry. Me have no present for her. No money."

The woman lowered her useless, ceremonial sword. She felt not the slightest bit threatened by the pathetic figure of the young man who stood before her begging her not to call the police.

"At least we have one thing in common," said Doña Rosa. "We both dislike the police."

"Dislike?" repeated the man.

"Police bad!" she said. "No police!"

The man managed a faint smile

"Thank you," he said, "No police. I go."

"No!" rebuffed Doña Rosa. "Not so fast."

She was just about to say something when a voice shouted from across the street.

"Doña Rosa!" a man's voice yelled. "Are you all right? We heard a lot of noise, and we wondered whether..."

"I'm fine," the widow shouted back. "Fine! Just practising my swordswomanship by moonlight!"

She gave a chuckle which both reassured and annoyed the man from across the street.

"Please, Doña Rosa, try to be a little quieter! It's only two in the morning!"

"Shh!" The widow held a finger to her lips for the man. "Inside, quick. You'll catch your death of cold out here."

He followed her cautiously into the kitchen. She put the old sword on the table and turned to face him. He was even shabbier than he seemed in the garden, with several days of growth on his chin. She felt truly sorry for him.

"On here," she said, tapping the table and pointing at the man's booty laden suitcase and potato sack. He opened the suitcase for her and took out one of Don Pedro's precious books.

"Why?" she asked, looking at the title of the book.

"I read books. Learn Spanish. Then bring back."

Doña Rosa burst into laughter once more. "Spanish? Sorry, but this one's in Latin. And this... and this..." she said, pulling out another two ancient, leather-bound volumes. "No, I think you'd do better picking up discarded newspapers from the street. They really *are* in Spanish. And what about that sack?"

The man opened the potato sack and sheepishly extracted the large silver candlestick.

"Don't tell me!" Doña Rosa said. "You needed a light with which to read your... or rather *my* books."

Far from being angry, Doña Rosa seemed amused by the whole event, and this made the man feel distinctly uneasy.

"Will you put them back for me, please? Where they belong," continued the widow. She left the kitchen, heading for the sitting-room, expecting the man to follow her.

"No!" the man called out. "Cannot! Not go!"

"Excuse *me*," frowned Doña Rose, "are you now refusing to return my things?" Her smile had vanished.

"No," insisted the man. "Not refuse. No go back in there." He paused. "Monster," he added. "Monster with yellow eyes.

First, the man saw a return of Doña Rosa's smile. Moments later, she was speechless with laughter. She laughed so much that she had to return to the kitchen and support herself by holding onto the table.

"Oh dear, oh dear!" she giggled after she got her breath back. "This just gets funnier and funnier. Paño a monster? If he's a monster then *I'm* a goose with three heads. Follow me. I will protect you from the 'monster'."

Still wondering whether the woman was, after all, some sort of a demon, the man followed Doña Rosa along the short corridor, keeping his distance, then across the dining room before proceeding, warily, into the living room. This was now brightly lit, and there, on the settee, lay a large, furry, grey cat with its head on its paws. Big doleful yellow eyes stared at the animal's mistress who bent down and stroked him. A loud purr filled the room.

"Come and meet Paño, my monster."

The widow, smiling, motioned for the intruder to join her. Feeling utterly foolish, the young man did so and gave Paño a tentative prod.

"Are you from one of those Romany gangs?" Doña Rosa enquired, before sitting down beside a thoroughly contented Paño and beckoning the man to sit on a comfortable armchair.

"No gang. Romanian, not Romany," the man answered.

"Ahah!" exclaimed the widow. "Romanian! And your name, young man?"

"Name be Ion. Like Spanish 'Juan'."

"Well," the widow continued, smiling at Ion, "you are quite diminutive, so I shall call you Ionito. Okay?"

Ion looked puzzled.

"Okay," he replied. No point in upsetting this strange lady, he reckoned.

"And your sister? What's *her* name?"

"Sister be Juliánna."

"Juliánna. Pretty Name. And you came from Romania hoping to find work here in Granada?"

"No work!" he replied sadly, shaking his head. "Try hard, but nothing!"

"Tell me about yourself and your family, Ionito. And tell me about Romania."

Doña Rosa was no longer joking. He could tell from the look in her eyes. She was serious. *Dead* serious. In broken Spanish, with repeated prompting from an attentive Doña Rosa, the man she now called Ionito talked about his childhood in a village to the north of Bucharest, about the appalling hardships his family had suffered under the dictatorship of Nicolae Ceauşescu, and how, although he now tasted freedom, there appeared to be no chance of making a decent wage with which he might allow his poor mother to have a better life. He showed Doña Rosa the missing fingers on his left hand, and she nodded her understanding.

"And you wish to get a wedding present for Juliánna?" she asked.

Ionito smiled for the first time.

"You must be very fond of your little sister," said the widow.

"She is a good girl," said Ionito. "*Very* good girl."

"So," said Doña Rosa, "you can't find work here in Spain?"

"No," said Ionito, self-consciously holding his left hand in his right hand. "Many here not like my people."

"Can you blame us Spanish if your compatriots go around stealing from us?"

"Must live," replied Ionito.

67

Doña Rosa could see beyond the thief who had broken into her house. She saw before her an intelligent young man who, despite appalling difficulties in his life so far, came across as caring and, in his own way, principled. "Do you wish to learn to speak Spanish properly?" she asked.

"Please?" queried Ionito.

"If you wish to learn Spanish you may stay here in this house. I can give you lessons. In return, you could work in the house and the garden. That hand of yours. You seem to be able to do things with it. Like stealing. But here you can do better. The house is so big I have difficulty keeping things in order. You could clean, sort out the laundry and (she paused, then grinned) polish the silver?"

She raised her eyebrows and looked at Ionito. The man appeared to have understood most of what was said and seemed moved. Struggling to hide his emotions, he cried like a child.

Why should this woman, whom I tried to rob, now be so kind to me? he asked himself.

Doña Rosa continued, her voice now gentle:

"And when we've paid for the hole in the kitchen door you will, of course, get a wage. We can sort out the details later. When we've both had some sleep. Meanwhile, we'll have to move Paño over onto one of those chairs so that you can stretch out here on the settee. I'll get a blanket for you. And if the monster starts to snore again just try this."

Dona Rosa gave Paño a gentle prod and a smile brightened Ionito's tear-stained face.

Later that morning, Doña Rosa reappeared. Daylight brightened the room, although outside it was still cold and windy. Ionito was already up. She heard him moving around in the kitchen where, as she soon found out, he had set the table for breakfast, and where the smell of freshly brewed coffee tantalised her nostrils.

I think this is going to work out rather well, the widow told herself.

And so Ionito, as the young Romanian became known in the village of Monachil, moved into the grand house as housekeeper to Doña Rosa. A contract was drawn up and signed by both parties, all the necessary paperwork for the young man was sorted out, and plus the widow paid for him to have a whole new wardrobe of clothes, for the post of housekeeper to Doña Rosa Piñeda Galdós was to be regarded as an important social position in that little corner of Andalucia. And not only housekeeper, for the widow proudly told her neighbours how she now had a housekeeper, a gardener, and, after finding out that the Romanian was also an excellent chef, a cook. Actually, she said that she now had a head chef and laughed about it. It wasn't long before Doña Rosa felt the need for the services of a chauffeur. After all, most of the other wealthy Andalucian families had chauffeurs. Ionito was given time off for driving lessons, and she bought him a Mercedes together with, of course, a chauffeur's cap with white gloves to perfect the image.

The Romanian's sister and mother? Mysteriously, money was found to buy Juliánna a wedding gift that she could never have imagined: a beautiful silver dining-service. As for Ionito's mother, Doña Rosa wished to meet the woman herself. Now that there was someone to look after Paño the 'monster' she could get away by herself, so the widow arranged a flight to Bucharest and, after taking a bus out to a little mountain village in the heart of

Romania, she met up with the woman. The two soon understood each other very well despite the fact that neither knew one word of the other's language.

Ionito was particularly good with the children of the village, and Doña Rosa's house became an even more popular haunt in the evenings and at weekends. Also, new visitors began to show up. Older, marriageable girls, who seemed to have taken a great interest in paying the widow visits whenever possible. Always beautifully made up and beautifully dressed, and all *very* eager to teach Ionito the ways of the Spanish. That, however, is another story.

Paño loved the new occupant of his house. And, thankfully, Ionito did not snore, for two loud snorers in one house would simply not do. At least that is what Doña Rosa Piñeda Galdós told the good people of Monachil.

I'm Only a Guest

Hotel 'Belvedere'? From the outside appearance, more 'Hammer House of Horrors'.

Perched on a clifftop facing south-westerly gales, the pompous Victorian building, with thirties add-ons clinging to its dark sides like timidly obedient children, seemed an unlikely venue for our local gastroenterologists' club annual weekend get-together. I suppose the reasonable conference room hire price was reason enough. Plus the view. *It* truly was 'belvedere' provided the wind allowed you to remain upright for long enough to take it in.

Inside, a dated, austere décor added a certain charm. An enormous, lavishly framed painting of a hunt scene occupied the first landing wall-space, whilst the carved, oak banisters had probably acquired their first sheen from gentrified, sliding Victorian hands belonging to lives so different to what we twenty-first century doctors experience. But, like the hotel, the bannisters had retained their purpose.

The staff, too, had a purpose. To make us feel welcome. Mostly young, and several Polish (pre-Brexit!), they were wonderful. As was the food. However boring the Saturday morning scientific papers promised to be after a sumptuous Friday night dinner, I was determined to enjoy the weekend...

Until two in the morning the day following that meal.

"You've got to help me!" It was a soft, Irish female voice. A light sleeper, I awoke with start. I had been dreaming about being back at the hospital and, for the initial few seconds, the young woman's face, framed by long, straggled red hair, I took to be that of a patient.

Middle of the night. Lights off. Not the hospital. And that face, exquisitely pretty, only a few feet from mine, shone. Patients' faces *never* shone.

I edged backwards till my head was pressed hard up against the bed rest. The bed cover, gripped by hands too scared to shake, was pulled up to my nose. My own eyes remained fixed on those green Irish ones hovering above me.

I rationalized as any human would. Staff. Had to be. Although I failed to recognize her. Maybe she worked in the kitchen. Or as a chamber maid. There would have been a master key. Access no problem. And I dismissed the face's strange luminosity. Plus the fact that it was only a head.

She spoke again:

"You've got to help me!"

"Sit down," I urged.

What an odd thing to say to a head—*just* a head—I'm thinking, in retrospect. I guess I felt vulnerable, 'it' being right above me. As I eased myself up, the figure—I was beginning to see the rest of her—sat down. Dressed in a nightgown, she appeared waif-like. Now my eyes were above hers, so less scary. *She* was frightened, *I* no longer.

"Do you work here?"

Looking away, she nodded.

"Kitchen?"

She shook her head.

"For her ladyship, sir," she informed me.

"I'm not a 'sir'. Just a doctor."

"Oh... I'm so sorry, doctor. To be sure, I didn't mean

to—"

"Don't apologise! You've nothing to be sorry for. Is her ladyship another hotel guest? Like me? I'm only a guest, you know."

A frown troubled the girl's face. She obviously had no idea what I was talking about.

"I'm here for the conference. A gut doctor. Terrific meal last night. The beef was…"

She started to cry. I wanted to hug her, but I'm a married man, with a family, so I desisted.

"Please say you can help me."

"What's your name?"

"Sheenagh."

"Lovely name." I wanted to add '…For a lovely girl' but maintained professional respect.

"I feel far from lovely just now."

"Tell me."

"Her ladyship doesn't know yet, but when she finds out she'll send me back to Cork. My Da'll turn me out and…"

The tears took over. She trembled. I could no longer hold back. I placed my hand over hers as it gripped the edge of the bed, but all I felt was the bed. Our hands appeared to have merged. That's how I knew. Her ladyship was no more a hotel guest than I was Lord of the manor. And the girl was a ghost.

But how could I help? Doctors spend half their working lives listening, the other half trying to make sense of what's told to them. I needed to listen.

"You're in some kind of trouble?" I asked. She nodded. Taken in by her beauty, I guessed what that might be.

"Terrible," she said.

"I'm a doctor, so whatever you say'll not leak out of here."

"I can't. Too ashamed. But if she finds out…" She stopped.

"Was it his Lordship? Or the son, perhaps?"

She stood up. A look of horror altered the beauty of the girl's face.

"How could you say that? Sweet Jesus, I'm not some cheap whore who throws herself at any man!"

She was growing dim and I felt awful. My twenty-first century interpretation of nineteenth-century events was seriously off the mark.

"I am so sorry. Please forgive me. Just that, with your looks…"

"My looks? My looks have nothing to do with what happened!"

"Please, please sit down and tell me. I got it wrong and beg forgiveness."

Beg forgiveness? I was beginning to sound Victorian myself. She sat down again, looking troubled beyond belief as she stared at her small, translucent, white hands. Then, somehow finding courage, she turned to face me. The anguish in those eyes played havoc with my insides.

"I found a cross. With our Lord on it. A silver one."

What could be so terrible about that, I wondered?

"Where?"

"On the stairs. My wee sister Caitlin, she doesn't have a cross. Da hasn't the money. She's so upset. I told her when I have enough I'll buy her one but… but her ladyship pays me so little for cleaning her room and putting out her dresses and preparing her baths. Then I saw this little gold cross on the stairs and I wanted to give it to the butler but

I thought of little Caitlin and I told myself..." She looked down and a fresh tear emerged.

"Told yourself what?"

"I committed a terrible sin, doctor."

"How come?"

"I persuaded myself it was a gift from the Good Lord to take home to Caitlin."

"Perhaps you were right. Don't worry about it."

Again the Irish girl shook her head.

"She asked me. 'Have you seen that cross I was to give to my granddaughter?' she said. I could've died. I think she..."

The girl paused.

I knew what she thought. With a face as innocent as hers, how could the guilt have been concealed?

"She guessed, right?"

She nodded.

"But you said nothing."

"I couldn't! Stealing, that would've been. A terrible sin, to be sure."

"So?"

"Just now. The butler had us all in the hall. He's going to search everyone's belongings."

"Go back to your room. Fetch the cross and... just put it somewhere. Back on the stairs, maybe?"

"We're not allowed in our rooms till it's been found."

"Oh!"

Not the usual 'doctor's dilemma'.

"Tell the truth?" I suggested.

"They'd have me whipped and sent straight back to

Ireland."

"But your belief? If you truly believed it was a gift from God they can't be so hard on you."

"Do you not know the butler?" My turn to shake my head as she fixed me with those green eyes...

"A temptation from the Devil, he'll say."

Thoughts of time-space wormholes whirled in my confused mind like mental mini-galaxies. If only there was some way of transporting this poor child out of her Victorian Hell into the comparative calm of the twenty-first century. Could I squeeze her into my bag and, back home, search for some magical treatment in the hospital where I worked to bring her forwards to the contemporary world? Would the resuscitation room have ghost-reviving equipment?

"You can't help me. I know it," she sighed.

"You're a good girl," I said. "Even if God didn't mean you to take that cross, he'll know you did it to make your sister happy."

She was fading fast. I reached out to try to stop her from disappearing but clutched only a handful of nothing. My last memory of her was those sadly beautiful green eyes and the senseless pain crying out to me through them.

I did finally get back to sleep and was almost surprised by the normality of the hotel in the daylight the following morning. But the rest of the weekend was not enjoyable, despite the gourmet food, scintillating company and smiling staff. I could not get that poor young girl's green eyes out of my head. As a doctor, I had failed her and I needed to know whether this had been the ultimate failure.

"May I see the manager," I asked on checkout.

"Is there a problem sir?" the polite young Polish receptionist asked.

"No, not at all. A wonderful hotel."

"Oh, you wish to give praise, perhaps?"

"Praise is due. Don't get me wrong. Just something personal."

The way he looked at me... had he also seen her?

The manageress appeared about twenty minutes later...

Some terrible disaster in the past?

What?

A ghost?

No!

An Irish girl, accused of stealing?

No!

Killed herself?

No!

"Never mind," I said. "But this is a wonderful hotel. Should have five stars, I reckon."

The manageress smiled.

"Thank you so much. I do hope you'll come again."

Now there's a thought. Surely, nowadays, there must be 'help-a-ghost' charities. I'll never sleep easily again until I've found a way to help poor Sheenagh.

Hit and Run

If Jim had not been so preoccupied with thoughts about his wife, Giovanna, perhaps it would never have happened. Unaware that his attention had been wandering before the car swerved out of control, the thud of the impact was sickening, but it was so sudden he failed to see how he could have taken any action to avoid hitting the man. Nevertheless, he *had* been distracted, worrying about Giovanna, when it happened.

He could not understand why she had been so cold towards him of late. *He* was the one who worked away all hours, supporting her and the children. It was *he* who provided Giovanna with the means to buy beautiful clothes and jewellery so that she still looked like the attractive young Italian air stewardess he married ten years previously. Surely she could repay him with a little warmth and love after he came home, exhausted, every night. A year, even six months back, things were different. They joked and made love as always, but recently it was as though she had simply switched off all marital passion. At times, Jim felt like a stranger in his own home. When he kissed Giovanna, it was like kissing a manikin, and in bed, after offering him her cheek, she would tell him she was 'too tired' and roll over to face the other way. *She* was tired? Damn it, *he* was the one slaving away; the one in need of a little comfort from his wife at night.

Jim had been turning all of this over in his mind, even wondering whether Giovanna had become a bit depressed and that perhaps he should talk to their doctor about his concerns, when he hit the man.

He appeared from nowhere. Jim had swung the

vehicle round a bend, possibly a little further towards the wrong side of the road than he should have been, and certainly too fast, but he was tired and there were those things going on his mind, Giovanna amongst them...

Saw the man, then bang!

The figure was thrown upwards, and for an awful fraction of a split second it seemed as though he was suspended in front of the windscreen; a broken marionette held motionless in the amber of timeless eternity. But time returned. In a nightmare flash. The car skidded sideways, hit a fence, then bounced back onto the road before jerking to a halt.

Jim knew, on approaching the body, that the man was at least seriously injured, but the stillness of the body made him fear the worst. The man's head was twisted sideways onto his shoulder like that of a broken, discarded doll, and the whole of one side of a lifeless face was caved in. The eyes told Jim that the man was dead. Wide open and frozen in a final moment of terror, Jim saw there was not a flicker of life behind them. No life, although blood, the elixir of life, still oozed onto the road from the smashed face.

Jim panicked. Who wouldn't? Later, he wished that he hadn't. Over and over he wished this, just as he wished he had been driving more slowly and not trying to solve marital problems festering inside his head. But when he looked at the man's head, knowing that he had been killed by himself, all Jim wanted was to escape from the nightmare.

There were no other cars around. No one to be seen. It was late at night. Few lights on in the houses lining the road. Sheer animal panic made Jim run back to his car. With the door still open, he leapt into the driving seat, turned the ignition, and sped off.

Trembling, he drove the car as lights went on one by one, pressing down on the accelerator until well away from the scene when he slowed and proceeded home at a funereal pace, barely able to focus on steering the vehicle let alone the road. He pulled into the drive. There was a light on in the upstairs bedroom, so he knew that Giovanna was awake. He got out and examined the front of the car. Considering the man's injuries, there was little damage. The paintwork along the nearside doors, where the car had hit a fence, had been scraped, one front wing was bent inwards and the bumper and grille, where the car had slammed into the man, were buckled.

Then Jim saw the blood. He felt sick. For the first time, the sheer horror of what he had done hit him like a punch from a champion boxer.

Blood was spread over the bonnet of the vehicle and splattered across the windscreen. Gripped with fear, he wondered, again, whether to call the police, but, having left the scene of the crime, things had already gone too far. Besides, he still had an overpowering urge to escape, perhaps to return to a blissful state in which he might be able to persuade himself that it had never actually happened.

If the blood was washed from the windscreen and from the car bonnet, all traces wiped off, maybe he would be able to erase from his mind the memory of the scene. The lifeless body, the caved-in face and the horror-movie ooze of blood. He had a job to do and getting on with this helped to control the nausea whenever that ghoulish image reappeared in his brain. There were some old rags in the garage, and he soaked these in water, using the outside tap at the back of the house. With the rags, he rubbed and scrubbed away at the car, stood back, rubbed again, walked around the car and then once again set about cleaning off every smear, every fleck. When finished, it looked like a showroom vehicle, apart from the dents and the scratched paintwork. He placed the rags in a plastic garden refuse sack, covering them with leaves, sticks and uprooted plants. He did not even check to see whether these were weeds or cultivated flowers. Just wanted to get it over with, go inside and live the lie he had planned in his head.

Giovonna was awake, in bed, when he entered the bedroom. She looked so beautiful it brought tears to his eyes. He wanted to tell her this, but his mind was too jumbled to focus on meaningful words.

"What took you so long?" asked Giovanna, looking up from a glossy magazine. No 'darling'. No smile. There was a time, not so long before, when she would have leapt out of bed and flung her arms around him. How lucky he had been back then. Was he taking her for granted? Was that the problem? But now she seemed even more lovely. Sex, however, was the last thing on Jim's mind.

"I was finishing off some work on my laptop in the car, darling," he lied. "Didn't want to disturb you. Thought you might be asleep."

"Light was on outside," said Giovanna looking down at her magazine again. "Never done that before, have you?! I wondered what on earth you were up to out there. Heard the outside tap running, too."

Surely she would not have heard the tap.

He said whatever came into his head:

"Got some mud on my shoes. At work. Walking to work. Big puddle."

Jim began to undress. Slowly.

"Some puddle, when it's not raining!" said Giovanna without looking up. Then, to Jim's relief, she changed the subject. "The children spent the evening with Sam. I was going to be late back from the hairdressers, so they're having a sleepover."

Samantha was Jim's long-suffering sister. She would frequently look after their two daughters to help out. They had gone to Sam's place a lot more often over the previous few months. Jim knew how much the girls loved Aunty Sam and their three young cousins, and he had never questioned this with Giovanna, but that very morning Jim had wondered. Nevertheless, he had attributed this to depression.

"Oh!" exclaimed Jim. "Was that okay with Sam? She's been awfully good to us recently, taking them so often."

Must keep the conversation away from what I was doing outside.

"'Delighted to have them,' she said," replied Giovanna still looking at her magazine. Jim continued the pretence:

"What about us taking the boys?" he asked. "Maybe one weekend, just for a Saturday night or something."

Giovanna looked up.

"You must be joking," she said. Her voice was razor-sharp. Not that of someone who was depressed. "What on earth would they do here? And where would they sleep? You know that Sam has bags of room in that huge house of theirs. What a crazy idea! *Sei pazzo*[7]!"

Giovanna seemed unreasonably upset by Jim's suggestion, and she always resorted to Italian when angry. He was taken aback. The suggestion had only been

_____

[7] You're mad!

mooted to steer the conversation away from the car cleaning.

"Sorry," Jim apologised. "It's just that I thought we owed her one. That's all. Perhaps we should get her a little present or something. Some nice wine, huh?"

"You know they don't drink. Look..." Giovanna put the magazine down beside the bed and fixed Jim with that cold stare with which he had become only too familiar. One of the things that had invaded his mind just prior to the accident. "Look, do you have a problem with the girls staying over with Sam? Because if you do, then you're the only one who does. The girls love it, the boys like showing off to their cousins, Sam adores them and it gives me a break. So if you think we should make other plans, let me hear about them."

She folded her arms. Something else she did whenever she was *particularly* annoyed.

"No," responded Jim, struggling into his pyjamas. His arms were shaking and his legs felt like jelly. "No problem, dear. Just me being stupid again."

Giovanna raised her eyebrows, as if to say, 'you can say that again.' Jim climbed into bed, still trembling, but Giovanna did not appear to notice. She seemed to be lost in her own thoughts as he turned off his bedside lamp. He leaned across and kissed her cheek before she turned off her own light. Her cheek felt so warm and soft. He remembered the excitement he felt on touching her skin with his lips back in the days when they seemed to be held together by passion; a passion that he had stupidly assumed would last forever.

"Good night," said Jim.

Giovanna replied with 'Mm!' in a tone that informed her husband there was nothing 'good' about being in bed with him.

The night was one long nightmare, eyes open or closed. Jim spent much of it wide awake, the image of the dead man's face with staring, unseeing eyes filling the darkness. In one of his brief dreams, the man came to 'life' as a corpse pointing an accusing finger at him for all the world to see. When he awoke, Giovanna was still asleep, but on hearing the newspaper come through the door, he slipped out of bed and went downstairs, picking up the paper from the doormat. He quickly scanned it but saw nothing about the accident. He took it upstairs and laid it on the bed beside Giovanna who was beginning to stir.

"Newspaper," Jim said. Then he went downstairs again to make himself a cup of coffee. He wasn't at all hungry, but he just wanted to get on with his day as though nothing had happened the previous night. A cup of coffee would at least help him to stay awake after a sleepless night.

The shock was almost as great as when his vehicle had hit the man. From the kitchen window he saw a police car. Two uniformed police officers got out together with what he assumed to be a third officer in plain clothes. All wore latex gloves. One bent down beside the offside front wheel of Jim's car and began to scrape something from the tyre into a small polythene bag. The other two went straight to the garden refuse sack into which Jim had stuffed the rags used to clean the car. Mouth agape, Jim watched as the rags were pulled out from their hiding place under leaves and uprooted plants and placed, carefully, into another polythene bag.

Jim's mind went blank. He ran through the house to the back door. Whether he was thinking of escaping, of running away dressed in his pyjamas, he did not truly

84

know. Ever since that moment of impact, all he really wanted was for the horror to end and for normality to return to his life. Visible through the long vertical window beside the door was the form of a fourth policeman standing with his back to the house. Jim returned to the kitchen to watch the live detective drama unfold in front of the house.

The doorbell rang. He went to the door and opened it. The plain clothes officer offered him a crocodile smile. The uniformed man beside him did not. His face was dead pan, and he held up a polythene bag filled with blood-stained rags. Jim tried hard not to look at those rags.

"I know why you're h-here," stuttered Jim. It was so unreal, and yet it was happening. "I'll get dressed," he added, pulling at his pyjama top. The plain clothes officer, still smiling, simply nodded his head.

Slowly, Jim made his way up the stairs. He wished he would never have to reach the bedroom. Only a few minutes earlier he had hoped that Giovanna might never get to know, and that things might soon be just as they had been before. He opened the bedroom door.

"Giovanna..." he began.

Giovanna was staring at her mobile phone, her hands trembling, whilst tears streamed down her face. She hardly seemed aware of Jim as he talked about having to go to the police station to sort something out. She kept shaking her head saying:

"It's him! Oh my God, no! It's him! Alessandro!"

Jim, his hand shaking, took the phone from his wife. The screen was filled with the image of a man's face. Then...

'The body of a thirty-five-year-old man was found late last

night lying in a street on the outskirts of Woking. The man, identified as Alessandro Taddei, was believed to be the victim of a hit and run incident. His relatives in Italy have been notified. The police are following up a lead from an eyewitness who saw the accident and who was able to identify the vehicle registration. A police spokeswoman told reporters that this was being treated as a serious crime.'

Giovanna looked up at Jim, her face uglified with grief.

"I was going to tell you, Jim. I was. I could never find the right time to do it. It's him, Alessandro. I knew him before. In Italy. And yes, we were lovers. Again. Here. I was alone so much. He contacted me. Had a new job here. In England. We... well... I was going to tell you... but... Oh, Alessandro!"

Unable to stop sobbing, Giovanna fell forwards onto her bent up knees. Jim, staring at the mobile, was standing beside the bed, motionless, speechless, when two police officers entered the bedroom. One held a pair of handcuffs.

The Shrine

It was his first pilgrimage to the shrine. He had come of age and, like his male ancestors for over a thousand years, could now venture out beyond the fields and forest to the great shrine of Quŏm-Pŏo-Tah. Many sunsets would pass before they reached the shrine, and the path was alive with danger.

Most who died perished on the hills where none could escape the ferocity of the sun. The sun was merciless and always angry. Only through her servant on earth, Quŏm-Pŏo-Tah, could she be appeased to allow the women and children to survive. Men knew that risking their lives was necessary to save the tribe from annihilation by the sun.

His mother wrapped provisions in a cloth and fixed this to the end of a pole to be carried over the shoulder. This might also serve as a weapon against animals and the wild men of the wastelands. Strapped about his waist was a belt from which hung flasks of water, and survival depended upon also finding water along the way. His mother came over to hug him and bid him farewell knowing she would possibly never see her son again. She begged him to heed the wisdom of his elders. Wiping tears from her face, he asked her to be strong for his sisters.

The men left at first light, their heads protected from the sun by layers of white cloth. They emerged from the forest and passed through fields and along riverbanks, waving at the women and the children working the fields before the heat became unbearable. Their path followed the river, passing clusters of docile animals, drinking. The animals showed no fear, for their instinctive terror of Man withered in the face of the overriding need to quench thirst. Normally the men would have picked off the weaker animals to take back as food for their families, but now they had no time to stop and kill, and the animals stood motionless apart from the in-out flicks of pink, parched tongues.

The fields gave way to scrub and grassland. He found himself on the edge of a vast barren plain across which they would follow the river to the hills, an easy three-day journey. The River God was their friend, but his power was as nothing compared with that of the sun. If their pilgrimage were to fail, the sun would destroy the river and its god.

Watching the sun set each evening, he wondered how that merciless celestial body could create such wonderful, changing colours in the sky, before retiring to rest, yet also destroy life on earth and all those other gods who failed to appease her? Why was she so wrathful? There was much he did not understand, but the elders were wise and, if this pilgrimage proved successful, his family might live for another year.

Climbing the hills, he became increasingly wary of the true dangers confronting him. There were tales. Tales of terrifying evils lurking in the gullies and valleys which cut through the hills. Gruesome creatures, rumoured to leap out at pilgrims and drag them away as quick as the flight of an arrow; wild men, like those who would occasionally attack their village in the forest and carry away their women. But worst of all, there was the unsheltered heat of the sun. On the crest of a hill they would be closer to her... and to her anger.

He had been told that they would come across streams on the way up the slopes. If dried out, then they would have to rely on their flasks. This seemed plentiful when they set off, but they would need a lot of water to get over the hills in the searing heat. Here, in the hills, he began to have doubts as he struggled to keep up with the stronger, fitter, older men. He feared that being so close to the sun, she might be able to read his doubts. He tried to keep his mind blank.

After the fifth sunset, things began to look bleak. They discovered that the first stream, then the second, and the third, had dried out. The men were forced to start drinking from their flasks. The elders tried to reassure him, and other first pilgrims like himself, that this was not unusual, but he sensed that even the elders were worried. More so when they learned that stream after stream had turned into stony, dusty paths. The steepest of the hills were yet to come, and all the time their bodies cried out for more water.

He could think of nothing but water. As the sun began to sink, after he had half-crawled, half-scrambled to the crest of the steepest hill he had ever seen, he was down to his last few drops. They were at least a day from the shrine, and for most of that time they walked on exposed to the sun in the dry, waterless hills. Now, only a miracle could save him now from certain death. He prayed to Quŏm-Pŏo-Tah for that miracle.

That night, constantly licking his parched lips with a dry tongue, he lay huddled, with other men, beside a boulder and fell asleep after the sun had dropped out of the sky. He had an unsettling dream about giants hurling great rocks, tearing up the hillside, to stop them from reaching the shrine. Then he awoke with a start. He heard excited voices, and his face was wet. At first he thought it must be sweat, for he felt even more thirsty, but it was a cool wetness, and it kept on coming out of the sky. He opened his eyes and closed them again as the large raindrops landed on his face. Like the other pilgrims, he put his head back and tried to drink the rain as it fell from the sky, but this did little to quench his thirst. He stood and followed a group of pilgrims who had walked on down the hillside, in the dark, towards the sound of running water.

They had heard it from afar and ran on weakened legs until they were able to fall forwards and immerse their faces in the fast-flowing stream. This was surely the greatest moment in his life so far. His prayer had been answered, and the Rain God had bowed to the might of the sun's servant on earth, Quŏm-Pŏo-Tah, and given up his water. They drank and drank until they felt their stomachs felt close to bursting, and then they filled their flasks. This done, they ate from dwindling rations, picked themselves up and continued on along the path. Although their flasks were once again heavy, their hearts were light, for they knew they had sufficient water to take them to the shrine. The rain persisted and there were other streams along the way from which they could drink. The distant roll of thunder indicated to him that the Rain God was now paying homage to the sun, and that she should be well pleased when they reached the great shrine of Quŏm-Pŏo-Tah.

He felt good, but better was yet to come. On scaling the last of the hills, and as the sun began to sink down through breaks in the Rain God's clouds, from the crest of the hill he was able to look across the plain of Quŏm-Pŏo-Tah. There he saw another great river winding its way towards a hazy blue horizon. This plain was green, not brown and yellow like the plain between the forest and the hills. There were trees. Many trees. Some solitary, trailed into the river, others stood in clusters. Large trees, with sturdy boughs and branches. There were dwellings, too, and he knew these to be the dwellings of the priests who guarded the shrine. The priests had fields with crops and fields with livestock animals.

Then he saw it. White and glistening in the light of the sinking sun. The temple of Quŏm-Pŏo-Tah. The temple of the great shrine of the servant of the sun. He was not the only one to be excited by the sight of the temple, for this is why they had come. Why they had risked their lives by crossing the barren plain and treacherous hills. The pilgrims descended from the hill towards the plain of Quŏm-Pŏo-Tah, and, after reaching the river, followed it until they arrived at the priests' dwelling places. They bowed to the priests, and the most senior of their elders spoke with one particular priest, the man who would guide them to the shrine. The elder gave the priest gifts of cloth, of tools and of honey, for there was much honey to be had in the forest, and the priests considered this a great delicacy. Then, a long trail of tired-but-confident pilgrims followed the priest along an easy and well-worn path that led to the temple.

The temple that held the shrine was smaller than he imagined, but all the same it was truly amazing. It was a building made from material that was both hard and smooth, and which appeared to contain no wood, mud, branches nor moss. It was as white as a cloud, and there were several curious dark rectangular spaces on its edifice. These glistened in the sun's intense light. At first he thought they looked like water, for he had the impression he could see into those spaces as he might when looking into water, but they were unmoving and did not give off the sound of water. Indeed, they were quite solid. At the very top of the temple was a vast grey panel made up of many large squares. The man beside him said that this was the ear of Quŏm-Pŏo-Tah, through which the sun would speak with him. It was rumoured that the priests took it in turns to care for the great ear and, at all costs, keep the ear clean.

The pilgrims followed in single file through a large doorway. He had never before passed through a doorway without having to crouch down. The door was made from wood, he could see that, but wood that had been so beautifully smoothed and crafted that this could only have been created by a god. Through the doorway they went into a place that seemed to be from another world. There was a long narrow passageway, lined throughout by the same sort of smooth white material that he had seen on the outside of the temple. Above were bright round globes that lit up the passageway. These were like miniature suns, doubtless there to remind everyone who entered the temple that Quŏm-Pŏo-Tah was the sun's only servant here on earth. There were many doors along the sides of the passageway, again made from that exquisitely god-crafted wood. The priest opened one of these and led them into a large space in the temple with many of those miniature suns looking down at them. He was simply dumbfounded, as were the other first pilgrims. The space was large enough for all of them to gather together, and then they were asked to sit on square pieces of wood raised up onto four thick sticks. He felt nervous, thinking his weight might break the sticks, but they were strong, and these perches must have been made by the same god who had crafted the doors, another servant of the sun, for sure. He found the perch to be comfortable, particularly since it bore a wooden rest against which he could lean his weary back.

The elder who had given the gifts to the priest told the pilgrims to maintain absolute silence whilst the priest contacted Quŏm-Pŏo-Tah. Not a single sound should disturb the priest, he said. They were also told to copy whatever he did. Bow when the priest bowed and repeat the chants. They knew the chants would be in that strange language from the past that only the priests understood, but chant they must if they were to appease the sun through Quŏm-Pŏo-Tah.

The shrine was on a raised platform, for all to see, also supported on thick wooden sticks. He had never before beheld anything like this and the shrine was so different to what he had imagined. It was smaller. In fact, not much larger than a piglet, although, like the building, it was smooth and angular at all corners. It had no legs and did not breathe out fire, as he had been led to believe. When he looked more closely, he saw that it had tails. Several of them, narrow, winding off in different directions.

It was then that he noticed that the shrine was linked to the wall by one of these tails. Afterwards, they told him that this was not a tail but a slim, black snake. A very special snake, such as only the Sun Goddess and her servant might possess. A snake that could carry in her long, curled body the words of the sun from the ear of Quŏm-Pŏo-Tah to the shrine. Already, he knew that the part of the shrine on that platform was the eye of Quŏm-Pŏo-Tah through which he could look out at the earth and speak in that strange and wonderful language to his mistress, the sun.

The snake connected the eye of Quŏm-Pŏo-Tah to

the wall, and behind this, they knew, were the heart and soul of the servant of the sun. And only the head priest knew about the beat of that heart. To touch this meant instant death. And he learned, later, that should a priest fail to keep the great ear clean when it was his duty to do so, death would come swiftly. He thought that the life of a priest was perhaps not as wonderful as first seemed, although the priests did enjoy ample food, water, and women. Every priest would have two or three women, and the women worked the fields and brought up the priests' children whilst the priests tended the shrine of Quŏm-Pŏo-Tah.

Suddenly, a strange noise emerged from the shrine.

"Bow, for the great Quŏm-Pŏo-Tah speaks," the elder whispered as the priest fussed around the shrine, touching and pressing things. The voice of Quŏm-Pŏo-Tah was the strangest sound he had ever heard. Quite out of this world, and almost like music. Then the great servant of the sun went silent as He opened His eye to look upon the pilgrims. The boy knew then that he was being scrutinised, that his innermost thoughts were being read, and that now he must keep his mind as pure as on the day he was born.

They were ordered to look at the eye of the servant of the sun. Like the others, he gasped as soon as he beheld the eye. This was indeed no ordinary eye. It shone, like the sun herself. It was large for an eye, and rectangular like the temple and like the spaces within the temple. Now he knew why the temple was built as it was. To look angular, like the eye of Quŏm-Pŏo-Tah. Suddenly, a picture appeared on the eye. It was beautiful, and recognisable as the hills over which they had passed, only now covered by bright green grass. The picture was so real that it was just

94

like looking at the hills with his own eyes.

He'd been told that Quŏm-Pŏo-Tah's eye can see into men's minds, and from what he saw in the eye it was clear to him that one of the pilgrims must have been secretly praying that there would be more rain before their return journey, and this would turn the hills green. Without a doubt, this picture that he beheld came from the mind of another man as seen through the eye of the servant of the sun.

To the side of that image of the hills, the eye of the shrine bore strange little colourful signs, only just visible from where he sat, and underneath these were markings that looked like some sort of script. Later, he learned that these very markings were indeed a form of writing. The writing of the gods. Then, for the first time, he noticed that the priest was bent over a flat tablet covered with small square stones of identical size with markings and which sprang down and up as he tapped at them. He also guided a smooth shell-like silvery stone over the platform that bore the shrine. He moved it this way and that. The movements of this shell stone seemed both random and purposive, and every time the priest paused with his hand over the stone, he would tap it with a finger. Gently. He knew how gentle the priests had to be with the shrine, for they too did not wish to anger Quŏm-Pŏo-Tah.

The priest spoke, and the elder repeated his words. Solemnly, all the pilgrims echoed the elder, without knowing what those strange words from the world of the gods could possibly mean.

"Oh, Quŏm-Pŏo-Tah!" they repeated after the elder, "Mowce! Aí-konz!"

They all bowed respectfully. Suddenly something flashed. They looked up, and gasped, for the green hills had gone from the eye of Quǒm-Pǒo-Tah, and they found they were looking into a square piece of white sky. He knew they could never look into the sun herself, for those who did became blind. Was this also true for Quǒm-Pǒo-Tah, the sun's servant on Earth? Had He to keep his gaze to the side of His mistress and look only at the white or the blue of the sky?

The sky in the eye of Quǒm-Pǒo-Tah was like no other for it bore more of that strange script and many small yellow squares. Being yellow, these were surely to do with the sun. Then he noticed something. For the first time. Whenever the priest moved the shell stone, a little tiny white arrow moved across the eye. When his hand stopped, the arrow stopped.

The priest spoke again. The elder repeated what he said, in that strange tongue, and the pilgrims dutifully copied the elder, as they bowed their heads again.

"Maí-Dǒkkoom-Ants," said the priest.

"Maí-Dǒkkoom-Ants," repeated the elder.

"Maí-Dǒkkoom-Ants," echoed the pilgrims in unison.

Another flash, and a picture appeared once more on the eye. A baby, wrapped in strange clothing like the outside of a sheep. The baby was most certainly real, but it did not move. It just smiled and smiled and smiled. There were sighs of relief from the pilgrims. No one owned up to being the father of that baby, but they knew that Quǒm-Pǒo-Tah had seen into the mind of one of the men, and that the smile on the baby's face was a good omen. Later, someone told him that the eye had seen the same baby the previous year, but he did not believe them. How could a baby remain unchanged after a whole year had passed?

For a while, the priest continued to move the shell

stone whilst the arrow simultaneously darted about across the eye, and the eye would constantly be seeing different things. People with impossibly strange faces, grown men without beards, beautiful women with very red lips, more babies and children, and even strange animals. With each new vision in the eye, the priest would chant something different, they would all bow their heads and repeat the chant, after the elder.

A very strange animal indeed appeared, with hugely long ears, and a frightened staring face.

"Rab-beet!" chanted the priest, and they all echoed his speech. Surely this animal must be one of Quŏm-Pŏo-Tah's special creatures, endowed with extra long ears to listen to His mistress, the sun.

Then there was a flash and more sky appeared.

"Maí-Krowsoff-Wurd!" chanted the priest, followed by the elder and then the pilgrims. The sky in the eye filled with that strange, ethereal script.

"Now we shall pray," said the priest, in their own tongue, before starting to chant in the language of the gods:

"Deah-sur, it iz wiv ree-grĕtt Aí-wish to kán-sul maí subskríp-shon for dur kummin yee-ah…"

There was a pause. Then the priest continued: "Yeorz sin-seahllee, Gee-Ahr Bĕmbrij. Amen!"

"Gee-Ahr Bĕmbrij, Amen!" repeated the pilgrims together, heads devoutly bowed.

Surely this prayer to the sun, through her servant on earth, would seal the good fortune of the village for the coming year.

The priest returned to moving the shell stone over the platform, and as he did so, the arrow shot across the sky in the shrine's eye. He stopped, pressed the stone with one finger. There was another flash and another chant.

"Quǒm-Pǒo-Tah Pleh-Steh-shón," the priest said in a low solemn voice.

The elder raised his hands up before the pilgrims to indicate that they should now leave, and so, in silence, they stood, heads still bowed, and shuffled towards the door. There were changing lights in the eye, and Quǒm-Pǒo-Tah spoke again. It was strange and terrifying to hear him. His voice was loud, and there were noises like thunder and falling rocks. Lightning flashed in that rectangular eye, and as the pilgrims took their leave, he saw moving figures there. Figures of real people who bore sticks that erupted into fire with crashing sounds that caused other figures before them to fall as though dead. He seemed to be witnessing some terrible battle through the eye of the Quǒm-Pǒo-Tah, far fiercer than their own battles with the wild men of the hills, and he became fearful.

His last glimpse of the priest was of a figure bent over the shrine, jerking and jumping about with great excitement as the arrow in the eye darted crazily all over the place, amidst exploding men dressed in the most extraordinary costumes.

"We leave now. The priest must be alone," whispered the elder, leading the pilgrims away from the shrine.

Outside, a younger priest took the pilgrims to their huts of logs, sticks and moss, where they would get a good night's rest before a long and tedious journey back to the village in the forest. They were thankful that the return journey would be so much easier. The streams over the hills would, for sure, still be flowing with cool water, and the priests would give them sufficient provisions and refill their water flasks. As he fell asleep, his head full of the strange things that he had witnessed in the temple, he felt reassured that for another year his mother and his sisters would be safe, protected, again, by the Earth's servant of the sun, Quŏm-Pŏo-Tah.

Beijing Panda

Lady Hermione had spent most of the night making generous contributions to the Beijing sewage system. The urgency of each call was such that she left the bathroom light on for fear of not finding the switch in time in the dark. The following morning, feeling weak and unwell, she tapped on the door of the adjacent room of the five-star Beijing hotel. Her son, Algernon, opened the door. He was grinning from ear to ear. This was the last day of their ten-day luxury tour of China before taking an evening flight back to Heathrow. They had the day to themselves, and Algernon was really happy. No more pagodas, museums or palaces. His mother had promised him a visit to the Beijing Zoo to see the pandas. She knew that Algernon had loved pandas ever since his Uncle James had given him a toy one for his birthday all those decades ago. For Algernon, this was to be the highlight of their trip.

"It's no good, Algie dear," said Lady Hermione, holding on to her son for support. "I feel dreadful. Up all night. Washed out, so to speak. Some frightful tummy bug. I really don't think..."

She suddenly went a strange shade of grey, spun around and shot back towards her own room with remarkable agility for someone with advanced osteoarthritis. Algernon shuffled after her in his bedroom slippers. His smile had vanished. In his mother's room he stood addressing the en-suite bathroom door, from the other side of which came a machine gun burst of explosive farts.

"But Mummy, I really must see the pandas. You promised. Just put me in a taxi. I'll be fine."

Lady Hermione re-emerged from the bathroom, backed by the sound of a flushing toilet cistern. Her face was drawn. She looked at her son. Outwardly he gave the appearance of a senior business executive. Even more so when he was dressed in his usual attire of a neatly pressed flannel suit complete with a white coloured blue striped shirt and dull conventional tie. His hair was grey at the sides and at the back, and thin on top.

Looks, however, belied the true Algernon. His father, his lordship, a philanderer who could not have been more different from his son, had fled 'home' at the earliest opportunity leaving Lady Hermione to raise Algernon by herself. Private teachers came and went. They usually went as soon as they learned from her ladyship that young Algernon was *not* to be treated just like any other child. According to Lady Hermione, Algie was delicate and sensitive, and the boy had to be protected from the awful ways of the world. Most of his education came from Lady Hermione herself with brief periods of tutoring from the numerous 'governesses', as she insisted on calling the temporary home-schooling teachers. School itself was simply out of the question, she would say to her increasingly concerned family, including her brother James. Later *he* tried to help by introducing young Algernon to some of the less wicked ways of the outside world, but to no avail, for Lady Hermione would trust no one but herself on the matter. The result was a middle-aged man, time-warped and with the mind and ways of a young child. "Honestly I could, Mummy," continued Algernon. "Remember when I took that taxi to the London Zoo five years ago?"

Lady Hermione looked at her son. The thought of him not being around her feet all day long, within the confines of their hotel rooms, did appeal just so long as he was 'all right'.

"Well," she agreed, later, together with their Chinese tour guide in the hotel lobby, "as long as he'll be all right."

She was attracting interest from quizzical Chinese hotel guests as she stood in her long, purple dressing-gown and pink satin slippers, talking to other members of their tour group. She could not understand why no one else appeared to relish the idea of taking her Algernon to the zoo to see the pandas. However, the tour guide, a young woman who spoke good English, was very reassuring about the Beijing taxi service. She agreed that Lady Hermione should rest at the hotel all day before their long flight back to Britain and had kindly offered to get 'very good Chinese medicine' to ease her ladyship's troubled digestive tract.

Algernon felt so grand climbing into the back of the large blue taxi that arrived outside the hotel just for him. Lady Hermione stuffed a fistful of Chinese banknotes into her son's hand.

"Now do be careful, Algie dear," she said, anxiously, as the man stared wide-eyed at the small fortune that he clutched. Never before had he had so much pocket money all at once.

The taxi finally came to a stop in front of a drab façade which, it appeared, belonged to the Beijing Zoo. And to Algernon's absolute delight there was also a giant poster with huge pictures of pandas on it. This had to be the right place, he reckoned. The taxi driver was somewhat surprised to be given such a large collection of banknotes. He was an honest man and returned all but one of these, together with some coins and a few extra smaller notes. The taxi drove off, leaving Algernon standing on the pavement looking up at the images of pandas.

The woman appeared from nowhere. Algernon was all alone at the kerbside, trying to work out where the entrance to the zoo was, when he felt a gentle tap on his arm. He turned round.

"Welcome Beijing!" said a softly spoken, pretty Chinese lady standing right beside him. She must have been about thirty and she wore a long colourful dress and shiny, high-heeled, black shoes. Algernon had never before seen such an attractive woman, and he, including a certain part of his anatomy, felt peculiarly happy when she smiled at him.

"Oh, I say! Jolly good," he guffawed. "Thank you. Yes, that's awfully nice of you."

The young woman rested a small, delicate hand on his arm.

"I show you nice time. Come with me," she continued.

Algernon liked her. He liked her *very* much. She made him feel important and sort of warm and excited inside. Plus something down there stirred. Something he could never talk about to Mummy.

"Oh! Erm! Oh! Well, all right then," he said. "The pandas. There!" he added, pointing up at the panda poster.

She smiled. "Come. We see pandas together," she urged, gently steering Algernon towards the Zoo ticket window. "You have money?" she asked, leaning on his arm. The faint expression of anxiety tarnishing her pretty face vanished as soon as she saw the collection of banknotes that Algernon pulled from his pocket. She patted Algernon's hand before relieving him of the cash. "I look after for you. Give you good enjoy in Beijing. Come me!" she said.

Algernon had no wish to refuse her offer. After purchasing, and handing Algernon his ticket, the young woman put the remaining banknotes into her handbag.

"Safer!" she said. "Here many pockpickets!

"Erm... pickpockets?" Algernon suggested. "Yes. Quite right. Thank you. So awfully good of you."

The woman slipped her hand under Algernon's arm and looked up at him with an enchanting smile.

"You name?" she asked as they walked together into the zoo.

"Me... name? Me? Oh! Yes, my name. How jolly. Yes, my name. Well... erm... Algernon. Algernon Manlegge. My father's a lord, you know."

"Please?" She smiled that sweet smile again.

"Algernon Manlegge," he repeated, slowly.

"Ah!" she said. "Al—ger—non Man—leg," emphasising each syllable carefully and with such a serious look on her lovely face. Then she laughed. Algernon laughed as well. He was really beginning to enjoy his little outing.

"Oh!" she exclaimed. In mock shyness, she covered her sweet, pretty mouth with her hand. "I like man leg. *Special* leg!" She laughed again, and Algernon added a few very British guffaws, although he had no idea why.

She looked serious again.

"Me Hua Mei Ling. Mean beautiful blossom. Please call me Mei Mei!" She tugged playfully at Algernon's arm.

"Oh! Jolly good. Mei Mei," repeated the aristocratic Englishman.

Together, Mei Mei and Algernon saw two jaded,

static elephants, a collection of unhappy looking, skin-diseased monkeys who sat scratching away at festering sores, and, in a dull concrete building, they passed by a row of prison-like cages containing terminally bored tigers. The smell of animal urine in the large cat house became so overpowering that they ended up with handkerchiefs over their noses. They giggled as they emerged, gasping, from the building.

"Um... I think... erm... well... do *you* think we could see the pandas now?" Algernon asked his newfound friend.

"Of course!" Mei Mei replied. "Me silly. These animals are not nice! Smell bad. We go see pandas!"

Her brow furrowed.

"Pay more for pandas. Okay?" she added.

"Oh yes. Rather!" replied Algernon.

Algernon loved the pandas. One was stretched out in the sun on his back looking straight up at him and Mei Mei standing together. Or so it seemed, for its eyes were lost in the two large black patches on its face. These made the animal appear rather sad. Another panda was also on its back, exposing a large, rounded, white belly, and surrounded by branches of bamboo. Like a playboy sipping cocktails and eating goodies on a Florida beach, it reached out, with its paw, pulled at a clump of bamboo and began to chew, nonchalantly, at the stalks.

Mei Mei and Algernon lunched in the run-down zoo cafeteria. Mei Mei giggled at Algernon's valiant attempt to eat noodles with chopsticks but she rescued him from further embarrassment by asking a waitress to provide him with a fork. When finished, they merely sat for a while in silence before this was tentatively broken by the young

Chinese woman...

"Now I give nice enjoy for you, Algernon." She said. Totally serious. Algernon looked at her. He had no idea what she was talking about.

"Oh!" he said, "that's awfully jolly of you."

An anxious frown appeared across Mei Mei's face, followed by an expression of resignation.

"Come with me!" she said.

Mei Mei's husband had been killed in a workplace accident two years previously. She had received a pitifully small compensation package and had lost the apartment which came with his job. She also found herself without work. Orphaned in her late teens, and without siblings, there was no one that she could turn to for financial help. It was a friend who suggested she should use some of the compensation money and make the best of her good looks by buying some fine clothes and make-up to earn a living 'entertaining' foreign men. Mei Mei hated the idea, but she was desperate.

The hard-headed Japanese businessmen were the worst. They treated her like a throwaway consumable, but the money kept her alive. In fact, the money became so good that she found she could be more selective about the men whom she 'entertained'. She far preferred Western men, like the man she was now with, although never before had she encountered anyone quite like Algernon.

*****

The taxi pulled up outside a scruffy hotel in a small side street not far from the zoo.

"But..." began Algernon looking up at the dilapidated building, "This isn't Mummy's hotel."

Mei Mei took hold of his arm.

"You... me, good enjoy!" she said, smiling so sweetly. She guided Algernon into the dimly lit building.

"Oh, rather!" agreed Algernon. "Jolly good show!"

He wondered whether Mei Mei had a trainset. He so loved playing with his trainset back home. The one that Uncle James had given him. He followed her into the hotel. She spoke briefly with a grumpy concierge who handed her a key, and together they climbed a dank and dingy staircase, adorned with cobwebs and littered with cigarette butts and scraps of paper, skirting around a vivid yellowish splash of vomit. They passed along a narrow corridor and entered a tiny room, bare except for a bed, a chair and a small, rickety table. No trainset.

Mei Mei, aware of the look of disappointment on Algernon's face, gently took hold of both his hands and asked him, "What those English ladies teach you?"

Algernon thought for a while. He really did enjoy looking at Mei Mei's face as she held his hands in hers. These felt so soft and warm. Not like his mother's cold, gnarled paws.

"Well, Mummy taught me joined-up writing and..."

Mei Mei looked in puzzlement at the man, seated beside her on the bed. Suddenly her face lit up.

"Come!" she exclaimed, before gently helping Algernon off with his jacket, followed by his tie, then shirt and, finally, trousers.

"Oh... well, I never!" uttered Algernon after Mei Mei had removed her own clothes and placed them neatly over the back of the chair.

She wore only a pair of pretty, pink panties. Algernon had no idea anyone or anything could be so beautiful. So much nicer than a trainset, he reckoned. Once he had caught sight of a photo of a bare-breasted

108

woman in a newspaper at the dentist's surgery. It had inspired many pleasant thoughts and wet dreams for quite a while but they were nothing in comparison with the lovely, near-naked Mei Mei who now stood, shyly, before him. This was far, far better than the pandas.

During the following two hours, in that dingy little Chinese hotel room, Mei Mei taught Algernon so much. With her tender, caressing body moving gently up against him, Algernon learnt the most extraordinary things about his own body. Things beyond his wildest imagination, and hitherto unused parts of him simply sprang into action. He loved her warmth and her silken skin, and her legs felt so soft wrapped around his own as he entered her.

It was an exhausted but a very happy Algernon who, later, sat watching his pretty, newly acquired Chinese acquaintance dress herself. Somehow, in Mei Mei's company, it seemed quite natural for him to be wearing nothing at all. With his mother it was always trousers, shirt and tie at the very least.

"Where you now go?" Mei Mei asked when fully dressed, putting an arm lovingly across his shoulders. "Um... well... erm... London," mumbled Algernon.

There was an abrupt change in Mei Mei's expression. A look of sheer horror now distorted her beautiful face.

"You what say?" she asked anxiously.

"London," replied Algernon. "We fly back today. I do like airplanes. On the flight here I watched Mr Bean, and..."

Mei Mei interrupted him, a note of alarm in her voice:

"You fly to London today? England?"

"Yes," said Algernon calmly. "Mr Bean, I must say—"

"When? What time flight?" interrupted Mei Mei. She

sounded frightened.

"Well, Mummy said be back by five. The bus is taking us to the airport. Oh, I do hope they have Mr Bean again."

Mei Mei glanced at her watch. It was three-thirty.

"Fast dress!" she exclaimed, pulling Algernon up off the bed and over to the chair where his clothes lay strewn. She seemed seriously agitated. "Fast dress," she repeated in desperation.

"They had cartoons as well, but Mr Bean's the best!" Algernon prattled on about Mr Bean as he casually slipped into his trousers and shirt, appreciating Mei Mei's help with the tie and jacket.

When fully dressed he was hurriedly pulled along towards the door by the young Chinese woman. He felt a great sadness to be leaving that dirty little room in which such wonderful things had happened. As he looked at the bed for the last time, he knew it was where he had experienced the happiest moments of his life.

Downstairs, at the reception desk, Mei Mei talked frantically to the sour-faced concierge who finally responded to the urgency of the situation after being handed a generous helping of Algernon's Chinese banknotes. Telephone calls in Beijing Mandarin were made whilst Algernon stood in smiling blissful ignorance, his mind reliving, over and over, that heavenly time he had in bed with Mei Mei.

"Okay!" the concierge said at last.

Mei Mei reassured Algernon that the taxi would soon arrive. The fear of Algernon being left behind in Beijing, and the terrifying repercussions with the Chinese authorities this might have caused her, had galvanised her into a state of frenzy. She was so relieved when the taxi turned up. Having paid the hotel lady, she handed the taxi driver his fare, together with a handsome tip 'to make sure the Englishman gets back to his hotel in time,' as she put it, in Mandarin, to the driver. Of what seemed to her a small fortune when Mei Mei first met Algernon, nothing was left.

Algernon did not want to say 'Goodbye.' He so wished to ask Mei Mei if she could come on the plane with him back to England, but things were happening too quickly. She slammed the taxi door shut as he was still thanking her profusely for everything and wondering how to ask her. He did try to tell her that it had been the happiest day in his life, but all that came out was "Jolly good, how lovely."

The taxi drove off at break-neck speed. He just had time to turn to wave at the beautiful, tearful, young woman standing on the pavement, and he thought she must truly be an angel of the kind his mummy had talked about when he was a boy. Thankful that the Englishman had been successfully dispatched, the woman smiled and waved back at him. Engulfed by the pleasure, and the sadness, of seeing that smile for the last time, Algernon felt a tear trickle down his cheek, but he never saw the sorrow in the smile of the young Chinese woman.

Fortunately, the tour guide had given Algernon a card on which was written, in Chinese characters, the hotel address. The taxi driver had no difficulty in getting Algernon back to his hotel in time, and the Englishman rather enjoyed the excitement when the taxi wove between oncoming vehicles at Formula One speed. On the wrong side of the road.

Back at their five-star hotel, Lady Hermione, who had miraculously recovered from her night of intestinal torment, was pacing to and fro in the lobby when her son finally appeared. She immediately cornered him and scolded him as though he were a child.

"Really, Algie dear, this *won't* do!" She tapped at her watch. "Only fifteen minutes before the bus leaves. What *have* you been up to?"

"Well, Mummy," began Algernon, embarrassed by the amused expressions on the faces of their tour group members assembled in the hotel lobby, "you see, Mei Mei and me—"

"Look, Algie dear, I know how keen you are on those pandas, but this is ridiculous! Anyway, the porter has brought our cases down."

"But Mummy, Mei Mei is a—"

Lady Hermione never understood why they gave pandas such silly names like Wa Wa and Lu Lu... and Mei Mei. She grabbed her son firmly by the arm.

"Now be a dear and just take those case over there by the door. We'll be leaving in a few minutes. And Algie, I do want back the rest of the money I gave you. We have to give our charming guide a nice tip. That Chinese medicine of hers really worked a treat."

"Well you see, Mummy, I gave all the money to Mei Mei, and—"

There was a momentary pause as her ladyship stared, dumbfounded, at her son. Then...

"You gave all that money to a panda?" she bellowed. What on earth came over you, Algie? How *could* you?" she ranted, her voice still raised. Someone behind her ladyship chuckled but immediately stopped when Lady Hermione turned around to give him one of her withering looks.

"No, Mummy, Mei Mei is—"

"Oh, *do* get a move on!" Lady Hermione nagged, pushing Algernon towards the suitcases.

On the bus back to the airport, Lady Hermione remained tight-lipped whilst Algernon just stared out of the window as the vehicle sped along the highway.

"She had such soft legs," he said dreamily.

"What *are* you talking about?" snapped Lady Hermione, turning to look at her son.

"Mei Mei has really soft legs. And such a lovely—"

Lady Hermione was too irritated to listen to any more of her son's nonsense.

"Do stop going on about that beastly panda, Algie!" she angrily interrupted.

Later, as the plane taxied onto the runway, Algernon was thinking about Mei Mei's pretty face, her soft, silken body up against his own. As the aircraft lifted its great glistening metallic bulk into the air, Lady Hermione, her forehead furrowed in an aristocratic frown, sat puzzling over a panda with soft legs.

Kidnap

David knew something was wrong from the way his secretary burst into the middle of the executive meeting.

"Mr Linton..." she began, causing a row of heads to turn, in unison, and stare. She paused, "Mr Linton, I'm really sorry," the woman continued, "but your wife's on the phone. She sounds pretty upset. Forgive me for interrupting."

David Linton frowned.

"Please continue without me. I shan't be long," he apologised, clearly annoyed.

Jayne, David's young wife, would never call him at work. Even before he became chief executive, he could get angry if bombarded with trivia over the phone. *Something exceptional?* he wondered. Perhaps one of the children had had an accident at school, or maybe there had been a disaster in the house. He tensed as he picked up the phone, totally unprepared for what followed:

"Yes, what is it? I was—"

Jayne, sobbing, cut him short...

"David darling, this is so awful. Something—" There was a scuffling noise then a heavily accented man's voice took over.

"Mr Linton, sir," it began. "Your wife here. She is well and, oh yes, very pretty, your wife. But you listen! She not being so pretty if you don't do right thing. And you speak to no one. *No* one! Hear?"

A feeling of faintness forced David to sit on the edge of the desk as his secretary discreetly left the room.

"No say anyone. No police!" the man continued. Although it all seemed so unreal, David knew that Jayne had been kidnapped. Something that he imagined only occurred in the Middle East, in Latin America or in Hollywood movies, had happened to his own wife in London, England. Or was it a joke? *Please God, make this a joke,* he thought. His knuckles turned pale from gripping the telephone.

"Mr Linton, you go home now. You find instruction there."

David's only choice was to obey. Over the phone, in the background, he heard muffled sobs. Jayne's. Anger kicked in, but he remained speechless. Then, that awful voice again...

"Yes," it continued, "very pretty." Then the phone went dead.

David was still holding a purring phone to his ear when Mrs Fogarty, his secretary, returned. A kind, middle-aged woman who always concerned herself with other peoples' problems, but in a way so unobtrusive that those in need were hardly aware of the support she gave them. Kindness seemed to flow from Mrs Fogarty like a river in a desert.

"Is Jayne all right?" she enquired, sensing something was wrong. David craved her support, and desperately wanted to tell her, but knew that to do so might destroy his chances of ever seeing his beloved Jayne again. That hateful, heavily accented voice still echoed in his ear.

"I must go," said David. "I'll call you from home. Please give my apologies."

On the doormat, back home, an untidily folded scrap of paper awaited him. Standing in the open doorway, trembling, David reached down to pick it up. He stared in disbelief at the terse message crudely scrawled across the paper in large block capitals. Hopes that this might turn

115

out to be a hoax were dashed…

YOUR WIFE. GIVE £5 MILLION. HAVE 2 DAYS.
COME MORE INSTRUCTION.

A huge emptiness opened up forDavid. His wife, his family life, all that he had worked for, could all come to an abrupt end. David looked blankly at the paper in his hand as thoughts and images tumbled about in his mind. Poor Jayne sounded so upset. He could not bear to think of her in the power of the owner of that voice. What was the bastard doing to her right now? Even the unthinkable crossed his mind. *Rape! Oh my God, no!* He screwed the paper into a tight ball. *Screwed? Jayne?*

Jayne and David had always been so happy together. As he lowered himself into a chair to steady himself, he recalled their first meeting eight years back. He was a youthful thirty-eight on a skiing holiday, Jayne the beautiful chalet girl. It was unbelievably idyllic. Truly love at first sight.

Jayne, just turned twenty, was trying to earn a little extra cash to support her during her final year at art school. The age gap did not bother either of them, and Jayne's parents seemed delighted with her newly acquired, mature and wealthy boyfriend. David was already successful in business, and, before they married, a year later, he had found her part-time employment in the design section of his company. They went on to have two sons, Michael, now seven, and Peter, who was five, both of whom David was immensely proud. They reminded him so much of Jayne, particularly Michael, whose open friendliness was the epitome of his mother. Jayne, still in her twenties, had retained her youthful appearance, her

116

sleek black hair beautifully trimmed at shoulder length. Whenever David looked at his wife he could not believe his luck. He, himself, had become quite middle-aged. His protruding belly pushed his trouser waist downwards and his hair was grey at the temples. But Jayne never gave him any cause for concern about the age gap.

The next twenty-four hours were a living nightmare. David had to fetch the boys from school, prepare their food (he hardly ate anything himself) and do all the other things he would normally take for granted but now had to consciously think about whilst imprisoned in a nightmare. He kept hearing that chilling voice in his mind causing him to freeze with fear for Jayne. As for the boys, he hated having to lie to them about their mother. He had told them she was visiting their grandmother for a few days, but they could not understand why they weren't aloud to call Granny on the phone and talk to their mother. They were even more puzzled when David burst into a fit of sobbing as they pleaded with him to let them telephone her. They merely stared at him with blank little expressions.

David phoned Mrs Fogarty from home and told her that there had been a family crisis. She knew from the sound of his voice that something dreadful had happened but did not press him for details. David almost wished she would. He needed her help, her kindness. He felt so alone and miserable, but knew that this was how he would have to face things if he was to get Jayne back alive.

He worked out how to obtain that huge sum of money, five million pounds, and quickly. The nagging fear that he might never see Jayne again gave him purpose and drive to do whatever was necessary. It gave him focus. If he were to follow the kidnappers' demands to the letter, then surely his reward would be to see Jayne again.

Or so he tried to reassure himself.

He arranged an urgent meeting with his bank manager and managed to secure a loan on the strength of his assets which were considerable. It did not seem to matter to him that he would be bankrupt when it was all over. The bank manager, a pleasant man, whom David knew well, was sensitive to David's unease and offered help in 'other ways' as he put it. As with Mrs Fogarty, David desperately wanted to offload, but couldn't.

At midday, after seeing the bank manager, David sat alone, beside the kitchen table, staring vacantly at the telephone handset in front of him. All he had taken since the previous evening was a cup of strong black coffee. His hands trembled. The phone rang. His body jerked as if hit by a heavyweight boxer's punch. After a pause of a few seconds, seconds that seemed to fill an eternity, he picked up the phone.

"Mr Linton, you have the money?"

David could make out other voices in the background. His own sounded remarkably calm.

"Yes, I will have," he said. "Soon."

"No say to anyone?"

"No."

There was a scratching sound, then Jayne's voice. Although distraught, it lifted David's spirits to hear her and know that she was alive.

"Oh David, please do as he says. Please, please. These men mean business. Please don't go to the police. I... Ow!" She let out a shriek that cut into him like a meat cleaver. Then that foreign voice again...

"Tomorrow morning eleven o'clock. Man's toilet. Marble Arch near Hyde Park. You find instruction. Black bag. Talk tomorrow. Same time. Your wife sensible woman. No police, she say. She..." There was a pause. Then, with a nauseating leer, "She *very* pretty."

The phone went dead.

Another twenty-four-hour ordeal for David. The children, their clothes, the meals, their questions and entreaties to telephone Granny, over and over, whilst his mind was paralysed with fear for Jayne's safety, what she might be going through and what horrors might yet be in store for them both.

David found the black bag in the Hyde Park toilet. It was an empty leather briefcase. Later, he found himself seated in the kitchen, back home, again waiting for the phone to ring. It did so at precisely the pre-arranged time, but still he jumped as though punched.

The nightmare continued. David listened carefully to instructions as to where he should leave the case full of money at seven the following morning. This time, the gent's toilet in the underpass at Marble Arch, beneath a wash basin. If the money was not there, or if the police were to turn up, he would never see Jayne again. After the drop off he should go to work as though nothing had happened. He would get further instructions at work the following day if he did as he was told to do.

"Let me speak with her, please," David begged, but he was cut off. Later, in the afternoon, David collected the money from the bank manager himself. He was unable to sleep that night. At five-thirty in the morning, he crawled out of bed and, after three cups of strong black coffee, picked up the black briefcase loaded with cash. Every note had been counted and recounted, and the case had spent the night on the side of the bed where Jayne should have lain. The bank manager had pulled out all necessary stops to come up with such a large amount of cash in a such short time. He had no choice other than to bring the boys, hastily bundled into their school clothes, with him. They yawned their sleepy heads off as he pushed them into the car. With the briefcase stuffed full of money on the front passenger seat where he could keep an eye on it, he drove through near-deserted London streets. There were plenty of free parking bays off Oxford Street. David pulled in, fed some coins into the meter, un-strapped the boys who had fallen asleep, and hurried off, holding the case, the boys tripping along behind him on rubbery little legs. They were too sleepy to ask their father what it was all about and followed like obedient puppy dogs.

David found what he took to be the drop-off point in the gents' toilet near Marble Arch, paused, looked around, went back up the steps of the underpass and down again before finally reassuring himself that this had to be the correct location. He left the case of money and, taking each of his sons firmly by the hand, walked quickly back to the car.

"Why did you leave that black case in the toilet, Daddy?" asked Michael, now wide awake.

"I had to leave something for a man, Michael," said David. He did not dare to say too much, not even to his son. Something might leak out at school. The teachers could inform the authorities.

Pete piped up.

"Is it because of Mummy?" He looked directly at David with wide, enquiring eyes. David silently cursed the boy for being so bright.

"Mummy will be home when you get back from school," he said. He had to believe this. The boys remained quiet all the way back to the car, and throughout the car ride in the early morning traffic. He stopped off at a café in Hampstead to snatch a quick breakfast before taking the boys on to school. David then drove to work, leaving the car in a nearby twenty-four hour parking lot.

Why had they told him to go on to work? He tried to give himself hope. Perhaps it meant that they would drop Jayne off at home when he was out of the house. He could understand why they might do this. However, what he dreaded most of all was that he might now hear nothing more from the kidnappers and never see Jayne again.

It was an awful day that never seemed to end. It was as though time stood still. He sat in his office, idled with his laptop, fumbled through some paper files, all the time feeling like a bad actor in a second-rate Hollywood movie who had forgotten his lines. Mrs Fogarty helped him to survive merely by being there. He had heard nothing by two-thirty and feared the worst. Why no contact from the kidnappers?

David left for home, feeling so heavy inside himself that he worried his legs might give way any moment. He looked towards the house from the gate, still open as he had left it early that morning. Those last ten yards up to the door of the house now seemed to stretch for miles. Every yard could be divided into feet, every foot into inches. And each inch of those last few steps up to the house saw his brain invaded by hope, by doubt, by uncertainty and with that terrible fear of the worst possible outcome: that the house would be empty because Jayne was dead. Having heard nothing further from the kidnappers it seemed that way to David as he reached for the door with his key.

David's heart leapt in his chest when, on turning the

121

key, he found the door unlocked. Quickly, he flung it open. It was a dull day and the hallway was dim. It appeared empty. He failed to notice Jayne's jacket, which lay on the chair in the hallway. He called out. Silence. The warm feeling that enveloped him on finding the door unlocked wavered. Had he just forgotten to lock it that morning?

"Jayne!" he called out. Again, silence. He entered the living room. At first he could not see her as the settee upon which she was lying had its back to the door. He saw something move before spotting Jayne's hair above the back of the settee. David ran round to the front of the settee. She lay there, wearing only a flimsy dressing gown and staring ahead at the empty wall opposite. David dropped to his knees, crying like a child, and draped himself around his wife's motionless body.

"Hello, David," Jayne said. Softly. She seemed distant and unemotional, in total contrast to his own explosive sobs whilst he explored her body with trembling hands, as though he was discovering it for the first time. Despite his tears, never before had David felt such happiness as at the very moment he knew that Jayne was still alive. *She must be in a state of shock,* he thought as his fumbling hands sought some sort of response from his wife. Then, slowly, she ran her fingers through David's thinning hair, but still stared blankly ahead, her mind elsewhere.

David could not stop talking through his sobs, but Jayne remained silent. Whether she was listening, David was unable to tell, but it did not matter. Before, he would have been furious if he felt she was paying no attention to him, but now he knew that the words tumbling out of his mouth were unimportant. Jayne was alive.

David jerked up, staring at his watch.

"My God, Jayne. I forgot about the boys. I'll go and

collect them from school. Do not move from here. Don't answer the door, don't answer the telephone, although I'll leave it right here beside you. Any suspicion of someone outside and call the police right away."

"David..." Jayne began as David was about to leave. "The police. Have they been in touch with you?" She sounded concerned. The first sign of any emotion since David had got back.

"No, darling. I took no risks. Made no contact with the police."

"Oh," said Jayne. "Perhaps tomorrow."

"Tomorrow what, darling?"

"Tell the police. Tomorrow. If they haven't been round by then."

David left to collect the boys, somewhat confused about why Jayne seemed so concerned about the police. When he returned with the boys, Jayne was in the kitchen, preparing tea for them. It all seemed too normal after what both she and David had been through.

"Mummy!" shouted Michael, before rushing forward and encircling her legs. Pete copied his brother. "Why couldn't we call you at Granny's? It made us both very sad!" Michael asked.

There were tears in Jayne's eyes, for the first time, when she crouched down and hugged her sons together. David answered for her.

"Granny wasn't well, was she Jayne?" he offered. "We were worried about waking her up by telephoning. But now that Mummy's home that doesn't matter anymore, does it?" Jayne looked up at David and smiled. How he loved that smile.

"Thank you, David," she said.

123

With the boys around, everything seemed back to normal, but after David had put them to bed Jayne became quiet again. Several times, she checked with David about the police. She seemed obsessed with the idea that the police might call on them. David unwisely talked about getting help through their GP.

Possibly some counselling, or maybe a session with the practice nurse? In confidence, of course.

Jayne exploded when David suggested this.

"What do they know about kidnappings? Do you have any idea what I've been through? What's a quiet little chat with some ignorant practice nurse going to do for me, eh? How bloody stupid!" Jayne's rage was unprovoked and inappropriate. He was completely thrown by the suddenness of her verbal attack. In the past, he was the dominant one, the one who set the pace. He now saw a side to Jayne that she had kept hidden. He edged towards the door, backing away from her.

"I'm s-sorry, Jayne. We've both been through hell and we need a rest. Let's go to bed, darling. I've hardly slept since... since they... erm... they took you. I feel shattered."

"You go. I'll be up later," replied Jayne.

David went upstairs. He heard Jayne weeping downstairs. Why she was so cold towards him he could not fathom, but he was still so insanely happy to have her back he hardly cared. Besides, he reckoned, she would still be feeling traumatised, barely aware of what she is saying.

Jayne finally came upstairs about an hour later. She undressed in front of the mirror, her back towards David. His bedside lamp gave a little illumination and to his horror David saw marks and bruises on his wife's youthful

124

body.

"What the...? he began, startled by what he saw. Jayne swivelled, fixing him with tear-filled eyes.

"They weren't *all* like that!" she said.

*****

Jayne was walking along the empty street beside the school, having just left her two sons at the entrance, when a white van pulled up alongside her. A young woman wound down the window, waved an A to Z at her and called out in a strong cockney accent.

"Excuse me, miss, is this the right way for Marble Arch?"

Jayne should have been suspicious, but the girl seemed pleasant enough. She felt she could hardly offer more than the A to Z, particularly as she had no knowledge of the one-way systems. She was trying to think of the best way to get to the Edgware Road, this being the most direct route, when she was grabbed from behind. Her assailant had the strength of an ox. Her arms were held as if in a vice and a rag placed over her head. There was an awful smell, then, quickly, she lost consciousness. When she came to, she felt horribly uncomfortable, lying on her side, arms tied tightly behind her back, her short skirt up around the tops of her thighs, her legs bent and secured to stop her from kicking, plus there was a strip of sticky tape across her mouth. Also blindfolded, she could only grunt. Jayne was bumped about, like this, in the windowless back of the van from which the young cockney woman had asked for directions. Several times her helpless body slid sideways as the van swung around a corner, causing her head to bang, painfully, against the side of the vehicle.

Finally, the vehicle came to a halt. The front doors

opened then slammed shut again. There was frantic talking in some foreign language, then the back doors were opened, noisily, and, through her blindfold, Jayne became aware of bright daylight illuminating the interior of the van.

"Quick!" someone shouted in English. Jayne felt her legs being grabbed and pulled then roughly turned this way and that before getting rolled over till she felt a tight pressure encircling her body. She realised she was being wrapped in something, possibly a carpet. Someone removed her shoes. Like a helpless animal trussed for slaughter, she was pulled out backwards and clumsily carried by two people up some steps, through a door, into a house, then up a steep staircase, when her rolled-up body was more upright than horizontal. Then, along a corridor and through a door until she and the carpet were thrown down onto the floor. The carpet was unravelled against a background babble of foreign male voices plus the unmistakable voice of the cockney woman, although she, too, at times, spoke in that same unfamiliar language.

When her blindfold and the tape covering her mouth had been removed, Jayne saw that she was lying on the floor of a small room, bare except for a table, a few wooden chairs and a mattress in the far corner. There was only one door. A pair of drab green curtains had been drawn across the only window. Jayne was terrified beyond words. Her captors stood around her in a circle, grinning like hunters proudly displaying their quarry. She blinked with frightened eyes at the young cockney woman.

"'Allo, luv," the woman said. "'Ave a nice ride, did yer?" She cackled like a witch. Jayne knew she would receive not one shred of sympathy from her. She glanced at the three men: a young man she recognised as the driver of the van, of similar age to herself; an older balding man, late fifties or early sixties, in a well-cut dark suit, and, finally, a very unpleasant-looking, thick-set, swarthy man with curly brown hair in his thirties or forties. It was this man and the cockney woman whom she feared the most.

"Welcome to your new home, Jayne, darling," said the swarthy man. He gave the impression of being in charge. "I'm Sergei..."

"Just call 'im Serge, luv," interrupted the woman. "I do!"

Sergei repeated himself. "I'm Sergei. This young lady, she Anna, over there, he Yuri and this clever man here, he be Boris. You call Boris, 'Sir'. He big boss guy!"

Like a confused and frightened rabbit, Jayne peered from the unrolled carpet at the faces peering down at her. The four of them began to speak again, amongst themselves, in what Jayne took to be Russian. Sergei stooped down to untie the ropes binding her legs and her hands. As soon as she was freed, he grabbed one of Jayne's arms and roughly pulled her up. For a few moments things went blank, and she thought she was going to faint, but gradually her head cleared and her vision returned. She was pulled by the elbow towards the table where she was forced to sit on a kitchen chair. Jayne reckoned that the safest thing was to quietly acquiesce to all her captors' demands. All she wanted was to stay alive so that she might get back home to David and to her sons.

Sergei took out a mobile phone from his pocket and dialled a number. He gave Jayne the phone and asked her to get David. Jayne wished she could have explained her plight to Mrs Fogarty, but she knew that would have been too dangerous.

"Yes, what is it? I was…" David began. Jayne knew from his angry tone that some important meeting had been interrupted. She was sobbing.

"Oh, David darling, this is awful. Something—"

Sergei grabbed the phone from Jayne. He ogled her, his ugly mouth distorted into a bestial grin, then spoke to her husband. The way he spoke was terrifying. Jayne was revolted by the man, and by his lecherous leer when he told David she was 'very pretty.' With her short skirt still up around the tops of her thighs she felt dangerously vulnerable.

Jayne knew that Sergei meant every word of what he said. They would kill her should David go to the police. And those demands with which he must comply… what were they, she wondered? Would they demand money from her husband? Poor David. How awful he must be feeling. She was everything to him, and she knew that his world would simply fall apart if anything happened to her. But David was strong. He would do everything possible to get that money if money was all that they demanded. She had a chance as long as David followed Sergei's instructions and did not lose his legendary temper or call the police. David never liked being told what to do. She soon learned this after they married. Now, for both their sakes, he would have to be the one being dictated to. He would become the underling.

Jayne's fear of Sergei proved to be well founded. A few hours after that awful telephone call to David, Sergei put a plateful of cold tinned spaghetti on the table in front of Jayne. She had no appetite whatsoever and felt like throwing up when she saw what her captor offered her.

"Eat!" Sergei demanded. Anna was lying on the mattress, browsing through a fashion magazine.

"Better do as 'e says, luv," advised Anna, without looking up.

"I'm not hungry." Jayne offered, weakly. "Later, perhaps." Jayne was not prepared for what followed. Without warning Sergei grabbed a handful of Jayne's hair, pulled her head back, and, with a crazed look in his eyes, struck her across the face with the back of his hand.

"I say eat, you eat!" He released his grip on Jayne's hair. Her head flopped forwards. She sobbed.

"Told you, luv," Anna said, glancing up at Jayne. "'Ere, Serge, she'll now need water an' all. Jus' look at them bleedin' tears. Be all dried out, she will." She witch-cackled, again, whilst Jayne forced herself to eat the cold spaghetti, repeatedly gagging.

Jayne soon learned more. It *was* money that was being demanded in return for her life. Five million pounds. And within two days. Where would David find money like that? And so soon? Jayne began to feel there was no hope. To make things worse, Sergei and Anna took obvious pleasure in her wretchedness. There were more beatings. The two of them clearly enjoyed abusing Jayne. It seemed to sexually arouse them, for on a few occasions, after beating her, they would make love together on the mattress in the corner. The same mattress on which she would have to sleep. When Sergei and Anna made love it was as if Jayne's presence in the room was of no consequence to them whatsoever. They were like wild animals, and Jayne found it hard to believe anyone could be so subhuman. Curiously, she did not hate them. No more than she could hate a pair of crazed dogs. But she feared them. She wanted to live. Oh, how she wanted to live to see her children and David again, but it was these two crazed dogs who would decide whether this could happen.

The man in the suit, Boris, did not reappear until the last day of Jayne's captivity. He was the faceless man behind the scenes, the one who had masterminded everything, and whom the other three clearly feared. The moody young Yuri was in the room on guard duty for a lot of the time. Fortunately, Sergei and Anna were not around too often, but enough for Yuri to see how they treated Jayne. When all three were in the room together with her, Yuri sat quietly in the background without saying a word.

On one occasion, as he was sitting at the table, opposite Jayne, whilst Sergei and Anna mated noisily on the mattress, Jayne caught sight of Yuri looking at her. So many human feelings seemed to flicker across his dark eyes. She found herself staring back at Yuri. They both remained silent against the background of grunts and gasps from the rutting couple. Yuri had just witnessed Jayne being beaten by Sergei, he had seen her crying and rubbing her bruises and there was a mixture of fury and tenderness in his eyes. When Sergei and Anna had finished copulating, and had left the dingy room, and Jayne was alone with the young Russian, he spoke with disgust:

"Animals! I will kill them! This, I promise."

Jayne looked across the table at Yuri. She had barely heard him speak before, and indeed had been unsure as to whether he spoke English at all. His accent was almost perfect. He got up and came over to where Jayne sat sobbing and pulled up a chair alongside her. "I am so sorry for what they are doing. This is not how it should be."

Jayne edged away from Yuri. She felt true anger for

the first time since being kidnapped.

"Should be? *Should be?* What do you mean, should be? I shouldn't bloody be here at all. Did you know that? I should be at home. I should be with my family, my sons. So don't you give *me* any more of your 'should-bes', you Russian bastard! Just take me home now if you really feel this isn't as it should be. Go on, take me home!" Jayne challenged. She even found the courage to thump Yuri on the arm when she said this.

"I wish I could. I really wish I could. Boris has his men outside. If I try anything, they'll kill us both. These men, they have no hearts."

"Speak for yourself, you coward!" Jayne was seething.

"Right about bastard," said Yuri. "And my mother, she died when I was only five. Can hardly remember her. Father was murdered by the KGB. Orphanage was full of other bastards, like Sergei. I ran away. Lived on the streets in St Petersburg."

"Oh, cut out your sob story. Just leave me alone," said Jayne, turning away. Then she heard the strangest of sounds. That of a man sobbing. She looked back at Yuri. Head hung forwards, he cried like a child. At first she did not know how to respond, but her anger seemed to just melt away as she sat staring at her weeping captor.

"I'm so sorry. Please believe me. What we do is so terrible. I know. I cannot forgive myself," he said before looking up at Jayne.

She had always felt there was something about this young man that set him apart from the others. Slightly built, almost thin, with tousled black hair, he looked Romany. His eyes were deep set, and there was something

131

about those eyes that held Jayne's attention. They were not the eyes of a hardened criminal and certainly not those of a murderer.

Jayne and Yuri talked. Jayne desperately needed someone human with whom she could communicate. She asked him more about his childhood, his background in Russia. She learned how he had left the Russian army with engineering skills and had found employment in a garage. He told her of his dream to find work in Britain, and how he had worked hard to learn English at night school. He explained how this dream seemed to have come true when a 'friend' in St Petersburg put him in touch with a man from Moscow. The man took all the money he had and arranged his passage to England. He even found him a job in a garage in North London, but there were conditions. He would work for 'them' otherwise his life expectancy would be brief. 'They' were the Russian Mafia. Yuri knew little about Anna and Sergei, except that Anna was half-English and half-Russian.

Jayne listened to all of this as she would have listened to a friend. In return she told Yuri about her own dreams, her life with David, how they had met whilst she worked as a chalet girl in the Alps, about her home and her two sons. She found it difficult to stop talking and Yuri listened with such an intense look on his face that she wanted to laugh. How could he *really* want to know her full life history? After all, he was one of her captors. It all seemed too bizarre. Even more so when she found out that it was Yuri who had done all the spying on David and herself. He admitted going through their rubbish bags when they were out. Amazing what can be found out that way, he told her, credit card details included. It was largely through Yuri that 'they' had found out Jayne was the ideal target for their purpose, although, as she was well aware, it was Sergei and Anna who did all the dirty work.

Gradually a bond formed between Jayne and Yuri, for as well as being captor and captive they were also just two young people who had been thrown together in circumstances from which there was no escape. Both needed support and reassurance. After witnessing Sergei's repeated brutality inflicted upon Jayne, Yuri's guilt for his involvement in her abduction became unbearable. Jayne believed that he really had no idea that the kidnapping would have taken the course it did. Boris had reassured him that David would pay the ransom and that their captive would be set free, unharmed. Neither had taken into account the devilry of Sergei and Anna, but Boris was too removed from the action to actually care. Jayne knew that Yuri was not a criminal at heart, and that his real wish truly had been to start a new life in Britain rather than becoming caught up within the evil machinery of the Russian Mafia.

Yuri was in tears again. Jayne came up close. She put an arm around his shoulders and tried to comfort him, although her words gave no comfort to herself. For both, this action proved to be like the flicking of a switch. Their tears mingled as their cheeks touched. They kissed. Lightly at first, but the kisses became stronger, more intense, as they felt and fondled one another. They moved across to the mattress, still feeling and fondling. They abandoned the words and the talking. Their physical passion began to burn with an intensity that neither had previously experienced for a very long time. It was as though an unmet need had become all the more urgent after years of dormancy. Yuri was so gentle that Jayne, too, started to cry. He stroked her tear-stained cheeks. When her clothes had been removed he caressed her bruises, swearing vengeance against Sergei. They made love and, shortly after collapsing into each other's arms, exhausted and breathless, they began to make love all over again. Later, Jayne felt like a person reborn as she and Yuri put their clothes back on. No one had ever made love to her with such passion before, and she felt a strange strength well within her. Somehow, she felt no guilt whatsoever for, at that very moment her life, David and the children belonged to another world. Now she felt only a certain inner strength, and she sensed the same strength in Yuri. He kissed and fondly comforted her; he told her that he would look after her and make sure she came to no harm. Jayne believed him.

The following morning, the money was to be picked up. Jayne had every confidence in David. He would do exactly as he was told to. He had confirmed, over the phone, that he had the money. What was unclear to Jayne was exactly how she would, afterwards, be released. She was thankful that Yuri was there, with her, in the morning, although neither gave any hint of what had happened between them the previous day. Jayne was aware of Yuri looking at Sergei through narrowed eyes whilst the latter again bound Jayne's arms and legs before taping her mouth and blindfolding her. Once more, she felt the fear that had engulfed her when she came to in the van following her capture. If things were to go wrong, what could young Yuri do, unarmed, against a thug like Sergei and the Russian-Cockney witch, Anna? For the second time, Jayne was trussed in a rolled-up carpet, bounced down the stairs, then out into the street and pushed headfirst into the van. She heard the doors slam shut, the engine rev, and felt the vehicle move forward. She had no idea whether or not Yuri was with them although he had reassured her that he would be the driver.

Yuri drove the white van through the almost empty streets. He drove slowly, which irritated Sergei. The excuse he gave was not to arouse suspicion, but the real reason was to make the journey less traumatic for Jayne. Yuri prayed that Sergei's stupidity would be the brute's undoing when the time came; but he feared that Boris had an alternative plan to the one given to David. Boris was that sort of a bastard. When Yuri pulled up in a parking bay, a few blocks away from Marble Arch, he saw Sergei fumble through some papers and documents. These included Russian passports. He studied one for a Nastasya Nevsky. He had never heard the name before, but he recognised the young woman in the photograph…

Jayne!

Yuri tried to sound casual.

"Who's that for?" he asked in Russian, nodding at the forged passport.

"You'll find out," replied Sergei in Russian. "Let's just say, we'll give Hampstead a miss when we have the money. First, we leave that with Boris. Then our little friend in the back is going to have a nice long holiday in our mother country. To enjoy good Russian f---s. Boris says we need girls like her back home for his friends. He's already fixed the price. Get a lot of rubles for an English girl like her. Then move her on to some other country once tamed and when her looks have faded."

Sergei grinned. Yuri had to hold back from slamming his fist into the bastard's face there and then. He knew Sergei was armed, and tried to stay calm, act at the right time, then act quickly.

135

Sergei placed the documents in the glove compartment and left the van to collect the money. Yuri had five, if lucky ten, minutes to sort out Anna. As soon as Sergei had turned the corner, Yuri was out of the van. He slipped round to the back of the vehicle and opened the van doors. Anna was sitting to one side, resting her feet on the rolled-up carpet concealing Jayne.

"Where's the...?" Anna began in Russian but got no further. With one well-aimed blow, Yuri rendered her senseless. He crawled into the back of the van and quickly unrolled the carpet to free Jayne. She reached up to touch his face.

"No time!" he said. "Quick, help me tie her up and roll her up in the carpet. But first, take off her clothes."

Yuri and Jayne worked in perfect unison, as they'd done when making love. In no time, Anna was trussed up, gagged, blindfolded and rolled up into the carpet. She was beginning to come to, uttering a few guttural grunts. Jayne knew what to do with Anna's clothes. The half-Russian woman was of heavier build, and Jayne easily slipped her jeans up and over her own small skirt. She covered her shoulders with Anna's denim jacket, then sat in the same position in the van that Anna had taken, giving Anna a heartfelt kick in the back after she leant against the side of the vehicle. Yuri slammed the doors. Jayne sat and waited.

Soon, she heard one of the van's back doors open. Yuri spoke in Russian, and Sergei replied. He sounded agitated. After that, things happened so quickly that Jayne had no time to feel real fear. The back door slammed shut, the passenger front door opened. Sergei's face appeared and spoke in Russian. She leaned forward, from the back, to face him. For an instant, the brute stood frozen, disbelief written across his face. That brief moment of shock on seeing Jayne, and not Anna, in the back, gave Yuri a split-second advantage. He appeared behind Sergei and in an instant grabbed the larger man in a strangle hold, bent his head back, and with alarming strength and agility, had Sergei pinned down in a flash. With the man's arms pulled back in a full Nelson, rendering him helpless, Yuri pressing his knee into the base of Sergei's spine. Then, in a movement so fast it was barely perceptible, he whisked out Sergei's gun, flicked up the safety catch and held the weapon up against the other man's temple.

Sergei's bloodshot eyes peered sideways at Yuri. There was sheer terror in those eyes.

"Don't shoot me!" he begged in Russian, followed by, "It's not loaded."

Yuri remained calm.

"If it's not loaded, I can shoot!" He started counting in Russian. *"Odin... dva..."*

"Niet, niet!" screamed Sergei. Yuri reverted to English when he spoke to Jayne:

"Take the bastard's shoes off, take the laces out and use them to tie his feet together. *Really* tight. Make his feet drop off if you can. But first, give me Anna's jacket and jeans. I'll use them, too."

Sergei whimpered like a baby as Jayne and Yuri set to work to immobilise the fiend. A handkerchief was stuffed into his mouth, whilst Anna's jeans, which Jayne had taken off, were pulled firmly around his mouth and eyes then wrapped twice around his thick neck before being tied at the back. Anna's jacket was used to bind his arms up behind him, then tied to the jeans. Not even Houdini could have escaped from such bonds. With Anna and Sergei both bundled up, like market-bound livestock, in the back of the van, Yuri leapt out, and offered Jayne a hand to help her down. She retrieved her skirt, the doors were slammed shut, the two lovers ran round to the front of the vehicle, climbed in and Yuri started up the engine. He drove off slowly, quietly, towards Hampstead.

They left the van in a secluded side street off Fitzjohn's Avenue, the black case with the money still on the passenger seat. From there, they half walked and half ran to Jayne's house. Jayne still had her key. She opened the door. What a relief for her to be back home, but at the same time it all seemed so strange, even more so with her young Russian lover at her side. She closed the door behind Yuri and flung her arms around his neck. She kissed him all over his face, and, leading him upstairs to the bedroom, she kept on kissing him whilst she peeled off her own clothes. In between kisses, Yuri also managed to undress. They sank onto the bed together, their entwined nakedness feeling and moving like a single being. Their lovemaking was even more passionate than it had been back in that dismal room, now free from the heavy weight of doubt and fear that had haunted them both the last time they came together. Jayne loved, with her body, as she could not have believed possible. Yuri entered Jayne three times before they finally lay still, hands clasped together, both staring up at the ceiling.

It was late morning before they left the double bed and dressed in silence.

"The police. We should phone them. About the van. About the money. About..." Since arriving back home, this was the first time Jayne had even dared think about what she had been through earlier on that morning.

"The phone?" asked the young Russian.

"Yes, Yuri. I have Sergei's phone. I do." She fetched the mobile from the jumble of clothes beside the bed and switched it on. Jayne took the phone, dialled, for Yuri, the emergency services number asking for the police, then handed it back to Yuri. Yuri explained that there were two dangerous Russian Mafia criminals with stolen money in the back of a white van parked off Fitzjohn's Avenue. He refused to give details about himself and quickly rang off. He felt for the gun in his pocket. It was still there. He might yet need it.

"I go now," Yuri said to Jayne, standing up. "Your husband, he'll worry. He'll soon be back."

Jayne always knew the thing with Yuri would come to an end although she desperately wanted to hold on to him.

"What will you do now, Yuri?" she asked. "You've risked your own life for me. I couldn't bear for anything to happen to you. Boris, those others, they're still out there. And bloody dangerous. You could hand yourself in to the police. You might be safer in their hands. I'll stand up for you. I can visit you—"

"In prison? No, I don't trust the police. Only you, Jayne. I'll hide. Maybe get on a boat to Europe. Even go back to Russia. There I have friends. I can look after myself."

Jayne, tearful, knew only too well how true this was. Also, she knew that ending their brief but fervent love affair would be as painful for him as it was for her.

"Yuri, I *must* see you again. I have to. Tomorrow? Please don't go into hiding before tomorrow. You could..." Yuri took hold of Jayne again and silenced her with a kiss on the lips. He gently wiped away her tears, went downstairs, all the time holding her hand, and they stood awhile, in silence, together, at the door.

"You have David. You have two sons. Stay with them," he said. "I have only love for you. Nothing more. Nothing less. Now I must go."

Jayne, exhausted, went back to bed and sobbed herself into a fitful sleep. When she awoke it was about one-thirty in the afternoon. She had a bath, slipped on a dressing gown, went downstairs to lie on the settee in the living room, waiting for David to return home.

David and Jayne awoke early the following morning. Before the boys were up. David insisted on making Jayne a cup of tea and some toast. He wanted to do everything possible to make things easier for her, for he could only imagine how traumatised she must feel. Perhaps she would come round to his suggestion of counselling in her own time.

Jayne followed David downstairs into the kitchen. She turned on the radio before sitting at the kitchen table, across which she leant forwards on folded arms. After a short while the seven o'clock news was announced...

"A young Russian man is helping the police with their enquiries after the discovery of the bodies of a man and a woman in the back of a white stolen van at mid-day yesterday following a mystery phone call. The dead man is thought to have suffocated. The woman remains critically ill in the intensive care unit of the Royal Free Hospital in Hampstead. It is believed that the crime was committed in connection with the activities of a Russian Mafia network within Britain. The identities of the dead man and of the young woman are unknown, but the young man in custody, Yuri Kajensky, appears to be an illegal Russian immigrant. Detectives are busy tracing the source of the large amount

of stolen money that was found in the van. The police, who now have several important leads, ask for any witnesses to come forward. The number to ring is..."

The doorbell rang. Jayne let out a shriek.

"Boris? No, no, no! Please, God, please make it be Yuri!"

Boris? Yuri? David stood frozen to the spot, caught between his wife's sobs and the loud, persistent ring of the doorbell.

Karma

It's that time of year, isn't it?

I'm not talking about the ridiculous number of apples that threaten to break the boughs of our apple trees, or the splashes of orange and red daubing the maples beside the road to Galashiels in the Scottish Borders where I live. I don't even refer to the endless references to a summer that never happened north of Hadrian's Wall. No, it's when the spiders' thermostats tell them that there ain't gonna be enough flies out there any longer so they come crawling into our houses. Never polite enough to walk in through the front door, of course. They simply turn up. In the bath, in your bed when you pull back the duvet, or they come running out towards you from under the piano.

The piano! Perhaps if I played it more often they might be discouraged from seeking refuge there because of the discordant noise whenever I play at being a pianist,. Play all day long and our house might be spider-free come October.

It was early morning. Sunny outside, for a change. Perhaps this was the reason. Attempting to make the most of the fading summer warmth. Emerging from under the piano, it was large, black and distinctly hairy.

Funny thing, arachnophobia. Did it originate in the days of our pre-vertebrate ancestors when they were prey to giant arachnids that would make modern day pet tarantulas seem smaller than mites? But I'll never forget the bravery of our four-year-old granddaughter when she held a tarantula, red not black, in her wee hands at the Edinburgh Butterfly Farm.

"Do *not* drop it!" warned the handler. "They're terribly fragile. Break if they hit the floor. It happened here, once, when a child dropped one of our much-loved spiders. It was horrible, the way it died, innards spilling out. I was in tears."

My granddaughter just stood there with the huge spider straddling both palms, looking down at it in awe. The tarantula was facing the other way, but I wondered what it would have made of the little girl in charge of its immediate destiny had it been able to see her face.

Both granddaughter and the Mexican, red-kneed tarantula were fine. The arachnid was safely returned to its cage and the girl quietly the wiser for she now knew not to fear spiders.

No way could I follow her example. I would most certainly have dropped the poor creature and broken yet another beautiful spider. I guess they're expensive. Particularly the colourful red ones. But when a big, black arachnid with hairy legs ran out from its musical hiding place, I froze with fear.

Stamp, run or scream? Which was it to be? Old men with white hair, like me, cannot run or scream, so my options were reduced to stamping. No time to worry about the stain on the carpet. A black one, I imagine, seeing that the creature was black. Did that red-kneed Mexican Tarantula leave a red stain when it left its guts on the floor of the Edinburgh Butterfly Farm?

Why do they call it a farm? Puzzling. No sheep, cattle or wheat-fields. There are exotic birds there (some large spiders eat little birds) but the birds I saw were hardly *farm* birds. I digress...

The spider halted. Unlike the tarantula in the Butterfly Farm (do tarantulas eat butterflies?) who calmly sat on a little girl's open hands, it looked up at me. My raised foot hovered above the creature, having followed the spider's darting zigzags over the carpet. And I stepped back when the spider spoke...

"Karma!"

Parrots can speak, and they say dogs and apes can understand certain words of human speech. But spiders? It was a sweet, high-pitched little voice, not deep and gravelly as I would have expected. High-pitched seemed less threatening. Indeed, a speaking spider would allow me to address my arachnophobia in a way that did not involve holding the animal. As I said, I am not as brave as my then four-year-old granddaughter.

"What?" I questioned, peering down at the little creature that, after all, was no way as large when standing there on the floor as it appeared to me inside my head. No more than two inches across. Big for a spider, sure, but small for a talking thing.

"Karma!"

"You can speak?"

"So can you."

Speaking spiders were new to me, let alone those that question my own ability to speak.

"Look, I'm sorry. Wasn't really meaning to stamp on you. Only politely avoiding you."

"Liar!"

I tried to see where the voice came from. No moving mouth parts, no little hole. Just a squeaky voice.

"And stop staring. It's all about karma, like I told you. You do know what that means, don't you?"

"Sort of. If I were to step on—"

"One of our lot does the same to you. Bloody great

house-sized spider stomps you into the dirt. Get it?"

Perhaps my arachnophobia *is* well-founded, for the spider seemed pretty shirty.

"Okay. I *was* going to squash you, but—"

"Thug!"

"I said 'sorry' didn't I? Anyway why did you come out of safe hiding from under the piano when you saw me."

"Isn't that obvious?"

"Not to a human. You could've stayed there, unnoticed, till spring."

"God, you're stupid! Nice day outside. I saw the sunlight on the carpet. Wanted to see the sun. Maybe for the last time. That's why."

"Planning on going back outside, then?" I asked, hopefully.

"That's where the sun is, you human thickhead."

"Why go outside? Snuggle down for the Autumn. Anyway, where's your wife? She still hiding?"

"I am the wife, idiot!"

"Oh! Where's your husband, then?"

"Inside me."

I remembered. Maybe that's why I'm arachnophobic. Some female spiders devour their males after doing 'it' together.

"Erm... taste nice, did he?"

"Don't be rude. Sacrificed himself for our babies. Now, are you going to let me out of that front door or not?"

A thought occurred to me. If spiders can talk, maybe there really is something in this karma business. Who knows? I might return as one myself the next time. If so,

145

please, God, make me female. Or non-binary.

"I'll make it up to you by taking you outside. Okay? Put you down in an insect-ridden flower bed."

"How can I trust you?"

"By believing in karma?"

The spider tensed, backed away from me, then edged forwards again. Just as a human might whilst weighing out the pros and cons.

"Okay! As long as the postie isn't around. He once tried to kill me, you know."

"He avoids the flower beds."

I knelt down and held out my hand, palm up, on the floor. The spider walked towards me, tapped at my hand with hesitant, wavering front legs, then climbed up. She shuffled around to face me again.

"You won't bite, will you?" I needed reassurance as beads of sweat broke out on my forehead. "I told you, I'm not as brave as my four-year-old granddaughter.

"I'll not bite if I want to come back as something better than a spider."

"A human?"

"I said 'better'. Oh, do get going!"

As if walking with the crown jewels in my hand, I took the spider outside and gently placed her on a bed of dying pansies and spent nasturtiums.

"Just one last look at the sun. I'll soon be gone. Just a dried-out exoskeleton stuck in a web. Ex-mother of dozens of spiderlings."

"I'm sorry."

"About my babies?"

"No! Because you're life's so short."

"Thanks, anyway. We part on good terms, right?"

"Hope so. By the way, who taught you to—?"

But the spider had vanished. I returned to do what I came down from the bedroom for. Make my wife a cup of tea. And now I wonder whether I should finish by saying:

'I woke up when my wife gave me a nudge and asked where her cup of tea was.'

No. That would be a cliché to be avoided at all costs. Instead, she asked:

"Who were you talking to downstairs?"

"Oh... myself, as usual," I lied. How could I own up to having a conversation about karma with a spider?

"The surgery opens at eight thirty. Perhaps you should think about—"

"No. I've heard that many great minds talk to themselves," I assured my wife. Thank goodness human females do not behave like female spiders. Had that been the case the case, I would not have lived to see my lovely granddaughters.

Secretly, I thanked the grumpy spider for curing my arachnophobia. Will I hold a tarantula the next time I find myself in the Edinburgh Butterfly Farm? No. I've a good excuse. Far too clumsy. Would hate to drop it, because this could have an undesirable effect on my karma. Imagine being dropped from fifty feet up by a spider the height of the Eiffel Tower?

It's My Work!

'Torture? Bullying? What the f--- are you talking about? We're not North Korea, nor some Latino banana republic! Look, son, we're talking about terrorism here. TERRORISM! So we don't pussyfoot around. It's our work! Get it?'

Every image he created with his camera was, for Kamal Bukvic, like a newborn baby. His child. His creation.

He knew everything there was to be known about cameras. His work was selling cameras, but his passion was photography and the images that he produced with his cameras, of which he had a substantial number. Different cameras for different purposes. Portraiture, weddings, landscapes, wildlife. Into all types of photography, as a free-lance professional, he had built up a vast portfolio, but his heart was in capturing 'real people with his lens'. His term for street photography. For Kamal this was real work, and he loved it.

Kamal had nothing in his life to distract him. No family. The orphaned son of East European immigrants, his childhood had been spent as a loner in an orphanage. Brilliant, but alone. Media studies at university, then, with a degree in the bag, a diploma course in photography which, until then, he had only thought of as a hobby. But the hobby soon became his work, his life, his reason for existing. There were no lasting girlfriends. No time for emotional involvement. Only work. Photography. Creating his 'children', as he called his photographic images, alone.

It's easy to understand how the elderly woman, in good faith, mistook Kamal's appearance and behaviour one Monday morning in Mayfair, London, England. Kamal

148

cared not a jot about how he looked, or what the public thought of his antics behind a camera, but to many the scruffy, dark-complexioned, foreign-looking man photographing nothing in particular, only a street away from the American Embassy, might have seemed more than a little suspicious. Why should anyone in their right mind want to photograph such things as a lamppost and why take the same shot over and over again? A little to the right, up a fraction, then from close to the ground. Needless to say, Kamal was a perfectionist, like all true photographers, but your average man in the street would know nothing of such things. And for every image he took, there was so much he could always improve on. The angle of the shot, the aperture, the exposure, the shadows— shadows were so important—and Kamal was obsessive about attention to detail. Why not? It was his work, after all.

'Questions? Why? It's our job to protect people from terrorists. That's all. Those whom we catch deserve what's coming to them. F------ deserve it! What do you mean, 'brutal methods'? A bomb going off in the street, killing innocent people. Is that brutal or is it brutal?'

The elegantly dressed, well-spoken lady who observed Kamal from the other side of the street was commended by the police for reporting a man of foreign appearance taking undue interest in buildings and people that Monday morning in Mayfair, so close to the American embassy. How was she to know he was a professional photographer? But when, moments later, there were reports of a huge explosion just a minute's walk from where the lady had seen Kamal behaving so suspiciously, what else could they have done other than to rush to the scene with an anti-terrorism squad of eight heavies to catch the bastard and bring him in. His guilt was confirmed, as far as they were concerned, when examination of security camera footage showed Kamal, just before the blast, acting exactly as the good lady had described, in the street where the bomb went off.

A police van screeched round the corner and drew up yards away from Kamal. He already felt jittery after his focus had been fractured by an enormous bang that shook the pavement he stood on. Unaware, initially, that this was a bomb, the screams and the sickening smell, began to make him wonder.

The rear doors of the van swung open. Out leapt two, four... no, *eight* armed officers in black flack. Kamal was so taken by surprise when they pinned him against the railings that all he could do was to shout, "Jesus Christ, what the f--- are you buggers doing?" as he kicked and struggled. Eight against one. He was soon overpowered, and the muzzle of a gun pressed into his right temple made him want to throw up.

"Foreign, all right," said a red-faced Cockney officer into his mobile phone, clearly mistaking Kamal's Brummie accent for something dangerously Middle Eastern. "Anyway, we've got the bugger, and we're bringing him in, Charlie."

Kamal yelled abuse when they snatched his Nikon D2X from him. Two thousand pounds worth of top of the range digital equipment. But worse than this was the thought of losing all those images. His 'children' so lovingly conceived, coaxed and extracted from the dull grey streets of inner London. He 'f-----' and 'c-----' like crazy as they pulled and pushed him into the back of the police van. Kamal hadn't a clue why they were doing this. Only that these armed thugs were arresting him under the Prevention of Terrorism Act, as a red-faced brute had informed him. No explanation was given to link the loud bang with Kamal and his photographic work. Despite an outpouring of threats and expletives, inside, Kamal felt only bewilderment and blind fear. No... sheer terror.

'It's our job to keep terror off the streets. So that you lot can sleep easy at nights, go to your offices, do your shopping, make love at night, without the constant fear of being blown to buggery. Think of that, did you? Doing our job, and we know what to do. It's all about training, you see. Training, and, well, initiative, I guess. Enjoy our work? We can't all have that kind of luxury, chum.'

He was one of the 'best young photographers in London' he had been told. Many times. And boy, did he know about photography, about his work! So what the f---- was he doing in the back of this armed police response van being rushed to God knows where on some crazy, trumped-up charge? And things became no clearer, two hours later, in that Special Unit interrogation room somewhere in the back and beyond. Just a different set of thugs digging terror into him.

"Why did you do it? Who are your contacts? Come on, come on! We're just wasting time here. Be a lot easier for you if you just tell us all, son. Come clean. Your religion is it, blowing people up?"

They showed Kamal photographs and images. Him, a man of images! And the images made him retch, for they showed blown-apart bits of people, fragments of lost lives reduced to charred hunks of human flesh, scorched hair,

151

crispy, burnt skin and legless feet with bones sticking out. "Why are you showing me all this crap?" he wept. The pointless swear words had left him. Besides, he'd used them all up. His anger—and he was a guy who so easily flipped—had been peeled away by the constant, unending barrage of questions, and all that remained was terror.

"Why? Because this is what you did to those poor innocent people. This is all that's left of their lives. Proud, are you?"

They showed him the hand of a little girl, her tiny, charred fingers still gripping the ear of a blackened teddy bear. He leant sideways and vomited over the floor.

"Didn't think of her, did you?"

But the image only fuelled his anger. He kept on telling them, over and over again:

"I'm a photographer. It's my bloody work! I was building up a street photography portfolio for an exhibition. That's what I was doing there. Bloody working! What do you mean, you got a tip off? I knew nothing about that bomb. You're crazy, the lot of you. F--- you!"

After five hours of relentless interrogation, they took him down to a cell and locked him up. He was given food and water. Just a little. Then they brought him back up to that soulless room and started all over again. More intensely, for they had found out so very little about their 'man'.

Seemed he was a bit of a loner, and probably worked in isolation, they thought, not part of a cell, but there had to be contacts, and, by golly, they would get it out of him, whatever it took.

Whatever…

'Methods? What methods? I told you, it's our work, our job, and we're bloody good at it. You don't question the bus driver about his 'methods' every time you get on a number 62 bus, do you? Or a doctor trying to treat your cancer, or a teacher trying to teach your kids? So what's all this crap about questioning our methods? We do what we have to do so that no more little girls end up as barbecued stumps of arms with bits of charcoaled coat sleeve hanging off them. Get the message?'

Night followed day, followed night, followed day. Questions, questions, questions. Endless, stupid, repetitive bloody questions. Always the same simple answer:

"It's my work. I'm a photographer."

Sleep deprivation. Constant, humming sounds were piped into his cell. 'Faulty wiring,' they lied. "This ain't the Ritz, mate!" was all he got when he complained. Then there was the blowing hot and cold. One minute friendly and sympathetic, then a mental whack cranking the fear up to an even higher setting. Physical abuse? No, he couldn't say that. Just a little duffing up in the street before being bundled into the police van.

"Just getting on with my work," he repeatedly said.

"Like buggery! Some work, blowing up little girls!" came the reply, over and over and over.

Interminable days passed. He was allowed to see no one else. This was in the Prevention of Terrorism Act, they explained.

"No cushy-jobbed lawyers for you, young man," they said. "Not yet! Just come clean! Those contacts! Before any of you lot strikes again, f--- you!"

But he *had* come clean. Totally clean. He was only

153

carrying out his work, that Monday morning, by capturing images in the streets.

Two weeks, they took, puzzling over those images on his camera card. Those little masterpieces of light and shade, of shadowy street shapes, of passing people lost in thought or lively conversation. People! The very essence of life for the young photographer, as he balanced them with inanimate cars, metal railings, lampposts, buildings. People! He loved people. How on earth could they believe he was capable of blowing them up—little girls or old men—with bombs?

They could make no sense of those images, despite days on end using complex computer programmes to look for matches, patterns, links with terrorist targets and activities. Links? That's what they wanted to find. Before another bomb went off. Before there were further casualties, for sure as God made bananas that turn yellow and pigs that squeal, there would be more bombs, more people blown up. And then the public would complain that they weren't doing their job. Like f--- they would!

'So imagine this. You're on your way to work. Tube... bus, makes no difference, for you work anywhere and everywhere. You're thinking about that report you never finished, the pay rise that never rose, then... BOOM! If you're extremely lucky, you're on your way to hospital, ambulance siren blaring, and you're looking down, puzzled, at those bloodied stumps of meat and shattered bone that only fifteen minutes earlier were legs taking you to work, and you say, "how can this happen to me? Who's supposed to be protecting me from all of this?" And now you just go on and on about our 'methods'!'

They found nothing whatsoever to incriminate Kamal. No hard evidence. But they all knew that he was guilty. There was no one else. No other leads. They changed tactic. He was proving too tough for them, despite days on end without uninterrupted sleep, and ceaseless games of mental meltdown, he admitted nothing, gave them not one inch to play with. So they sent 'baby-faced' Dave to his cell to 'befriend' the man. No one could resist being open with Dave. He was that sort of a guy. 'Everyman's friend' some called him. Without asking a single question, Dave would get him to talk.

'Okay, so we got it wrong. Actor forgets his lines, circus juggler drops a plate, accountant makes a mistake with a list of figures, but you don't f------ crucify them, do you? Dave seemed our best bet at the time. And how did we know that creep with a funny accent might have been clean? After all, a respectable member of the public had fingered him. Okay, just one little lady, but she was well-dressed and well-spoken, and there was that footage on the security camera. Come on, don't try to tell me I was doing anything other than a day's work in the life of an anti-terrorist officer.'

Kamal was always suspicious of baby-faced men. It came from watching too many bad Hollywood movies in the orphanage. For them to start invading his only surviving private space, his prison cell, was bad enough, but to send him 'friendship' in the guise of 'baby-faced Dave' was the last straw. This Dave person even had the audacity to sit right next to Kamal, on his bed, put a comforting arm across his shoulders, and tell him he would do anything to get him out of this predicament and back to freedom. Kamal shrank from the false camaraderie. He got up and sat on the chair opposite the bed whilst inwardly seething in silence.

Fake-friend Dave embodied Kamal's anger and his hatred of the system. He had no friends, no family. Only work and his 'children'. His beloved images. He knew this, and they should have known it by then, and now, as a final insult, they were sending in baby-faced Dave as if to mock him since they could find nothing concrete to link him with the bombing. Dave tried, indirectly, to get him to talk by going on about his own life and thoughts, as though this could mean something to the young photographer from Birmingham with the funny name. Kamal felt himself slip towards boiling point. His anger swelled and he burst. What it was that made him finally flip is irrelevant. Perhaps a small remark, an insinuation. Whatever, it happened. Kamal so completely lost control, and he was so quick (street photographers have to be), that nothing could have prevented the outcome. And, of course, there it all was. Caught on camera. How ironic! Cameras were his work, his love, his life... and now his undoing.

Kamal sprang forward and gripped baby-faced Dave by the throat. By God, that small shrimp of a man with a funny name turned out to have superhuman strength. Dave, a far larger man, was seen to flail his arms, kick his legs, but the small photographer from Birmingham gripped, pressed and twisted the other man's head and neck until there seemed to be a kind of snap. Yes, they played that sequence over and over again. There was definitely a noticeable snap as Dave's head went back too far. They sat together, open-mouthed, watching the screen.

Dave went limp and flopped sideways. Kamal stepped back and gave the security camera a wild animal glance. Baby-faced Dave made a gurgling noise, his last, then slumped to the ground. They knew he was dead before a prison guard burst into the cell.

From then on it was a different set of officers. The murder squad. Kamal was taken to another jail in another police van. Nothing further was said about the original charge under the Prevention of Terrorism Act, for nothing in the way of hard evidence had been found. And this is how it appeared in the newspapers the following morning:

'A twenty-eight-year-old man, Kamal Bukvic, has been charged with the murder of a special investigations officer whilst being held under the Prevention of Terrorism Act in connection with the recent London bombing. The officer's name is being withheld for security reasons, and the man is expected to appear before a magistrates court within the next few days. Meanwhile he has been transferred to a high security prison outside the capital.'

The journalists were just doing their job. Reporting what they had been told. And Kamal? Well, he finally had a lawyer who was most encouraging. He was certain he could get the charge reduced from murder to manslaughter and was quite excited about the challenge facing him to achieve this. He was good at his work and kept telling Kamal this to reassure him.

"It's my work!" he proudly told the young man with the Brummie accent but failed to understand why Kamal never seemed to pay him any attention.

"Don't you think it's really great news that they have not one shred of real evidence against you for the original terrorism charge? Just think! Only ten years for manslaughter as a result of killing under duress? Released in eight years for good behaviour... perhaps?"

But Kamal knew he could never do 'good behaviour'. It wasn't in his genetic makeup. Whilst his lawyer prattled on as lawyers do (it's their work), Kamal thought only of a life that might have been. Contracts for magazines and advertising companies, exhibitions, international acclaim. He had hoped to write a book about street photography, about a life that was his work, his 'children'... himself. And now? Bare prison walls.

'So, maybe we made a mistake! Happens all the time in other lines of work. But what about that stuff we found on his computer? Can't say too much. Still classified information... but...?'

The hard-faced chief of the special interrogation unit leaned towards me across his desk, arms folded, as I listened.

"We found out that he spent time in Afghanistan and in Pakistan. Can't ignore that, can we? Coincidence, eh? I don't think so!"

"He did have family in both countries," was my response.

He switched off the digital recorder and thanked me. If only I could get another interview with Kamal Bukvic, I thought. Find a way to crack *his* shell. If only...

'Often, I wonder how people can truly say, 'Oh, I just love my work!' I don't. Most of the time it frustrates me. After all, how can I ever find the truth that you lot seek? Still, I try my best and I do work hard. Okay, sometimes I get it wrong, but...'

(Inspired by a press article concerning a photographer who 'looked foreign' according to a member of the public and was apprehended by eight anti-terrorism officers in the Docklands area of London because his behaviour was 'suspicious'.)

Panty Lines

"Sorry, old man, but it's been a hard week. Well, perhaps not hard enough for you! Sorry... joke! But, what with my mother coming last weekend, and all that palaver at work, it's just been just one thing after another. Too much! Anyway, I'll make it up to you this weekend. I promise. It's Saturday today, and what a great day for it!"

Mike stretched out, panda-like, on the top of his bed, clutching a cheese straw and gazed out of his bedroom window at the cloudless, azure sky shimmering above the Golders Green rooftops. He had, of course, been addressing his penis.

Thirty-five and still single. This did have *one* drawback. It meant that Mike was constantly seeking employment for 'Dick', as he called his penis. Mike was not into monogamous relationships. Why, he would argue to himself, should he, the world's greatest lover, be wasted on just one woman? That would be most unfair to the female sex in general and would certainly not suit his lifestyle.

But more than a week without sex was too long, and he simply had to give Dick what he needed so badly that very day. Mike rolled over and reached for his book of 'important telephone numbers' from the bedside cabinet. He flicked through the pages. Nothing to his liking under 'A'. Not on a glorious day like this, but what about 'B'? Brenda? It must have been weeks since he last slept with Brenda. What a figure that girl had. Pretty face too. Dick began to get excited. There was a downside with Brenda, but he was sure he would cope with that. And she was always better on sunny days.

"Okay, old man. Just hang in there... so to speak. Let *me* do the talking. Why do *I* always have to do the difficult stuff, eh, whilst you just enjoy the fun times?"

The phone rang three times before a soft, female voice answered. Mike gave Dick a thumbs up.

"Hi, Bru! Mike here. How *are* you? Sorry it's been so long, but really, I've been *that* busy. Look..."

A string of verbal abuse cut, like a butcher's knife, into Mike's bumbling soliloquy.

"Oh, Bru... you really do sound as though you need a little cheering up. Look..."

More angry words.

"What's that? The line's not too good. 'The cat's lost her sight', you say? I'm—"

The phone babbled, then went silent.

"Oh, sorry! The cat's not right. Vet?"

Loud, unhappy sounds from the phone.

"No need to shout, Bru. *My* fault? Why *my* fault?"

Serious accusations emerged from the phone.

"I *kicked* her? Oh Bru, surely...?"

Fury gushed from the other end of the line.

"Well, I didn't know she always slept across the bathroom door, did I?"

Mike held the phone away from his ear whilst it disgorged more high-pitched babble. Suddenly, the phone went quiet.

"No, I did *not* know that was her special pink mat."

Babble, babble.

"Of course I care about her, Bru. And I *do* know her name. It's...well, you know, it's... it's just there... Erm.. Of course! I've got it. It's Champagne."

A scream!

161

"What? The line's bad. 'Bubbles'? That's what I said. Champagne's short for 'bubbles'. Look, Bru, how about…?"

Sobs.

"What's that? Mummy's nettles are worthless? Not sure what…"

Loud yells emerged from the phone.

"Please don't shout! Mummy's kettle's not working? Fine, Bru, I'm great at fixing kettles. Do it all the time. Look…"

Sobs.

"Oh! Bru darling, you don't have a peabrain! It's just…"

"Migraine, not pea brain?"

Sobs got louder.

"Sorry! I'm giving you a migraine? Why, Bru?"

After another ten minutes of this Dick lost interest, so Mike put down the phone mid-flow from Brenda.

"Sorry, Dick," he said apologetically, "but Brenda's not having a very good day. Look, I think we should go out. Go a-hunting. Like last month. Remember those two Japanese girls?"

Dick came to life at the mention of the Japanese girls.

"Never seen you get so worked up! That's what we'll do. Take the tube to Marble Arch. Good hunting ground."

Mike spent a while choosing the right clothes. He was very fastidious about his appearance. Felt it was really important for making new conquests. When he was finally ready, he looked appreciatively at himself in the full-length mirror on the door. What a fine alpha-male figure he saw standing there grinning back at him.

He and Dick headed for the tube station. Those Japanese girls were quite something, he recalled as he sat on the tube train. What a pity they hadn't been able to spend the whole night with him. For reasons he was completely unable to comprehend, it seemed that their one week tour of Europe *had* to include a day at Loch Ness. The girls' minimal command of English had been no problem in bed, but when he tried to dissuade them from taking that flight up to Inverness early the following morning, he wished they had taught him Japanese at school instead of French. He told them that all they would see would be lots of mist, a few sheep, a ruined castle or two and, if they were *really* lucky, some old fart dressed in a kilt, but his attempts to dissuade them proved fruitless. The Japanese girls merely giggled to each other, coyly covering their pretty little mouths.

"Look," Mike said to them, "I'll buy each of you a cuddly little green Nessie off the internet and send them to you in Japan if you spend the whole night with me!"

"Ah so! Nessie!" the little one had replied, covering her mouth again as she laughed.

When Mike arrived at Marble Arch, he was faced with a dilemma. Oxford Street was teeming with shoppers, and many of these were gorgeous young women in light summery clothes. He had no doubt that some of these ladies would give anything to be swept of their feet by the lover of their dreams... by the one and only Michael Dibble. For a few moments, Mike feasted his eyes upon all that female beauty as he stood, indecisive, at the station entrance. Here, in Oxford Street, or maybe Hyde Park, where he met the Japanese girls, he wondered?

It was Dick who made the decision for him. From behind him, a blonde woman with exquisitely curvaceous legs exited the station and headed off up Oxford Street. Mike hadn't seen her face, but from what he *could* see she

163

was a real stunner. She wore a very short blue mini-skirt that covered her shapely bottom so tightly that her panty line was clearly visible, and, as she tripped along in her blue, high-heeled shoes, this moved up and down in a way that drove Dick to distraction. The woman's broad hips were accentuated by her delightfully narrow waist. Her pale blue bra straps showed through her wonderfully thin, white summer blouse. Her shiny, shoulder-length blond hair bobbed in rhythm with the playful movements of her panty line as she walked towards Selfridges with a determination that hinted at sheer heaven in bed.

Mike swivelled like a compass needle responding to the magnetic pole. He, too, headed off in the direction of Selfridges, his eyes glued to the playful ups and downs of the panty line decorating the woman's blue-skirted bottom.

"I won't let you down this time," Mike whispered to Dick as he dodged the shoppers in his attempts to keep up with the woman. She walked surprisingly quickly. "Means she'll be quick to respond to you, Dick, old fellow," he reckoned. And in Mike's mind he went through the various possible opening gambits, all of which had worked in the past. The faked recognition, followed by:

"But I'm *sure* we met... you know, at what's-her-name's place." Or the accidental bump, followed by a long and over-profuse apology, until the recipient of the bump would laughingly say, "Oh it's nothing, really, but are *you* okay?" Alternatively there was the asking for directions to New Bond Street, after which, "...You see, I have to buy a nice gift for my little sister's twenty-first, but I'm so green about this sort of thing! Would hate to get something she doesn't like." Mike knew that for whichever scenario he chose, timing was critical.

He saw the woman disappear into Selfridges. He ran to catch up and darted through the doorway in the wake of a startled customer whom he almost knocked over.

"It's okay, old man, just calm down," he muttered to Dick as he spied the woman in the blue miniskirt move swiftly through the cosmetics and past the stockings. Mike hurried off in her direction.

"She *would* look great in stockings, Dick. I do agree with you. Oh damn! She's moved on to the handbags. Oops, there she goes, up the escalator."

Mike still had not managed to catch a glimpse of the young woman's face, but somehow he knew she would look like a Botticelli angel. He ran in bursts to catch up with her. If only she would slow down or stop for a second, he thought, but she kept going with a sort of urgency and an almost unnatural determination. Mike stepped onto the bottom of the escalator just as the woman in the blue miniskirt disappeared from view at the top of it. When he reached the top, he caught sight of her hurrying past the skirts, blouses and pretty dresses. *A hat perhaps,* he hoped, as she approached the hats. No, she moved on past the hats. Suddenly he realised she must be heading directly for the shoes. Of course... with legs like that! He should have known. Beautiful women love beautiful shoes.

The woman in the blue miniskirt came to a halt, as he predicted, in the shoe department. Dick became *very* excited. Row upon row of beautiful shoes, high-heeled, low-heeled, no-heeled. Plenty for the young woman to choose from whilst he formulated a strategy. He watched her from behind as she looked at shoe after shoe, picking up, examining, looking at her feet, putting down. Mike decided. He would try fake recognition. Then it would all

165

fall into place. He was supremely confident, and Dick had already gone into a state of penile ecstasy thinking about his next little adventure. Mike had already obtained a tantalising side view glimpse of her fabulous figure, with her face still annoyingly turned the wrong way, but that glimpse was enough to urge him forwards to make the necessary move. Her shapely breasts and the curves of her bottom were sending Dick into overdrive. The woman was examining a silver-tipped shoe, turning it this way and that, when Mike tapped her on the shoulder.

"Why, hello there! I..." began Mike, before she had a chance to turn around. When she did, she looked him straight in the eye.

He reeled backwards from shock, and, for a few moments, stood there, numbed. His mouth remained open, frozen around a word that never came out. Dick flopped down like an empty, miniature Christmas stocking. The young woman, whose teasing panty line had fired both Mike's and Dick's imagination, had a face so indescribably hideous that it was *way* uglier to behold than the back view of her heavenly body had been beautiful. The thick, shapeless lips and irregularly-protruding, lipstick-stained teeth were bad enough, but it was the lifeless, stone-grey eyes that filled Mike with horror. These, and those awful cheeks contoured by hollows and bumps in all the wrong places, topographical irregularities accentuated by the woman's thick, heavy make-up. Her perfume, strong enough to mask the smell of a rotting corpse, was so pungent that Mike felt physically sick.

"Oh, I'm s-s-sorry," he stuttered, "I've made a m-m-mistake."

Rediscovering the power of movement in his legs, he

backed away. He was just about to turn and flee when the woman's face lit up as though in instant recognition. She spoke with a surprisingly normal-sounding voice.

"No," she said, "no mistake. So good to see you again. How *are* you?" Even her voice was as hard as concrete, and Mike could not believe his ears.

"No... no... I... well... really, I've m-m-m-made a mistake."

"No you *haven't*," insisted the woman. "You remember, don't you? At... oh, you know, at thing-a-me-bob's place. Last year? It's really great to see you again, darling. What a time we had together! Look, now that we've met up again, how about—?"

Mike turned and took off like a frightened rabbit. It was that terrifying smile of hers. He could not bear to look at it for another second. He even attempted to run down the ascending escalator in his confusion. Bumping into surprised shoppers, he rapidly retraced his steps, out of the store, until he reached Oxford Street where he paused to catch his breath.

"Phew, that was a close one, Dick." Mike whispered to his traumatized penis.

He wondered what to do next. Another go with the shoppers, or head off for Hyde Park? Maybe the park. At least he'd get a proper look, first, of the face of any woman he might think about approaching in the park. Before setting off, he just happened to glance over his shoulder. Briefly. To his horror, there she was. Right behind him. The woman in the blue miniskirt. With her crocodile smile. She waved as soon as she saw him turn around, again displaying a mouthful of horror-movie teeth. She ran towards him in rapid little high-heeled steps.

Mike shot off like a released greyhound in the

direction of Marble Arch Station. He cared not about people who got in his way. A few of these toppled over as he tried to reach the station entrance by the fastest and the shortest route possible. He simply *had* to get away from that woman. He could not bear the thought of being the recipient of yet another smile from her, let alone what was clearly on *her* mind. Dick would just have to wait as far as that other matter was concerned. This was all *his* fault, anyway.

Giggling teenagers, smart, middle-aged women and their bag-carrying male partners were scattered asunder in Mike's desperate flight to reach the underground where he knew he could disappear. Twice, Mike turned around, and each time she was there, not twenty paces behind him, tripping along in hurried little steps with a dangerous determination. Mike darted into the station taking the stairs two at a time. Fortunately, he had an all-day ticket, which he immediately showed the machine. He slipped through and ran to the escalator which he descended as rapidly as possible. At the bottom, he looked back up. He could scarcely believe it. There she was, the woman in the blue miniskirt, about halfway down, and again waving at him.

"Shit!" he exclaimed, loudly.

He rushed onto the platform, knowing that the woman was now aware of his direction of travel. Thankfully, the platform was crowded, and a train was just coming into the station. Momentarily, he hid behind a group of large West Indians oblivious of Mike's serious game of hide-and-seek. As the train doors opened, he slunk sideways into the carriage, crabwise, drawing puzzled looks from other passengers. Mike breathed a sigh of relief and calmed down after moving along to the

168

safety of the far end of the carriage. In his mind he could still see that face. He shuddered. He thanked God for his escape, but...

He could not believe his bad luck. Nothing like this had ever happened before. In his book, a beautiful female body was always blessed with a beautiful female face. He simply did not understand.

He changed onto the Northern Line at Tottenham Court Road. Here, he found himself repeatedly looking over his shoulder. Just to be certain. He thought he might have glimpsed a woman in a blue mini-skirt, half-hidden from view before reaching the platform, but did not see her again and reassured Dick and himself that he must have been mistaken. The Golders Green train was half-empty. He slumped onto a seat and tried to put the events of the previous forty minutes behind him.

As the train slowed into Golders Green station, Mike felt that he and Dick were slowly returning to normal.

"We'll go home, then decide what to do," he told Dick.

As he alighted from the train, he promised his unused member that he would have another look through that telephone book back home. Dick failed to respond, for at that very moment a woman in a blue miniskirt got off from the adjacent carriage. She waved at him, sporting gravestone teeth through that ghastly smile.

"Oh my God!" Mike exclaimed.

Driven by runaway panic, he made the exit in lightning time, repeatedly muttering, "How on earth... how on earth?" He ran along Golders Green Road, not daring to look back. At last he reached his home, fumbled for the key, opened the front door and slammed it shut behind him.

"High heels," he reassured himself. "She cannot

possibly have kept up with me in those high heels." Nevertheless, he bolted the door, as a precaution, before going upstairs to his bedroom where he collapsed on top of the bed. For a while he lay there, completely still. The solitude and the silence were a welcome relief. He glanced with disinterest at the phone and at the telephone book, both of which lay where he had left them earlier that morning.

"*Your* bloody fault," he accused Dick. "Next time—" But Mike never finished his sentence. The doorbell rang. Loudly and for a long time. First, he sprang upright, startled. With the second ring he felt a wave of nausea. The third ring seemed even louder, and it just went on and on and on. Persistence added to insistence. There was a determination in that ring that he knew only too well and the nausea was replaced by terror.

Pink Crab

A large, pink crab scuttled out of the pool and came to a standstill. Beady eyes on stalks searched the warm sand, independently, until fixing on a grumpy-looking, curly brown-haired boy seated upon a rock clutching a stick. He was poking irritably at popping seaweed whilst his big sister enjoyed herself, with their dad, in the sea. Earlier, he had sunk into a bad mood because they said he shouldn't go in the water because of his ears.

"Never heard of anything so daft!" he muttered angrily as the seaweed went pop... pop... pop!

Why having an infection in the ears should prevent him from swimming in the sea had not been properly explained, so he decided to remain crabby for the rest of the afternoon.

"Hey, dude!" he said on spotting the crab. "You on the run from crab catchers, then?"

Sean did not expect an answer, and nearly fell off the rock when he got one.

"Na! Looking for a boy called Sean," the crab replied.

Sean pinched himself. It hurt, so he knew he was awake. He peered around, expecting to see a ventriloquist trying to make fun of him, but the closest human was half a football pitch away. A girl in a two-piece, stretched out on her back with a stripy blue blouse covering her face. She reminded Sean of a dead body in one of the boring, yawn-a-minute TV crime flicks to which his dad sat glued, but he knew for sure she was not a long-distance ventriloquist.

"Crabs don't talk," he said to those round eyes on stalks staring up at him.

"Do!" answered the crab. "I'm living proof!"

"Nope! They don't!" insisted the boy. "Crabs most definitely cannot talk!"

"What am I doing then?"

"Standing on the sand. You're just a crab standing on the sand. That's all."

"No! The other thing. What else am I doing?" The crab sounded annoyed.

"Looking at me. With silly little eyes."

Sean had never before had the opportunity to 'get up a crab's nose', if, indeed, crabs had noses, so, feeling bad-tempered, he decided to make the most of the opportunity.

"No! What am I doing with my mouth? The sound coming out of it. What d'you call it?"

"Crab burps!" This was the rudest thing Sean could think of on the spur of the moment. "Like crab sticks, only burpy!"

The crab changed tack. He decided to enjoy the encounter. At the very least, he might stop the boy poking at, and popping, the seaweed.

"Oh forget it!" said the crab. "Have you by any chance seen a boy called Sean? I need to know."

Sean stopped poking the seaweed and squinted at the crab. It was large, for a crab, with scary-looking pincers, but his stick was scarier. At least, for a crab. He tightened his grip on it.

"Yes!" he replied.

"Yes what?"

"Don't need a 'what' with yes. Like, 'Yes, I've seen a boy called Sean.' At school. So now I've answered your question you can just crawl back under that rock before the crab catchers get to you."

"But you don't understand. I *must* find him."

"Why?" Sean began to feel intrigued but remained suspicious of the crustacean. What might it do if he were to admit to being Sean? Pinch off his toes?

"Can't say," answered the crab.

Hmm! thought Sean. *Two can play at this game.*

"My mum's told me about the likes of you," he said.

"Your mum?" The crab sounded ruffled.

Got him! thought Sean.

"Yeah," persisted the boy. "Crabs who go around annoying kids. Causing trouble, like!"

"Honest," objected the crab, "I really don't mean to cause trouble. Just have to find this boy called Sean."

"Tell me why, then."

"Can't do that. Against the rules."

Rules? Sean hated rules. Like not swimming because of infected ears. He had a good mind to send his doctor a letter pointing out how those rules had ruined his weekend by the sea. Did the stupid man believe his ears might drop off in the water just because they were infected? On second thoughts, he reckoned, perhaps he should tell his mum instead. Besides, he did not have enough money for a stamp.

Sean's mum was at the far end of the beach seated in a deckchair with a woman's magazine across her face. A sort of sunshade. Like the stripy blouse on the girl who wasn't a ventriloquist.

"Rules are stupid!" Sean said with conviction. "Don't trust anyone who sticks to rules."

"Can't change them!" insisted the crab. "Rules say I am only allowed to tell this boy called Sean."

173

Sean began to wonder what it was he should be told by a crab. He thought about those little crabs he might have annoyed with his stick because of his anger. Perhaps they were related to this talking brute with big pincers. Sean reckoned these were even larger than his sister's feet. He could lose all his toes to pincers like those. He waggled his toes, causing ripples to spread out across the still pool.

"Any relatives?" he asked the crab.

"Dunno," replied the crab. "Anyway, they only mentioned a boy called Sean. Not his relatives."

"No. You. Any little crabs of your own? Son and daughter crabs, like?"

"Of course! What's the point of being a crab who doesn't produce little crabs?"

Sean tried to think of a good answer. The only one that appeared in his brain was another, more obvious, question. 'What's the point of being a crab at all?' Glancing at those pincers again, then his toes, he decided against posing the question.

"Dunno!" he replied. "Do little crabs talk, by any chance? Did *they* say anything to you about the boy called Sean?" He was wondering whether he might have wiped out a few baby crabs by poking at the seaweed.

"Can't say! Lips are sealed!"

"Crabs don't have lips," observed Sean.

"Do!" came the response. The funny looking bits beneath the crab's stalked eyes made a weird, curly shape, but Sean wasn't convinced they could be called lips.

"Look," the boy began, "why don't you ask that 'body' over there on the sand? See if she knows a Sean!" Sean would have preferred for her to get her bottom pinched by those pincers than for him to lose his toes to them.

"Great idea!" responded the crustacean. "They told me to keep trying till I find him. Thanks for your help whoever you are."

The crab scuttled sideways across the sand. Sean relaxed his grip on the stick and went back to popping seaweed. Periodically, he glanced up to see how the crab was getting on with the crime scene body. He grinned when the crab tapped at the girl's leg. Wondering what her face was like, he watched as she pulled away the striped blouse. No longer just a body, the girl sat up. Sean knew he was too young to think of girls as pretty, but he recognised some were nicer to look at than others. His big sister was most definitely not one of those, but the girl who was no longer a body, was. Older than he'd imagined, too. She had well-formed boobs.

She smiled sweetly at the crab, nodded then stood up, dusting the sand off her legs. She walked across the beach towards the rocks between where he sat and the sea, and the crab scuttled sideways after her. A fair-haired boy, about his age, appeared from behind a large rock and ran towards her. A brother? 'Why couldn't *his* sister look like that?' Sean asked himself.

Fate, he decided. He had read about fate, and reckoned that fate was now on his side having narrowly escaped being de-toed. Should he warn the other boy? Instead, still feeling peeved with his mum and the doctor, he sat and watched and grinned.

'Maybe I'll feel less upset after seeing someone else lose their toes to those pincers!'

The boy and the girl followed the crab back towards him. They halted beside a cluster of rocks just a stone's throw from where he sat.

175

"Wait for this!" Sean muttered to himself. "Bet a whole army of crabs will run out from behind those rocks and remove those kids' toes because I've been annoying little crabs with my stick. The Great Toe Massacre, huh?"

It never happened. The girl and boy knelt on the sand and began to dig away with their hands.

"Dopes! Digging graves for their toes and don't even know it!" Sean mumbled.

He dropped his stick, picked up the seaweed and began popping it between his fingers until interrupted by a loud shriek from the girl. Sean turned to look, assuming he would see her hopping about and clutching a toeless foot. Instead, she and her brother were bent over a box that had been buried in the sand. The boy reached in and removed his hand, showing something to his sister. Sean stood up for a better view. A handful of baby crabs, perhaps?

"Wow, Sean!" the girl exclaimed to his namesake, her brother. "Awesome! We can afford to go on holiday now! Dad'll get a new car and..."

"And you can afford to go to uni, Jenny!" the other Sean said.

The boy's cupped hand was filled with gold coins, a tiny fraction of what clearly remained in the box.

Sean frantically looked around for the pink crab to let him know that the correct Sean was himself, after all, but the creature had vanished. Walking back across the beach, alone, towards his snoozing mum, he thought that if he hadn't been so worked up about not swimming because of his ears then he might have been holding a whole new future for his family in his hands rather than having a head full of anger.

Skylark

Every year, on June the third, he would travel to one of a list of particular places with a very particular purpose in mind. The third of June was the anniversary of his wife's death. He would visit one of those many places they had visited, and enjoyed, together when she was alive. He had done this for fifteen years. For the first few years following her death, perhaps he went in the forlorn hope that she that might magically reappear, but as the years rolled by it simply became an annual routine.

Although fit for his age, his daughter began to feel concerned about the trips. That year he would be seventy-eight, and the thought of him alone and clambering over the cliffs near Seaford, on the South Coast, was too much. She decided to put her foot down.

"I'm coming with you, Dad," she insisted over the phone.

"No! I'll be fine," he objected. "Always go by myself. Just something that I... well... that I *have* to do. Besides, it's a Wednesday. You won't be able to take time of work."

"Will and shall!" his daughter replied. She could be every bit as stubborn as he was. Unhappy with her invasion of his privacy, he struggled to find an excuse to put her off.

"What about the children?"

"Heavens, they're old enough to do without me for a couple of days. Anyway, Dennis will be around. No problem. I'll come down the day before and we can drive over to Seaford together. Stay the night in a B&B, drive back the next day. How about it, Dad?"

He knew he could not argue with his daughter once

her mind was set. Arrangements were made, and, on the second of June they were driving together towards Seaford.

"So, why Seaford, Dad?" she asked. She was driving.

"Well..." he began, "Mum and I went there a few times when we were courting."

She smiled. She found it hard to imagine her white-haired old father courting, although in old photographs she had seen he was certainly a handsome young man.

"Glad it worked," she said.

"What?" he asked, distracted.

"The courting," she replied, turning briefly.

"Yes," he murmured, clearly not taking in what she said. His mind was too full of thoughts about his late wife.

He always became sad in June. On closing his eyes, he could see her there, lying in bed, the light from the window picking out her pale, skeletal face as she looked up at him. She knew she had only a few more days at the most, possibly only hours, and he refused to leave her side. She had fought the cancer so bravely, but there came a time when she seemed to welcome death. It wasn't that she had given up on life; more that she knew she had to move on to the next stage of her existence, whatever form that might take, whether just inanimate molecules or a new life. They waited together, each knowing he would be left behind, but no words were spoken.

Was the annual trip something to do with being left behind? A futile attempt to communicate with her? A private call to someone, somewhere unknown, beyond the grave?

Their daughter had been wonderful. She took time off from teaching to stay with them during her mother's last few weeks. She did everything possible to allow her parents to be alone and together all the time.

He saw, in his wife's eyes, how happy her daughter's presence made her, for mother and daughter had been so very close. There was a bond between them that even he, who loved his wife so dearly, did not fully comprehend, but respected. After her death, during difficult times, he felt sure she was still with him, silent and unseen, and this kept him going, as did the annual trip on the third of June.

His daughter knew that he had gone quiet for a reason, so she drove on in silence. They discovered a pleasant B&B, at the edge of Seaford, where they found rooms for the night. The following morning, when he awoke, his bedroom was illuminated by a shaft of sunlight that cut through a gap between the curtains, streaking his bed cover. He was pleased. It reminded him of when he and his young girlfriend, later his wife, would arise early on a sunny Sunday morning whilst spending a weekend with his parents in Brighton, and decide, in whispered love words, to go for a walk together along the cliffs at Seaford.

He met up with his daughter over breakfast. He was still mute, but his daughter sensed his excitement. They parked the car near the start of the walk up to the headland. It was already warm in the strong sunlight, but there was a pleasant, cooling breeze lifting off the sea. He walked slowly, his daughter always by his side. Not only was he now resigned to her joining him, but he was strangely happy. He began to open up, first telling her stories about his courtship with her mother, anecdotes of events long passed but never forgotten. She listened in silence. She knew there had been something special between her parents, and her father's tales described the events that had helped to cement their fond relationship. She loved to listen and he loved to tell her.

"I think you need a rest, Dad," she remarked on noticing how he had slowed down, stopping every few yards to catch his breath. "We can sit on the grass. It's quite dry."

"I shouldn't walk and talk at that same time. Not at my age," he joked as she laid out a rug on the grassy slope.

"You're doing fine, Dad," she said, after they sat down. "Hungry?"

But he did not reply for at the same moment he heard something that took him back nearly sixty years to when he and his young girlfriend walked, talked and kissed on the very same stretch of clifftop grassland. For a few moments, he held his breath and merely listened. Even the sound of his own breathing seemed to interfere with the magic of it. He squinted into the sun. All he could see was the cloudless, impossibly blue firmament. He remembered it had been the same when he last went there with his girlfriend-come-wife-to-be. They heard a skylark but could not see it. It was as though the sky itself sang, and such a beautiful song. It used to bring tears to his wife's eyes. Tears of happiness. She would say that she was so pleased that she could never see the bird itself when he told her it was a very ordinary and uninteresting looking little thing.

"I don't want to look at anything uninteresting when I can just listen to something so wonderful," she said to him. So they would sit and listen to the song of the skylark and look out to sea.

"Isn't it beautiful?" he said to his daughter.

"Yes," she replied, "I never tire of looking at the sea. Looking at it and smelling the ocean."

"No, the skylark. Don't you think it's lovely? Magical?" He looked up again at the sky.

"What skylark?" she asked puzzled.

He raised his hand. To silence her. "There," he said, lifting his hand towards the sky. "You'll hear it now. Up there somewhere." His hand up high, he craned his head back hoping his eyes might catch a glimpse of that uninteresting little bird. All he saw was an intense blue nothingness. "But you can never see them, the little buggers," he added. "Didn't worry Mum, though. She preferred not to see them."

Ecstatic with joy, he grinned at his daughter. "I'm afraid I still can't hear it, Dad," she said. "There," he whispered. "Listen! It's so clear." They sat in silence for several minutes.

"Isn't it just amazing? A tiny bird like that, and such a sound," he said.

"Sorry Dad, I really can't hear it, but I know what you mean. They say the song of the skylark is one of the most beautiful imaginable. Captured by a poet. Meredith, wasn't it?"

"You honestly don't hear it?"

He seemed disappointed.

"Dad," she began "it's what *you* hear that matters. Remember, it's your special day. You heard a skylark, and I think that is fantastic! Besides, sometimes we only hear what we're meant to hear. Perhaps today only you were meant to hear that skylark." She smiled at him and he saw his wife in that smile. Suddenly, it all became so clear.

Of course! There's no need for her to hear the skylark. Her mother is here, within her. It's taken me all these years to

181

realise. I've been truly happy today for the first time in such a long while, even before I heard that skylark. And it's because I'm here with my daughter. I knew today would be different from all those previous years, and now I know why. How bloody stupid I've been!

"Yes," he said, "I did need to hear the skylark, but I've heard it now. I don't think I'll need any more of these little trips in the future. After all, I am over three quarters of a century."

They chuckled together as they sat looking out to sea.

Tobikomi

(Inspired by a true event)

The man breathed a sigh of relief when the long-awaited train finally drew into Lewes Station. There was no reason to panic but he had a thing about punctuality. A part of his obsessive personality. He was a control freak. Something he could not change. After boarding, and glancing again at his watch, he settled into a seat in a first-class compartment with only one other passenger. It was one of those old-fashioned carriages with individual compartments each with its own door.

Three-forty. He would be home by six and their flight from Heathrow wasn't till eleven. He placed his briefcase on the seat beside him, rather than on the luggage rack, so as to keep an eye on it. Another obsession. Workwise, he was ahead of schedule, as always, and he snuggled into a corner by the window, closed his eyes and tried to doze.

Half awake, David Mason, businessman extraordinaire, was unable to prevent his brilliant mind from being invaded by those travel brochure images of Kenya; of the animals they were sure to see and the mind-boggling vistas. He had been working far too hard and truly needed this break. So did Ann. Her moodiness of late even irritated him. She did not seem the least excited by the prospect of going on holiday, but he felt certain that, once there, she would love it.

After twenty minutes, the train jerked to a halt. He awoke with a start, peered out of the window and frowned, for it wasn't Haywards Heath. They had come to a standstill in the middle of nowhere surrounded by fields dotted with cows with seemingly only one purpose in life:

to chew grass. Living, milk-making machines! The sun was already low and a windbreak of trees, bordering a field, stretched long shadows across green, unripe wheat.

David sat upright and glanced at his watch. He used his mobile to call Ann, but the line was engaged. He questioned the tired-looking, flannel-suited fellow businessman diagonally across from him.

"Why have we stopped? And where the heck are we?"

The man shrugged his shoulders, then explained how they'd been delayed coming into Lewes because of an electrical fault. Perhaps the same fault had happened again, he suggested.

As the minutes ticked by, David started to become anxious. Anxiety did not agree with him. Every time he tried to call Ann the line was engaged. She must have left the goddamn phone off the hook!

Why does she have to be so bloody absent- minded?

He knew he was forever nagging her, but this was only because of her thoughtlessness of which this was a prime example. Maybe, after Africa, he might persuade her to mend her ways. It would make life so much easier for him and, God forbid, he had enough to contend with without coming home every evening to a pile of unwashed dishes.

Like a slowly sinking giant orange, the sun continued to drop down onto the horizon whilst tree shadows lengthened across the field. Another twenty minutes passed before an announcement was given over the intercom. David did not like what he heard:

"We apologise to all our passengers for the delay. There was an accident further up the line and all rolling stock has

come to a halt. I am afraid we don't have further details at present but we will let you know as soon as there is more information. Thank you for your patience."

Stuck out in the middle of bloody nowhere! Accident? A dead deer, perhaps. Surely it doesn't take that long to clear the line.

The man opposite did not seem particularly perplexed as he sat reading *The Financial Times*. David interrupted him:

"Bloody marvellous! Have to catch a plane from Heathrow tonight. Can't they pull their flipping fingers out and do something?"

The man looked sympathetically over his paper at David, raised his eyebrows and shrugged his shoulders.

"Going anywhere nice?" he asked politely.

"Kenya," replied David. "My wife and I. Always wanted to go on one of those Safari trips but the wife was never overly keen. Anyway I got this brochure and it all looks pretty civilised so I somehow managed to persuade her."

He offered the man a lukewarm smile. He was about to expand on the programme he had planned for their holiday when the intercom voice started up again:

"Well, ladies and gentlemen, I do have some more information and thank you again for your patience. We've been told a person jumped in front of an oncoming train at Gatwick Airport and, as I said earlier, all trains in both directions have been halted. They are doing their very best at the scene but as you can imagine there will be a considerable delay and we'll have to wait here until we have clearance to move on. There's a stack of three trains in front

of us. After they are able to move these forward we would hope to get you to Haywards Heath. We do apologise for this delay to our service but I am sure you will understand that it is due to circumstances that are out of our control."

"Out of their control?" David was livid. "How can they just let someone jump in front of a train? Aren't there people employed to prevent that sort of shenanigans? Guards or something?"

The other passenger suggested it might be impossible for station staff to stop members of the public from doing anything stupid.

"You can say that again. *Bloody* stupid!" echoed David. "Selfish, too! Jumping in front of a train and causing havoc for innocent people like us. How on earth am I gonna get home to pick my wife up and get to Heathrow in time?"

"The fast train service from Paddington is pretty good. You should still make it." But the man's reassuring voice only stoked the fire of David's fury.

"Should make it? Should? 'Should' is not good enough! Have you seen the time? Nearly four-fifteen and out in the middle of the bloody Sussex wilderness. It's worse than Africa. Plus my wife has gone and left the damned phone off. Can't get in touch with her. Otherwise I'd have taken the connection from Gatwick to Heathrow and asked her to make her own way to the airport. If she can manage that. Women, ay?"

"Let's hope they'll get us to Haywards Heath soon," the other man said quietly, but his calm manner only irritated David and for a while both remained silent.

Six-thirty... Six-forty... Seven o'clock. No further announcements. David flipped. His deadline had passed.

He was leaving the train.

"Well," he said to his co-passenger, "I'm off. Can't hang around on this bloody train a minute longer. Make my own way, I will!"

Thankfully, it was one of those old-fashioned compartment-carriages with handled doors, probably brought out of well-earned retirement, he reckoned, as they hadn't enough of the newer carriages. Whatever, to the other man's surprise, David opened the door, picked up his briefcase and jumped from the train. He slammed the door and ran back alongside the track until he found a gap in the hedge. From here, he cut diagonally across a field, half-running, half-walking. The cows glanced up with passing interest then got on with keeping the grass cropped. At the far end of the field was a gate over which David clambered. He was angered to see mud on his suit trousers.

Perhaps, if it's not too much bloody trouble for her, Ann will take them to the dry cleaners when we get back from Africa.

Ann? He tried to phone her again. Line still engaged.

"Stupid woman!" he muttered. Across the field, he spotted a clump of trees and houselights.

I'll phone for a taxi from there. Should get to Croydon before eight. Might just make it if Ann has everything ready. Like I told her to. Surely she won't let me down again. If she's not ready, then there's no way we'll make it to Heathrow in time.

Being overweight, by the time David arrived at the cottage he was panting for breath. He rang the bell.

All this running about cannot be doing me any good, he thought. *Ann's bloody fault again... as always! If only she'd not left the flipping phone off.*

He rang the bell a second time.

"Come on, come on," he urged through clenched teeth. "What's keeping you? I know you're in there, whoever you are."

Finally, a scuffling noise from the other side of the door, and bursts of barking, preceded the sound of a catch being released. The door opened and a small, off-white terrier burst out, yapping and jumping up at David. He backed away, lifting up his briefcase.

"Oh, hello," said a bent little, grey-haired lady who smelt of mothballs and wore bottle-bottom spectacles. "Would you like to come in? You must be from the church?"

"No," answered David, keeping an eye on the terrier, "I'm not from the church, but yes, I would like to come in. I wondered if I could use your phone. You see, there was an accident and..."

"Oh, I am sorry. Are you hurt? Please come in. I'll call the doctor."

David eased himself past the dog and spied a telephone on a table just inside the door.

"Look," he said, "you're very kind. I've not had an accident. My train stopped *because* of an accident and I need a taxi to take me home. I wondered if I could use your phone."

Somehow, he managed to smile as he stood in the small hallway holding his case out of reach of the jumpy little animal.

"You've not had an accident?" confirmed the lady. "I'm so pleased. Then I won't need to call for the doctor, will I?"

"No," sighed David, "you won't. But I'd be most

grateful if I could use your phone, please."

"Is it my telephone then?" she queried, looking up at David. "You want to check my telephone?"

"Yes, please. I would be—"

"It's there. I didn't think it needed fixing but you'd know better. Would you like to sit down?"

David shook his head. He focused on the terrier, now busily sniffing his shoes, and remained standing whilst he searched through the Yellow Pages. He held this open at 'taxis' as he dialled a number. Thank heaven, it was answered instantly.

"Quick Link Taxis. Can I help you?"

David explained his plight over the phone, plus the need for a taxi to take him urgently to Croydon where he lived.

"No problem, sir. May I have an address?"

David had no idea where he was.

"Your address?" he asked the lady. "Where are we?"

"Oh, thank you," she said, "you really are kind."

"No," persevered David, his impatience swelling like a puffer fish. "What... is... your... address? Where are we? The name of this house, please."

"Why? Is it important?" asked the lady, clearly puzzled. "We're called Hawthorn Cottage."

David handed her the phone to explain the whereabouts of Hawthorn Cottage.

"They say they'll be here in fifteen minutes. It really is good of you to go to all this trouble," she told him.

"Thank you, too. Look..." David continued to eye the terrier with suspicion. Its interest had travelled upwards from his shoes to his mud-spattered trousers. "I'll wait outside now but let me leave you something for the telephone call." He put a five-pound note beside the telephone then, gingerly stepping over the terrier, opened the front door.

"Well I never!" the lady exclaimed. "They don't usually pay you to fix things."

"Glad to be of service," David said. "Must hurry." The taxi arrived promptly. David checked his watch again. Eight thirty-five. He reckoned that, with luck, he should make Croydon by nine thirty. *I'll be okay,* he repeatedly tried to reassure himself.

The taxi driver was sympathetic. David spilled the full story as the driver took a detour, using back roads, to avoid the M25. He told David that he had already heard about the suicide at Gatwick Airport station on the car radio.

"Terrible thing," he said. "My wife's brother committed suicide three years back and her sister-in-law never got over it. She really suffered. Two young kids. And so hard up now. We've tried to help them out. You know, only the other day the wife said how selfish he was to have done that to her. Lovely girl, her sister-in-law, and lovely kids. But, oh my God, what they've been through! So selfish, doing that to himself." The driver shook his head.

"Absolutely!" agreed David. "I was thinking exactly the same thing myself when I was stuck there on that train fearing my wife and I were going to miss our holiday of a lifetime. How selfish, I thought. Us innocents having to suffer like this."

"And now you've no need to worry. Get you there in time. Guaranteed! Thank goodness for taxis, ay?"

"Yes, thank goodness for taxis," echoed David.

There were several traffic jam hold-ups. David glanced anxiously at his watch every few minutes, but the taxi driver skillfully used his knowledge of all the byroads and suburban streets. It was almost nine o'clock when the taxi turned into his home street. David felt so relieved he could have hugged the taxi driver, and again thought about the holiday. Once there, Ann was sure to like it. How could she fail to enjoy all the things he'd read about in that brochure, including early morning tours in a four-wheel drive, barbecues and a three-day stopover at a beach resort?

The taxi slowed.

"Yes," said David, "that's it. Number thirty-one. White gate."

David had seen the car parked outside the gate from the top of the street.

A police car?

"The cheek of it!" he mumbled. "How dare the police bloody block my drive! The road's empty!"

He paid the taxi driver, adding a generous tip.

"Thank you very much, sir. Hope you enjoy your holiday!"

"Well, you might just have saved my life," joked David, winking at the other man.

"The Japanese call it *tobikomi*, you know."

"What?"

"Suicide by jumping in front of a train. Very popular in Japan, once, I was told by my last passenger. Before I picked you up."

"Hmm!" grunted David. Carrying his briefcase, he approached the white gate. As the taxi drove off, the police car doors opened on both sides. A tall sergeant and a young policewoman emerged, as if choreographed.

"Are you Mr David Trent, sir?" the sergeant asked.

"If this is about my damn partner's embezzling, I spoke to..." David halted mid-sentence. There was something about the expression on the policewoman's face.

"Y-Yes. I am David Trent. Why? Is there anything wrong?"

He looked from one police officer to the other. For a few moments neither said a word. Then the young woman spoke:

"I think we should go inside, sir."

She took David's briefcase and held his elbow. His head felt swimmy as he was being escorted to the door.

"Your key, please, Mr Trent," requested the sergeant.

"No," said David. "Ring the bell. My wife's in. We're going on holiday tonight. Africa. Kenya. One of those safari holidays, you know," he told the policewoman who had not taken her eyes off him.

"Your key, please, sir!" repeated the sergeant.

David, limp, responded like an automaton. He handed over his house key and allowed himself to be helped into the soundless house. The need to sit down became overwhelming as he was ushered into a cold, familiar-yet-different living room. He could smell Ann's perfume but Ann did not appear. The young policewoman sat beside him on the sofa. He knew what was coming but only stared, blankly, ahead.

"I'm afraid we have bad news, Mr Trent. It's about your wife, Ann Trent."

She paused. Tears snail-tracked down David's cheeks.

Please don't say it… Oh Lord, do not say it, was all that went through his mind during the brief eternity of deathly silence that followed.

"There was an accident at Gatwick Airport station this afternoon. Your wife. I'm afraid something terrible has happened." The policewoman paused. "I have to tell you, she was hit by a train. She would have died instantly. They… they think she jumped."

Gatwick? Can't be! It was Heathrow where we were to…

Then he remembered their honeymoon night at a Gatwick Airport hotel before two magical weeks in Corfu, perhaps the last time Ann had been truly happy. The young policewoman kept her arm around David. He turned and hid his face on her shoulder. A pain that he had never before experienced racked his insides. A pain that found no relief from sobbing, the sound of which echoed in the empty house. Beyond the sobs another sound tore at his soul. A terrifying scream cutting into that of a train hurtling towards him.

(In the Netherlands, ten percent of suicides are rail related. Suicide by 'tobikomi', jumping in front of moving things, was once rife in Tokyo, Japan, but has been reduced since some Japanese rail companies took families of suicide victims to court for damages over lost income, and glass barriers have been installed on platforms.)

The Tepee

A tepee appeared one morning in the field at the edge of the town. Old Jock's field. Sergeant MacLean slowed his car, looked at, then puzzled over it. No law had been broken, so he pressed the accelerator pedal and drove on.

By midday, the town was alive with gossip about the tepee.

"What is the world coming to?" remarked Major Findlay-Smith when he bought his daily newspaper at the corner shop. "Invaded by Red Indians, I ask you. Whatever next?" he grumbled.

"Simply awful!" agreed Mrs Fullerton as she poked and prodded the tired-looking vegetables on display in boxes in front of the counter.

By the time the bars had opened, folk talked of nothing else. Only one occupant had emerged from the tepee, and everyone knew that he was up to no good. Even on the day of the tepee's appearance, Mr McLachlan dropped into the police station and demanded Sergeant MacLean evict the town's latest resident. The sergeant shook his head.

"No law has been broken," replied the burly police officer.

"Not yet!" complained an irritated Mr McLachlan before leaving. "And what secrets has he got hidden away in that tent thing of his, I'd like to know?"

Then the thefts began. Someone broke into the newsagent's. Bella's jewellery shop was burgled, plus surrounding housing estates reported multiple robberies over the following two weeks. The tepee-talk became aggressive. Few doubted that the gaunt, young hippie who wore shoulder length hair, and who had set up the tepee, was the culprit. That is, apart from Sergeant MacLean who was told to 'go and arrest that man' so many times that he was barely able to get on with the job of investigating the crimes. He and his two constables worked flat out. One had already had 'the freak' in for fingerprinting. There were no matches on file nor at the burglary scenes.

Then the unthinkable happened. A young woman, who worked at the pharmacy, was assaulted in the park on her way home late one night. She screamed so loudly that her hooded assailant let go and slipped away into the dark. All she could make out were a black balaclava and jeans.

"It was *him*, wasn't it?" they suggested to Aileen. "*He* always wears jeans."

"I don't... I couldn't..." the bewildered girl struggled to reply.

"Well," they asked, "what about the shoes? You'll recognise *them*, won't you? Then we'll 'ave 'im!"

"Honestly, I didn't get a chance to—"

Jimmy MacLean was told to get out there and check the man's shoes to look for matching footprints in the park.

"Why didn't Jimmy think of that? Do we have to do his job for him now?" they complained.

"Porn!" muttered Mr McLachlan. "That's what they'll find if they raid that tent thing. Porn and filth and... and... stolen goods. Those'll be his grubby little secrets."

The following day, women invaded the pharmacy in twos and threes. They decided that the man's jeans would give him away. They told Aileen to make sure Sergeant MacLean got hold of the jeans. Of course she would instantly recognise the jeans.

"I honestly couldn't say..." wept the confused girl.

"Well, we'll tell Jimmy to get hold of the bastard's jeans. So you can confirm he's the beast who attacked you. Then the sergeant can arrest him and lock him up for good."

The men got together. Aileen's father spoke with his friends, they talked to *their* friends and soon some thirty or so men met in the Fox and Hounds. The beer and whisky flowed liberally. Fuelled by alcohol, the tepee-talk and the atmosphere became increasingly agitated. If Sergeant MacLean was not going to do anything about it then they would have to act. They would confront the freak, make him confess then drive him out of town and tear down his tepee.

"And we'll find out his dirty little secrets," a tipsy Mr McLachlan informed the assembled throng.

Thirty plus men met up before work in front of the war memorial. A few children tagged along for fun and to brag about it at school. Dawn had just broken and the light was dim.

*****

Before the loud procession of steel-faced men arrived, the damp, morning air around the tepee had been still and quiet. Inside, a scruffy young man sat on the edge of his camp bed absorbing the silence of the dawn. It was his favourite time of day. A time when at least nature seemed to be at peace if not mankind. He wrote most of his poetry during the early hours of the morning.

When the man heard the commotion of advancing townsmen, he put down his pen, his poem unfinished. Cautiously, he opened the flap of the tepee and stepped outside where he was met by a line of hostile faces. The tension of their anger dispersed the peace of the dawn and he felt troubled, for the air was heavy with hatred. He knew they could never know nor understand why he was there, not with all that hatred, as his kind, Godly eyes searched the hatchet faces for a soul that might listen. But he saw only violence written across those faces and felt only sorrow and compassion whereas *they* felt only anger and revenge.

He spoke:

"Not yet! It's too soon," he said, softly. "My mission is yet unfulfilled."

"Its too bloody late, son," muttered Aileen's father edging forward, oozing menace. The young man repeated his words:

"It *is* too soon. You would never believe me if I tried to explain. Just... please... not yet."

In silence, the townsmen closed in on him. He felt no fear, but he had to act. It *was* too soon, as it had been the last time. Like a deer, he leapt over one of the ropes securing his tepee and took off across the field. Never before had the men seen anyone run so fast. They knew this meant that he was guilty. Guilty as hell, which was where they would send the bastard. They chased after him, like hounds after a quarry. Nothing would prevent them from ridding the town of this monster. The men spread out in a semi-circle, cutting off the man's escape when he reached the far end of the field, and where a steep embankment overlooked the bypass. At this time of day, the bypass was alive with traffic. The man turned to face the crowd of townsmen.

"Please," he begged, "not now! Truly, it is too soon to

save you all from eternal doom."

The men did not hear, nor wish to hear, his quietly spoken words. They merely watched, their faces distorted with devilish smiles, as he lost his balance, toppled backwards and, when his feet slipped on the dew-laden grass, disappeared over the embankment. There was no immediate sound, but, just as Aileen's father reached the edge of the steep slope, he heard a sickening tyre screech followed by a loud bang. Then another and another bang before the others joined him to peer at the wreckage of smashed vehicles strewn about on the road below. There were more tyre-screams and more noises of metal impacting with metal. Then silence. Lying face up on the road, his arms outstretched, like a crucifix, was their quarry. Blood stained his hands and streaked his forehead. Blood drawn by the brambles covering the embankment.

"That wasn't our fault!" reasoned Aileen's father, turning to speak to his friends. "He should've given himself up." Besides, he thought to himself, the minister had told them in church, the previous Sunday, how they must stand together against those outside the faith. Those guilty of unspeakable crimes. God was on their side and he grinned victory for God. He went to church every Sunday, so *he* should know. "Serves the bastard right!" he exclaimed.

Each man high-fived with a fellow 'Christian' and they left others to sort out the mess on the by-pass.

*****

It was the sergeant's duty to identify the body lying in the hospital mortuary, but before this he went to investigate the tepee. He truly did not know what to expect. Why were they all so certain the young recluse had been responsible for the thefts and for the assault upon poor Aileen? Mr McLachlan had been convinced the sergeant would uncover his sordid secrets inside the tepee, but the officer was not only unsure but unprepared for what happened after passing beyond the tepee flap.

No words could express the feeling that overcame Jimmy MacLean as he stood inside that tepee. It seemed as though he had passed through into another dimension, his mind now filled with a mix of detachment and of indescribable peace. Nothing outside the tepee appeared to matter any longer. Inside, the space seemed immense. Like a huge cathedral, the vault of which was in another world.

Jimmy MacLean stood alone in the vast emptiness of the tepee multiverse, yet it was not *truly* empty. The very air seemed alive with unseen things; with compassion, with love...

And with sorrow.

The sergeant sat down, uneasily, on the edge of the camp bed at the far end of the small tepee. How could such a tiny place seem so large, so limitless? Why had meaningful dimensions, even reality itself, changed so much on entering the humble, canvas dwelling? And as he slowly became more aware of a feeling of limitless space pervading the tepee he knew *this* was reality. Not that other place where crime and hatred ruled.

Neatly placed beside the camp bed were some books and loose sheets of paper. Jimmy MacLean picked up one of these.

A cultured man, despite the demands of his job, Jimmy had a good knowledge of literature and of the arts in general. He found himself looking at handwritten poems unlike anything he had read before. There was

199

something extraordinary in the way all human feelings, life itself, seemed to flow through the words. How come those words meant so much? Why was he so moved?

He looked up, frightened by the power of the words. He had entered the tepee seeking answers and now he was searching his own mind for the questions. Whatever they were, he had found one answer. The man had nothing to do with those crimes out there; crimes that seemed of vanishing importance to what he experienced in the tepee.

Jimmy had never fully understood why the locals persecuted the man. They took against him (Him?) before any crime had been committed. His only crime was to look and behave differently. He never stood a chance.

"They've killed Him," the sergeant whispered to himself as tears moistened his cheeks. "They've killed *Him,* again, and for no real reason. Like the last time." He had no idea why he said that, nor why he grieved so much.

Sergeant MacLean's search of the tepee gave him no other clues as to the identity of the man in the mortuary, although deep down he knew. Apart from a neat pile of folded clothes, some cooking utensils and washing things, there were only books and poetry. No official papers, no cards, no name. He stuffed the poems inside his uniform jacket leaving everything else for the forensic boys.

"No secrets here," he muttered, glancing back for one last look before leaving. "We should all know this, anyway, but how *can* we now that He's been killed… again?"

He said no more.

The following day, the pathologist submitted a report to the Procurator Fiscal. Looking at the body on the slab, he was overcome with a feeling of sadness such as he had never before experienced. He spoke gently as his assistant carefully sewed up the autopsy incisions:

"No doubt they'll record this as an accidental death." He shook his head. "Too soon. And no one will ever know. Or learn. Again."

In the town the break-ins and thefts continued. A week after the young man had fallen to his death, a female primary school teacher was raped and murdered in the park on her way home, plus a doomed world never got that second chance.

Mucus Guzzlers

"That's her, Dennis. Cute, isn't she?"

Dennis Huntley of Huntley Pharmaceuticals peered through a microscope at a grey mucus splodge at the margin of which hovered a determined, sausage-shaped thing that repeatedly pushed its rounded end in and out of the splodge. With the eye of faith, Dennis could just make out a tiny mouth at the end of the little sausage which, without a shadow of doubt, was carving a deepening hole in the splodge.

"How do you know it's a 'she'?" asked Dennis, looking up. "Looks pretty sexless to me."

"Because it's a *good* bacterium. That's why. Like Acidophillus and Lactobacillus. I like to call the good ones 'she'. And boy, is this a good one! Just think, Dennis. Can you not see the headlines? 'Mucus Guzzling Bacteria... Massive Breakthrough in Medical Research!' Who knows where this might lead? If you give me an advance of ten million, Dennis, I'll get the first batch of these little beauties to your lab by next week."

Dennis looked again down the microscope. The hole in the splodge around the business end of that agitated little sausage was getting larger by the second as he watched it tiny mouth attack a blob of laboratory mucus with the relish of a shark on a feeding frenzy.

"A *good* bacterium, eh?"

"Sure thing, Dennis! A colony of those little blighters could sweep up and down your respiratory passages like clones of council cleaners tidying up the streets of London. Imagine! Not a discarded wrapper, fast food carton or Coke can in sight. Not *one* fleck of mucus to rattle around your respiratory tract."

No denying it, Dennis *was* impressed.

"Eight million?" he suggested.

"For you, Dennis, old fellow! *Only* for you. Dirt cheap. Most of the research completed. All the files are here. You can check them out for yourself. Just a few clinical trials and you'll be reaping the benefits. Many times over. Many, *many* times over! And a knighthood, I expect. For services rendered to the national health. That sort of thing. Just think of all those hospital beds freed up because our little mucus-guzzling friends have kept all those respiratory sufferers out of hospital, huh? Dennis, this is big. *Really* big! Just what your company needs judging by the latest FT report."

"Bunch of wankers, those news boys. But it does have appeal, I have to admit. Just one thing, though. How can you be sure those sausage things are good and mucus is bad?" On peering again down the microscope, Dennis Huntley saw that the sausage had already devoured half of its tasty mucus meal.

"Dennis, oh Dennis! How *can* mucus be good if you nearly drown in the stuff whenever some horrid respiratory bug hits your lungs? *And* the sinuses. *And* those other biological nooks and crannies where it gunges up the works. Take my word for it, these mucus-guzzlers will be a miracle cure."

Later that afternoon, when eyelids drooped around the table at the board meeting, Dennis Huntley, under AOCB, brought up the issue of an advance to Plumley Microbiologicals for supplying the 'good bacteria' to be tested for treating respiratory conditions. There were a few soporific grunts and a several sleepy nods of assent from those around the table although, later, no one could recall an actual figure for the transaction being quoted.

"I take it you're all in agreement. Then that draws our meeting to a close, ladies and gentleman. Same time next Friday? All right?"

All weekend, Dennis could think only about that microscopic, mucus-guzzling sausage. Could it really be? A knighthood? Early retirement? The Bahamas? Alice had always wanted to live somewhere warmer.

"Of course I'd love to live in the Bahamas, Dennis," she agreed. "You know me and sunshine. But hardly likely, what with all that financial bother the company's been going through, eh?"

"Wait and see, darling. Just wait and see."

There was a definite twinkle in her husband's eyes, but Alice merely shrugged her shoulders. She had heard it all before. Like when he was conned into believing there was a vaccine against cancer just around the corner, and when he was persuaded that a particular combination of vitamins would stop dementia in its tracks. The company had barely recovered from those little ventures.

"Just be careful. Please!"

But over the weekend, out there in the streets, in the supermarkets, Dennis kept seeing '£' signs hover over the heads of anyone who happened to cough. Soon he would be collecting all those '£'s. No, millions of '£'s! And that house in the Bahamas? It had a swimming pool. In his mind's eye. He could barely contain his excitement.

"Came by special delivery this morning," Dennis's secretary told him the following Monday. "'Open with care', it says."

"I know what it is, Sarah. Very hush-hush. Top secret.

Something really big."

Sarah recalled the placebo dementia treatment and the cancer vaccine fiasco, and she worried about her pension. She eyed her boss with suspicion as, clutching the package, he skipped joyfully out of the office and headed for the laboratory.

"Now be sure you take extra care with this, Jones," he said to his chief research scientist. "These are the good bacteria I spoke about on Friday. The basis of our new product, Mucalieve. Got a cold coming on, so I'll be the first human guinea pig. Tomorrow! Guinea pig, ha-ha! Oh, to be a guinea pig and get the good things in life, Jones. Right?"

Dennis Huntley gave an almost maniacal chuckle as Mr Jones placed the eight million pounds worth of Petri dish in the incubator. He, too, worried about his pension.

At coffee time the following morning, Jones said to his boss, "They've come along very nicely."

"Who have?" the other man asked, his mind still in the Bahamas.

"The subcultures of that bug you gave me. Growing extremely well, they are."

Dennis rubbed his hands with glee.

"The little angels, eh?" His grin stretched from ear to ear. "Daughters of fortune, Jones. No, daughters *for* fortune!"

"Not sure I'd ever call any bacteria 'angels', sir. Helpful sometimes, maybe, but 'angels'?"

"Jones, you have no idea what a great day this is. I can feel that mucus rattling around in my chest already. And you know, if I were elderly, or poorly for any other reason, that mucus could just tip me into hospital. Those little beauties you're now growing, well, they might just keep me out of hospital. Think what this could mean, Jones. Millions saved on the NHS budget. No, billions! The value of our shares could shoot through the ceiling overnight." Precisely what Mr Huntley had said about the breakthrough treatment for dementia. Actually, shares fell to a record low.

"Oh, I am so excited I can hardly keep still. How should I take them, Jones?" He began hopping about from one foot to the other.

"As an aerosol. But is this wise, Mr Huntley? I mean we need time to check on the veracity of the data from Plumley Microbiologicals."

"Totally trustworthy, Jones. You have my word on that."

As he'd had on the fake dementia pills and the cancer vaccine scam.

"Well, sir, if you're determined to go ahead so soon, the way they're growing I could have one of those subcultures ready as an aerosol within an hour."

The hour flashed by. Dennis Huntley arrived back in laboratory on the dot, with a bottle of champagne in one hand and two glasses in the other. Jones eyed the bottle with suspicion.

"Isn't it a bit premature for all that, sir? Besides, we don't know the effects of alcohol on these bacteria. We know so very little about them."

"Nonsense, Jones. We know they'll make us all stinking rich, the lovely little creatures!"

"But sir, there *is* one thing. The speed with which they multiply. I made some more plates an hour ago when you were here, and those new colonies have already completely covered the dishes and swallowed up all the available agar. I think..."

"Great news, Jones! Wonderful! They're trying to tell us how rich we're gonna be. Got that nebuliser thing ready? We'll have the little darlings guzzling the mucus in my air passages in no time. But first a drink to celebrate, huh?" The cork shot from the bottle, hitting the ceiling. With shaking hands, Dennis Huntley poured a bubbling glass for himself and one for Mr Jones.

"To the mucus guzzlers!" he exclaimed, raising his glass.

The chief research scientist took a tentative sip then, when his boss wasn't looking, tipped the rest of contents of his glass into a nearby beaker. Dennis Huntley downed one, two, then three glassfuls before wiping his sleeve across champagne-smeared lips.

"Just put the mask over your face, sir, and I'll turn on the nebuliser. It'll take a few minutes before the vial's empty."

With an asinine grin, Dennis Huntley sat on a laboratory stool taking in deep breaths of mucus guzzlers.

"Can feel them doing me good already," he announced within seconds.

"Don't talk yet, sir. Wait till it's empty."

There was a curious sucking noise as the remaining contents of the vial disappeared into Dennis Huntley. Jones turned it off and his boss removed the face mask. The director of Huntley Pharmaceuticals drew in a deep breath.

"Not a single rattle of mucus. What do you say to that, eh? No doubts now. Not a single one, Jones. Mucalieve will be a miracle cure. An *absolute* miracle." Dennis Huntley swayed a little as he stood up.

"You all right, sir?" asked Jones as the other man

tipped from side to side like a flagpole in a gale.

"Never felt better, Jones. Never felt... erm... look, I'll take a little... you know... yes! In my office. Mucus! Mmm! Lovely, delicious mucus!"

Dennis Huntley lurched forward, gripped the edge of the laboratory bench, hiccupped, and turned to address his chief research scientist:

"We really need more mucus, Jones. Where can we get it?"

"Sir, shall I call the doctor?"

"Is he made of mucus? Ha-ha! A mucus doctor. A lovely, slimy mucus doctor. Very tasty, Jones. *Very* tasty!"

After which Dennis Huntley zigzagged to the door before leaving the laboratory. Jones, frowning, returned to the row of Petri dishes now overflowing with colonies of mucus-guzzling bacteria. For each dish, he plated out another ten cultures and began to worry about having enough incubator space for this latest project.

"He's gone awfully quiet," said Sarah over lunch. "And all he said when he went back into his office was, 'We must get more mucus. More, more, more!' Not himself at all. Do you think I should check on him? Take him a coffee? I mean, he's usually first in the canteen at lunch time."

All agreed that Sarah should check on Mr Huntley. Plus a nice hot cup of coffee for their boss was most definitely called for. But no one was prepared for the scream. Or the sound of breaking china when Sarah opened the door to Mr Huntley's office. For several moments, everyone stood, huddled around the trembling secretary, frozen in horror...

There, wedged in the company director's chair, slumped forwards onto the desk, and showing a distinct interest in his employees gathered at the door, was a vast, living, slippery sausage. Worst of all was its gluttonous mouth clearly searching for something with large rubbery lips hungrily opening and closing.

"Mr Huntley?" Sarah queried, faintly. "Oh, Mr Huntley..."

That Holiday in Tuscany

"Umberto, Umberto... che cosa fai? Oh, mio bambino cattivo!"

"What the devil's the woman talking about?" I said, as I tried to crawl away from her. The annoying thing was, my words came out funny. Not proper words at all. Just a string of idiotic 'goos' and 'waah's. And could I crawl away? Damn it, I could not escape from that giant of a woman. My arms and legs only flailed about as I kicked my toes on that marbled flooring before she picked me up. That was the worst of it, being lifted up close to her face. Her *awful* face! Then, bugger it, I began to scream. Me scream? Well, *you* would, wouldn't you? Scream when enveloped by over-generous wafts of garlic breath.

I peered at the floor. It was a long way down and there were bits of broken china all over the place. The large vase, a potential weapon that I had been peering up at, was no longer on its pedestal and the pedestal lay on its side. Luckily, I hadn't cut myself.

What a bloody awful place! Little wonder I screamed and screamed and screamed. And then—Oh, my God— then I was dangled in the air inches from that woman's pimpled face. I could see every spot and every mole, each fold and each blemish on her cheeks and on her chin. I even saw the hairs sticking out from her nostrils. I yelled like a banshee, but all she did was to shake that large head of hers. Then there was that weird language. Like school Latin gone wrong. She shouted abuse at me. I could tell it was abuse from her facial contusions as she shouted and yelled. At me! A university lecturer in information technology, for God's sake!

The shouting and abuse was one thing, but what came next is almost too humiliating too relate. I was taken to the white room again. This kept on happening. Still screaming, I would be rolled over onto my back and, as always in that white room, half my clothes would be removed. The lower half. Then the woman with the large face would do things with my bum. Cold, wet things. This was invariably followed by a furious rubbing of my bum, then clothes would be put back on. That place, that white room, stank like a sewer.

'Where is she?' I thought when back in the other room. *'My beloved wife! Where?'*

I found myself staring at a brightly-coloured ball inches from my nose. If only I could have controlled my hands, I would have reached out, grabbed the ball and chucked it at the woman with a large face. I'm a good shot. You might not believe it, but I'm an expert at clay pigeon shooting.

'But damn the woman with the large face,' I thought. *'Where is soulmate for life? My gorgeous wife?'*

I remembered. She had been so impressed, so proud, when she saw those clays explode in the sky in response to my pull of the trigger. Could I do that now? I wondered as I kicked and jerked about on my tummy on the floor. If I went out with *her*, now, with my girl as she was then, but now my wife, and tried to shoot at a clay, would the same thing happen? With my limbs flapping about all over the place, would the clay still explode?

More to the point, where is she? What am I doing in this place, and where is my wife? I've been without her for too long. I so miss her eyes.

Oh, those eyes! If I didn't see them again, and soon, I

was sure I would go mad.

Her body too. The shape of her hips; her breasts. How soft against my chest are those breasts of hers.

But here, in this awful place, there was only the woman with the large face and the large breasts and a strange man, although I didn't see much of him. He disappeared every morning. The woman with the large head, she would push my face into her huge breasts. Swollen breasts. And believe it or not, she would make me drink from them, and I did drink because I had this damnable thirst. I even craved for those swollen breasts, and then, when full of milk, I would wonder why the woman with a large face had such a hold over me. She was hideous. And, whenever replete with warm milk, I would think of my wife, of her own sweet, young breasts, her smooth belly and her yielding lips, and I would cry because she wasn't with me.

I gave up asking questions. It wasn't answers that I needed. I only wanted my wife. But day after day, it was the same thing. The woman with the large face shouting, *'Umberto, sì! Umberto, no! Umberto, vieni qua, mio bambino!'* Those swollen breasts, the coldness on my bum in the white room, the helpless sprawling on the marbled floor and futile grabbing for things forever just out of reach. The day all of this changed, I was perched on the brink of madness itself.

She came back into my life but something was horribly wrong. The door opened, and there she was, standing in the doorway. The sweetest moment of my life, to see her again, at last…

But my body could do nothing about it. My arms and legs moved and jerked aimlessly as I looked up from the marbled floor at my wife.

"Oh, he's so cute!" my wife exclaimed as soon as she walked into the room.

"Yes, it's me, my love!" I cried out. At least, that's what I tried to say, but all that came from my mouth was, "Goo... gaa... grrrr... b... b..."

"Kiss me, darling. Take me away from here!" I called out, but she only heard, "Maaa... waa... gooo!"

Then, ignoring me, my wife spoke to the woman with the large face and the milk-swollen breasts.

"Such a lovely pensione you have, signora. Erm... *bella! Molto bella!* Um... *mi piace!*"

Even *she* spoke that funny language. But...

Oh my God, who the f--- is that? I asked myself.

A man carrying a suitcase followed my wife into the room. The swine put an arm around her waist, and she smiled at him. As she always smiles at me.

"My husband," my wife said, looking at this man. *"Il mio marito!"*

"Sì! Ho capito. Buon giorno, signor," replied the woman with the large face, shaking hands with the man.

My lovely wife spoke again, and... Sweet Jesus, *she* put her arm around *his* waist!

"We must take a walk around the town, dearest. There's so much to see in Arezzo."

The woman with the large face and the swollen breasts looked blankly at my wife.

"Noi, um..." my wife began in that weird language, indicating the man and to herself, *"vedere* Arezzo."

"Ho capito, signora! È bellissima, la nostra città!"

"Very *bellissima*," my wife said to the man, smiling again. For him. I could have killed the bastard. Could have?

Wrong tense. *Will!*

She turned to look at me again.

At last, I thought.

"Oh, he really is so cute!"

Cute? Her husband cute? That man? Or was she perhaps talking about me? I wondered. I thought again about tenses. And about time.

"Come si chiama, il bambino?" she said to the woman with the large face.

"Umberto, signora. Si chiama Umberto."

Oh my God, here we go again, I thought. *All that Umberto business. Who the f--- is 'Umberto'?*

I felt desperate. I had waited so long to be with her again, and now this. I tried to call out to her, over and over. I attempted to turn my 'goos' and my 'gaas' into meaningful words because I needed to tell her how much I loved her, but she only laughed. Laughed so sweetly that I longed for her even more. Longed to hold her, kiss her, make love to her. And I so needed to ask her what on earth she was doing with this strange man, and why he had been introduced as her 'husband'. *'Me! I'm your husband!'* I tried to make my useless voice say, but "Goo... w-w-w... ma!" came out instead.

"Darling," she said. To him, not to me. "Take the suitcase upstairs please. I'll wait down here. I must ask the lady if she's got a map or something that we could use."

'At last,' I thought when that man had left the room. *'Now perhaps she'll look at me. At her true husband!'*

"Per favore, signora, ha una mappa?" The woman with the large face looked puzzled, again. Then, suddenly, her face lit up.

"Ah, sì! Lei vuole un piano della città?

214

"Please."

"Un momento!"

The woman with the large face disappeared. Finally, I found myself alone with my wife... my girl... my soulmate.

I rocked, turned, pulled and twisted, fixing all the time on her beautiful face, and I swear that she was looking at me in the same way. I honestly swear it. Her eyes widened a little, perhaps. I don't know, precisely, but there was something about the look in those lovely eyes. She just stared as I edged slowly forwards, on the marble floor, towards her. I could definitely tell, from her eyes, that she knew who I really was as she stood peering down at me. She *had* to know. Her true husband, for heaven's sake. But what about that man?

Something I needed to know. Had they—you know... in bed together? I could not bear to think about it. Not just then. I would forgive her. Of course I would, if only so that we could be together again, and for me to escape from this hell and the woman with the large face and big floppy breasts.

I was moving forwards, inch by inch, making headway, at last, on the cold marble floor, getting closer and closer until my hands touched her legs. Her skin. I had longed so much for the smoothness of that silky, soft skin, and now I was touching it. Feeling it. I traced the gentle curves of her calves with my ridiculously small hand as I reached higher. I caught hold of her skirt, and I tried to pull myself up to my full height. She reached down and held my small hands with her fingers. How silly that my hands should be so small!

Now upright, on my feet, I seemed to be looking at

my wife's knees, not her face. Then a strange thing happened. She stooped down and picked me up, as if I were a small doll. Her husband a doll? She lifted me up high, holding me in front of her face.

I hope you will believe me when I tell you that my wife is the most beautiful woman in England. She has to be. But knowing that, you will surely understand how I must have felt inside, suspended in the air just inches away from that gorgeous face, once again, but completely helpless to do anything about it. How many times had I been that close to her face when our heads rested together on a pillow as I caressed and stroked her young body? All I wanted then was to be in bed with her again. To feel the pressure of her hips against mine. To make love to her again and again and again.

She looked at me. Her brow knotted. There was a troubled look in her eyes. She lowered me onto the marbled floor, and once more I became an unpleasant, helpless, crawling, bawling thing after she abandoned me that cold, foreign room. I did not see her again all day, but that evening I heard her voice. I had been placed in that moveable, wooden prison with bars, unable to get to her.

The following morning, with my stomach full of milk from the woman with a large face, and my bum ignominiously washed then rubbed dry, I was back on the floor when my wife entered the room together with that man. As they sat down together, at the table, I tortured myself with that awful question:

Had they done 'it' together in a bed the previous night?

The way he looked at her, and the manner in which he placed his hairy, ugly hand over my wife's small, yielding hand made me worry more and more.

216

"Buon giorno!" It was the woman with the large face. *"Fa bel tempo, oggi. Davvero!"*

"Sì!" my wife agreed. "A beautiful day," she added for his sake.

I had been thinking about it all night. My plan. To get rid of him and claim her back for myself.

"It's lovely to be in Italy, Frank," she said to him. "You know, David and I had talked about it so much. Coming here to Tuscany for a holiday. He badly needed a holiday with all that overtime he'd done for them. And he so loved art and old buildings. We'd even booked it. This very pensione. Then he got ill."

My wife paused. She looked sad.

David? That's me! David! I tried to call out to her, to tell her that *I* was her David, and that if this was actually Tuscany then why didn't we just go off together. Needless to say, only more of those meaningless, idiotic sounds emerged from my mouth.

"Darling," I tried to say. "It *is* me, Your David. We have a lovely house in Reading. We got that room ready for the child we're wanting. Remember?" But she only heard "Gooo... gaaa.... waaa... brrrr!"

My wife continued to talk to that animal of a man:

"You know, I should feel sad being here without David. It would have meant so much to him. He loved the work of Piero della Francesca, too. What Arezzo is all about. But being with you, darling, I no longer feel sad. Not with the baby on the way."

Baby? What baby? His baby? Inside my head I began to scream. The thought of them together in bed was bad enough, but my wife being pregnant with his baby was unendurable.

"Oops," my wife continued. "That reminds me. I

217

forgot my folic acid tablet. Just a mo. I'll go get it. Baby won't be happy if I forget his tablets."

"Or her tablets?" the man suggested, picking up my wife's hand and kissing it.

'Oh, My God,' I thought, *'this cannot go on!'* My wife stood up, kissed him on the cheek and left the room without even acknowledging me. *'Now's the time,'* I told myself. *'I don't have a gun, but...'*

I craned my neck and looked up at the towering glass cabinet just behind the man's seat. He was too busy opening a bread roll and plastering it with butter and red jam to notice me as I seal-flopped my way across the marble floor towards the cabinet. So engrossed with stuffing his face, he didn't notice me pull myself up at the corner of the huge cabinet. I stood there, feet apart to help me stay upright, emitting the occasional grunt, as I tried to rock the cabinet to and fro, I remember feeling so frustrated that I no longer seemed to have any strength. I simply could not understand what had happened to me since I last made love to my beautiful wife, but one thing was certain. He, this animal in front of me, had made her pregnant.

My anger boiled and gave me the strength that I needed. The cabinet began to move. It wobbled slightly, then—now this was the strange thing: there was no noise—then it tipped forward as he carried on stuffing a breakfast roll into his gaping mouth. As if in slow motion, the gap between the glass cabinet and the wall became wider and wider, and the gap between the glass doors of the heavy cabinet and the man below less and less, although, in truth, it was over in a split second...

The cabinet crashed down onto his back with the sound of an exploding bomb, showering the room with

218

splintered shards of shattered glass. Having lost the support of the cabinet, I slumped down onto my bottom, and I giggled and giggled and made *'goo... goo'* noises as I patted the glass-strewn marble floor with my tiny hands. The crushed body of the man, pinned down onto the breakfast table by the fallen cabinet, remained still. There was a piercing scream when the woman with the big face appeared. My wife, who must have heard the commotion, rushed in, after her, to stand staring at the motionless body of the man pinned down by the fallen cabinet. There was a lot of blood. Then... more screams.

"It's okay!" I called out, to stop the screaming. "He's gone now. We can be together again. At last we can have that holiday in Tuscany. The one we so often talked about. Don't you remember? We were sure a baby would come after a holiday together in Tuscany, and, if a boy, we were going to call him 'Piero' after my favourite painter!"

I said all of this to my wife, but she did not seem to hear, nor could she have made sense of the 'goos' and the 'gaas'. She just stood there and screamed and screamed.

"Umberto, Oh Umberto!" cried the woman with the large face. *"Che cos'hai fatto, Umberto, che cos'hai fatto?"*

A Seventy-Thousand-Year Reunion

The three women belonged to the same tribe. A group of some two thousand men, women and children whose ancestors had left the great plains and the mountains to the south, and who moved northwards following the coastline in constant search for food. Those three women were strong in heart, and wise. They chose their men well. Not weak or foolish men, but men skilled in hunting. Men who would use their cunning to win in battle; men whose blood might mix with their own strong blood to produce young ones who would also become leaders. And the three women were friends. They helped each other with everything, and, because of this, their men also became friends. Times had become hard for the tribe. The land was drying. Some had tried going even further north in search of richer findings of food from the sea, but the desert there reached down to the sea and the land was harsh and unforgiving. A few returned to warn the tribe not to venture further up the coast. Others wanted to turn back, to return to the lands of their forebears and hunt the large animals there, but the three women and the wise men in the tribe knew this could destroy them. Their ancestors had been driven away from these lands by fierce warriors from the south. If they were to return, they would probably all be wiped out.

Each evening, the three women would sit by the shore, in a circle, and talk. Their speech was simple. To survive they needed simple speech. There was no place for ambiguity of meaning, for argument or for discussions that failed to alter anything. Their tribe was starving and, if unable to find somewhere with more plentiful food and fresh water, they would all die, the tribe gone forever.

The three women talked about the land across the sea. One could see this land in her mind's eye. There were hills there, and trees. This women knew that if there were trees there would also be animals, and therefore food. She, the one who could see in her mind's eye, knew there was no limit to that land. At least not one they could ever reach. So the three realised it was not just an island too small to sustain the tribe. The women thought only of their tribe when they spoke with the men and with the other women. All listened to those three women who were so wise and so strong in heart.

There was great excitement in the tribe about their plan. A plan that might save them all. Inland, there were still a few trees. The tribe had used the branches for shelter and the sticks for spears and clubs. They knew how remarkable the wood from trees was. The three women had seen how the sticks used to spear the fish would float on the water. They realised that the larger branches and the trunks of these trees would also float. They found strong men to cut down sturdy trunks and branches with their stone axes. The men would carry these to the shoreline, whilst the women taught the children how to swim in the water of the sea. The very young would be lifted onto strong shoulders where they could cling onto long hair. The very old and the sick would have to stay behind, but the three women said that with fewer mouths to feed, those left behind should find enough food for their shrunken bellies.

The women chose the time carefully. A time when the air would be clear, the water calm and with less pull in it to drag them out to sea, for the women knew about that mysterious pull in the water. They knew it was worse at certain times of the day, and they knew in which direction the pull would take them. They would use their wisdom to decide when and how to launch the logs, and how they could use the pull of the water to help them reach the land across the sea.

The three women decided when the time was right. The logs fringed the shoreline, like waiting crocodiles. The women knew that for many of them the logs would mean a final journey to that other place, the land where their ancestors now dwelt. However, if the tribe were to survive, they had to attempt to cross the narrow sea. The three women had too much of the Great Spirit of Life in them to give up and allow death to claim victory over the whole tribe.

When they left, it was the three women who directed the stronger men. The other women, the older men and the little ones clung onto the twisting logs as the men pushed these away from the shore and in the direction of the land across the water. Then the three women followed with the stronger men. The three women had chosen their time wisely. Slowly, the tribe, bobbing on the water, in huddles, edged it's way across the neck of sea they called 'The Gate of Grief'.

They travelled in a great arc, swimming against the pull of the water, then used this to bring them back on course towards the opposite shore. Some of the older women and men, who had little strength left, were carried away on their logs and disappeared. The three women reassured the tribe, later, that these people, being old and weak, were, anyway, ready to join their ancestors. Those who remained, exhausted as they crawled onto that other beach where a new future awaited them, looked back at the horizon beyond which was the land that they would never see again. They knew that the fierce people who lived to the south of that land, and who had driven away the tribe, shared the same ancestors as those old people who had now been swept out to sea on their logs. Together the people of the tribe spoke to the ancestors in a prayer for the old people. They also asked that their children's children be allowed to return to the great plains, one day, and make peace with the fierce people. The three women led their prayers.

The tribe found some food, but soon realised this would be insufficient to sustain them all. The three women sat apart from the tribe and talked. They agreed with one another, for each one of these three women had the wisdom of her ancestors. They would have to separate. Each woman would take a group of some six hundred people—including strong men, young ones, plus her own children—and each group would become a new tribe. They could go their separate ways. If they did not, they just knew the tribe would start fighting itself, as had happened in the old land, later to be called Africa, told in the stories handed down to them. The spirit of life was strong in these three women, and everyone knew that they were doing this to save the tribe.

So three new tribes were formed, some joining the first of the three women, others the second and the remainder of the tribe the third woman. When they parted in search of new lands, and in the hope of finding better food sources, the tribes were still as one with each other. The three women were sad. Their faces were wet with tears as they touched foreheads and noses together. This was how they would both greet and say farewell to those close to them.

They knew that this time it would mean farewell

forever for them, for their children and for their children's children, but together they prayed to their ancestors that one day, when they too had become ancestors, that their new tribes would come together again. They prayed that there would be a reunion of the souls of these tribes on the soil of some distant land. After saying tearful farewells, the people in their new tribes did not look back. The farewells were over, and they moved forward, each tribe having one of the three wise women.

The first of these women was both beautiful and graceful. She had been a great dancer in the old tribe. Back then, folk would sit in a large circle and watch her supple limbs writhe and twist as the music men used sticks and rocks to knock a rhythm out of a tree trunk or a fallen branch. Sometimes her torso would arch back, so that her face was turned upwards, towards the lands of their ancestors; other times she would stoop, gracefully, as though looking deep into the ground where the trees and plants found their life force. Those now with the first woman felt they were fortunate to be in her tribe. Her children, too, were beautiful and graceful, like their mother. This tribe followed the coast to the east then struck north, away from the midday sun.

The first woman grew old and, one sad day, she too joined her ancestors. Her children's children, also beautiful, were by then already growing up. The tribe split into several different tribes as the people spread across the new lands, forever heading eastwards towards the rising sun, and northwards to enter the lands of snow and ice. The children's children led new tribes, these tribes moved on, some merging and taking over great areas of land, others searching for new territories to call their own and in which to raise their children and their children's

224

children. Some of these lands to the east, and to the south again, were lush and warm. The people in these lands remained dark of skin like the three women who left the lands of the ancestors. Others, in colder inhospitable climates, gradually lost the darkness of their skin as the children born to lighter skinned parents survived better in the cold, and they soon begot more fair-skinned young ones. Those who had been born with smaller, more rounded noses, and with folds to protect the corners of their eyes, fared better as the cold winds from the frozen deserts of the north blew harshly against their faces. These people, many as graceful as the first woman herself, had a new and delicate sort of oriental beauty.

Mei Li awoke, as usual, before her parents, put on her pale blue school tracksuit and ran to the park, near where she lived in Nanjing, to spend at least a full hour practising her jumps, leaps and twists in the air. Winning the gold medal in the junior world gymnastics championships had only spurred the girl on to do even better. Her coach had told her that with hard work she should win an Olympic gold and what glory that would bring for her motherland, China. Mei Li needed no encouragement to work hard at her gymnastics. She was a bright girl who easily achieved high grades in all the academic subjects at school, but every minute of her spare time she would spend going over and over her routines in the gym until they were perfect. Then she would start all over again to improve on that perfection.

Mei Li's father was both proud and respectful of his sixteen-year-old daughter. Proud that she had been ear-marked for the Beijing Olympics, proud that she lived up to her name, and respectful of the beautiful young woman she had become. Many had told him that she was by far the prettiest girl in her school. Plus he was respectful of her determination and that strength of spirit which meant she would never give up. He called this the 'Spirit of Life'. Others saw where this spirit had come from. Her father. He had been a handsome and gifted acrobat. His leadership skills soon saw him heading an acrobatic team that became renowned throughout the province. All this he gave up to allow his daughter to concentrate on her gymnastics when the coaches told him that she would lose out by travelling with her parents all the time. They settled in Nanjing where Mei Li's father owned a very successful sports shop. Mei Li knew, later on, that her father would feel sad to see her leave home, but she also knew how proud he was for her to have been selected for entry into a prestigious gymnastics school in Beijing. She would neither let him nor her country down. She would win that Gold for China in the Beijing Olympics. Her own coach had jokingly said that her opponents would not stand a chance competing against her.

When Mei Li got home that morning, her father was sitting with her mother, eating breakfast. Mei Li joined them. She showed no sign of feeling tired after her punishing workout in the park.

"Last day at the old school, father," she said, smiling. Her father saw both beauty and a zest for life in that smile. "From now on I will work really hard."

"Mei Li, you are already junior world champion. Don't put yourself down. You have always worked hard. Your grandmother told me that Mei Li's genes are strong, from her great grandfather, and she was right. It's always been in you, to work hard and to do well."

"Father," began Mei Li, as she hurried through her

breakfast, "if I do get chosen for the Beijing Olympics it won't be just about China, will it? I mean, what would excite me as much as winning anything is the thought of meeting all those other athletes from the other countries. I love to see them on the television, and it was so good to actually be, and talk, with these people at the junior world championships. Wouldn't the Olympics be the same, only ten times better? They tell us that that is what the Olympics is about. People getting together, ordinary people from all over the world who are equal in all other ways." Mei Li's father knew then that there was a third reason for him to feel so proud of his daughter. Her wisdom.

The second woman was tall with long limbs, and she was the fastest runner in the tribe. Even the men could not outrun her. Her link with the ancestors was strong. She was the one who could feel their presence in the land, in its soil and in the trees and the plants that came from the soil. It was she who saw the land across the narrow sea in her mind's eye. Wherever she went, she felt as one with the land, and her tribe loved her and respected her for her knowledge. Like the first woman, she led her own people to the east, but they followed the coastline and did not travel inland to the north. Her own children's children, and their children's children, all kept their darker skins as they took their own tribes into warm jungle areas. Some settled in these parts and grew to know the jungle well, becoming a part of it, over countless successive generations. Other tribes moved further east and south to those islands now known as Indonesia. A woman from one of these tribes looked across the sea, like her ancestor, the second woman, and somehow knew there was a great land beyond the water. And like her ancestor, she got her men to cut logs and these logs became boats that took them across the swirling waters of the sea. They kissed the new land when they came ashore off their log boats. Was this the land where her great ancestor meant to bring her own tribe? The land that tens of thousands of years later became known as Australia.

Betty was the only Aboriginal girl to have won a national sporting event for the under eighteens that year. She was not powerfully built. Indeed her long slim legs almost gave her an appearance of fragility, but how misleading this was. When she ran, people saw another side to this quiet, contemplative girl, for she ran like the wind. No noise, no fuss. Within seconds she would streak ahead of other competitors, never showing the slightest sign of fatigue to slow her down. The press spotted her talent, and in the sports pages she was called a 'phenomenon'. That she would try for the Olympics in Beijing was without question. Betty herself, now sixteen, did not speak about this, but deep inside she knew that she would compete in Beijing, and that the banner she would bear would be for her Aboriginal ancestors as well as for the nation of Australia. The fact that she had already beaten the world record for two hundred metres did not stop Betty from running the track every evening during the school week, and every weekend.

Betty was quiet, and yet made friends easily. Everyone who met her loved her. She would listen to people with a warm smile on her face, and her speech was always comforting, reassuring. If chosen for the Beijing Olympics, Betty knew she would then be meeting with athletes from all over the world, each of whom would strive for perfection in his or her own event, undeterred by anything. She wanted so much to meet these other athletes. Betty knew that if this dream were to become a reality she would have to train as hard as she could, then train even harder.

The third woman was as agile as a goat. She could climb where no one else in the tribe would dare to go and show no signs of fear. Her men in the new tribe had a great respect for her. She taught them to abandon all fear, and the tribe grew proud of the courage of their men. This courage and agility was carried through to the children of the third woman, and on through to the children's children, and to their children's children. These tribes moved northwards, over the high mountains, through a land now called Turkey, and northwards to a land of cool summers and freezing winters. Again, in these colder climes, the children with lighter skin were stronger, and had more offspring, than those with darker skin. Over the millennia the people of these tribes became paler than their ancestors. Their hair became long and straight as this gave them an advantage during the bitter winters. The men with hair on their bodies survived tedious hunting trips better than those with smooth hairless skins. The many tribes that had stemmed from the children's children of the third woman moved across the lands of Europe and, over the millennia, formed many great countries.

In the small town of La Chappelle-sur-Erdre, in the Loire region of France, a young woman called Claudine practised jumping in a field at the back of her grandmother's cottage. She had just left school, where she had not only won trophies in the high jump for the region, but also where her athletics teacher had also given her private coaching most evenings. He had recognised something quite extraordinary about this girl, now eighteen. She seemed to have no fear whatsoever, and a determination that was almost frightening. He had arranged for her to go to Paris where she was to be trained with the aim of possible selection for the Beijing Olympics. In a week, she would leave behind her family, village life, and her friends in Nantes. Claudine's mother and father knew their daughter would have to make sacrifices if she were to be chosen to represent France at the Olympics, but her mother also knew that the fearlessness and the determination that she saw in the daughter were deeply ingrained in her family line. If Claudine had decided to go for the Olympics, her mother somehow knew that the girl would not only be selected, but that she would be content with nothing less than a gold medal.

Claudine was so looking forward to Paris. She had secured a part-time job in a shop to help with her keep, and her father would pay for her to be taught by the best coach in the country. She realised she had a very good chance of both being selected and of winning a medal, but what really excited her was the chance to mix with others sharing similar feelings and thoughts.

The girl was determined to work hard at her sport to enable her to go to Beijing where she was certain to meet people from the world over who, like herself, would never give up if they had set their minds on something. For Claudine this would be like a reunion of souls with a single purpose: to show to the world that there was only one thing that really separated the peoples of the all many different countries across the globe, and that was the way in which each individual responded to that great inner spirit of life, the most precious thing that her parents had passed on down to her from their parents' parents, and which they had inherited from long-forgotten ancestors.

(Some scientists have suggested that mitochondrial DNA analysis tells us that all the people in the world, outside Africa, are descended from just three women from a tribe that left the continent *between eighty-five to sixty-six thousand years ago by crossing the Red Sea into southern Arabia, from where they spread across to Asia, to Australasia and to Europe.)*

The Piano

It began when Steven was four. He climbed into his parents' bed, one night, and snuggled up against his mother.

"It's that piano, Mummy," he cried. "I don't like it."

Only half awake, his mother placed a comforting arm around the small, warm shape huddled beside her.

"There's no piano. Don't worry, Stevie. Just a bad dream," she said, stroking his hair. Although she heard nothing herself, she could not think why her little son would be so upset by the imagined sound of a piano. In fact, they *did* have a small upright in the corner of the living room, left to her by a deceased aunt. No one played it, but it was useful for putting things on. She had noticed, however, that Steven always avoided playing near the piano.

In his sleep, Steven's father mumbled something incomprehensible.

"There we are!" Steven's mother said, kissing the boy's forehead. "Daddy says you should go back into your own bed now."

Reluctantly, Steven pushed himself backwards and out of the comfort of the large, warm, parental bed. Clutching a tatty Eeyore, he headed for the door. "It wasn't a dream!" he muttered, grumpily, without looking back.

Sometimes this scenario would be repeated for nights on end. Steven's mother grew weary of being awoken for no good reason and even expressed her concern to the doctor.

"Please don't worry about Steven," was his reply. "Children have great imaginations. This sort of thing is perfectly normal for a small child."

It did not seem normal to Steven's mother when he started to go on about the piano during the daytime whilst eating lunch. Nevertheless, there were periods when Steven made no mention of it for months on end and, once, for almost a year.

After he was thirteen, the piano seemed to stop. In fact, he had almost forgotten about the torment it had caused him as a small child until one sultry Friday afternoon, in early June, almost seventeen years later. Steven, now married with two boys of his own, was facing a class of fidgety children in the school where he taught. As always at that time of day on a Friday, he could hardly wait for school to finish and for the weekend to begin. The children before him, clutching their pencils, struggled with the figures on their worksheets. Steven was checking lists of stock items for order. It was remarkably quiet until...

Quite suddenly, the sound of a piano, only just audible, being played a long way away just as it had always been when Steven was a child. He looked up at the class. The children remained bent forwards over their tables. Steven glanced at his watch. He knew no one would be playing the school piano at that hour. Besides, the piano he heard was far too distant for it to be the school piano along the corridor in the assembly hall. Nor were there any houses adjacent to the school to account for the sound. No! Steven knew this was the piano that had haunted his childhood, and the thought that it had started up again sparked a panic tinged with a strange nostalgia.

The music of the far-off piano was unlike anything that was ever played on the school instrument. The notes seemed to breathe a life of their own as, in distant cascades of sound, they tumbled into faintly audible melodies of incredible beauty. Steven felt that same powerful lure of the unseen piano that had troubled him as a small boy.

A young voice jolted Steven's attention.

"What's the matter, Mr Horley?" asked a little girl at the table nearest to his desk, fixing him with an astute stare.

"Just that piano," replied Steven, without even thinking that the child might not hear it.

"What piano, Mr Horley?" enquired the child. She looked puzzled, and her small hands gestured that she had no idea what he was talking about.

Steven's heart sank. He was reminded of his failure to persuade his parents about the piano, a failure that ultimately made him keep quiet about the whole thing. And he knew that there was nothing wrong with the girl's hearing.

Steven heard the piano many times over the next few weeks, both during the day and at night. It was clear that his wife and two sons did not hear it, and, eager to avoid causing them alarm, he simply did not mention his apparent auditory hallucination. He had read somewhere that some people might hear a particular strain of music before taking a fit, but his consciousness was never affected and his doctor reassured him that there was no possibility of this being a manifestation of epilepsy. Besides, the music played by the piano was constantly changing. Never the same tune as would be expected with an epileptic aura; the chords and arpeggios flowed with endless variety and invention.

What troubled Steven most was an intense feeling of sadness evoked by the faraway music. He almost yearned to hear it played more clearly, from close by, seated in a grand recital hall where he could listen properly to those extraordinary melodies. As in his childhood, there were periods when Steven did not hear it at all, but when present the sound of the piano triggered memories of profound feelings of longing and of loneliness, almost unbearable when he was a boy.

Thankfully, the piano stopped as the term drew to a close. Once again, he felt that delightfully light and airy sensation of the last day of the school year. He thought only about the coming vacation with Susan and the boys.

"At last! Wonderful!" Steven exclaimed, as he lugged cases and bags from the house to the car the following day. They were heading for the Norfolk Broads, a part of the country he had always felt drawn to, and planned to spend a few days getting there so that they could take in some of the quaint old Suffolk and Norfolk towns and villages. Steven had a passion for old Saxon churches, and Norwich Cathedral was, of course, an absolute must.

"F---!" Steven uttered an unrepeatable swear word under his breath when the piano started up again as they were driving along a quiet B road towards a small village described in the guidebook as 'quaint'. The boys were asleep in the back of the car. This time, the piano was so loud, the music in a minor key, that it startled him. The car swerved as he momentarily lost control. Susan, who had been perusing the map, grabbed the door pull and glanced sideways at her husband.

"Please be careful," she begged, frowning.

"Sorry!" mumbled Steven, his mind now flooded with a haunting melody and rippling broken chords. The magnetic lure of the music was stronger than it had ever been, the yearning it provoked unendurable. He gripped the steering wheel and sat forwards, using all his powers of concentration to focus on his driving and on the road ahead.

"What's wrong, darling?" asked Susan, still clutching the door pull.

"N-Nothing, dear. It's been a long drive. That's all."

"Only an hour and a half, Steven," Susan said, glancing at her watch. "That's nothing."

"Well..." Steven continued, trying hard to smile against the crescendo of music in his head, "...I need lunch, I suppose."

"It's only eleven o'clock."

For a while there was no further exchange of words. Steven drove on, grim-faced, Susan tense and clearly cross. Finally, they arrived at the small village.

"Not much here," scoffed Susan, looking again at the map. She did not share Steven's enthusiasm for Saxon churches.

"Just a short stop, then," said Steven before getting out of the car. He could barely hear himself speak above the overpowering music in his head. He felt he had to find a place where he could sit and make sense of it all. Maybe, in a few minutes, the piano might stop playing. Susan did not drive, so their safety was entirely his responsibility. If the music failed to stop, he would have to tell her. For reasons he could not understand, this was something that he dreaded.

"Look!" exclaimed Steven. "There's a small park with a slide and some swings over there."

He pointed across the street.

"Take the boys and I'll go for a little walk. Clear my

head. Join you in about twenty minutes."

He handed Susan the car key and headed off for a narrow lane some fifty yards back where he had spotted a signpost to the village church. For the first time ever, he felt that he was actually walking *towards* the piano, although he knew this was only in his head. No longer a faraway sound, it had welled up inside him to such a volume that the louder passages were deafening. Even in the quieter phrases each note could be clearly distinguished, and somehow the music seemed to mean so much to him. There was a sense of urgency as the sound of the piano pulled him towards the church.

He walked quickly, turning at the end of the small lane to find himself facing an insignificant-looking little church. He passed through the gate. A gravel path led to the door which was shut. Another veered off towards a jumble of gravestones, several of which leaned at garish angles, half obscured by weeds and overgrown grass. Steven followed this path as the piano music, now in A minor, swelled into a series of sweeping scales. It had become so loud that he felt his head might burst any minute. He stopped just as the music reached an intolerable, frenzied fortissimo.

Steven found himself standing beside one of the more modern, marble gravestones. Almost white, it stood out amongst the others, its top gently curved, casting a strong shadow in the midday sun. The gold inscription had been clearly carved, and, for several minutes Steven merely stared at this as though in a trance. At first, he only saw words and figures. The frantic music drumming into his brain seemed to prevent him from making any sense of what was written. He was aware of tears cooling his cheeks. Slowly, the writing on the gravestone formed itself into some sort of meaning. He read:

'In Sacred Memory of our beloved Son and Brother John Gautier, Pianist and Composer, taken from us so tragically and so suddenly on October 5th in the Year of our Lord, Nineteen Hundred and Ninety-Three, aged thirty years.'

Steven wiped away the tears with the back of his hand to read the words carved in smaller italics at the bottom of the gravestone:

God asks us only to understand through His love.

Steven, now kneeling on one leg, looked up again at the name... John Gautier. It seemed so familiar. Aged thirty. His own age. And the date of the man's death was some nine months before he himself had been born. Slowly, he stood up, and it was only then that he realised that the music had stopped. The silence that followed was almost as intense as the sound of the piano had been. During that silence he spent time clearing the weeds and tall grass surrounding the gravestone. It was the least he could do for his own grave.

The silence was suddenly broken by the noise of a car engine starting up. Gradually, Steven became aware of more sounds. Someone shouted; a dog barked; loud and bold, the shrieks of other children playing in the park. Then, the most wonderful sound that he could imagine... that of the shrill voices of his little sons. Just as the haunting music of the piano had drawn him to this secluded graveyard, he now felt the vitality and the joy of his two boys pull him back, away from the sadness of that place where a past life was half-remembered... away from death and towards new life. Steven ran to the park to be with his wife and the boys again. His excitement at seeing them, after a separation of only fifteen minutes, was so overwhelming that he rushed over to a rather surprised Susan, embraced her lovingly, and then romped around with his sons as though he had been away for months.

"You've made a quick recovery!" remarked Susan, laughing.

"Like I said, darling. Just needed a bit of a breather," said Steven.

Thereafter, the piano remained silent.

The Badger Set

'I, too, was once a man. Remember?'

She read the message scrawled, on the torn slip of paper, in a hurried writing that she knew so well, by a man she thought she also knew. Looking up, she opened her fingers and the paper fell, soundlessly, from her hand to the floor...

The first snowflake of a winter of perpetual sorrow.

A good opportunity to try out those new night vision binoculars, he thought. He'd not told Jennifer about them. In fact, he'd not told Jennifer about a lot of things.

It was a clear evening in late spring, and he reckoned if lucky—*really* lucky—he might catch a glimpse of the badger cubs. He knew exactly where the badger set was. Just across the ditch beside the road that curled around the lake beyond the golf-course. It was a quiet road; the golfers never went that far.

There was a small layby, a few hundred yards back from the site of the badger set, occasionally used by young lovers to do what young lovers do in cars. He reckoned this should not be a problem. They never get out of their cars, those young lovers, and their grunts of carnal ecstasy would be inaudible to passers-by, let alone badgers a quarter of a mile away. Thank goodness, for he hated hearing those endorphin-triggered gasps and moans, painful reminders of his own sexual inadequacy.

He could not remember when his attractive young wife, Jennifer, last gasped in response to his fumbled penetration of her. His impotence was a cause of nagging guilt for not only was Jennifer fifteen years his junior, but she was also pretty and exceptionally young looking for her thirty-five years. She surely had latent sexual feelings just waiting to burst free, waiting for that wonderful endorphin surge that follows unbridled erotic desire, the romantic tenderness culminating in gasps, moans and grunts.

Their love life had dwindled to nothing over the previous two to three years although he still loved her passionately. But the passion had been reigned in for fear of failure. It was as though their love had been hidden away, buried deep, and all that showed was a sexless friendship.

Jennifer deserved more. Still young and attractive, she *had* to have more. Of course, she was very understanding, but that was the worst of it. At first, when it all started, he would kiss and cuddle her, and they would both be roused even though he remained limp and useless. She wanted him, yearned for more, desired his manhood, he knew it, but nothing happened, and he became angry with his limpness, with his failure and with himself. She deserved more, needed more, and he could not give it to her. Who could, he began to wonder?

Who would?

The question frightened and excited him at the same time. Would she find a lover? How come the thought of this brought a little firmness back to his flimsy member in that bleak desert of impotence? What a strange thing the body is, he would tell himself, as he tried to coax more than a little firmness back into his prick. But it remained a useless thing, and the cuddles and the caresses in the matrimonial bed ceased.

Neil thought only of Jennifer as he drove along the narrow, tortuous road towards the beauty spot and the badger set. She looked so lovely when she had left for her dance class that evening. She said she would be late back. "Going for a drink with the girls afterwards," she told him.

The girls?

A little firmness returned to his penis as, in the darkness of his mind, he saw a potent stranger tear away her clothes before searching his wife's pretty body for those secret places of arousal. He was the fly on the wall, watching. Watching Jennifer being roused.

Watching her being f-----!

The car swerved dangerously, and Neil gripped the wheel more tightly as he tried to concentrate on the dark road, the kerb, the shadowed trees. He passed the beauty spot car park. It was empty. No bouncing cars. He drove the vehicle into a layby a few hundred metres further up the road. What a perfect evening, he thought, as he set up the night vision binoculars on a tripod, hidden discretely behind a bush. The cold, white light of the moon rendered the binoculars almost superfluous. He was less than fifty metres from the badger set, and he waited.

It was getting cold. He zipped up his jacket. He realised patience was required, and that he would wait all night if necessary. Waiting for the badgers and wondering about Jennifer. *Being f-----!* He thought of himself as a patient man, and his doctor had gone on about the importance of patience when they'd first talked about his problem

"Relax, Neil. Be patient. It'll come back. It usually does, you know."

It didn't. And he *was* patient, but nothing happened down there. He knew all about his illness, his diabetes, he knew impotence could be a problem for diabetics, and he knew it was his body failing both him and Jennifer. What

242

do you do when something fails? You get another one. *He* couldn't, but *she* could. As Neil stared at the hole in the ground through his night vision binoculars, he wondered how it would be for Jennifer, getting another penis for her own sweet hole. Would it feel the same for her, or would it simply be so much better? Had he been a poor lover? Would she discover that? Would he lose their past as well?

There had been a time when he thought he should talk about it to Jennifer. Have it out in the open. Could they then share the problem, for surely it was hers as well? But he did not know how to. He was afraid. Afraid it would, for her, merely put the seal on it. Turn his fly-on-the-wall fantasies into nightmares.

"Are you telling me to take a lover, then?" she might have asked. "Is that what you really want? So that you can just lie there and masturbate about it?"

How could she possibly understand? A passionate woman is receptive. What happens when there's nothing to receive any longer? Nothing physical. She waits, as he now waited for the badgers to show. She waits for a stallion-mounted knight to appear over the brow of the hill, praying she's still young enough to attract him. Oh, Jennifer was *certainly* that. A young thirty-five, and very, *very* attractive!

There were tests. He waited patiently for all those tests to come back. It was a lonely business, like waiting there, alone with his binoculars, for the badgers, for Jennifer did not know he had been to see the doctor about it. When the results came back, they told him nothing, gave him no hope.

The Viagra hadn't worked (Jennifer never knew about the Viagra either). Finally the doctor came to the conclusion that it was 'multifactorial'. When Neil asked what that meant, and whether there was treatment for it, the doctor, shook his head and said,

"...Diabetes, psychological stress and anno domini."

Anno domini? For God's sake, he wasn't yet fifty but had already lost the thing that allowed him to turn the very essence of his life, his love for Jennifer, into something tangible, something physical. Another baby. A child who might stay alive. Their loss still pained him beyond words, as it must have pained Jennifer back then.

There was a rustling from the ditch ahead. Neil froze. He peered into the darkness ahead where black tree shadows, cast by the moonlight, patterned the path and the ditch. The sound emerged from that shadowed darkness, but he was unable to make out anything definite.

Slowly, cautiously, he crept forwards with the night vision binoculars trained in readiness on the badger set. Inch by inch, each unblinking eye hovering over an eyepiece, until there, in the centre of his field of vision, appeared the pale triangular snout of a badger. Seen through the night vision binoculars, her eyes burnt like bright coals. Had she spotted him? For a few moments he held his breath for fear of disturbing the wonderful creature with the sound of his breathing.

She was unbelievably beautiful. Her pale snout twitched, her head turned, and those bright torch eyes were gone. They flashed again when she turned her head back to face him once more. Then, in a flash, she vanished, after retreating backwards into the set.

He remained statue-still, waiting, waiting, waiting... all other thoughts obliterated by his concentration on that little space on the side of the ditch where he had seen her snout appear from out of the dark earth. And in that concentration, for a few moments, he forgot his illness, his inability to perform, to satisfy his very own woman.

There she was again, her snout and her torchlight eyes, moving, unsure, turning, moving to the right, lost from view, back again, foraging, searching. Then, oh joy, another white snout, tiny in comparison, and another and another. Three badger cubs tumbled out into the ditch, and began to wrestle, yelp and dart about, randomly, but never far from their mother who continued her search for food.

At first he blamed it on their daughter's death. Now this seemed like a different existence altogether, their life with Emma, their little bundle of happiness. Lovemaking came so naturally to them back then. Nothing could dampen it, for it was a thing of mystery that had given life to the little girl, and Emma *was* their life. Her death from a mysterious illness at the age of five puzzled the doctors and destroyed that existence, turning joy into a pain that Neil would never, before, have believed possible. He and Jennifer clung to each other in their grief, but for a very long time the sex was gone. At first it seemed wrong to Neil, for the sex that had created little Emma no longer had a safe place in their lives. It felt wrong. After a while, the grief turned to sorrow, and the sorrow to numbness.

Jennifer healed more quickly, more easily, than Neil. Her circle of female friends gave her support, she began to do things in the evening to occupy her. She even joined a ballroom dance group. When they started to make love again, it was automatic for Neil, fumbling, heavy with guilt, and over far too soon for Jennifer. He made excuses. The usual ones. Headaches, tiredness, too much on his mind. Later when he did try, he usually failed. More excuses. Strangely, his failures made him desire her more. The

245

urge, the lust, returned, but still nothing happened.

The mother badger reappeared. Her head, then her whole body. Followed, again, one by one, by the cubs. They played, tumbling, snapping at each other, darting, zigzagging, bumping into their mother, always running... just as little Emma always used to.

Why did she run out of life? The doctors had been open and truthful. It was as though her young body had given up. All systems failed. Probably triggered by a virus infection, they said. Even when the child was on a life support machine, he refused to give up all hope, like a climber dangling over an abyss and clinging to a straining rope. And when the rope broke, and he fell into that abyss of sorrow and of death, it seemed as though he had been there all along. That interlude of happiness with Jennifer and with Emma was just a drop of liquid gold in an endless, black ocean of pain.

The badger cubs abandoned their play. They must have sensed their mother was heading off on a serious foraging expedition, maybe hoping to bag a chicken or two, and they ran after her in little bursts of energy as she waddled along the ditch, up and over the far side and on into scrub where the family vanished. The mother badger probably had no inkling of her cubs' vulnerability. Would death take them, too, before life could unravel her own secret mysteries for them? Would they turn into car-flattened, fur-covered remnants of unlived lives decorating a country lane tarmac?

Neil suddenly felt utterly useless. No longer a father, unable to satisfy his wife, the only person who now mattered to him, he had been powerless to warn the mother badger of the inevitable emptiness of life should her little youngsters be killed. He put the binoculars back in the bag, folded his tripod and returned to the car.

As he drove back towards the beauty spot, he saw a car in the lovers' car park. He braked, turned off the headlights and cut the engine. It was Jennifer's car. He could read the number plate. There was a light on in the car. He made out two heads in the back.

He got out of his vehicle and walked slowly towards his wife's, ensuring the tread of his feet on the grass verge was soundless. Beneath a tree, he stopped about twenty yards short of her car. And he watched. There was no need for him to worry about being spotted, for he could tell Jennifer was far too engrossed in...

Oh, God, this was so unlike those private erotic thoughts he had of his wife with another man. She really was being... Jesus Christ... being f-----!

In his dreams about Jennifer being fondled by a naked Adonis his penis would stiffen, but he could hold her there in his mind, have control. Out here in the dark, lovers' car park it was like watching a movie from which he was excluded, and his penis hung limp as he saw his wife jerk, now frantic, in response to the rhythmic thrusts of the other figure in her car. Her breasts were free, soft and pliant in the man's hand, and Neil remembered feeling those same breasts, their nipples firm, against his chest in a past that had been stripped from him. Jennifer's eyes were closed, her lips parted, and the silence was broken by her muffled gasps as she climaxed. The car window was open, so he could hear everything.

He turned and ran to his car. He switched on the engine, revving, angrily, with bursts from the accelerator pedal, slipped it into gear and the car shot forwards. He could not bear to look again at Jennifer as he sped past her and her lover. Could not bear to see the testosterone-driven bounce of her car. It was over. Everything was over. The drive home was just a blur, for all he could now see was the rapture on her face in that lovers' car park, her yielding breasts, the dark silhouette of the unknown man's head and shoulders. Back inside their house, his and Jennifer's, he scribbled a note and placed it carefully on the door mat. There was a tow rope in the back of the car. He would use that. He went outside again and removed the rope from the boot. The night vision binoculars were still there, in their bag, with the folded tripod. What use could Jennifer make of them, he wondered? Sell them, perhaps? She would now get nothing from his life insurance cover. He kicked the car, angry with himself for being such a total failure, and went back into the house. He chose the banister. There seemed to be nothing else appropriate. He practiced a few times with the knot. It would have to easily slide tight around his neck to do the job properly when he jumped. The drop, they used to call it, when this sort of thing was a part of the legal process.

On her way back home Jennifer felt no guilt. She knew Neil hated to talk about his problem, which meant nothing to her, she loved him so much. It was her friend at the dancing class who suggested it. Non-penetrative sex, she called it. Being a lesbian, the butch woman knew about that sort of stuff.

It all came out when Jennifer and her friend went for a drink after one of the classes. The other woman had hoped Jennifer had the same sexual inclination as herself, but Jennifer had laughed at the very thought of it.

"I'm sorry, but I'm terribly straight, you know. And I've got the most wonderful husband you could imagine."

"No, I can't imagine, I'm afraid," laughed the other woman.

They became good friends, secure in the knowledge of each other's differences. And her friend would ask her, curious, about sex with a man, and Jennifer would laughingly say, "I hardly remember," and her friend, serious, would respond, "But how awful!"

"It no longer matters," Jennifer said the day her friend came out with her suggestion.

"But what about your husband? How do you know it doesn't matter to him? Did he say as much?"

Jennifer had to admit that she and Neil never discussed sex. She told her friend about little Emma, and how he never got over the child's death.

"Won't it help him forget the past? To have sex again? You're still young enough to have another child."

It was then that she told her friend about her husband's problem, but her friend merely shrugged her shoulders.

"You don't have to have penetration to enjoy sex. *I* should know! You're such a funny lot, you straight people. So bloody inhibited!"

She came up with her suggestion. Jennifer was horrified, at first, but she knew the woman well, and realised that she was only trying to help, for Jennifer had said how distant Neil had become of late.

"He probably no longer feels wanted. Needed!"

How could this lesbian woman understand her husband better than herself? Nevertheless, her doubts had been fanned. She would try anything for her Neil. And so, the following week, after the dance class, the two woman drove to a secluded beauty spot, in the dark. Jennifer felt sure it was the right thing to do, for Neil had been so terribly withdrawn before she left for her class; muttered something in that soft, almost inaudible voice of his, about a badger set, but gave her no explanation of what he was on about. Her friend would teach her things. About erogenous zones, about responding to caresses, about sex without penetration, and *she* could teach Neil and together they might rediscover that closeness that had brought little Emma into the world.

She had only been able to go through with it by persuading herself, all the time, that the other person *was* Neil, and by keeping her eyes closed. Although with her short male-style haircut and thick neck, her friend could have passed for a man in the dim light, imagining she was aroused by some other man was almost worse than the thought of being aroused by a woman. No, it had to be Neil, she told herself, after removing her blouse and bra and skirt, and after those strong hands began to stroke and fondle those secret places that only Neil had touched before. He had been her first and only lover.

She had mixed feelings as she drove home. Her disgust at being touched and felt by another woman was made bearable by her determination that, in her mind, it had been Neil doing those things. Neil who had released those emotions in her head that allowed her to climax. But how would she get him to do the things her friend had done without upsetting him, making him feel inadequate? "Be open with him," her friend had said. "Och, you straight-laced straight folk! What a waste of a beautiful woman."

They both laughed, and, oh, she so wished she could make Neil laugh again like that.

She saw Neil's car in the drive. The lights were on in the house. She parked behind his car, walked up the drive, her erogenous zones still tingling from a strangely artificial orgasm, and she rang the bell. She had planned it in her mind: that he would open the door, she would fling her arms around him, take him by surprise, and whilst still smouldering from a sex session with her 'teacher' before becoming teacher herself, she would undress for him and put his hands, real man hands, in those tingly places.

No response. But he was definitely in. She tried again. The same. She took out her key, opened the door and stooped down to pick up a note she saw lying on the mat. Her smile and the tingling gone, she looked up, dropped the note and her bag... then she screamed and she screamed and she screamed...

The Wheel

From the way he stared at her, she knew that he knew.

She glanced down at her hands resting on her lap, at the mud spattered hem of her long dress, her cape and at his shiny patent shoes pointing at her, accusingly. She peered up at the smart, brown leather case on the luggage rack above the man. Terrified, she tried to keep his tall black top hat in focus. Anything but his face and those eyes, all the time fixed on her. Was it so very obvious? Perhaps he was trying to imagine her body swinging from the end of a rope, her miserable life jerking free in a final ghoulish death dance. She'd heard how it excited some men to see a young woman hang on the gallows. *He'll be one of those,* she thought as she fought the urge to fling open the door and leap from the moving coach and, if she were to survive the fall, run...

Run where? Anywhere! Across fields, through woods... keep on running... never stop... not until...

But *they* would catch her and hang her.

It was on such an impulse that she *did* run after it had happened, the thing from which she was so stupidly trying to escape. If only she had gone for help, explained everything, told the whole story, they might have believed her, and she would not now be fleeing for her life. Her fingers stroked her neck, feeling the smooth skin there. A pretty neck, her uncle in London had once said before she got married off to that fiend. *What happens to a pretty neck when they hang you?* she wondered. *Does it snap?* Her fingers trembled.

She'd had good reason to run. To escape from him. An opportunity she had only dreamt off for so long, but not in that way. Not running from the gallows. It had been bad before their son died the previous summer, but after her husband blamed the accident on her, accused *her* of taking away his only son, the torment of verbal abuse became unbearable.

The boy had fallen from a tree whilst collecting thrush eggs and his skull smashed against a rock like a cracked egg itself. He would have died instantly. She was beside herself with grief as she cradled his broken body in her arms, and yet, during the very worst moment of her life, the man swore and shouted at her. Perhaps if she had killed him back then she might have got sympathy from others in the village, her sentence commuted to life imprisonment. After all, life alone with that man had been nothing less than endless incarceration. But burning the stew? Could she expect any sympathy for killing him because he got upset when she burnt his stew?

Her fingers traced the cold trail of tears on her cheek. She wiped their dampness onto her cape and, with head bowed lest the gentleman opposite should see and misunderstand those tears, she fumbled for a handkerchief in the scruffy, hastily put together bundle on the seat beside her.

I must not give the man that pleasure, she told herself. *It'll only excite him all the more to think of me standing there on the scaffold with my face wet from crying.*

"Allow me," the gentleman said, leaning forward, offering her his handkerchief.

She looked up.

"I hate to see a young lady in distress. Please, if I can be of any assistance...?"

She watched his lips. No smirk. Her husband's turned-down lips had only ever smirked at her. He was clean-shaven, so unlike her husband whose chin was stubbled like a worn scrubbing brush and whose bitter face was crisscrossed with scars. *His* features—the man opposite—were unblemished. Almost aristocratic.

"You show me great kindness, sir, but I'll not be wanting to waste your time with my worries. Anyway..."

She stopped on seeing his searching blue eyes without a flicker of malice. *Not* the eyes of a man who would enjoy watching a young woman swing from the gallows. She could hold back no longer. Her hunched body shook as she sobbed into the large, clean, gentleman's handkerchief.

It truly was an accident. Although she had so often wished her husband dead, she had no intention of killing him when she swiped at his legs with the blacksmith's hammer. She only did this to stop him because she had barely recovered from that last belt beating. As he dragged her off to his work shed, his heavy buckled belt dangling from his hand, and with all that anger in his eyes, she knew she could take no more. Not with the bruises from the previous day's beating still racking her body. Yes, the stew was burnt, but she apologised. On her knees. Begging him not to hit her again. Trying to tell him how distracted she had been that day, for it was the anniversary of their son's death, but this only incensed him all the more. His anger and blame resurfaced, magnified to grotesque proportions.

"I'll beat some sense into you, you good-for-nothing, miserable bitch!" he screamed, pulling her backwards by her hair across the yard. In the shed, horseshoes lay strewn on the ground beside the anvil. A buckled iron gate rested against a workbench near the anvil and the coals in the brazier glowed, red as the portals of Hell. She felt their heat as he yanked her towards the rope dangling like a hangman's noose from the rafter.

Her husband was certainly one of those men who would have enjoyed seeing a girl hang, only he was usually too busy to go into Marlborough whenever a hanging came up. He worked hard. Indeed, some said he was the best blacksmith in the county. Of course, no one else knew about the beatings and the mental cruelty, and from the way other villagers had spurned her after her boy's death, she was certain he had poisoned them all against her with the blame of it.

He was going to tie her arms to that dangling rope again and, as he loved to put it, 'beat the living daylights out of her.' Since her son's death this had happened regularly, and it was far worse than the usual beatings he inflicted in the cottage with a stick. Sometimes she could barely walk for days afterwards, and that particular day she could no longer face it. She fought back. She needed time to herself to recall those interludes of happiness with her son, now fading memories. If only she hadn't confided with the boy about the eggs, she was thinking when the stew got burnt. She had forgotten to buy eggs in the market the previous day, and it being Wednesday, her husband would demand eggs with his lunch. Their son hated to see his mother get beaten, but she had no idea he would go to the lengths of raiding a thrush's nest in the old birch tree to prevent the inevitable chastisement. So when her husband blamed *her* for the child's death, the guilt was already there, gnawing at her heart.

"Tell me about it. You're running away, aren't you?" She nodded without looking up. "From your husband?" Again, she nodded. *Oh God,* she thought, *he'll turn me in.* "What you tell me will get no further than the confines of this carriage," he reassured her as if reading her mind.

Her hand holding the handkerchief dropped. She allowed her gaze to return to his face for a brief instant but immediately looked away because his eyes were kind and she knew there was no kindness in the world. Only cruelty and death. Soon, her own death. An illusion of kindness seemed worse than none at all.

"Everything!" he insisted. "I want to know *everything.*"

Gradually bits of the story emerged, fragmented. In between choking sobs, she told him about the beatings and the verbal abuse... and about her loss. The words that emerged from her mouth were barely intelligible when she reached the bit about the death of her darling boy... the blame... and the eggs.

"He went to collect eggs for his mother. And why shouldn't he? He was doing it for you. It shows how much he loved you. No, the blame is with the father. For treating a young wife so cruelly. Maybe now that you're gone, the man will come to his senses. Realise how lucky he is to have such a gracious wife. How could he...?"

She started to shake uncontrollably. So much so that he came across and sat beside her. Not to take advantage, for she sensed he wasn't that sort of a man. He didn't even touch her. He had too much respect. It was a gesture. He was letting her know he wanted to help her and closeness does that. It shuts out the uncertainty of the unknown. By being beside her, he was excluding the rest of the world, yet *still* she could not tell him. She only shook her head, slowly, as her mind filled with awful images of herself grabbing the hammer from the workbench whilst her enraged husband dragged her by the hair towards the rope. Of her swinging the hammer at his legs and of him falling, like a felled tree, landing on the brazier and screaming when yellow flames leapt from his clothes, crying out with pain and prancing about before he dropped to the ground when his legs finally gave way, his hair on fire, the smell of smoke and burning flesh filling the work shed.

"I should have..." she began, about to say more—a lot more—about the threat of being beaten yet again, the hammer, the brazier, her husband catching fire and how she had dithered for a few brief moments, wondering whether or not to call for help before fleeing with a quickly-prepared bundle of clothes and the money she found in her husband's wooden chest behind his barrel of beer in the pantry.

She never got to tell the gentleman these things. A terrific bang was followed by a scraping sound and sudden jolt, flinging her violently against her travel companion and knocking his hat to the ground. The carriage tipped sideways, jerking to a halt.

"WO-AAH!" shouted the coachman against a background of agitated whinnying from the two horses.

"I... I'm so s-s-sorry, sir," she stuttered when she realised she was clutching the gentleman's arm. She edged away from him. Reluctantly. It was so different to that awful animal closeness when her husband forced himself on her. She was sensing something she had never before felt, and she blushed.

"Don't apologise!" he insisted, reaching down for his fallen hat. "You've nothing to be sorry about. Are *you* all right, though? Your arm... is it hurt?"

"Nothing, sir. Just a fright. But what...?"

"Broken wheel. Axel must have snapped. Wait here."

The man opened the carriage door and jumped down. How agile, she thought, her blush deepening. He spoke to the coachman but she wasn't listening. Fear had gripped her again now that she was alone. They'd give chase as soon as the body was discovered. Marlborough was the only place she could flee to— she'd taken the only coach that morning—then from Marlborough on to London, then... to her uncle? How could she ever have believed that she might escape? And now this wheel! She was doomed and the tears streamed as she realised this had to be God's punishment. Not for hitting her husband, but for telling her son about the eggs. Oh, how she feared death, the only possible outcome of His punishment.

"The metal axel's snapped, as I thought."

She looked up. The man was back at the coach door.

"Coachman says he's never had this happen before. He'll have to wait for the coach coming the other way from Marlborough. Then they can take the axel back to Avebury. A good blacksmith there, he says. You should go with them. I'll have to leave you, though. See if I can borrow a horse from a farm a few miles up the road. Have to get to Marlborough urgently."

For a few moments, when their eyes met, it seemed as if they shared a thought: that she should come with him. But neither spoke and she instantly dismissed the notion as the madness of one soon to be condemned to death.

"You *will* be all right, won't you?" he asked. "He'll want you back so much, I'm sure of it. *I* would... erm... I mean he'll realise now how much he's wronged you."

Oh, I wish to tell you everything. Everything! And I want to die.

But she only nodded.

"Take care," he said.

She looked for his handkerchief lost somewhere in the folds of her dress.

"Keep it! In memory of one who'd have done so much more if only he could have."

He turned and walked away. She was certain she heard him repeat the words *'so much more'* to himself before she flung herself across the carriage seat and wept.

"It'll not be long, Miss, the carriage from Marlborough. No need to fret. There's one this afternoon. Were you to be met there? In Marlborough?"

It was the coachman. She said not a word. Not then, nor on the coach from Marlborough, in which a small boy travelling with his mother stared at her throughout the journey. And she said nothing to the constable waiting for her when they arrived back at the coach station of her hometown of Avebury. She knew him. One of her husband's drinking companions. As he bound her wrists, she wished he would hang her there and then to get it over with. That afternoon, she was on the coach bound for Marlborough again, with the constable and the coachman.

The jail was a cold, windowless stone cell, four foot by six, with nothing but a bucket and some straw on the floor, and the jailer a toothless hunchback who seemed only able to grunt, but from the way he looked at her she could tell he was a man who would enjoy watching a young woman swing. That night he brought her a bowl of cold broth and a crust of bread. Before handing her the bowl he spat in the broth. From the leering grin he gave her, she knew what he wanted. She threw the bowl to the ground, and, when he had gone, she crouched in the corner of the cell, her head on her knees, and cried. All night, she cried.

In the morning, the jailer was back with an officer of the law. She was to be taken upstairs to the magistrate's court, where, without a shadow of doubt, she would be committed to trial before a judge and jury and thence to the gallows. Her head was swimming from lack of sleep, her vision blurred.

"See you in Hell, my pretty one. Might find you more willing there, ay? They're *all* willing in Hell!" the jailer shouted after her as she climbed the stairs.

There was a flight of wooden stairs leading up to the court room. When the door was opened she was hit by a wave of raucous voices. A young woman up for murder and the promise of a hanging? The courtroom was packed! She entered and, as she was taken to the dock, the noise of jeers and whistles rose to such a pitch she thought her head would burst.

"Hang the murderess! Let her swing! Send her to the gallows!" they eagerly shouted, over and over, shaking their fists at her.

The little door to the dock slammed behind her, and she tried hard to shut out the jeers and whistles as she stood, eyes swollen, bound wrists aching. She wondered how it would be up there on the scaffold. More yells and catcalls? And her hair? What would they do about her hair? She loved her long, wavy, dark auburn hair. Her uncle had often said how pretty it was. She liked her uncle. He was a kind man, like the gentleman on the coach. If only she had escaped and fled to London *before* it happened, before the 'murder' for she now believed she truly *was* a murderess, for she *had* wished him dead.

"Silence!" roared the clerk.

A hush blanketed the courtroom. The magistrate entered, causing subdued murmuring from the public gallery which was cut short by the thud of the hammer on his desk. She looked down at her bound hands in shame. A murderess! She deserved to hang for her carelessness in telling her son she had forgotten to buy eggs for that ogre.

There was talking. Strings of words. She wasn't fully listening, but the word 'accused' kept on recurring. *Her.* The accused. Soon to be condemned and hanged.

The door to the dock was opened.

"Didn't you hear the magistrate?" the court officer asked, pulling her roughly by the arm. "He wants you down there. Before his desk. He often does that. In case the accused can't hear properly, I s'pose. There's many lose their ears before their lives, ay?"

She stumbled on the steps down to the magistrate's desk and she was aware of tittering from the gallery. Alone, in front of the desk, she kept her head bowed whilst staring at the ground which she wished would open up and swallow her forever.

"Unbutton the good lady's dress at the back!"

That voice? No, it can't be!

"Hurry, man. I don't have all day!"

It *was* him, without a shadow of doubt. Her shame felt a thousand times worse. Why should he humiliate her even further by exposing her back to the public? Doubtless to show what a slut she had been to enrage her husband so. 'Such a decent man,' she had already heard the constable tell the court room, referring to that monster of a husband of hers. It felt cool on her back as the officer pulled apart her unbuttoned dress. Cool and sore, and there was a hum of unease from the gallery when the recent injuries inflicted by her dead husband's belt were exposed.

"Shame on you all!" the magistrate bellowed. "Shame on every man and woman here who shouted at this poor young woman before I entered. Oh yes, I heard you! Heard your abuse! Well, I'll say just one thing. There is more goodness, more nobility in this woman you see here than in all of you put together."

Tears trailed her cheeks. She couldn't look at him. She thought she *must* be dreaming and that by looking at him he might disappear and she'd find herself back in that hell of verbal torment.

"I want you all to hear the truth. From the woman herself. And..." He paused, turning to face her. "You can look at me now, young lady. And take all day should you need to. Believe me, I have time for your words. And spare them no details," he added, addressing her alone, his tone turned gentle.

She looked up. In a faltering voice, after her dress had been re-buttoned, and without taking her eyes off the magistrate, she continued the story she began on the coach. There was not a whisper, not even a cough, from the public gallery. And when she had finished, silence hung heavy in the courtroom as she waited for reality to vanish, for the nightmare to return.

It didn't.

"The woman goes free," announced the magistrate. "She has suffered enough. I record death by misadventure, not murder nor even manslaughter. The only accused here are those of you who showed her no pity. Take your shame with you. Think about it. And pray to God that one day He may forgive you!"

No one spoke as they filed out of the courtroom. Soon there was only her and the magistrate left, still looking at each other in disbelief.

"Well, thank heaven for that broken wheel, ay?" he said at last. A slight frown disclosed her puzzlement. "If you'd gone on to London *they* would have caught up with you," he explained. "Who knows what would have happened if you'd been thrown to the legal wolves! Tell me, now that you're free, what will you do? Will you still go on to London or will you return to the forge?"

She did not know what to say. She had only given thought to the gallows and final public humiliation.

"Well then," he continued, "I have a proposal to make. You see, since my wife and son were killed in a coach crash—yes, I know how you, too, must have suffered when your own boy died—and since then it's been difficult for me to... well... erm ... to keep house on my own. It's too large a house for one person, I suppose. So my proposal is this. Would you at least consider a position as my housekeeper? That is, if you'll put up with my untidiness. And my moods... although, in all honesty, I think the moods might become less of a problem if you were to accept."

She wiped her sleeve across her eyes to clear her vision and to get a better picture in her mind of the man who spoke those words. The mysterious gentleman on the coach, with the top hat and the shiny shoes. She opened her mouth, but nothing emerged from it.

"Please... if you're not sure just say so. Should you need more time, then—"

"Yes, sir!" she interrupted. "Yes, yes, yes!"

And his smile reflected something she had all but

forgotten since her son had died. Love. Here was a man she could love.

The Lady on the Train

Keith sat down, awkwardly, on the only empty seat in a carriage of the Yamanote Line train. The conference was over, but he had a day free in which to see a few of the sights of Tokyo. Still jet-lagged, his head full of the arguments and controversies from the meeting, and feeling totally confused by the Japanese subway system, he remained on the edge of his seat, as the train slid out of the station, sandwiched between a neatly dressed, expressionless lady of indeterminate age and a sleeping businessman in a dark suit.

Keith was not used to having time off from work, even if it was just for one day. He opened the Tokyo guidebook. What, he wondered, might he see of this vast city in a single day? Seated opposite was a young man in a leather jacket and dyed reddish hair fashioned into a nineteen-eighties punk cut. Between him and an extremely pretty girl with long, sleek hair of a similar artificial colour shade, sat two salarymen with shiny briefcases perched on their laps. All four had their eyes closed and appeared to be asleep. At the end of the row a studious-looking youth was reading a book.

Keith peered at his watch as the train slowed into a station. Considering the distances involved with the itinerary suggested by his conference hosts, he realised he would be spending a lot of his short stay in Tokyo on the subway. He needed to modify this.

Keith found it easy to make quick adjustment decisions. Still single at thirty-eight, he had gone through life alone. His career was the only true motivating force in his life. No one else to complicate the decision-making process, and this suited Keith fine.

It wasn't that he found the opposite sex unattractive. Indeed, at that very moment he was finding it quite difficult not to look at the shapely legs of the sleeping Japanese girl seated opposite. Over the years Keith had had several girlfriends but he had never met a woman with whom he felt prepared to share his personal space and for whom he might abandon his freedom. Plus there was another thing. None of these girlfriends could compare with the woman in those dreams.

They started when Keith was a teenager. He began to have recurring dreams about a girl, a dream friend, with whom he shared everything. His love for her was intense. He would always awake from such dreams feeling happy and fulfilled. On those days, what happened afterwards, during the waking day, seemed unimportant, almost unreal. As Keith grew up so did the girl in his dreams. The dreams recurred, sometimes nightly, sometimes not for months. He and the girl, now a woman, became closer and shared this dream life like man and wife in a city he new so well when asleep, but which bore no resemblance to anywhere that he had ever visited... until he found himself in Tokyo.

In his real world she was without name, this woman of his dreams, but she was always there, inside himself. Perhaps this was the reason that would have made it difficult for him to marry. Any other woman would have seemed like a stranger to Keith.

The train stopped and one of the salarymen suddenly opened his eyes as though preprogrammed to wake up at that precise moment. He immediately stood up and got off the train. Meanwhile, Keith scanned his guidebook, flicking through the pages he had marked in an attempt to prioritize the key sights in Tokyo. He prided himself on his ability to make instant decisions. That was surely why he had become so successful in business.

The doors closed and the train started off again, accelerating rapidly out of the station. Keith looked up.

For a while he sat in total disbelief, unable to move. He could hardly take in a breath, as he stared at the lady in the seat vacated by the salaryman. He looked away, then looked back at her. A sense of total confusion and near panic overcame him. He tried to feel and think rationally. There, sitting opposite him, was just another Japanese woman. Yes, she *was* pretty and young looking, but... *here in Tokyo most of them are, anyway,* he thought. And she was, of course, a complete stranger. Then his mind stopped being rational. This *was* the woman of his dreams. Of this, he was in no doubt. For the first time in his life he was looking at her whilst awake. As certain as though his own mother had walked onto the train and sat down in front of him.

He tried to be rational. A successful businessman, he simply had to be. *She,* the woman of his dreams, did not exist. Also, this lady was Japanese. How could the woman of his dreams be Japanese? For once in his life he had to be wrong.

But Keith knew that he was never wrong. He continued to stare at the lady opposite him. She was dressed in a blue skirt and matching blouse. Her legs were crossed, and, for a while, she sat looking down at her hands; hands that had caressed him a million times.

When she looks up I'll see her eyes properly, he thought to himself. *Then I'll see how stupid I've been.*

She looked up. She looked straight into his eyes. It *was* her. Even that brief, momentary eye contact was enough for Keith to feel once more all the warmth of their lifelong passion, her humour and her understanding of his funny little ways. Enough to make him realise how much he loved her, and how much he missed her during his waking life. He wanted to call out to her, knowing now that she was for real, but his head could not come up with a name. Never had he felt so uncertain, so lacking in confidence.

This lady, a total stranger whom he loved and understood more than anyone else in his life, now looked at him as though expecting an announcement. His mind was awash with words, with thoughts, but he merely sat and stared. She smiled, as though trying to help him, as always, with his difficulty, his embarrassment, but this simply made things worse.

How he loved that smile. His return smile was little more than a facial contortion. Her eyebrows lifted, in amusement, as they sat looking at each other and as Keith tried to think of something to say. Perhaps she spoke no English. He tried to remember what language they used in his dreams. Was it English?

When the train entered the next station the lady raised her eyebrows again. He knew that expression so well. One she always wore if something inevitable was about to happen. Something that they would have to face together...

Oh, to be together with her, and in real time!

The train stopped. A group of chattering, mini-skirted, Japanese schoolgirls crowded onto the carriage. To Keith's annoyance, they moved along in front of him and, holding onto the straps, stood between himself and the woman in the blue skirt. The doors closed, and one of the schoolgirls, who kept looking down at him, and who had not stopped talking since boarding the train, whispered in her friend's ear as Keith leaned to one side in an attempt to make eye contact with the woman again. The other girl glanced at Keith and giggled into her hand, unaware that this strange '*gaijin*' had no interest in her and her friend, and that they were simply getting in the way. The schoolgirls continued to whisper and giggle as the train sped off into the tunnel. Keith just wished they would move.

Once more, the train slowed as it arrived at the next station before groaning to a halt. Keith panicked on seeing the lady was now standing and making her way towards the door. Never had Keith felt so helpless. He simply did not know what to do. *She* was leaving the train. An unknown Japanese woman in this strangely foreign city, his brain informed him it would be madness to approach her. She might call for the police, claiming harassment. He envisaged himself surrounded by a crowd of aggressive, gesticulating Japanese shouting in their incomprehensible language.

She slipped through the doors as soon as they slid open. Keith remembered that briefly shared gaze and, like a Jack-in-the-box, he shot up out of his seat, rudely pushing aside the schoolgirls who gasped, their startled eyes wide with disbelief. He grabbed the two doors, which had already started to close, and for a moment the Englishman stood trapped between them as they continued to open and close against him like the jaws of a large carnivore trying to tackle something indigestible. Finally the doors opened fully and Keith was disgorged, alone, onto the platform.

'Shinjuku' was the name of the station spelt out in understandable '*romanji*' letters beneath the Japanese script on the wall. The place was teeming, but, to his relief, he glimpsed the woman further along the platform: a small figure with long black hair, in a blue skirt and blouse, heading for the stairs. Keith zigzagged between commuters who politely ignored him. She had already reached the top of the stairs as he started to scale them two or three at a time.

At the top of the stairs, sweating and breathless, he was overcome with fear. Fear of losing her. A huge passageway confronted him. As far as he could see in both directions, it was almost solid with a moving throng of Japanese. There was a confusing array of signs and notices in Japanese script, and huge advertisements with grinning oriental faces adorning the walls. In mounting desperation he searched the ceaselessly moving hordes... then, as if by some miracle, he saw her again.

She was heading for the west exit. Again Keith took off, quickly weaving through the crowd, but he never seemed to get any closer to her.

"I must reach her, I *must*," he muttered aloud, now forcefully pushing people out of the way. Once again, she disappeared as the west exit veered off towards the right. When Keith reached the same spot, he was confronted by yet another vast space filled with black-haired people moving in all directions. However, to his relief he could still see her. She was standing still and appeared to be searching for something in her handbag. This would surely be his last chance to catch up with her, and it was imperative that they should have 'real' time together. He would talk to her, even if she understood no English. He would try to explain everything to her. He simply had to be with her, however briefly.

As Keith pushed on, through the crowd, the lady

passed quickly through the exit gates without looking back. Had she done so, he might have caught her attention. Thankfully, she stopped again, just beyond the gates.

At last he reached the exit, just yards from the woman. His heart was racing and his hand trembled as he fed the ticket into the slot. He rushed forward…

Slam! He bumped into the gates as they snapped shut in front of him. Then he remembered. They had told him to get the cheapest fare and then pay the difference at the fare adjustment window. He called to the lady in blue as she pulled out a mobile phone from her handbag. Unaware of his attempts to draw her attention, she keyed a number into the phone, held it to her ear and started to talk. Keith shouted, in vain, clumsily backing out from the exit before rushing over to the fare adjustment queue. After fumbling in his pocket he pulled out a crumpled collection of yen notes. He looked up. She was still there, talking into her phone. He now saw her face so clearly and was in no doubt. It was *her*, and he had to reach her.

"For God's sake hurry up," he muttered, impatiently shifting from one foot to the other. A small lady with frizzy black hair, standing in front of him, turned around and looked at him, her full-moon face expressionless like that of a Buddhist nun. Keith kept his eyes on the lady in blue still speaking on the phone. Her conversation appeared animated and she smiled. Her last smile had been for him, he remembered. Whilst the frizzy-haired lady paid her fare adjustment, Keith told himself he just had to make it, he so needed to reach the woman who lived in his dreams and they would, at long last, be together, however briefly.

Keith handed the metro official a fistful of notes, shrugging his shoulders when asked a question in Japanese. The man examined Keith's ticket, quickly keyed numbers into a machine then returned all but one of the notes together with a few coins. Keith grabbed these and looked up.

She was gone. It had taken only seconds, but she was no longer there. He scanned the merging columns of moving people stretching in every direction. Shinjuku station seemed like a living being, and the lady in blue, the stranger whom he knew to be his partner in another life, a dream life, had been swallowed up by this creature. Any further search for her in this alien world would be pointless. His only chance of ever meeting up for real with the one person who mattered to him was gone. The knowledge that she *was* a real person, and not a fabrication of his dreams, seemed to change everything. The confidence of being in total control of his destiny, a hallmark of his life to date, had, in those brief moments, been replaced by hollow despair. Forever, he would remain alone. She was real and there could be no one else. Never.

(Note: Over two million passengers pass through Shinjuku station, in Tokyo, every day... Every day?}

The Island

The sun always shines on the island so close to the shore that even the weakest of swimmers should be able to reach it. Whatever the weather on the bleak beach where I stand, the island basks in sunlight illuminating a paradise of lush vegetation and gentle rolling hills, plus, even from the beach, you can read the joy on the faces of folk on the island.

I thought I was a reasonably good swimmer. Not strong, but all right. *'The distance from the shoreline to the island is trifling,'* I remember thinking. *'Even a child can do it!'* Children must have swum to the island for you can see them there at play, running about. Hear their shrill laughter. Yet I never made it.

Every time I dived into the sea, waves rose up and burled me back onto that wretched beach. Plus evil-eyed monsters, unleashed from the depths, their snapping jaws crammed with razor-sharp, ivory teeth, made sure I would get no further than the first line of waves, whilst shark fins cut sinister curls on the still surface beyond these waves. Bedraggled and exhausted, I would crawl back to the beach, then sit, watching, whilst others, including disabled people, happily waded into the water. For them, the waves, reversing their direction, became gentle hillocks bearing them out to the island, The monsters became harmless floats onto which the swimmers clambered. So, of course, I would return to the ocean where, again, the waves and the monsters would repel me. Again I would end up panting on the beach. Again, again and again!

Why did I so desire that island? The answer stood behind me, hollow-faced and black-cloaked, leaning teasingly on his sharpened scythe, watching me fail *ad nauseam*. He could wait for all eternity, but for me time was running out. Fast. He knew that.

And now? I'm dead, of course. My bones lie bleached on that beach, my only consolation being the knowledge that there is no island.

Highland Fling

No reply. She tried his mobile phone. Turned off. Panic set in.

Guilt? Was this why she panicked. As she waited for the taxi to take her to the station, all she now wanted was to speak to him, hear his voice. She would know from his voice whether he knew.

Her mind, jumbled like the clothes she had hurriedly pushed into her suitcase, was making things worse. So was the cold. Middle of May, and she felt cold, standing outside peering at the empty driveway leading up to the hotel whilst waiting for the taxi. Was she a cold person, she wondered? Had that been the trouble all along? Was this why David had become so withdrawn and boring? Why the sex had stopped?

'Depressed,' her brother suggested when she told him about David. God, why did big brother have to complicate things? How she needed sex when that e-mail appeared on her iPhone.

'Highland Fling?—Stefan.'

That's all that her boss, Stefan, had written, but it sent her heart, like that of a lovesick schoolgirl, into a gallop as she sat at her desk grinning to herself. The two of them had already been there, in her dreams, naked and at it like rutting deer, but this was for real. She knew all about the contract for a new hotel in Perthshire, and she knew he fancied her from the way he ogled her legs, her bosom, whenever he passed her by on his way to his office, and, right enough, her mock bashfulness on catching his eye must have sent him messages. That e-mail pieced things together. Perfectly.

Stefan had a reputation, but what did she care? Sex again. At last. Sheer heaven! He had chosen her, and why shouldn't she have a fling? She needed to escape from the dreary day-by-day drudge with Dave for however long the fling might last.

She clicked on reply and typed *'Yes!'*

It was all too easy. Stefan, the architect assigned to the job, needed a secretary to go with him. He said. Why he had to see the site again remained a mystery to her, but she had no desire to argue the point. Only to get into bed with the hunk. The evening before, Dave sat slouched in front of the telly, his usual morose self, whilst she packed her case with the most revealing of dresses and skirts in her wardrobe and the prettiest of the panties in her undies drawer.

I will try, she thought with the merest pinprick of guilt when Dave finally crawled into bed that evening. *Try to rekindle our dead passion.* She wrapped her arms about him, pressed her breasts against his back. He merely grunted.

That did it. Why should she feel any guilt?

She must have tried phoning at least ten times on the train between Perth and Edinburgh. It was the way he sounded on the phone that made her feel so awful. And he *never* phoned her, just like he never talked to her. So why then, of all times? When she was in bed with Stefan, so electrified with sex she expected sparks might fly from her as she picked up her mobile. What a lover her boss was. If only she had turned off her phone, but she had been in too much of a hurry to give herself to Stefan—every square inch of her body—to think about piffling things like phones.

Thoughts of sex again, at long last, had clung to her mind like decorations on a tired Christmas tree as they toured Perthshire in his Lexus, stopping off at the House of Bruar for lunch. He kissed her, properly, on the walk up to the waterfall. Even carried her a short way in his arms when she complained that high-heeled shoes weren't the best footwear for a highland fling. She could not imagine David even lifting her toes off the ground. And he bought her a brooch in the shop there. It was beautiful. An elaborate Celtic design superimposed over a thistle.

"In memory of our highland fling!" he whispered in her ear.

But why a thistle? This pained her.

"What's she like?" Dave asked after giving his wife a chaste kiss on the cheek before she left the house early that morning.

"Who?"

"Your boss."

"Oh, fine! Smart! Yes, always smartly dressed... and... erm..."

She blushed as she imagined her boss without any clothes on. Of course, Dave somehow assumed it would be a woman. Stefan was always merely referred to as the 'boss'.

"Don't forget to bathe the children. And take those ready meals out of the freezer. Bye darling! Love you!"

True, she thought as she climbed into the taxi. She loved David. *So why am I doing this? Why is the lure of a highland fling with my predatory boss driving me crazy?* Then she recalled the grim silences, the grunts, the rows, although now David rarely flew off the handle. She so desperately needed a break from all of this. And with Stefan. It was as if heaven had fallen into her lap. She tried to imagine what it would be like to be kissed by him as she sat on the train towards Pitlochry watching fields, houses, hills drift past the window.

The train hurtled towards Edinburgh, but it was still not fast enough. The woman opposite stared, plainly puzzled, as she dialled home every few minutes. She avoided the woman's gaze, for she would have surely broken down if asked why she could not stop trying the same number. She wanted no sympathy for what she had done. Only a return to the past, however dull, however awful that had been. At Edinburgh Waverley, she used the public call box. In case David might answer a call from an unknown number, and hoping the past from which she had tried to escape was still there, safe, comfortable… dreary.

How stupid to think one phone might work whilst another wouldn't, but the whole sordid affair was stupid. Most of all, her expectation that she could have a fling on the side, enjoy sex again, and afterwards everything would fall neatly back into place as though nothing had happened.

She couldn't help herself. To be kissed like that again after so long, to feel his strong hands searching her body as though already naked, it caused any lingering traces of guilt to evaporate like spilt wine in the heat of a tropical sun.

"Can we go back to the hotel now?" she asked.

The words seemed to come from another woman's mouth. A woman without the burden of a loveless marriage and forever demanding children. A woman who would give herself to a man she barely knew.

Barely?

"You're in a hurry!"

She didn't know whether to laugh, to cry or to slap him across the cheek. But it was true. She wanted it there and then, in the House of Bruar.

She remembered once, as a child, running breathless into the sea at North Berwick.

"You wouldn't dare," challenged her elder brother. It was cold enough for others to be wearing sweaters, although it was midsummer.

"Who says I wouldn't?"

She ran, and the cold water hit her with shock waves that turned her legs into jelly and made her scream out, but she did it, she splashed and dived in and came out and she survived.

"Wow!" her surprised brother exclaimed as he handed her a towel. She felt like a tribal Pictish queen who had just proved herself in battle. And now she had won again, a break from tedium, a highland fling, because of her looks and her figure.

Or was it just sordid sex that had won on behalf of that selfish Pictish queen's carnal pleasure?

She climbed into the taxi.

"Can you please hurry?" she asked the driver.

"Hurry? In Edinburgh during Festival time? Sorry, hen, but I cannae afford to lose my licence!"

The brooch. It was still there, on her blouse. Shakily, her hand trembling, she removed it and hid it at the very bottom of her bag. Why the bottom? David would never search her bag. Like he'd not searched her body for over two years. Perhaps it was the guilt that she was trying to hide?

Oh God, she thought, *David must not find out. It'll kill him.*

The taxi stopped outside the familiar row of austere, terraced grey stone houses. The light was on, up there, on the third floor. She felt relieved. He must have got back since her last attempt to call him at Waverley Station. The taxi left her standing alone in the street, uncertain whether to phone again, and talk to David from her past, or whether to go on up and dive, like that teenage Pictish queen, into a cold, uncertain future.

He almost tore the clothes from her as they embraced in the hotel room. She fumbled with his shirt buttons, pulled at his sleeves and felt for his belt. And when they tumbled together onto the king bed, neither had on a stitch of clothing and, as they came together as one, she gasped and called out his name over and over again. She felt as though she was being reborn when she climaxed and she hung onto the man, holding him close for fear of losing forever the sheer joy of it.

It was only three in the afternoon, but she and Stefan remained there, in bed, until early evening, and she marvelled at how he often came, and how many times she accepted him, during those hours of sexual bliss.

"Mr and Mrs Grzwybowski, eh? Can't even pronounce it properly!" she giggled as they sipped red wine later in the dining room.

"No matter!"

She felt hurt. If this was a proper relationship it *did* matter. To her, at least. He was supposed to have taken her hand and given her a little lesson in Polish

280

pronunciation.

"How come? The name? You sound Scottish enough."

"Grandfather came over as a free Pole during the war. To see how many Scottish girls he could please."

"I'm sure he... I mean, I don't think..." She was aware that she had turned deep scarlet.

"And you know a thing or two about free poles now, huh?" He pointed at his crutch. She wanted to hit him. It wasn't just the crude gesture, it was the triumphant look on his face. God, what an actor! In bed the gentle smiles, caresses, the soft words of love, and now he was mocking her. Of course she'd known all along this was only a pleasure thing for 'Stefan the Polish Prick', but surely he could go along with the deception of it for a little longer? "So what is it with this nameless husband of yours?" he asked.

Nameless? She was certain she'd told Stefan he was called 'David'.

"What's what?"

"You know! Can't get his end up, then? With a girl like you?"

A girl? Like me? What am I like?

"That's nothing to do with..."

"Oh, but it is!" insisted Stefan placing his hand over hers on the table. "Any children?"

She had definitely told him that she had a boy of six and girl of four. Plus how having children had changed her marriage. It was after their daughter was born that David lost interest in sex, and she thought at the time that Stefan might read between the lines and understand, but it was clear to her now that he hadn't even been listening. She was just a toy to play with, then, afterwards, to throw away.

"Shouldn't we be talking about the hotel you're designing?" she asked.

Change of subject, leave David out of it, finish the meal and then more glorious sex?

"You? A mere office girl? Ha! I like it! Shows you've got spirit, though. Mind you, you showed me plenty of that upstairs. Not had such an eager bedmate for a long time!"

"Bedmate? Is that all you think of me?"

"It's all you wanted, isn't it? You're a married woman. Why else do you think I chose you for a nice little highland fling?

Why else? He chose me because I'm married. So he can boast about it in the pub

"I'm really not feeling hungry!" Was this all she could come up with?

"Look I'm sorry! Why don't we... you know...?" he began. She withdrew her hand, still staring at the delicious, untouched meal on her plate. "Mrs Grswybowski?"

She laughed. Such a silly name. And such a silly predicament. In the Highlands, having fling with a predatory womanizer who happened to be her boss, and having already sinned enough to get a dozen one-way tickets to Hell with a body still hungry for something much more than food. She knew it could not last after the things he said, but the sex had been mind-boggling, and, well... Why not? One last time?

Back in the bedroom, on that king bed, she let it happen all over again, but now it was different. She felt cheap and unclean and, although she got back into bed

282

with Stefan intending to turn the tables around, and to use him for *her* enjoyment, it did not end up like that. Once again it was she who gave herself to him, she who climaxed and cried out for more... and more...

And that's when her mobile phone rang. Breathless, with Stefan both on her and in her, and giggling mischievously, she answered it.

"Sarah? You okay?"

He sounded so worried, poor David. *Was she okay?* she asked herself, as an orgasm set her ablaze?

"I... I..." she began, panting.

"You're desperate for more, girl. Tell him!"

"Who was that, Sarah?"

"Working, David. That's all. We're working. On the project," she replied.

"Sarah, *that* sounded like a man!"

Stefan's lips touched one of her breasts, triggering a tingle that travelled around her body.

"Um... what?" She could not think of a sensible reply. Not from underneath Stefan whilst still in a state of sexual ecstasy.

"I'll call you back, darling. Do you mind?"

"Sarah, who... ?"

"Not now. Please. Love you!"

"It's a man, isn't it, Sarah? I'm not a complete idiot." David was crying.

Clutching the phone, she rolled over and away from Stefan. She wanted to shut out the man who had just lit up her body like a Roman candle and made her feel so alive. The enormity of what she had done exploded within her. A veritable volcano of guilt. She felt as though the lava flow of her deception would cover the whole world as it poured out from her soul.

"David, it's nothing! Look, I'm coming home. I'll take the next train. Don't go worrying yourself."

"The children are with nan." These were his last, abrupt words before hanging up.

"So that was him?" asked Stefan. "No harm done. Might even get a stiffy himself if he realises his little wife's been having a bit of a fling!"

She hit him. The orgasm over, she walloped him across the face as hard as she could before getting out of bed. She hurriedly picked up her clothes strewn about the floor and disappeared into the bathroom. She now wanted to hide herself from the man on the bed who lay rubbing his cheek and gawping at her through narrowed eyes. She wanted to drag the whore she had been away from this place, purify her and bring home the other Sarah, the mother... the wife.

"You bloody shouldn't have hit me!" Stefan called out.

"It's only your pride, Stefan. You got what you wanted. Just let me go home. You don't need me to design that crappy hotel of yours!" She appeared in the doorway in knickers and bra. "We both got what we wanted, right? Just call it quits and pretend it never happened!"

"Oh it happened, all right. And you, you bitch, you just couldn't get enough of it!"

Sarah, knowing this to be true, vanished into the bathroom. She did not want to give the bastard the pleasure of seeing tears streaming her cheeks. When dressed, she re-emerged, briefly, to stuff her clothes back into her suitcase. Her mobile phone was still there, where she'd lain, as a whore, on that bed.

"Stop being so stupid, Sarah! Come back to bed!" Now *he* was begging *her*. She snatched up her phone. "You'll regret this! As soon as you reach the station, you'll be wanting to come back for another f---. I know your type!"

Type? What type am I? she wondered as she ran downstairs to reception. She did not wait for the lift. *The uncaring adulteress? The mother who would abandon her two children for two days and a night. Is that the type I am?*

She so longed to be back with David, to beg his forgiveness, to pray that he would make love to her as...

Oh God, what have I done? She rang the bell. She had her key but decided to ring the bell first. Nothing. Perhaps he would forgive her between then and reaching the door to their flat. She could not blame him if he didn't, but she prayed that he would. She wanted to touch him, hold him, tell him how much she loved him, and, with the children being away, they would be honest with each other for a change. There would be tears, of course, but the tears would pass like her infidelity had passed, and they could move on. Together.

No response. Using her key, she opened the street door and lugged her case up three flights of stairs. She banged on the flat door. No response. She tried her key, upside down in her confusion, her vision blurred, then the right way up. Then on into the living room, leaving her case out on the landing. She froze...

At first she saw only protruding legs on the other side of the settee. David's legs. When she saw the whole body stretched out, gun in hand, the snake-stream of blood on the carpet beside his head, she gaped in disbelief.

Rigid, she could not scream, cry, move or, for a few awful moments, even breathe.

It was when she went to phone for an ambulance that she saw the answerphone light winking at her. She pressed the 'play' button...

'Oh, I forgot to say, in case you hadn't noticed... she's got a mole just above her pussy on the right. Cute little thing, that!'

The bastard had got her home number from her mobile whilst she had been with him in that awful hotel bathroom. He'd told David everything. She felt like smashing the phone, destroying every trace of her highland fling. Instead, that other woman, David's wife, calmly dialled '999'. David still breathed, thank God...

Invisible Curtain

The door opened almost as soon as Aila rang the bell. A dumpy, red-faced woman, wearing a flowery, pink apron, stood there in the doorway grinning at Aila.

"Aila, ain't it! I'm Mrs Babbage," she said cheerily before the Finnish girl could utter a word. "Like in cabbage!" the woman added with a chortle. "Come in, luv."

Mrs Babbage stepped back enough to allow Aila to squeeze past her rotund frame.

"My, you are lovely," remarked Mrs Babbage when Aila smiled nervously at her new landlady. She gave the girl a nudge and a wink, saying it was a good job her son was not at home as she would have had her time cut out trying to keep him away from Aila. But the Finnish girl did not feel at all lovely as she followed Mrs Babbage up the narrow staircase, clutching her small suitcase. In truth, she felt she must be the plainest girl on earth. Why else would Simon have abandoned her? With Simon still occupying her thoughts, she fought back the tears. Mrs Babbage babbled on about the bathroom, the shower and the washing machine downstairs. Aila was told that she had free use of the kitchen, any time. For a brief moment, Mrs Babbage stopped talking. Her forehead furrowed slightly as she looked, caringly, at the well-built, but by no means overweight, girl standing in the doorway of the small, cosy bedroom. Aila's beautiful blond hair almost reached down to her waist.

"Lovely!" she said again, with a smile, patting Aila's hand. Aila grinned back but said nothing. "Come and 'ave a nice cuppa with me in the kitchen when you've unpacked, luv," she said, cheerfully.

"Oh, yes. Thank you," replied Aila. For a while, Aila sat motionless on the edge of the small bed in her newly acquired bedroom whilst Mrs Babbage pottered about, noisily, downstairs, occasionally humming in loud, tuneless accompaniment to strains of Daniel O'Donnell emerging from a CD player. Tears streamed Aila's pale cheeks as, in her head, she went over the events of the last few days again and again.

Aila's lover, Simon, had been the only person to whom she had ever felt really close. Before they met, six months previously, she was resigned to being the dull and dumpy foreign girl in the corner. The one whom no one ever spoke to. Not because she could not understand English. Her language skills were excellent. Back in Finland, at school she was always top in English, as with most other subjects. She just felt certain that no one would be interested in what she had to say. Somehow she had always felt that she was on the wrong side of that 'invisible curtain'. The curtain that separated her, her father, too, from a world where life was to be lived and enjoyed. She and her father lived in a different world. One whose occupants could only see and watch enjoyment from afar. A world that seemed, to young Aila, to be little more than a waiting room for death. Aila's father, a lawyer, lost his wife , to whom he had been deeply devoted, when the girl was only three. He had brought up his young daughter, unable to remember her mother, by himself. He never remarried. Although immensely proud of his clever daughter, he rarely showed her outward affection.

As she grew older, Aila would sometimes stare longingly at fading photographs of her mother, wondering what her life might have been like if the woman had not died so young.

The Finnish girl spent much of the time desperately trying to please her inscrutable father. Just a little praise or show of love would have been like magic to her. Not only did Aila lack confidence in herself, as she grew up she also began to dislike her own image: that of a sturdy young girl, the result of finding solace in food, although not obese. Nevertheless, Aila only saw herself as fat and unattractive. It hurt her to see boys hanging around her slim, female classmates. She hardly ever went out and was never *asked* out. Her uncles and aunts tried hard to introduce her to young men, in the knowledge that Aila's father would give the girl little encouragement in that area. Poor Aila barely had the self-confidence to show her face in their company, let alone offer scintillating conversation. At business school in Helsinki, she had no close contact with the opposite sex. She wore her hair long, matching her long dresses, hoping that this would make her appear slimmer, but no one ever dated her. Every evening she scurried home, alone.

It was after pressure from his family that Aila's father suggested a year in England, using, as a pretext, the importance of her becoming more fluent in English. They all felt that Aila and her father were just too much alike, and hoped that having time on her own, away from her father, might draw the girl out. But Aila felt she was going to London only to please her father.

As Aila sat on the bed in that tiny room, staring at the open suitcase beside her, she could not help but think how small her world had become now that she was back on the joyless side of the invisible curtain. It seemed to the girl that those previous six months on the other side of that curtain had been but a dream.

After arriving in London, she found part-time work at a Burger King and soon got used to being the unattractive, foreign blonde whom no one bothered about. She was only a year or two older than most of the other young workers there, but she felt she belonged to a different generation. Then Simon came into her life.

She first saw him that pervious winter when he kept looking at her from the line of cold and hungry shoppers queuing up for burgers. No one had ever looked at her like that before. She felt nervous when it was his turn to be served; more so after he boldly asked her where she came from. Her face turned crimson as she stared at him in silence. He repeated his question.

"Finland," she replied, quietly. She even smiled. Such a rare event for Aila.

"Lucky Finland!" said Simon as he handed her his payment.

Aila felt confused. She kept looking across to where Simon sat huddled over his hamburger and chips. She was disappointed when she saw that he had gone, but her heart did a little summersault after the girl at the cash till handed her a scruffy piece of paper.

"That tall man said to give this to you," said the girl. On the outside of the folded paper was scrawled, in pencil, 'To Finland!' On the inside, a phone number. Aila's hand trembled as she dialled the number after work, and from that moment on she started a new life that she could never even have dreamt of before. A life on the other side of the invisible curtain. Simon, about forty (she never asked him), had split up with his wife 'for good', as he put it. He saw his two children, of whom he was extremely fond, once a week, but until Aila appeared on the scene, he had been living alone in a cramped suburban flat. Simon was so attentive towards Aila that, for the first time in her life, she began to feel like a real person rather than a transparent presence sitting alone in a corner. She felt happy. *Supremely* happy. She smiled most of the time when Simon was around. Most of all, she talked. She wanted to tell Simon anything and everything. Plus there was their love life.

Aila had been a virgin when she first slept with Simon. Seated alone on the bed at Mrs Babbage's, she even managed to smile to herself as she recalled their wild and amorous antics. With Simon she had even learned to love her own body. For the first time in her life she felt truly alive. But this all ended as quickly as it had started.

Aila knew by the look on Simon's face that something was not quite right when he got home that awful evening. It did not stop him from making love to her, later, but the following morning he came out with the truth.

"I'm going back to live with her. I'm sorry, but it'll be best for our children. It's *because* of the children. You do understand, don't you?"

Aila did not want to hear any more. She had difficulty taking it in. She became hysterical. Something she had never before experienced. Far from trying to comfort her, Simon became more distant. Her love shattered, her close friend and companion for six glorious months no longer there for her, Aila once again felt that oh-so-familiar loneliness in a cold and confusing world.

She was given twenty-four hours to find somewhere else to stay. She saw Mrs Babbage's advertisement card in the local corner shop window later the same morning.

Although she still desperately wanted to be with Simon, she knew it had all come to an end. Having been thrown back across the invisible curtain, discarded like refuse, it seemed an even more desolate place, more painful, now that she knew what life *should* be like; not just a long, slow wait for death.

Aila splashed her face with water to wash away the tear smudges before going downstairs to the kitchen.

"Come and sit down, luv," said Mrs Babbage. She showed the Finnish girl to a chair. Aila thought the woman resembled a mother hen. "I do 'ope you'll get to like it 'ere", continued the girl's landlady before pouring out a large mug of tea for her. They sat together for over an hour. Mrs Babbage did all the talking. Aila remained her usual monosyllabic self, but she listened intently to every word that emerged from the babbling Cockney woman. She learnt how Mrs Babbage had been widowed when young, just like Aila's father, and had to bring up three children by herself.

"And wiv no 'elp from 'is family, I can tell yer!" Mrs Babbage proudly added.

She could not have been more different from Aila's father. Open and friendly, but also sensitive, not prying into Aila's own life. She came over and gently placed her arm across the girl's shoulders and asked her jokingly whether she minded her passion for Daniel O'Donnell. She even joked about this when she asked her new lodger,

"What 'as ninety-nine legs and no teef?"

Aila shrugged her shoulders, puzzled by the question.

"Front row of a Daniel O'Donnell concert, luv!" chuckled Mrs Babbage before giving the girl a hug.

Apart from Simon, Aila was unused to anyone showing any sign of affection towards her. Bizarrely, such warmth and kindness made the girl want to cry again. Feeling awkward, Aila excused herself, saying that she had to go to her room to study her English.

"Nuffink wrong wiv your English, luv. Much better than my Babbagelish!" chuckled the plump landlady. Her bright eyes twinkled as her red face rounded into an impish grin.

Back in her room, to Aila it seemed that the sound of Mrs Babbage's clattering about, and her bursts of loud, tuneless humming, out of sync with Daniel O'Donnell, belonged to another world. A world on the bright side of that invisible curtain and a world where she had lived, so briefly, when together with Simon. Now she hated her own existence even more than before the affair. It appeared to the girl that her short-lived spell of happiness and love only happened to show her how miserable her existence would be from then on. She could see no end to it, and perhaps 'Simon' should never have happened anyway. Of one thing she was certain; that interlude of closeness to another soul would never repeat. Before she met Simon, Aila had learned to live herself on the dark side of the invisible curtain. Now it seemed that 'self' was not worth living for.

Aila sat for a long time on the edge of her bed staring at the unemptied suitcase beside her. She had already sent the letter to her father. An apology for all the trouble she had caused him. She had never even told him about Simon. She looked down at her hands clutching that small brown plastic bottle which, for Aila, contained, in pill form, the answer to questions about the future. Meanwhile, the noise of Mrs Babbage moving around downstairs blended with strains Daniel O'Donnell.

Aila tried to open her eyes, but her lids felt too heavy. There was an intense brightness and she was vaguely aware of two figures at the foot of her bed. Her mouth felt dry, and when she tried to turn over something tugged at her left forearm. Painfully. From the corner of one eye she glimpsed a white pillowcase and sheet. She thought this strange as they were definitely pink when she went to bed.

And those figures? Perhaps she was dreaming. One of her eyelids flickered into a narrow slit. Why, she wondered, was there a piece of plastic tubing sticking into her left arm?

"What a shame!" said a voice from beyond the foot of her bed. "And such a lovely girl. You will take care of 'er, won't you? I want 'er back soon. *Very* soon. Mrs Babbage is the name..." There was a pause, then, "...Like in cabbage," followed by a mischievous chuckle.

Slowly, it came back to Aila as she lay there, tears leaking from her closed eyes. Not for the loss of Simon, nor the unhappiness that led her to swallowing all those pills the previous night. The tears began to flow when she realised that someone she hardly knew actually cared about her, and the tears washed away that invisible curtain. Thank God the pills failed to do their job.

The Door

"Ropes, Jimmy?" he asked, gazing at the great white cliffs.

"Aye, Callum. Ropes," replied the other man, slipping a coiled rope off his shoulder. Jimmy secured one end to his harness, handing the other to his companion. They were standing in several inches of thick, brown muddy water. The white cliffs stretching high above them were streaked the same dirty brown. "Too soft," complained Jimmy, stabbing at the cliff face with the handle of his pick. "Pitons won't hold. Have to carve out footholds and rely on these," he added, holding up his pick.

"Do you think we'll make it?" asked Callum.

"We bloody have to. No choice. You looked over the edge of the precipice back there. The only way on is up. Then... well, we'll just have to see what comes next, eh?"

Jimmy began to climb. His boots sank into the soft, white earth. *Like climbing on snow*, he thought... only the snow was curiously warm. Thankfully, it wasn't slippery like snow, and slowly the two men eased their way up the cliff face.

"Hey, Callum, it's not bad, this stuff," Jimmy called down.

"Like you said, Jimmy," his friend answered, kicking his boot into a foothold.

They crossed a traverse, balancing above a sheer cliff face. Soon, Jimmy reached a narrow, mountaineer's chimney. He waited for Callum.

"Better without a rope from here on," he suggested after his friend had joined him. "This stuff's not gonna hold if one of us slips."

With the rope coiled, once more, over Jimmy's shoulder, the large man wedged himself in a chimney of soft, pale soil, and, by using his back and his outstretched legs, started to lever himself upwards, inch by inch, towards the gleaming white crest of the cliff. Gasping for breath, he finally reached the top. Moments later, Callum's head appeared.

"Wow!" exclaimed the smaller man as he eased himself up and over onto level ground. He went to stand beside Jimmy staring at the vista beyond.

For some distance, the terrain appeared easier. A wide plateau, and then a series of gently rolling hills of the same white soil. But appearances proved deceptive, for with each step their boots sank deep into the soft soil, just like its cold equivalent, snow. In the distance, they saw a great, rounded, green hump of a hill.

"That's where we're making for," said Jimmy. "I'm sure of it. It was in that picture I saw. The master plan. A great green hill made up of rounded boulders. It'll be tough going, Callum, but it's our only chance. Follow me, and stay close, laddie."

Jimmy plodded on, painfully slowly, sinking into the soft white soil with each step. By the time Callum had caught up with him at the summit of the first of the series of hills, both men were exhausted but they had to press on, down the slope, up another hill, down and up again until they reached the green hill. From where they stood, Jimmy could now make out individual green boulders. They were smoothly rounded and considerably larger than he had reckoned on. He had no idea how they were going to climb the hill but, once again, they had no choice. There was no other means of escape. He could only pray that they would see a way on from the top of the green hill.

Not only was the going tough, but the heat was becoming unbearable and it was coming from the ground. The heavy, clinging white soil was hot. Layer by layer, the men removed their clothing, until they were stripped to the waist with sweat glistening bared torsos.

Jimmy and Callum were in a state of exhaustion and despair when they finally reached the foot of the great, green hill. Callum sat on one of the boulders to recover his strength and immediately slipped down, onto the ground, his bottom sinking into the soft white earth. He extended his legs, lay back and made a large 'T' with outstretched arms, staring at the cloudless sky. And he laughed.

"Used to do this as a child in the snow back in Perth, Jimmy," he said, moving his arms up and down. "Only that was always nice and cool. Not like a bleeding sauna!"

Callum sat up and looked at his friend resting back against a green boulder.

"You know, the sky up there's funny," he said. "No clouds, but no sun and no blue sky either. Where are we?"

"What the hell!" groaned Jimmy. "I don't have the energy to look up, Callum. Few more minutes of rest here, then we press on. Tackle these ruddy great slippery green boulders. Hopefully, we'll be able to bump-slide down the other side after we reach the top of this bloody hill." He jerked his thumb at the tumble of green boulders behind him.

A short while later, the men began the climb. The boulders were too slippery to scramble over, but they found that by wedging themselves between two boulders, and pressing with their knees, bottoms and elbows, they could edge their way upwards to the next layer, climbing higher and higher. At least the green boulders were not hot like the white soil. Only warm. Nevertheless, it was a

297

death-defying climb. At one point, Jimmy thought it was the end when a boulder became dislodged and bounced and crashed down to the white soil way below. Callum only just caught Jimmy in time, pulling him back in between two boulders when the larger man began to slide downwards. Gradually, there was less of an incline, until, at last, the ground levelled off.

They had reached the top and were relieved to see that the slope on the other side was far less steep. The green boulders curved gently down to a broad, flat brownish plain, separated from the green hill by a murky brown lake.

"Okay to press on?" Jimmy grinned at Callum.

"Aye!" And the two men laughed and joked with each other as they bump-slid on bruised bottoms over the smooth, shiny green boulders down towards the murk of the brown lake.

"Funny, but this reminds me of those bumpy slides in the park near where we lived in Crieff when I was a bairn," observed Callum pausing halfway down.

"Everything seems to remind you of your childhood, laddie!" remarked Jimmy.

"It's strange, but I can remember some things perfectly, but the rest is a total blank."

"All a blank for me, Callum. Everything. Like it's been wiped out."

Callum shrugged his shoulders.

"Game for another ride?" he joked, before bumping on down over the boulders, giggling as he went. Soon, both men were at the foot of the green hill, looking out across the brown lake above which hovered small clouds of steam. Jimmy crouched down and stirred the thick, brown water with his hand.

"Pretty hot, but no worse than my morning bath."

"Bath? Crikey, can't remember when I last had one of the those," Callum joked.

Jimmy stood staring at the plain beyond the lake and at the heat shimmering above the brown earth. His expression changed.

"Hope the ground here doesn't burn the rubber off my boots," he said.

"Would spoil the delicious smell here, that would," said Callum. "Have you noticed the smell? I really like it. Feel it should remind me of something but I can't think what."

Jimmy did not reply. He waded into the warm lake followed by Callum.

It was hot. Only just bearable. The water got deeper and deeper until they were forced to swim. It was thick and heavy and they made little headway. The energy expended to go just a few yards exhausted them, but slowly, with sweat streaming their red faces, the two men edged forwards until, quite suddenly Callum stopped, gasping for air.

"I... I... I can't! Not..."

"Callum!" screamed Jimmy, his shoulders and chest appearing above the water. "It's okay where I am. I can feel the ground beneath my feet. And it's all soft and springy. Look!" Jimmy proceeded to make bouncing steps through the brown water towards the shoreline, laughing hysterically.

"I can almost run!" he yelled, demonstrating the point.

A weakened Callum stood and staggered on to join

Jimmy on the lake shore. Already, Jimmy was jumping up and down on the springy brown ground.

"Its like a bloody trampoline!" he cried.

"A what?" said Callum.

"Trampoline, laddie. Hey, I just remembered something. Boy next door had a trampoline in his garden. When I was a kid. How about that, Callum?"

Callum pushed a booted foot into the soft earth, and watching it spring back up. Suddenly he was thrown backwards. The earth seemed to move away from him, and both men were sent sprawling onto the ground as it tipped from one side to the other. Now on his knees, Callum gripped onto the strange brown carpet-like ground with both hands.

"An earthquake, Jimmy. A bloody earthquake," he called out.

Jimmy giggled.

"It's okay, Callum. Nothing here to fall on top of us, seemingly!"

There was a sort of a jolt, and the ground went calm. Jimmy sat up.

"See over there," he said. "Way in the distance. That white horizon. All smooth, like. It's where we're heading for, Callum. Fancy a run? Should be easy on this springy ground."

"Aye!" replied Callum.

"Ready..." began Jimmy.

"Steady..." added Callum.

"Go!" shouted both men together.

Laughing, they ran like antelopes across the soft brown ground. With each bound they seemed to cover a greater distance than with the previous one. The gleaming white horizon got closer. And closer. And closer...

*****

"Someone left the lid off the jar," the waiter said timidly to the huge, red-faced figure seated at the table. "We think a couple may have escaped."

"What?" bellowed the red-faced man. "Who? How? Why? Bring him here at once! The one responsible. Hear me? Now!"

"S-Sir... but...?"

"At once!"

The red-faced man glanced sideways at the fearsome three-pronged pitchfork resting against the wall behind him. A warning that caused the waiter to tremble.

"S-S-Sir," he stammered, bowing obsequiously. "Roast beef, Sir. Roast beef, peas and mashed potato. Erm... medium rare. Just to Sir's liking. As always. Medium rare. Sir! Keeping nice and warm for you."

The waiter bowed, again, then backed away from the dining table and from the mumbling, cursing, red-faced creature-come-man. At the other side of the door he turned then ran back to the kitchen where he grabbed a plate of food being kept warm on the enormous Aga.

*****

It happened again. Jimmy and Callum were thrown to the ground by another violent upheaval.

"Jimmy, this is no bloody earthquake," yelled Callum.

"Earthquake or not, we've got to run for it," screamed the other man as the ground tipped and turned in all directions like a slippery raft in a gale at sea. The two men staggered to their feet and ran in short bursts towards the horizon. Towards the whiteness and the land beyond.

301

At last, at last!" grunted the red-faced monster when a plate of food appeared on the table in front of him. "I'm famished. Hear that? Bloody famished!"

He turned his ugly face and fixed the quaking waiter with hollow, evil eyes.

"Have you found the culprit?"

The waiter frantically searched his mind for safe words as those hollow eyes bore into his soul.

"Yes, Sir, straightaway. Famished. Culprit. Roast beef, medium rare… like always… and… and the culprit? Sir… yes. I'll see to it right now… Sir!"

The huge creature, to the waiter's great relief, looked down at his plate of roast beef, peas and mash, made an appreciative grunt then reached for the knife and fork.

*****

The ground went still. An ominous stillness. It had become darker. A lot darker. Neither man looked up at the sky, but each had the impression that there was red in that darkness. Like blood. They had reached the very edge of the springy, brown plain. There was a drop of about ten feet to a smooth white surface below. The men's toes curled as, balanced, they prepared to jump. Then it happened again. A violent force threw them over the edge…

*****

'Too tough!" roared the Devil, pulling and stabbing at the meat with his fork before pushing the plate away. "Waiter!" he shrieked.

The waiter ran back into the room. What else could he do?

He had searched everywhere for a scapegoat to drag,

kicking and screaming, into the red-faced man's dining-room, but he'd found no one. He seemed to be the only person around. There was no other culprit. And now *this!* The meat was tough.

"Beef's tough!" repeated his master.

The waiter remained silent. Through the corner of his eye he saw the pitchfork with its spear-like prongs, and he knew that the pain from the thrust of that pitchfork into his soul would last for all eternity.

*****

"It's like the whole world's gone crazy," shouted Jimmy, sliding about on the shiny white 'marble'. "The edge, Callum. Make for the edge!"

*****

Slowly, the Devil turned his great horned head to look at the waiter. This was the moment the man had always dreaded. And it was the emptiness of those eyes that filled him with fear.

"Not only tough, but crawling!" thundered the red-faced beast from Hell. To demonstrate his point he flicked away two 'insects' that had been slipping and scurrying about at the edge of his plate. He looked again at the servant who visibly cringed. "And waiter, you've not yet brought me that culprit, have you?"

The waiter shook as he watched his boss reach for the pitchfork.

"I... um... well... must, yes I will... erm..." The waiter turned abruptly and ran for the door. He ran in circles looking for the door leading to the kitchen but no longer could he find it. The door was gone. As he ran and he ran, everything seemed to become redder and redder. He failed to notice two minute figures on the floor. They, too, were running. Running towards a door. *Their* door was wide open. A door, smaller than a mouse hole, that he would neither reach nor pass through.

*****

"At last!" exclaimed Jimmy, now looking up at the bright sky after, unexpectedly, flying through the air as though thrown from a catapult. "Close the door behind you, Callum!"

But Callum was not there. The door, neither.

The Ravine

In the rain, with Pedro in her arms, she ran from the silence of the village to the roar of the ravine. She stumbled. Not through exhaustion for, heavy though the child was, she felt she could run with him forever to escape from the smoke and from the smell of death seeping up from the sodden ground of their village. For all she cared, they could have *her*, since the young Scot would have been slaughtered by Franco's troops like all the other men in the village. But Pedro? No! Nothing would stop her running to save him from a fate worse than Hell.

Or so she thought. A shell must have loosened the rock, causing a small landslide. Her ankle twisted, throwing her forwards. Her scream was drowned by the roar of the water whilst her mind clung to an image of Jock's face when her head bounced like a football off the rocks on her way down the precipitous slope.

*****

"Pedro, say '*hola*' to the man!"

Pedro came out from behind the bar, the evening before, to greet the gaunt young man with wild, red hair who had recently arrived in the village.

"His name's Jock and he's from Scotland. He's come to help us beat the fascists."

"*¡Hola, Señor Jock!*" the boy greeted, peering up at the stranger.

They had grown used to the rough foreign men who came to Spain to fight for a dream, and left their bodies, broken and bullet-ridden, in her streets. But Jock was different. There was something refreshingly gentle about him.

"Hello," said the Scotsman, his lips curving a reticent smile as he peered down at her son.

No one smiled in her village back then. War does that to a village. Stops the smiles and the laughter. But *she* smiled back at Jock. There was a nervous warmth about the man, and a depth that had nothing to do with fighting, nor with their cause, and it truly made her want to smile. To reassure him that at least *she* wished him to feel welcome in that Godforsaken place.

Her husband, fighting with the Republicans, had been killed early on in the war. The men in the village only wanted one thing from her and she fought to overcome the shame she felt for having been forced to give in to their lust whilst she sat and talked to Jock. They talked in English, for her husband had been a language teacher and had taught her to understand, and be understood in, the Scotsman's language. She learned that his father worked on an estate in the Scottish Highlands. They weren't poor, but Jock, a serious young man with a head full of dreams and communist lies, was determined to champion the cause of 'the people'. Spain gave him that opportunity.

And when he stopped talking and stared at her as though looking at the Holy Virgin herself, she blushed and looked away, wishing she could undo her recent past, erase what the village men had done to her and bare her soul just for him.

Carlos, a heavy brute who frequently demanded time with her, eyed the pair suspiciously.

"You any good with a gun, Jock?" he grunted in Spanish.

Frowning, she translated for the Scotsman. She was the only one in the village who spoke English. Jock looked embarrassed. Somehow she sensed he had never before fired a gun.

"Ana-Maria, put a cabbage up there on the counter of the bar."

"Carlos, you don't have to do this," she begged. "He's only here to help us."

"A cabbage!" shouted Carlos.

She fetched a cabbage and placed it on the counter.

"Now blindfold me!" commanded the brute. With trembling hands, she tied a cloth around Carlos's broad face. Jock appeared confused at the pointlessness of the exercise as the cabbage exploded into a thousand fragments, but Carlos only laughed. The first laugh heard for a very long time in the village.

"Waste of a cabbage," someone complained as Carlos pulled the cloth from his face. "And a bullet!"

But Carlos ignored the man. He stopped laughing and stared, coldly, at Jock, his eyes narrowed.

"If you can't do that you're a dead man, *Escocés!*"

She admired Jock's passive disdain for the anger in the eyes of Carlos and his compatriots who glowered at them as they talked on in private together. And she wanted to know why the Scotsman looked at her like that. Did he look at all girls in the same way? She hoped not. Oh, how she hoped he felt about her as she felt about him. Hoped there was no special girl waiting for him back in Scotland.

After the others left, with Carlos spitting his disgust on the floor at Jock's feet, they stayed on in the bar until two in the morning, talking, whilst Pedro slept curled up in a chair. But it never went beyond the talking and a shy kiss before she reluctantly bid him, *"Buenos noches."*

It had not rained for months. The land was parched,

the crops had failed, and the whole area was now sealed off by General Franco's troops. Jock must have been the last man in from the outside world. The villagers were beginning to starve, there was little water left and everyone prayed for rain. Prayed that clouds, not shells, would come their way.

That night, as she lay cradling Pedro in her arms, dreaming about the red-haired Scot, about telling him everything and begging him to forgive her past, it rained as never before. It hammered against the windows, driven by squalls, their tiny room flared by flashes of lightning and shaken by thunder as young Pedro clung, terrified, to his mother. In the early hours she was awoken by a different sort of thunder. The building shuddered when a shell exploded. She grabbed Pedro and carried him outside where people were randomly running about, screaming. One by one they were being silenced by the guns of Franco's soldiers who had attacked under cover of dark. The church was on fire, its roof gone. She ran with the child to the edge of town where she spotted a bombed-out farm. After splashing through a pig pen, ankle deep in mud, she squeezed herself and the boy into the pigsty.

"The pigs are all dead," she whispered to Pedro. "We can hide here till it's over."

Soon, the noise of exploding shells, the screams and the gunfire ceased, but she and the boy remained crouched in the pigsty until the black of the night had been replaced by the grey of the day. The only sound now was the monotonous patter of rain on the tin roof. All she could think about was getting Pedro to the safety of the mill at the foot of the ravine. Once there, Old Xavier could hide them, for the soldiers would never bother about Xavier, a wizened fossil of a man who belonged to no one. As she ran, tears streamed her face already wet from the rain. Tears for Pedro, too young to understand a war that was tearing his little life apart. Tears for Jock who never knew how much she loved him.

When she came too, the rain had stopped. Pedro was lying beside her. She must have been unconscious for hours.

"Pedro?"

She reached out and touched the back of his head, fearing the worst.

"Mama!"

He turned. Only a few scratches, and she wept for joy as she hugged and kissed him over and over.

"Oh, *Santa María* be praised, you're all right! Oh, my little Pedrito!"

"Mama, why did you sleep here after falling?"

She stroked his pale cheek.

"There are so many things Mama does not know, Pedrito! Come, we must hurry."

But when she tried to stand she couldn't. Her leg looked as though had been put through a mangle. Raw bone protruded from the gaping wound, and she cried out in pain, collapsing to the ground.

"Go!" she gasped, the knuckles on her hands turning almost white as she gripped her shattered leg in pain. "To the mill. To Xavier. Get help!"

But the boy refused to leave her. There was only one thing she could do. Gritting her teeth against the agony tearing at her brain, she started to crawl, dragging her injured leg and leaving a trail of blood along the path. It was at least a kilometre down to the mill, and how she made it was nothing short of a miracle. If it hadn't been for

Pedro she would have given up and allowed death to take her spoiled, guilt-ridden body, but the child's innocent presence kept her going...

"Mama, we must get there, we *must!*"

His childish voice hammered at her brain, urging her on. And in her mind, too, was the face of the Scotsman, his warm, green eyes still looking at her in that hauntingly special way. Thank God he never knew how bad Carlos and the others had forced her to be. 'Think of little Pedro,' they would threaten, if she were to refuse to sleep with them.

Five years later, thanks to old Xavier, she and Pedro were able to return to the village. The war was over. The church and the bar had been rebuilt, and she went back to working in the bar, but the new men in the village, Franco's supporters, they left her alone for she only had one leg.

It was raining again, like on that awful night, when a teenage Pedro, now on the brink of young manhood, came into the bar grinning from ear to ear.

"What is it, Pedrito?" she asked.

"There's someone in the plaza looking for you."

"Someone? Who? Tell me! No one ever comes looking for me now unless my wine tastes bad! No one—" She stopped mid-sentence on seeing the gaunt, red-haired figure in the doorway. She hardly dared blink for fear the apparition might vanish. She knew it could not be for real, and she felt angry with the Holy Virgin for putting such a cruel vision from the past in her head.

He spoke. That voice. She remembered it so well. Like a record, it had re-played in her mind every day since the night Franco's men destroyed her village, her leg and her future.

"Ana-Maria?"

A ghost, she thought. *It has to be.*

"It *is* you, isn't it?" he asked in English. "Pedro said I'd find you here."

Pedro's grin was unchanged. He often used to ask his mother about 'that nice foreign soldier with red hair.'

"You remember my name?" The only words she could come out with. He walked up to the bar. He seemed older, stronger and more self-assured, but he still looked at her in that same way and she had to hold on to the bar to prevent her only leg from buckling, for his stare made her feel as though it had just turned into rubber.

"How could I forget it? Or you?"

She looked down at her wooden leg. God's punishment for not preventing Carlos and the others from abusing her and destroying her innocence. At least he would never have to know about her past now for, even if he was real and not just a ghost, like Franco's thugs he would want nothing to do with a one-legged woman.

"Pedro's told me about your leg! But thank God the rest of you's okay! As beautiful as ever, huh?"

Head down, her tears streamed. She could not bear to look up at him.

"Why are you here?" she asked, her eyes still focused on the wooden pole strapped to her stump. "There's another war now. France. Germany. What are you doing in Spain?"

He laughed. She'd not heard him laugh before.

"Another war, another life, unending conflict, but the same you, huh? I enlisted to fight behind enemy lines. Help the Free French. It was the only way I could get back to Spain. To see you."

311

"You weren't killed, then? When Franco attacked that night. In the rain."

He laughed again.

"I'm not a ghost, if that's what you're thinking. Remember that exploding cabbage? What a waste! There's more to me than some men think, you know. I was the only one of our men who survived that night."

"I—" began Anna-Maria.

"I escaped," he interrupted. "Along the ravine behind the village. Saved my life, that ravine. And the rain. Franco's bastards wouldn't have wanted to get their dainty feet wet."

"I'm sorry, but I'm only…" She looked up and into his eyes and fell silent. It was that look of his. *I'm only a whore*, she wanted to say but his eyes said something so very different. He reached across the bar with his hand and stroked her cheeks, lightly brushing the dampness there with long, slim fingers.

"And I want *you* to find out how much more there is to me. I want you to come back with me to Scotland. You *and* Pedro."

"But…?"

"We can get you fitted with a proper leg. Called a prosthesis. As good as new, it'll look."

"But my past—"

"I don't want to know," he interrupted again. "The past is another life. I want you to have a new life. With me."

She glanced at Pedro, who nodded, grinning, her own happiness mirrored in his eyes.

"For Pedro, then," she said. "I'll come for Pedro's sake," she added, smiling in a way she hadn't done since that evening in the bar before she lost her leg.

(Some 40,000 foreigners fought with the Republicans during the Spanish Civil War which claimed between 500,000 and 1,000,000 lives, excluding those who died from starvation, or disease, as a result of the turmoil.)

Blue Rose Bush

"There's been an awful mistake!"

Before entering, he felt furious with the director of the crematorium. Once inside, internally he boiled with rage but it was not in his nature display emotion. "I can't believe this. Someone here got it wrong," he said, quietly.

The director glanced at his desk and at clearly written words on the crisp white paper. It was all there. A blue rose bush as well.

"Scatter the ashes in the garden of remembrance," he read. "Perfectly clear."

"But I expressly told the man I wanted them in an urn. I'm sure I did. To take home. It's all that's left of her, those ashes. And her dresses in the cupboard and her make-up and other things." His eyes moistened. "I slept with a blue dress of hers beside me last night. Could still smell her on that dress and when I closed my eyes I was certain she was there. With me. When I opened my eyes, I told myself all I now needed was her ashes in an urn. To put on the dressing table with her powders and her lotions and stuff. 'She'll be happy there,' I said to myself. In our bedroom."

His anger swamped by grief, he merely shook his head in despair.

"Well, Mr Wilkie, I can only apologize on behalf of my staff here at the crematorium. A mistake has obviously been made. But perhaps..." The director looked up at the distraught Mr Wilkie. "Maybe... well, you know how when people are *truly* upset they say things without realising they're doing it. Don't get me wrong. I'm not trying to make excuses. But it can happen, believe me."

The sorrowful figure on the other side of the desk shrugged his shoulders, staring blankly ahead.

"An urn!" he demanded after a few moments of silence.

"Pardon?"

"I want an urn."

"But Mr Wilkie, I told you her ashes are already scattered. In the Garden of Remembrance. You won't need an urn. We'll take you to where she's been laid to rest."

"I *must* have an urn," insisted Mr Wilkie. "For her ashes."

"But—"

"An urn. Please. *Your* mistake."

"Just an urn? It'll be empty."

"An urn. And take me to that garden."

"Garden of Remembrance?"

"Remembrance?"

"The rose bush."

"Rose bush?"

"Not yet planted."

"What?"

"Your wife's ashes are where—"

"An urn!" snapped the other man.

The director hurriedly left the office and returned moments later with an ornate brass urn. The very best they had. It was about the size of a rugby ball, and, of course, Mr Wilkie would not be charged. He needed mollifying, for should his employers hear about the mistake the director's job might be on the line. Mr Wilkie took the urn, removed its lid and peered inside. Bright and shiny both inside and out.

315

"Take me there," he insisted.

Soon, Mr Wilkie was on his hands and knees grovelling about in the Garden of Remembrance, carefully picking up small handfuls of ash and fragments of charred bone together with clods of earth, for he was determined not to leave behind one speck of Sylvie's ashes in the ground. Better to include extra mud and even an earthworm or two than risk leaving any of her behind. He would ask the council to arrange for DNA testing on each and every fragment, for surely that was the least they could do. He had read about things like that. Even her hairbrush or her nightdress might give them the information they would require to confirm these were, indeed, Sylvie's ashes.

"What on earth are you doing, Frank? You'll ruin your trousers!"

Mr Wilkie looked up. The girl in the blue dress with long, flowing blond hair, who had spoken, was Sylvie. His little Sylvie as he remembered her when they first met, both aged eighteen. He felt so old, all of a sudden, to be with Sylvie as she was then. How strange it was that he remembered every detail about the girl: her blue dress, her shoes, the band in her gorgeous blond hair.

He stood up and brushed the dirt from his trouser knees. Sylvie laughed.

"Oh you bad boy!" she joked. "But why are you filling that brass thing with all that earth, Frank?"

Old Mr Wilkie, trembling, pointed at the urn.

"It's you in there, my dear. I was just... I mean I must..." He truly did not know what to say to young Sylvie.

"It isn't and you mustn't," she interrupted with a frown that he knew so well. "Whoever heard of such nonsense?"

"But Sylvie, dearest, you're..." Mr Wilkie could not bring himself to tell Sylvie that she was dead. Felt unable to say the word, not with his pretty young wife standing right in front of him, more real even than the rose bushes.

"I *have* to do this, Sylvie. You were everything to me, and now that you're gone I've nothing left. Only this." Frank Wilkie looked down at the brass urn on the ground. "That's all I have!"

"Nonsense!" exclaimed the girl.

Frank Wilkie edged, shakily, towards Sylvie and reached out with his hand, but she drew back.

"No," she said, "you can't do that, you old silly billy! I'm not how I seem. I'm inside you. Have been all along. Didn't you know that?"

"But..." Mr Wilkie stared at his wife. He let his hand drop. "*Inside* me, you said?"

"Yes, you daft old goat!" Sylvie glanced at the urn. "Go on! Empty it out. That stuff belongs in the ground. I tell you, it's *not* me. Didn't you listen to the man at my funeral? 'Ashes to ashes, dust to dust'? That could never be *me* inside that brass thing there. I'm inside you, Frankie darling."

Sylvie had always had an endearing way of getting Frank to do things. He stooped to pick up the urn.

"Sylvie," he said, "you won't go away again, will you?"

Sylvie laughed.

"How can I if I'm inside you, you ninny!"

The old man scattered the contents of the urn over the flower bed.

Of course those little bits of burnt bone and ash could never

317

be Sylvie. She's been inside me all the time, he thought. *Oh my little Sylvie, how stupid I've been!*

A gardener watched with curiosity as the old man, who had been frantically scooping up handfuls of earth and putting them in the urn he'd brought along, was now, equally frantically, emptying the same earth back onto the rose bed. All the time he seemed to be in silent conversation with himself. The old fellow even appeared cheerful as he made his way back towards the crematorium office. The gardener shrugged his shoulders and carried on digging.

The crematorium director looked up when Mr Wilkie re-entered his office, puzzled to see a smile illuminating the old man's wrinkled face. "A beautiful day," the same face announced before placing the empty urn on the desk in front of the younger man. "It's okay," he reassured the director now staring anxiously at the urn on his desk. "It's empty. See?" Mr Wilkie lifted the lid and showed him the shiny brass emptiness of the urn.

"Yes. Empty," agreed the director. He had no idea where this was leading. Mr Wilkie was still beaming benignly.

Poor old guy's gone crackers!

"She's not there!" exclaimed Mr Wilkie.

"No she isn't," agreed the director, peering again inside the empty urn to reassure himself.

"She's in here!" an excited Mr Wilkie told him, tapping the side of his head.

"Of course she is!" The director offered a weak smile, now looking meaningfully at the phone on his desk.

"So I don't need the urn."

"No. You don't."

"Such a beautiful day!"

"Yes. It is."

"You know," continued Mr Wilkie, "before she told me where she was, I had no idea it was such a wonderful day."

"No."

"So?"

"Erm...?"

"Don't you see?"

The crematorium director appeared anxious. His hand edged, hesitantly, towards the phone. He was worrying about his job. If the whole affair had driven poor old Mr Wilkie mad, then his chances of holding on to it were poor.

"Thank you!" said Mr Wilkie.

"Thank you?"

The director's voice was barely audible. He withdrew his hand.

"Yes, thank you. I suppose your chaps knew all along. That she was in here!"

He tapped his head again.

"*All along*," echoed the director, cautiously eyeing Mr Wilkie.

"In my head!"

"In your head?"

Mr Wilkie offered the crematorium director his hand, and the other man stood and, like an automaton, shook it.

"No, erm... letter... then? No letter of complaint?" the director sheepishly asked.

"Complaint?" repeated Mr Wilkie. "What complaint?"

"Oh, nothing," the other man said hastily.

The two men remained with their hands locked together for a few moments.

"Had to put a *special* order in for a blue rose bush," the director added, grinning. "They're more difficult to get than the other colours."

"Blue?"

Mr Wilkie appeared surprised. The director began to worry again.

"It's... erm... written down here on the sheet of paper," he said. "In handwriting. Says must be blue. Someone must've—"

Mr Wilkie was smiling again when he interrupted the other man:

"Her favourite colour, blue. Always was."

The director, more relaxed, sat down.

"It'll look lovely when the flowers are out, Mr Wilkie. They're delivering it on Monday, but please come back in a month or so. You'll be amazed."

"*She*," corrected Mr Wilkie, tapping his temple again. "*She'll* be amazed."

"She," agreed the director.

"And thank you for being so kind and understanding," said Mr Wilkie.

"Oh, we always do try to please."

"So we'll be back next month. Both of us," Mr Wilkie said, before heading for the door. "Oh, by the way," he added, turning. "That's her writing."

"What?"

"On that bit of paper on your desk. About the blue rose bush. It's *her* handwriting. I told you she loves blue."

Mr Wilkie left in a remarkably good humour. The

crematorium director continued to stare at the piece of paper on his desk and the carefully handwritten insertion...

Blue rose bush.

Whispers in the Wind

Returning to Hell...

As the plane descended towards Singapore airport, Charles Grainger felt himself transported back sixty years to when, together with hundreds of other British conscripts, he was caught like a trapped animal whilst the Japanese Army poured into what had once been a tropical paradise. Within seven days, the British force at Fort Siloso was crushed. Why did they lie to him and all those others who had suffered and/or perished? This question had niggled Charles throughout those long years whilst the recurring nightmare of Hell in Singapore, and later, in the Malayan jungle, replayed over and over again in the cinema of his mind. Even more so since his beloved Jean had died.

'Won't stand a chance against our guns, those Nips,' they were told. *'Bow-legged and short-sighted. We'll finish 'em off before they get anywhere near us.'*

He had imagined little cartoon Japanese men with pebble-lens glasses bumping blindly into trees and falling over. How brutally untrue this turned out to be.

The British commanders were well prepared for an attack by sea from the Northeast. Instead, the invaders came out of the jungle, crossing the Jahore Straits during the night, supported by a ruthless onslaught from the air. Not only were the Japanese cunning and quick, but they also had a fearlessness and determination that seemed almost superhuman. It happened so quickly, and it was the Brits who stood no chance. The pounding of the Japanese guns turned courage into numb fear. Dumbfounded, Charles and his compatriots clutched their impotent weapons as the impregnable fortress on Sentosa Island, once named *Blakang Mati*—'The Island behind the Dead—'fell like a stack of dominoes. Following the British surrender came the ignominious herding into appalling makeshift prisons. The beginning of a nightmare of unbelievable terror in Changi and, later, in the Malaysian jungle. Charles' family told him it was madness to make a return trip to Hell at his age. Maybe the stubbornness that had helped him to survive his ordeal in Malaya had made him all the more determined to see this through. His son and daughters were, of course, unaware of the real reason for the trip. A secret enshrouded by shame.

This was not the Singapore that Charles Grainger remembered. As he checked into his four-star hotel, after a taxi journey through an alien, bustling modern city of spotlessly clean streets, he muttered, in front of the bemused receptionist,

"This cannot be the same place."

The meeting had been arranged for the following afternoon, at the main ticket office to the park on Sentosa Island. Strange how the word Sentosa, etched on his mind as a place of desperation and death, was now described as a place of leisure and of fun.

Sixty years had passed. Grainger knew it was going to be difficult to recognise his old enemy about whom he had felt so much shame. Even with the benefit of a recent photograph in his pocket, it would not be easy to pick him out from amongst thousands of East Asian faces. He, of course, would stand out. A pale, white-haired Englishman with a sizeable nose, sporting a Union Jack badge on his jacket lapel.

Then...

"Glainger-san, so preased you come!"

A bent, little man wearing a floppy hat approached Grainger precisely at the pre-arranged time. Not a minute sooner. He gave a formal bow which the Englishman returned. Grainger peered at the ageing, oriental face and immediately recognised the bright, twinkling eyes of the young Japanese soldier from that death camp all those years back. For a moment, both men stood looking at each other in silence, neither knowing quite what to do or to say. It was as though each expected the ghost of the other man, as he had been in the past, to materialise from out of thin air. Earlier, Grainger had scanned the crowds, almost hoping to see the smiling faces of his long-dead, slaughtered comrades to suddenly reappear in triumph over fate and time. Confronting his old enemy now, in this other life, compounded his guilt that he, not they, had survived.

Charles Grainger warmly shook the man's outstretched hand. It felt so weird, but for the first time he sensed shame at having felt ashamed about the meeting.

"Mr Takamata, I presume!"

"Come," said the wizened Japanese who resembled an ancient tortoise. "We walk. Here. I buy already ticket." He handed the Englishman a ticket for Sentosa Park. Or Hell? "No, no, no," he insisted, refusing payment from Charles. "Prease, Glainger-san velly special fliend. Come!" The fact that the old man still muddled up his 'r's and his 'l's made him all the more real.

The two men climbed onto the small train that looped its way around Sentosa park, both well aware that their last meeting had been in another life, in Changi prison, so long ago, and Charles began to experience such a strange mix of feelings and emotions that he found it difficult to adjust. It was all too bizarre. Perhaps his son had been right to question the sanity of his father's trip despite knowing nothing about Takamata-san.

After their initial, friendly-but-restrained reunion, and superficial conversation about respective travel arrangements to Singapore, and the hotels in which they found themselves, things grew tense. Each man searched his mind for the real reason behind this folly, the coming together of past enemies. But there was one thing of which Grainger was certain. Without the presence of a certain young Japanese soldier called Takamata, in that death camp, he, Charles Grainger, would have died. Together with several others in his unit, now still alive. It was a place where human life and human suffering were perceived as being of less value than horse shit, but somehow this made the humanity shown by the young Takamata all the more remarkable. So why should he have felt ashamed about a reunion with this man?

The two alighted from the park train at the old British fort where huge guns still pointed impotently seawards, and Charles recalled how useless they had been. They walked together, in silence, around the museum. Charles was experiencing painfully vivid flashbacks as each old soldier struggled with personal demons in a dimension of his own. It was the ex-prisoner of war who finally broke the ice:

"Tea, Takamata? Fancy a cup of tea? There's a café a little further on. It's marked on the park map."

The old Japanese said nothing, his face as expressionless as a Buddhist statue. They boarded the small park train again. In the café, they sat together, quietly. Charles had a small snack, whilst Takamata, using both hands, just sipped at his tea. He was staring, sideways, out to sea. Then, quite suddenly, he turned his head and looked directly into Grainger's eyes. His voice was shaky and charged with emotion.

"Glainger-san," he said softly, leaning forward, "I say solly to you." Takamata glanced down at his hands with their wrinkled skin and knobbly fingers. "Solly!" he repeated. "Tellible, tellible things. How can I—?"

"Look, Takamata, that's all in the past," interrupted the Englishman. "The war wasn't your fault. And remember one thing, Takamata. It was you who saved my life. Without you, I, and many others, would most certainly have died. I know it!"

"You are too kind, Glainger-san," the other continued. "But, you know, all that killing not Japanese way. We are mostly Buddhists. Buddhists no kill, no harm. Why? How?" He looked up at his old 'enemy' with moistening eyes.

"Takamata-san, you never really hurt me," Grainger insisted. "We agreed then that, at times, you had to appear brutal in front of your officers, but you weren't, even if you did manage to fool them."

Takamata smiled.

"Officers just turkeys," he added. "All noise, no—"

He tapped his head, unable to come up with the word 'brain'. They laughed together.

"Takamata, I really don't know how to thank you for giving me a life. Those morsels of food and medicines may not have seemed much to you, but they saved me and some of my chums in our unit. All I gave you in return were a few lessons in English, and a fat lot of good I was

326

as a teacher! You still get your 'r's and your 'l's mixed up!"

The two old men laughed again, together.

"Takamata, there is something I never asked you. Back then. Suppose they had found out about that food and those medicines. What would have happened to you?"

Takamata raised his right hand behind his head and brought it down chopper-style across the back of his neck.

"I thought so," said Grainger. "A beheading. See! You risked your own life for me. Your enemy."

"Not enemy! All my rife try to make good, Glainger-san." The old Japanese looked even more troubled.

"You're right, Takamata. We were never enemies. If it hadn't been for the war..." Charles paused. The other man shook his head.

"Those devils! Those poriticians and those army men! All face, no soul!"

Charles was eager to find out more about this extraordinary old man sitting opposite him. Their renewed contact had happened two years previously via the internet. He could scarcely believe it when, out of the blue, he received an e-mail from Takamata. Their initial correspondence had been very formal, and Takamata, in his politely succinct messages, gave the other man little information about himself or his own life since the war.

"Tell me more about yourself, Takamata," said Grainger. "Did you marry that gorgeous girl whose photo you were so proud of?"

"No mally, Glainger-san," replied the old Japanese man. He pulled out a wallet from his jacket pocket and extracted an old sepia photograph with frayed margins, handing this to his new friend from a shamed past. Grainger stared at the exquisitely pretty girl in the photograph. He remembered trying to teach the young Takamata to say 'pretty'—not 'plitty'—whilst looking at the very same photo over sixty years before.

"Yumi?" offered Grainger. How strange that he even remembered the girl's name. "Made me think of food. Like 'yummy'," he mused, still staring at the lovely, young, oriental face. "Food seemed like a distant memory to us back then."

"Tokyo bombs. Firestorm," explained Takamata. "Yumi and many, many others dead." He retrieved the photograph and stared at Yumi. "Only one Yumi. Yumi die. Takamata no mally!" He returned the photograph to his wallet.

Grainger felt a stab of guilt at the old man's words. He must have loved that girl so dearly, only for her young life to be snuffed out by the allies' revenge bombing. Some said, later, that the ferocity of that bombing was unnecessary since Japan was clearly losing the conflict. Back then, after experiencing, firsthand, the cruelty of the Japanese military, Grainger had no doubts about the need to 'flatten' Japan. Now, having seen, again, the haunting image of the girl, long dead, and hearing how there could never have been another woman for the old Japanese, he realised there had been another chapter in that awful story. A chapter of horror unleashed upon innocent Japanese civilians who had no say in what the Japanese Imperial forces got up to, and who almost certainly had no knowledge of the atrocities their soldiers committed in Malaya, in Korea and in China.

Takamata sensed his friend's disquiet.

"You, Glainger-san, you mally?" His eyes twinkled.

Grainger nodded.

"Marry? Yes. Very lucky, I was. Jean. A wonderful wife. Married soon after the war. Three children. Really lucky. Sadly, she died twelve years ago. Cancer."

"So solly, Glainger-san." The old Japanese truly did appear concerned to hear of the other man's loss.

"You know," continued Grainger, "I joined a pacifist movement. Later. When it was all over. And after I learned more about the horror of the nuclear bomb. The Campaign for Nuclear Disarmament. C.N.D. All that death, sadness, and suffering. To what end? We—me and a few others—we wrote to politicians, to heads of state, to public figures. But..."

Takamata's bright eyes shone with understanding.

"Whispers in the wind!" he exclaimed.

"Pardon?" queried Charles.

"Whispers in the wind," repeated Takamata. "What you did. Old Japanese saying. Wise words are only whispers in the wind for fool man. Fool man no want to hear wise words. Drowned by bad noise in heads of bad men. Poriticians, generals, other fool men. No hear your wise words. Fool man no soul. Must come back. Always come back, try again. Another life. Many times. This we Buddhists believe. Maybe after many, many times come back, no longer fool man. Maybe then hear those whispers."

Over the next three days the two old men became the greatest of friends. Sitting on the plane during the return flight, Charles Grainger felt like a new man. He was aware of a curious strength inside him. A strength that he felt sure would help him to confront, at long last, the demons of his past. He was so pleased that he had taken Takamata up on his suggestion of a reunion and was now

329

only too eager to tell his son and two daughters all about the man who had saved his life, allowing them to, later, exist.

The flight arrived at Heathrow in the early morning. Charles bought a newspaper at the station on his way home. He opened it out whilst waiting in the taxi queue; the date at the top of the paper was September twelfth, two thousand and one. He stared in horror at the front-page picture, then at the headline. Stunned by a sharp sting of shock, he placed the newspaper on top of his suitcase and stood, frozen, a living statue of anger, of disgust and of sorrow. All that moved was a tear that slowly found its way down his cheek towards one corner of his tight-lipped mouth. A gentle wind cooled the tear trail. He whispered aloud:

"Dear God, why, oh why, does the killing have to go on and on and on?"

He glanced at the others in the taxi queue. Ignoring him, they stared blankly ahead. Not one of them seemed to have heard his whispers in the wind.

(Strange how the internet can resurrect the past. The author once received, out of the blue, an e-mail from a play-group friend from well over half a century before.)

White Mischief

A mere filing clerk, Norman made no impression on Penny, the pretty, new, junior secretary. When he timidly asked her out she told him to, "F--- off!"

Back home things were so very different. He still lived with his parents, and, like his father, was as racist as a Mosley black shirt. Both were founding members of the local branch of the 'White Britain Movement'. The WBM. Their uniform was a white tee shirt sporting a Union Jack on which was superimposed a motif of a bent-up arm with a clenched fist. Underneath the arm and the flag bold letters screamed out 'WHITE BRITAIN!' The fist and the arm were pink, but Norman and his father saw nothing odd in that. Nor in the black (not white) trousers, the other piece of the uniform.

How important young Norman felt whenever he stood in front of the mirror wearing his WBM uniform. It added a certain strength to his puny frame and his lack of height. But at those meetings... wow! He felt so proud to be seated next to his dad at a gathering of fellow 'White Britainers'.

His father was the secretary of the local branch, and the lad often helped the man distribute WBM leaflets around the neighborhood. Norman could never understand the abuse he got from other White people, but he had his rights. At least, that's what his father told him, and it's what *he* told *them*. His mother never spoke about WBM activities with her son or her husband. Not that she contradicted the men in her family. She was forever saying, 'Yes, dear,' and 'That's right, dear,' quite appropriately, but somehow there was no passion behind her stance of passive agreement. Also, she talked to Black people in the shops, in the post office, and Norman had seen his mother smiling at the Black girl who worked in the library. 'Melanie' she was her name. Actually, Norman always looked longingly at Melanie whenever he took his books back to the library, but he did not dare to speak to her, and he would certainly never consider smiling at the girl. Strangely, Melanie *always* smiled at him. Not Penny. She only scowled.

Before breakfast, every morning, Norman would check on his WBM uniform to reassure himself that it was clean and tidy for the next meeting. He would also make sure his black (black... why not white?) WBM boots were nice and shiny, then, with welling pride, he would take out his medals.

The medals were not awarded for anything in particular since all WBM members had medals. Like his tee shirt, they bore the Union Jack and an upheld clenched fist. One of the medals was inscribed with 'WHITE BRITAIN!' in blue, another read 'NO MORE IMMIGRANTS' in red, and the third, his most prized, had on in it, in gold lettering, 'PROUD TO BE WHITE!' He would wear one of these at each WBM meeting, and at rallies he would wear all three together. Every morning, these medals were rubbed clean with a special cloth that Norman kept for this purpose in his bedside cabinet. His mother knew not to even touch his medals.

One morning, after checking on his uniform, and his medals, Norman stepped into the bathroom to take a shower, as usual, but could not understand why his skin had changed colour since the night before. He scrubbed and scrubbed, but nothing happened. Gradually, it dawned on him. He dried himself and peered again into the mirror. He turned round, wondering if someone was lurking behind him, but there was no one else in the room. He reached for the towel, furiously rubbed his face, then looked again.

No, it can't be!

Norman pinched himself, to see whether he was dreaming.

'Ouch!' he yelped.

Even his voice sounded different. Deeper. Richer. He put a dark hand up to his hair. Black and curled, although he knew it *couldn't* be since he was pure Aryan blond. Touching his face it felt normal. No different. But it wasn't a normal Norman staring at him from out of the mirror. It was a Black man.

The young man looking back at him had strong cheek bones and deep brown eyes, the whites of which sparkled mischievously. His lips were larger, somehow more important, and when his mouth opened a fine set of gleaming white teeth was revealed. Not his usual crooked, yellowish ones. Norman touched himself all over, wondering what the hell he should do. He tugged at his hair but it did not come off. He scratched at his cheeks. Nothing changed. Turning away from the mirror, he went back to his room and sat on the bed. He was still sitting there, chewing things over in his mind, wishing his body to turn pink again, when his mother called out.

"Norman, are you finished up there? Come and have some breakfast. It's getting late."

Norman remained silent. His mother called again, and Norman shouted back...

"I'm not feeling too well, Mum."

"You sound funny, Norman. I'm coming up.

"No, Mum. Don't!"

"Norman, I'm coming up!"

Norman had heard his father leave for work earlier on, so... just himself and his mother in the house. Perhaps this would be the best time to tell her, he thought, scrutinising his dark arms.

"Oh! Where's Norman?" his mother asked on entering the room. Norman was still sitting on his bed, dressed in his underwear.

"I'm Norman."

He turned to face his mother.

"No," she said. "Norman is... well... he's different."

"I *am* Norman, for God's sake," Norman stressed, looking at his mother with large, doleful eyes. He smiled, sheepishly.

"I do like your smile," said his mother, "but you can't be Norman. Your voice is different."

"I can be and I *am*," insisted Norman. His mother ventured closer to the bed and leaned forward, looking right into Norman's eyes.

"Well I never!" she exclaimed. "So you are. I can see it in your eyes. But you *do* look different. How did you manage that? It's awfully clever."

"Mum, this is *me*. It's how I looked when I got up this morning. I didn't do anything myself. But it *is* me, Mum."

"Oh, my word!" his mother said, holding her hand up to her mouth. "What *will* your father say, what with that WBM business and all? But... I do rather like it, Norman. You look so much stronger and kind of more important. Isn't that funny?" She gave a girlish giggle.

Norman and his mother had a discussion about things. He would go to work, as usual, with a note from her saying that she vouched for him being the same Norman. The same, only different. And his mother would prepare Norman's father for the change when he got home in the evening.

Norman quite enjoyed the anonymity that his colour change afforded him as he went to work. People whom he knew well, and who normally showed little interest in him when he greeted them in the morning, smiled back when he said, "Hi ya!" displaying fine white teeth through a friendly grin. At work there was a mixture of puzzlement, wonder and even amusement at the change, but everyone secretly agreed that Norman's new image suited him. *Especially* Penny. She kept on looking at the new Norman, smiling and asking him to do things for her and whispering about him to the girl at the desk beside hers. She frequently visited the bathroom to reapply her makeup and make minor adjustments to her hair, returning, on one occasion, with peach-coloured fingernails which she flashed at Norman when he glanced at her. She so hoped that he would ask her out again. Why, she wondered, hadn't he told her that he could look like this? But Norman did not ask her out again, to her great disappointment, because he was thinking about another girl.

On his way home, Norman found an excuse to visit the library. He hoped not only to find a book about adjusting to a new body image, but also that Melanie would be working that day.

She was. He found a book approximating to what he was looking for and gave Melanie a really friendly smile. He had so wanted to smile at her before, just as his mother did, but always worried that someone might notice. Now he cared not a jot about what other people thought.

Melanie took his book, scanned it, and returned the card and the book. She did not smile back at him.

"Did you see the name on that card? I'm Norman Braithwaite. You know... Norman! I often come here with my mother. I wondered if you would care to—"

"No," she said, "you can't be Mrs Braithwaite's son. He's really nice, and terribly good looking. A bit shy, maybe, but I live in hope that he'll ask me out one day."

"But I *am* Norman," objected Norman. "And I do want to ask you out. We're... you know... we're sort of the same now, you and me."

Melanie looked at Norman with those deliciously big brown eyes of hers.

"What do you mean? You turning into a girl, or something? Sounds weird if you ask me! No, give me the old Norman, any day."

She turned away and busied herself with a pile of books. Norman felt utterly dejected as he made his way home. He really liked Melanie. If only he hadn't been so stupid before, perhaps she would still recognise him now, as his mother had. It was beginning to look as though it would have to be Penny after all, but she wasn't half as pretty as Melanie and was painfully boring.

When Norman arrived back home, his mother was still busy preparing his father for the new Norman. She shooed her son upstairs, out of the way, until she felt it would be safe for him to come down. He left the bedroom door open and managed to catch snippets of the conversation going on between his parents...

"What do you mean Norman looks a little different? How different? Darker, you say? Hair different? But still our Norman, you say? Got a WBM meeting tonight, Alice. This is all very irregular, you know. And why do you say

Norman shouldn't come to the meeting tonight? He's my son, and I'm the secretary."

This went on for quite some time until Norman's mother came upstairs, quietly, and asked the lad to join them downstairs so that his dad could see for himself. She sounded so proud when Norman heard her announce, ahead of him, "...And this is our *new* Norman," that he even began to feel proud of himself. The disappointment over Melanie was still on his mind, but he suddenly had a brainwave...

Norman strode into the room.

"*You* could tell her, Mum. She likes you, and maybe if *you* speak to her, then... well, we could at least ask her back home. For tea, or something."

Mr Braithwaite looked at Norman. He looked at Mrs Braithwaite, then back at Norman.

"Mum?" he questioned. "What's been going on, Alice? What's *he* calling *you* 'Mum' for? Who's he talking about? And who *is* this man anyway? What's he doing in my—?"

"Look closely at him, Derek," interrupted Mrs Braithwaite. "This is Norman. *Our* son. And what a fine young man he is now. Just a little different, that's all. You can see it's Norman. In his eyes. Go on. Take a closer look, Derek."

Norman's father got up from his armchair came over and, for a long time, carefully peered at Norman.

"Well I'll be buggered!" he finally exclaimed, stepping back. "What have they done to you?"

"Nothing Dad," replied Norman. "Just woke up like this. Do you like it?"

"Like?" repeated his father, "Like? It's... well, it

won't... I mean... you know, it's irregular. That's what it is. Most irregular! Just won't do!"

"Why, Derek?" Norman's mother asked. "Look at his smile!"

Norman smiled. His father cringed.

"Well he doesn't *look* like our Norman. That's why!"

"Well, *I* think he's a lot more handsome, and *I'm* a woman," Mrs Braithwaite said.

"And what do you mean by that, Alice? No funny business in the past, was there?"

"Derek, this is *your* son and you're just gonna to have to live with it. It's the same Norman. Even you can see that. As for that stupid WBM stuff, why don't you just take Norman along? Tell them to change it to the White and Black Britain Movement. The WBBM!"

Norman's father stood rubbing his chin. He stopped and stared at his son, then rubbed his chin again. This always helped him to think.

"You might have a point there, Alice," he agreed. He sat down to turn things over in his mind whilst Norman explained his little plan to his mother.

"Melanie in the library?" he offered, attempting to jolt her memory.

"Oh, *that* Melanie," his mother replied. "Such a sweet girl."

"Well, I wanted to ask her out, Mum, but she says she preferred me as I was and I don't know how to change back."

"Oh, don't do that, dear. You're far more handsome as you are now."

"The point is, Mum, Melanie doesn't believe I'm really me. I never got to know her, before, because of all

338

that WBM stuff." He looked uneasily at his father. "But she trusts you, and if you tell her it *is* me, perhaps—just perhaps—she might allow us to invite her back here. Just for starters. If that goes well, she might even go out with me. Mum? Please!"

"I'll try my best, Norman. I do like that girl."

Mr Braithwaite took no notice of the conversation going on in the background. He was far too busy churning thoughts around in his brain. This wasn't something that he did very often, and it was a slow and laborious process, requiring a great deal of concentration on his part. He did rather alarm his wife and son, though, when he suddenly shot out of his armchair announcing that he had a brilliant idea.

"I've got it," he shouted. "Why don't we change the name of the movement altogether? We could call it the PBBM. The Pink and Brown Britain Movement."

Mrs Braithwaite winked at Norman.

"What a brilliant idea, Derek!" she said. "And Melanie will be more than welcome in our house too, won't she, darling?"

"Melanie? Of course, dear."

As Norman and his mum left the room, Mr Braithwaite called out,

"Who's Melanie?"

Author

After retiring as an NHS consultant physician in 2003, Oliver took to writing. Waking up one night with a ghost story in his head, he began to write adult short stories. Over fifty have been published, several winning prizes, and many appear in his first collection, **Walls of Words.** Short stories for younger readers were published as **Stories for Children Ages 7 to 77.**

His first young readers' book, **Moon Rabbit**, a magical journey to Mythological China (Oliver's wife is Chinese), was published in 2009. It was a winner of the *Writers' and Artists' 2007 New Novel Competition* and longlisted for the *Waterstones Children's Book Prize, 2008.* The sequel, **Monkey King's Revenge**, came out in 2011 and was a children's genre finalist for the 2012 People's Book Prize. **Northwards**, a young readers' dark fantasy, based in Texas and the Arctic, was published in 2010. *The Rainbow Animal*, a fun spoof on war, is also set in North America where Oliver's two eldest granddaughters live.

His debut adult novel, *A Single Petal*, which won the *Local Legend 2012 Spiritual Writing Competition*, is set in Tang Dynasty China. *Voices*, an adult novel of family love, intrigue, and deceit, is based in London whilst *The Parth Path* is set in a post-apocalyptic Scotland run by women for women and was inspired by Socrates' famous saying, 'Once made equal to man, woman becomes his superior.' *The Terminus*, Oliver's debut young adult novel, returns to the city in which he was brought up; a city called 'London' now changed beyond recognition from the drab post-World War II era and which, in a post- apocalyptic world, gives humankind a second chance. The *From Beast to God* trilogy, *The Golden Jaguar of the Sun*, *The Merging* and *Revelation*, follows a Texan boy and a Mexican girl on a life-journey involving drug gangsters, ancient Aztec, Mayan and Native Mythology, blending European and Native American beliefs; it was revised and republished as a single three-part novel, *Eyes of Fire*. *The Kelpie's Eyes* was inspired by a visit with Oliver's American granddaughters to a famous Scottish waterfall, the Grey Mare's Tale, and weaves Scottish mythology into a tale of sisterly love. It won the *2018 Georgina Hawtrey-Woore Young Adult Novel Award*. *Number Twenty-four,* a coming-of-age teenage novel, follows a Scots boy and a Chinese girl to 'Dogtopia', a land where human and dog roles are reversed whilst *The Zookeeper's Daughter*, co-written with the writer's nine-year-old Swiss granddaughter during COVID-19 lockdown, is about a brave little girl magically transported into the lives of animals, across the world, who are endangered because of what humans are doing to our planet. *No more Bamboo!*, illustrated by the author, for younger children, follows the adventures of a little panda who, fed up with eating nothing but bamboo, sets off alone, into the forest, to seek out more interesting food.

Oliver has also written several plays, one of which, *The Gap*, inspired by being caught up, with his Chinese wife, in the Great Sichuan Earthquake of 2008, and shortlisted for the *Rowan Tree One Act Play Competition*, went on tour in Scotland in 2012. Another, *The Other Cat*, a darkly humorous take on Schrödinger's famous feline, won the *2018 Segora International One Act Play Competition* and toured the Scottish Borders with two more of his plays in 2019.

Although not confined to any particular genre, Oliver feels most comfortable in that magical space between reality and fantasy; the space into and out of which children slip so easily in their play; the place of dreams and myths and legends and deeply ingrained in many cultures across the globe.

Websites:
www.olivereadebooks.org
www.oddproductionstheatre.weebly.com
Contact:
olivereade'at'googlemail.com, or via his website above.

Other Silver Quill Publishing books:

www.silverquillpublishing.com

Dream the Red Earth by Annette Reis, a debut novel for teens. Two girls, Keisha and Simi, experience loss in different ways.

The Stitched Record by Pamela Gordon Hoad, a historical novel about events just before and after the Norman conquest. Also ***Driftwood and Stone*** set in nineteenth century Sheffield and the ***Harry Somers*** series about a fifteenth century doctor-investigator.

Max's Diary-Tales of a time-travelling cat by Wendy Leighton-Porter to accompany the ***Shadows of the Past*** series bringing history to life, for children, through the adventures of brother and sister twins, their friend and the lovable and intelligent feline, Max.

The Atlantean Horse and other books for middle grade readers by the award-winning Cheryl Carpinello.

Autumn in August by Patricia Goodwin, for adults. Lucy carries a guilty secret. Will she maintain newfound independence or go with her heart?

The Pigeon Run by Robert Breustedt, for young adults. Four young teenagers stumble across drug dealing close to home and get involved with something far more dangerous than they imagined.

Crying Through the Wind, and other adult books

of the Oisin Kelly series, by Iona Carroll which take the reader on a journey from rural 20th century Ireland to Australia, taking in the horror of a war in Vietnam. Also **Other Peoples Lives**, a collection of adult short stories.

Susie in Spectra by Wendy Lake, a magical journey for middle grade readers over the Rainbow Highway to colourful lands of Spectra taken over by the evil Vileus. Can Susie and her new friend, Lemo, stop Vileus from plunging Spectra into eternal darkness?

No Relation by Christina Reis. An adult novel following the lives of two women, from different backgrounds, whose daughters later meet, unearthing disturbing and life-changing facts that devastate the two families.

The Adventures of Maxima and Coustaud, Books 1, 2 and 3, for children, by Sheikha Shamma, in which a magical horse and her funny bulldog companion must rescue a princess from a wicked witch... and more. Also, ***The Colour Thief*** about a young boy and his three pets who must save his city from losing all its colours to a mysterious colour thief, and ***Who is Corona***, a colourfully illustrated e-book that has a simple message for young readers.

From Simon Leighton-Porter, ***The Minerva System*** in which IT developer Mansell's Minerva system attracts the wrong kind of attention 'in the City where no one cares if you scream', followed by ***Death to Bankers***, '...simple, brutal and horribly real', adult

thriller novels. Also ***The Manhattan Deception***...
'Stike a deal with the devil or send one million people
to their deaths?' and 'a cracking story from a talented
writer', ***Bomber Boys***... a journalist and former RAF
officer, after devastating head injuries, is not only
haunted by the past, but haunts the past himself in a
struggle to return to the present day.